CRAWFORD SMITH

Fester

SWEET WEASEL WORDS
PORTLAND, OREGON, USA
sweetweaselwords.com

First edition

ISBN: 978-1-7332699-4-0

Cover art by Kenneth Huey
Editing by Paula Guran

This book was professionally typeset on Reedsy.
Find out more at reedsy.com

for Leah

Acknowledgement

Special thanks to Jess Truhan, Kim Smith, and Klint Finley, who provided invaluable feedback over the years while this book was being written.

Much gratitude also to Kenneth Huey and Paula Guran, who went above and beyond the call of duty for the cover illustration and editing, respectively.

Most of all, much thanks and love to my sweet honeybee NancyAnne, whose patience and advice made this book possible.

Chapter 1

In his tiny office, Inspector Martin Prieboy hunched over his notebook, filling it margin-to-margin with small, neat writing. The office was about seven by seven feet, with buzzing fluorescent lights and cut-rate ceiling tiles that occasionally rained white dust down on Martin's cramped metal desk. The first time it had happened, he sent a sample of the dust to the lab to test for asbestos. Martin was a firm believer in scientific analysis. Fortunately, the test came back negative, and now he always made sure to have a lid for his coffee.

Martin was slender, but solidly built, with fine blond hair brushed back from a high forehead. At first glance, one might assume he was quite young, but a closer inspection revealed subtle lines around his mouth and eyes, indicating an age closer to thirty than twenty. He wore a dress uniform that had recently come from the dry cleaners.

Martin was making notes regarding his latest case: an apparent murder-suicide in a dorm room at Prosser College. He had spent most of the previous day at the crime scene, estimating bullet trajectories and analyzing blood spatter patterns. He jotted down a few final notes, and turned to his typewriter to begin the official report.

Martin was no stranger to ugly crime scenes. In his time with the Fester Constabulary, he had dealt with much nastier sights than the scene in Adelaide Hall. Still, the scene of the murder-suicide was gruesome. The neat, all-American dorm room setting made the bloody mess seem that much worse by contrast. Martin pushed these thoughts away. He was a professional, and he had a job to do. That was all that mattered.

1

Behind him, a figure silently appeared behind the pebbled glass of the office door. A hand rose to knock, but before it could, Martin said, "Good morning, Chief. Be with you in a moment."

The door swung open and in stepped Chief Constable Billy Snyder. He was short, stocky, and barrel-chested, with a hard face that wore a permanently chiseled scowl. "Jesus, Inspector Prieboy," he said. "You must have the ears of a hawk. No, not a hawk—that sounds fucking stupid. What the hell kind of animal has good ears?"

"A bat?" suggested Martin. "They have good ears, for echolocation."

"Yeah, sure, a bat," said the Chief Constable. "Whatever."

"I figured it must be you," Martin replied. "I heard you coming a mile away. Well, a quarter-mile, anyway."

"What the hell are you talking about?"

"I heard your car pull into the parking lot. It sounds like the timing is about a degree and a half off—the engine makes a very distinctive sound. You probably ought to take it to the motor pool and have it adjusted. It could improve the gas mileage up to fifteen percent."

Snyder glowered. "Are you wising off to me, Prieboy? The last thing I need is you turning into a wiseass."

"No sir, Chief. You know I wouldn't do anything like that. It wouldn't respectful."

"Of course not. Those monks really beat respect into you, didn't they?"

Martin Prieboy had been born in Fester, but his parents were killed in a car accident when he was very young. With no other relatives, Martin had become a ward of the state. He wound up at an orphanage in Hershey called the Holy Jesus Christ Almighty Home for Unfortunate Boys. Run by an obscure sub-order of Capuchin monks, it was notorious for its strict discipline.

"My upbringing taught me respect and fortitude," said Martin. "I appreciate the way that Father McJaggar and the other brothers at the orphanage took the effort to instill discipline."

"That's terrific," said Snyder. "If only the rest of the constabulary were so disciplined." He gestured at the box of evidence on Martin's desk. "So tell me, just what the hell happened in that dorm room?"

"Yes, sir," said Martin. He thumbed back a few pages in his notebook. "Last night at approximately twenty-one thirty hours, residents of Adelaide Hall reported hearing three loud reports. The second floor resident advisor notified Prosser Campus Safety that he had heard what he believed to be gunshots. As per their protocol, they immediately informed the constabulary dispatcher."

"Stupid campus rent-a-cops," muttered Snyder. "Couldn't handle a popgun."

"Um, yes, quite, sir," Martin said. "After making the phone call, the RA went down to the door of this room, where a crowd of students had already gathered. He used his pass key to open the door and found the bodies of Michael Neff and Thomas Dreher, both dead of gunshot wounds.

"Constable Dirkschneider arrived on the scene at twenty-one forty hours and proceeded to clear the room rather, um, forcefully. Several of the students sustained minor injuries from his action."

"Do you not approve of Constable Dirkschneider's actions, Inspector?"

"It seems a bit . . . excessive, don't you think, sir?"

"He was successful in preventing a bunch of gawkers from contaminating the evidence, right? No point in making your job any more difficult."

"No sir, I guess not," said Martin. He cleared his throat, then continued, "It appears that Dreher shot Neff twice, then turned the gun on himself. I've managed to reconstruct the sequence of events. It seems pretty straightforward." He glanced briefly at his notebook, and then gave his boss a detailed step-by-step recreation of the murder-suicide.

"Jesus," said Snyder, when Martin had finished. "Any idea of the motive for this clusterfuck?"

"Unknown, sir. There were no witnesses. Neff's roommate dropped out of school in early February, and he'd had the room to himself since then.

"The deceased were locals and had known each other since childhood. Dreher had reportedly visited Neff in this room the night before the shootings. Thomas Dreher was not a student at Prosser, however. Apparently, he was not quite the scholar that Neff had been."

"That's for sure," said Snyder. "The kid was a major fuckup. I've known his father for years. Had to get that kid off the hook more than once."

"You mean you let him escape justice?" asked Martin.

Snyder eyed Martin uncertainly. "Christ, Prieboy, not everything is black and white, okay? Carl Dreher is a deacon at Calvary Lutheran and he swings a lot of political weight in town. Not as much as the Top Hats, but enough to cause trouble with Mayor Augenblick's re-election campaign if he decided to raise a stink. I let a few minor vandalism charges slide, nothing major. 'Escape justice,' my ass."

"I see, sir."

"I doubt it. Look, you handle the investigation and let me take care of the politics. Now, what about the weapon?"

"A Colt 1911 E .45 caliber semiautomatic pistol was recovered at the scene," he said. "The gun is registered to Carl Dreher, Thomas's father."

"Oh hell," said Snyder. "Carl's going to lose his shit when he finds out about this twist. Inspector Prieboy, you do understand that this case is to be handled with utmost discretion, correct?"

"Absolutely, Chief Constable. You can count on me."

"I know I can," said Snyder. "Have the staties come by?"

"Yes sir. Commander Johnson came by, just as the coroner was leaving. He was only there for a few minutes. He said it looked like things were in good hands as usual."

"Good deal," said Snyder. "Wally Johnson knows that we can take care of our own problems in Fester."

"Yes, sir."

"And another thing," said Snyder. "Why are you in your dress uniform? You know it's standard procedure for those with an inspector's rank to dress in plain clothes while on duty."

"Well, sir, I felt that it was important to let the students and faculty know that their constabulary was taking care of this, given the nature of the case. I wanted to fly the flag, so to speak."

"I see."

Martin look concerned. "I certainly hope that I haven't done anything

4

inappropriate, sir. It seemed like . . ."

Snyder waved his hand dismissively. "I trust your judgment completely, Inspector. You could wear a clown suit on duty if you felt it appropriate."

"Certainly not, sir," Martin said. He paused, considering. "Unless, of course, circumstances required that I go undercover at a circus or carnival."

Snyder's shoulders slumped slightly. "Indeed, Prieboy. I'm certain that you would make an excellent undercover clown."

"Thank you, sir."

"I'll want to see your preliminary report on this case first thing tomorrow morning." He glanced at the IBM Selectric on Martin's desk. "Why are you still using that old thing? Didn't you get one of those new word processors? Come on, it's 1993—get with the times, Prieboy."

"I was requisitioned a word processor, sir," said Martin. He waved at a box of computer parts and cables in the corner. "It seems, uh, promising. I thought I could improve its performance a bit, and made a few changes. I haven't had time to put it back together. No matter, Chief—I like using the old typewriter."

Snyder rolled his eyes. "Okay, fine, Inspector. You can write with a quill pen on a piece of parchment for all I care. Just have that damn report on my desk tomorrow morning!"

"Yes, sir," said Martin. He jumped up from his seat and stood at attention.

"Relax, Prieboy. You don't need to be so damn formal all the time."

"Understood, sir. I just want to make sure that I'm doing everything by the book."

"Don't I fucking know it," muttered Snyder. "Look, I can't stand around chatting all damn day. I've got things to see and people to do." He turned and let himself out of the office. Behind him, Martin leaned over the typewriter and got to work.

Chapter 2

Billy Snyder parked his unmarked cruiser on Morningwood Promenade, just below the pylons that marked the entrance to Morningwood Heights. He could see all of Fester spread out below him. The morning sun sparkled on the Black River to the east of downtown. Down by the Iron Bridge, huge plumes of steam rose from the Schmidt Pretzel Bakery as they fired up the ovens for another shift. The traffic on Route 17 and Route 23 began to pick up as Fester's workforce made their way into the city for another day. Billy watched the school buses from Fester's two school districts, Fester and West Kerian, trundling down the streets like yellow beetles.

He took in the view of morning in his town and he knitted. When he had given up smoking three years ago, his wife had suggested that he take up knitting as a way of keeping his hands busy and his mind off of cigarettes.

Billy had kept at it long after the last pangs of nicotine craving had departed. He enjoyed knitting gloves the most and was usually able to deliver several pairs a month to the Fester Men's Shelter. This civic-mindedness had paid off in a front-page story in the *Fester Daily Dispatch*, and personal kudos from the mayor and the city council.

Billy knitted and waited. From time to time, he glanced up at his rearview mirror as he worked on the thumb—always the trickiest part of the glove.

A huge black BMW sedan descended from Morningwood Heights and breezed by Billy's cruiser. It had a vanity license plate reading "ZIFF 1." It belonged to Dr. Michael Ziffer, chief administrator of Kerian Memorial Hospital. Billy observed the car with interest. He had recently learned that Dr. Ziffer may be involved in some sort of shady dealings with a large pharmaceutical company. Billy knew he was going to have to do a little more investigation into this, but not today.

In his rearview mirror, he could see a Mercedes 300-SL speeding down the hill. The little roadster tore past Billy's car, doing nearly sixty. Billy pulled out behind it and hit the flashers.

The driver either didn't see the flashers or didn't care, and it wasn't until Billy had come right up to the rear bumper and hit the siren that the Mercedes deigned to pull over just outside the gates of Highland Country Club. Billy pulled up behind it and waited until a count of sixty before getting out of his cruiser and cautiously approaching the sports car.

The driver of the Mercedes was Cecilia Schmidt, the CEO of the Schmidt Pretzel Bakery. Normally, Billy would have looked the other way if a Top Hat had been observed violating the speed limit, but Cecilia was a special case. First, she wasn't really a Top Hat—she had married the previous head of the company, Emile Schmidt III.

Emile hadn't been much of a corporate director—his real passion was deep sea fishing and he spent most of his time in its pursuit. Sadly, he dropped dead of a heart attack three years ago while battling a marlin off the coast of New Jersey. As per his will, control of the company passed to Cecilia.

The rest of the Schmidt family had been appalled. They had always considered Cecilia to be a gold-digger. However, they couldn't overlook the fact that she actually did a good job of running the company, and it had grown every year since she had taken over. Eventually, the family had—grudgingly—accepted Cecilia's control. After all, she was making them more money than Emile ever had.

Billy walked up to the car and rapped on the window. Cecilia sat staring straight ahead, not acknowledging him. She was in her early thirties, with a wave of bright red hair that cascaded past her shoulders. She was dressed to the nines, with an expensive-looking fur coat over a watered-silk peasant blouse. Her makeup would have been the envy of a New York fashion photographer.

Billy rapped on the window again. The driver's window slid down, unleashing an eye-watering cloud of Chanel No. 5, Cecilia's signature scent.

Still staring straight ahead, Cecilia said, "You must be new around here. Do you know who I am? "

"Oh, I know very well who you are, Ms. Schmidt," said Billy. "Don't I just."

"Well," said Cecilia. "If it isn't Fester's top pig."

"Yes, that's me," agreed Billy. "Did you know that you were doing sixty in a thirty-mile-an-hour zone?" He pulled out his ticket book and began writing.

"You son of a bitch!" Cecilia spat. "You really don't know your damn place!"

"Oh no, Ms. Schmidt, you've got it all backwards. I'd say that you're the one who doesn't know her place."

"Screw you. My place is running the largest business in town. I do a damn good job of it, too. I provide a good living to a whole lot of people in this crummy burg."

"Yes, you're a real pillar of the community," said Billy. "I think you've had a busy week, too. Caused a bit of a fuss in the Schmidt boardroom, from what I've heard."

"I don't see how that's any of your business," Cecilia growled.

"Well, a number of citizens—very *well connected* citizens—are quite upset. My job is to keep the citizens of Fester safe and happy. So it kind of *is* my business."

The day before, Cecilia had instituted a major shake-up at the company. She had fired half of the board of directors, all of whom were blue-blooded Schmidts. Even worse, she announced that the company was going to be renamed the Keystone Tasty Snack Food Corporation, and would soon begin producing potato chips as well as pretzels. The Schmidt family was outraged, but there was nothing that they could do. Cecilia had already called in the hyena-like law firm of Nasté, Brutus and Shore to make sure there was no way the rest of the Schmidts could thwart her plans.

"The problem is that you seem hell-bent on upsetting the apple cart," Billy continued. "You've got a lot of people very upset, Cici!"

"Don't you call me that!" Cecilia snarled. "And how I run my company is no damn business of yours, you overblown rent-a-cop!"

"I just wanted to give you a little friendly advice," he said. "You can waltz into this 'crummy burg' after things get a little too hot for you in Pittsburgh, and you can marry into the most powerful family, and you can even connive to take over the biggest business in town. But there are a few things that you won't ever be able to do."

Cecilia checked her nails and said, "Are you getting to that advice any time soon?"

"Let me explain it to you. You're a big deal in Fester. But you're not *from* Fester. You're not really part of this town, you've just managed to sleep your way into a position of power. But that doesn't really mean jack shit in the big picture, you understand?"

"'Big picture'? What the fuck are you talking about, Snyder? I think you've finally lost your little piggy mind."

"What I'm talking about, Ms. Schmidt, is that there are a lot of things about Fester that you don't know. This town is different from any other place in Pennsylvania, or anywhere else, really. We have our way of doing things, our own rules. Rules that have kept things chugging along nicely for a long time. It's not good when an outsider comes along and starts dicking with those rules. It makes important people very unhappy."

"Like I give a fuck, Snyder. What, did some of my shithead in-laws tell you to give me a scare?"

"Oh, no," said Billy. "Nobody asked me to do anything. I'm just performing my civic duty."

"Civic duty?" snorted Cecilia. "Don't puff yourself up, Snyder. You're nothing but the hired help. I ought to . . ."

"Ought to what? For all of your money, there isn't diddly squat you can do to me. What are you going to do? Complain to the mayor? That wheezing dimwit is my brother-in-law. You gonna sic your high-powered lawyers on me? I've known Pierre Nasté since grade school."

"Yeah, you're quite the big shot around here," spat Cecilia. "Well, here's a bit of news for you: you and me aren't all that different. For all your talk of important people and old money, you're no more part of this shithole of a town than I am. Talk about sleeping your way into power? You did the same damn thing, marrying the mayor's sister. You're just a fucking watchdog, owned by people like my dipshit in-laws to keep guard over their treasure. Nothing more. You're a dog."

Billy felt his anger flare up. He smacked an open palm onto the Mercedes' door, producing a hollow boom. "Hey! I'm done listening to your crap. You just better watch your step, because I'm keeping an eye on you. If there's any more bullshit like your little shake-up down at the factory, you are going to regret it. That's a promise."

Cecilia blew a stream of air through her teeth. She turned back to face straight out of the windshield. "Are you through yet?"

"Almost," said Billy, as he ripped the pink speeding ticket from his ticket book.

"You cocksucker!"

Without a word, Billy thrust the ticket through the roadster's window. Cecilia made no move to take it. Finally, he released the pink slip and it see-sawed down into her lap.

She turned and spat a fat loogie at Billy. It hit the seven-pointed badge pinned to his chest, slid down the bronze face, and soaked into the fabric of his tunic.

Billy had his baton out of its holster before he knew what he was doing. He almost used it, but his temper subsided quickly enough for him to realize he was about to make a big mistake. Slowly and deliberately, he replaced the baton in the holster. "I could take you in for that."

"Go ahead. Try." She reared back as if to spit again.

Billy remained perfectly motionless.

Something in Billy's stance must have made Cecilia think twice. She turned away from Billy and started the roadster with a roar. "Stay out of my business, you dog. Just fuck off."

"Careful what you screw with in my town, Cici."

The Mercedes pulled away with a screech, showering Billy's pants with gravel. A piece of wadded-up pink paper sailed out the car's window and came to rest in the middle of the road.

Billy watched the roadster roar around the hairpin turn at the end of the country club grounds and disappear into the trees. He looked down at the spit-stain on his shirt and the dust and gravel covering his pants legs. He'd have to go home and change into a clean uniform now. That pissed him off mightily, but not nearly as much as some of the things that Cecilia had said to him. "Dog, my ass," he muttered. He turned, walked stiff-legged to his cruiser and drove off.

Chapter 3

Randolph Warnke felt great. He was a few years past fifty, with a rapidly retreating hairline and a salt-and-pepper moustache. He was dressed in his typical wardrobe of sweatpants and a faded Pitt Panthers T-shirt. The clothes hung off of his frame, as if he had recently lost a lot of weight. He knew that he looked like crap, but he didn't care, because he felt great.

He vigorously polished the chrome trim on his kitchen table and whistled a jaunty tune as he worked. When he was done, he surveyed the rest of the kitchen. It was spotless. "Hell, yeah!" he shouted. He felt great.

He hadn't felt great in a long time. Before he'd had to move to Fester Fucking Pennsylvania, he had been a star. *That* had been great. For fifteen years, Randolph Warnke had appeared every weekday afternoon as Cowboy Bob, the rodeo clown host of WEVL-TV's *Cowboy Bob's Funtime Cartoon Rodeo Roundup*. Schoolchildren from three counties sat glued to their TV sets every weekday, watching Cowboy Bob's antics, along with afternoon TV staples such as Bugs Bunny, Speed Racer, and Deputy Dawg.

Warnke had enjoyed being a big fish in the small pond of central Pennsylvania television. WEVL's advertising revenues during the Cowboy Bob show were consistently high, and Warnke had been paid well. He'd had a big house, a fancy sports car, and plenty of groupies. A little celebrity went a long way in a place like Weaverville, and Warnke had made the most of it.

Most of all—more than the money, more than the women—Warnke loved being in the spotlight. When that red light when on, and the cameras swung around to face him, Warnke knew he was the absolute center of attention. All of the viewers in thousands of homes, all of the production staff on the set, and all of the kids in the studio audience were focused on one person only: him. There was nothing to match that feeling, and Warnke had lived for it.

Cowboy Bob had ridden high for fifteen years. Then things had fallen apart with stunning swiftness. It had started the day that Norbert Weevil, the station owner, had dropped dead of a heart attack on the golf course. His son had taken over the station. On his first day, Norbert Junior had announced that he was taking measures to "cut the fat" at WEVL-TV. This had included replacing *Cowboy Bob's Funtime Cartoon Rodeo Roundup* with back-to-back syndicated reruns of *Boscoville*.

Boscoville was a staggeringly popular prime-time animated sitcom. It followed the adventures of the Fergus family, who lived in the titular town of Boscoville. It was the typical sitcom family trope. Raymond Fergus, the father, was a lazy boob whose antics provided most of the show's gags. There were also the sitcom-standard long-suffering housewife, two precocious kids, and the family pet—a talking chimpanzee named Spanky.

Warnke loathed *Boscoville*. The show's continued popularity produced an almost endless string of merchandise and promotional tie-ins that rankled Warnke whenever he encountered them. Every time he saw a Boscoville product, he was reminded of his own showbiz downfall.

That downfall had been swift and merciless. Warnke had tried to find work with other TV stations with no success. There just wasn't demand for a TV kids' show host. The genre was too specialized, and hosted afternoon cartoon shows had largely gone the way of the dodo. Warnke's meager savings dwindled quickly. The fancy sports cars and groupies were soon ancient history. Warnke had been forced to relocate to a cracker box of a house in a run-down neighborhood of Fester, where he eked out a loathsome living appearing at supermarket openings and children's parties.

Fortunately, he'd found a way to supplement his income. An associate had introduced Warnke to a shady character in Philadelphia named Jimmy Francini. Francini promised to supply Warnke with all of the high-grade marijuana that he could move.

Warnke was all for it and found a ready market in his new town. Fester was such a depressing shithole that the residents would consume almost anything if it would take their minds off of their miserable existences. The high-grade weed sold well, and Warnke built up a network of distributors, mostly high school and college kids. He'd hoped that he would soon be able to afford to move back to a modest condo in Weaverville and put Fester behind him permanently.

This hope was now being derailed, and it was his own damn fault. Three months ago, during a run to Francini's place, his host had offered him a couple of lines of cocaine. Warnke had been offered coke many times before during his showbiz days. He had always refused, saying that he didn't want to "contaminate his craft."

Now that his "craft" was limited to the occasional ribbon-cutting at a new Food Ape store or twisting up balloon animals for snotty brats up in Morningwood Heights, Warnke figured he didn't have much to lose. Besides, he didn't want to risk offending his host, who was pretty damn intimidating. Warnke had gone ahead and given the toot a try.

It was an epiphany. For the first time since his show had been cancelled, he felt like the star that he always knew he was destined to be. The rush, the feeling of invincibility—these were what he missed most from his days in front of the camera. He felt great. *Really* great. Randolph Warnke had taken to cocaine like a pig to a cesspool.

That day, he'd brought a quarter gram of blow home along with the regular consignment of pot. On the next run, Warnke had purchased a gram, and on the trip after that, an eight-ball. Now he was going through an ounce every two weeks or so.

His newfound habit was cutting deeply into his profits. He was spending more on blow for personal use, which left him less to buy weed for resale. His solution to the problem was to get Francini to front him a bit more weed so he could increase his distribution network in Fester. It was risky, but Warnke knew he could pull it off. Because he was great.

Warnke looked at his watch. It was almost time for the Plummer kid to come by. Just enough time to do another line. He got his gear from the kitchen drawer and chopped out two big rails and snorted those puppies right up. His heart began to jackhammer, and he began to feel the slow Novocain drip in the back of his throat. It felt great.

There was a tentative tapping at the back door. Warnke jumped and nearly knocked the mirror to the floor. The little Plummer shit was early. He jammed the mirror back into the drawer and rubbed at his mustache, making sure that he was getting all of the residue off.

The tapping came again. Normally, Warnke would have made the kid wait a couple of minutes, just to let him know who's boss. No point in that tonight, though. He was feeling too good for that. Great, in fact.

He sprang to the back door and yanked it open, surprising Paul Plummer. He was a weedy-looking teenager who was five foot ten when he wasn't slouching. He had lank brown hair that hung down to his eyes, and a beat-up denim jacket that had some god-awful painting of a heavy metal band on the back. He jumped when Warnke yanked the door open. "Ah! Uh, hi, Mr. W," he said.

"My boy!" said Warnke. "Come on in, come in!"

Paul came into the kitchen reluctantly, nonplussed by Warnke's uncharacteristic *bonhomie*. "So, uh, how's it going?" Paul asked.

"Going great!" Warnke stepped over to the gleaming kitchen table and yanked back a chair. "Have a seat, Paul. Take a load off, as they say."

He slowly slipped into the chair. "Yeah, uh, thanks . . ."

Warnke deftly swiveled around the adjacent chair and straddled it, leaning into Paul's face. "So, my boy, how are you doing? How's school treating you? You ready for summer?"

"Uh, yeah, I guess so. It's, uh, y'know, not really for another couple of months, y'know?"

"Oh, yes, of course, of course," said Warnke. "It's just that it's so hot already and it's not even May. Whew!" He armed a puddle of sweat off his forehead. It *was* hot, at least to him. His heart was racing like a sprint car and his body temperature seemed to have gone up ten degrees. "Jesus! It's like summer already!"

"Uh, yeah, I guess so," said Paul. He started to take off the ratty jean jacket.

"Hey, I know!" said Warnke. "How about a nice cold beer? Nothing better than a cold beer when it's hot, right?" He bounced up from his chair, yanked open the refrigerator door and pulled out two Yuengling lagers. There were a few other bottles of beer in the spotless fridge and little else.

"Yeah, a beer sounds good, I guess," said Paul.

"You bet," said Warnke. He felt another rush coming on. All of a sudden he felt better than ever. He slipped into his Cowboy Bob voice and screeched, "Hey buckaroo! There's nothing better than a cold beer after a hard day on the trail! You betcha!" He capered around the kitchen, waving the bottles and singing the theme song from his old show. "Hey, boys and girls, it's Cowboy Bob time, Cowboy Bob time, Cowboy Bob time! Hey, boys and girls, it's Cowboy . . . WHAT THE FUCK IS THAT?"

"Wh-what?" asked Paul, clearly unnerved. "I don't kn-know . . ."

"Your shirt!" screamed Warnke. "Your *fuckin'* shirt!"

Paul's shirt had a picture of a cheeky-looking cartoon chimp in a pair of lederhosen, with the word "Spanky!" in balloony yellow letters underneath. He plucked at it helplessly.

"Why are wearing a fuckin' Boscoville shirt in here, you little shit? Take it off! Take it off right now!"

"What? You mean take it off? Here?"

"Hell, yes! Just take it off! Turn it inside out! I don't want to see the fuckin' thing!"

"Yeah, yeah, sure. Sorry!" Paul quickly inverted his shirt, then shrugged back into his jacket.

"Jesus! What the fuck were you thinking?" Warnke took a long pull off of one of the beers and put the other one on the counter. His good mood had suddenly been turned on its head. "Wearing that thing in my house! What do you want, anyway?"

"Huh?"

"What the fuck do you *want*? You didn't come here to chat about the weather, did you?"

"Uh, no, man, sorry. Sorry," said Paul. "I, yeah, I guess I want a zee, if

16

that's cool."

"No, it's not 'cool,' asshole," snarled Warnke. "I'm not screwing around with this rinky-dink shit anymore. Minimum's a kewpie."

"A quarter pound? I only have enough for an ounce." Paul pulled a wad of cash out of his pants pocket and made a show of thumbing through it.

"That's all right," said Warnke. He leaned in and snatched the bills from Paul's hand. "I'll front you the rest. I know you're good for it—your family's rich. I see your dad's face on billboards all over town, with his Lee Plummer Realty Trust bullshit. He got enough out of *me*, selling me this shitbox house, so I *know* you got money. Just get me the rest by Friday, okay? You got a problem with that?"

"No, no, that's coo . . . that's all right."

"Fuckin'-A it's all right." Warnke said. He opened the freezer and reached behind an ancient bag of frozen peas. "Ah, here we go!" He yanked out a fat plastic sack of pot and tossed it to Paul, who fumbled it.

"Hey buckaroos!" screeched Warnke. "That's some killer shit right there! Blow you right out of the saddle!" He laughed to see the look of confusion that spread across Paul's face.

Paul picked up the freezer bag, stuffed it into one of the jacket's inner pockets, and jumped up from his seat. "Yeah, okay, thanks, man," he said. He began backing towards the door. "I, uh, guess I'll be going."

"Yeah, why don't you do that?" said Warnke. "I'm gettin' sick of looking at you. And don't forget to get me the rest of the money by Friday. Don't make me come looking for you, snotnose."

"Yeah, no, problem, man." Paul stepped quickly to the door and pulled it open.

"See ya later, buckaroo!" screamed Warnke, laughing like a loon. Paul darted out the door and slammed it behind him.

After a few minutes, Warnke's heartbeat slowed down, but he was still pissed. That little shithead, wearing a fuckin' Boscoville shirt in here. Rubbing his nose in his own failure. That little fuck.

"Fuck it," he said out loud. He pulled the coke gear back out of the drawer and cut out another big line. He snorted it up and sighed. The rush was back. That was better. He turned to go into the bedroom to stash the cash.

Chief Constable Billy Snyder was standing in the kitchen doorway.

Warnke jumped. His heart seemed to seize up, then doubled its already frantic pace. He grabbed at his chest with one hand while flailing around with the other to find something to lean on. It hit the kitchen counter, and Warnke leaned back, breathing heavily.

Billy Snyder laughed. "Ha! That was fuckin' funny, Randy! You looked just like Redd Foxx. Y'know, you ought to go into show biz!"

"Holy shit!" gasped Warnke. "You scared the crap out of me! How the hell did you get in here, anyway?"

"With this," said Billy. He pulled a device from his belt that looked like a hot glue gun with a small saw blade on the end. He pulled the trigger a few times, producing a harsh rasping sound. "It's a lock-pick gun. Not entirely legal, but I've found it to come in very handy at times. This sucker will open up just about any lock. Well worth the investment."

"Shit, you could have just knocked," said Warnke. "You scared the bejesus out of me!"

"Nah," said Billy. "I don't knock, especially when I'm dealing with clowns like you. I like to see what people are up to when they don't think anyone's watching."

Warnke's mind raced. Had Billy seen him doing the coke, or did he come in afterwards? Would he even care? It was probably best to play it cool—although that was a difficult task when your heart was doing a drum roll from too much coke and a big shot of adrenaline on top of that. Cautiously, he reached for his beer and took a gulp. "So, what do you want?"

"We've got some business to discuss," said Billy. "I think we need to renegotiate our deal. Two thousand a month, payable immediately."

"Wh . . . what?" sputtered Warnke. "That's almost twice what I'm paying you now! Shit, I can't afford . . ."

"Bullshit!" roared Billy. "You're getting the deal of a lifetime, asshole! It would be cheap at twice the price. In exchange for your paltry two grand a month, you get to avoid going to prison. How's that sound? You're getting a fuckin' *bargain!*"

"Yeah, I guess so," muttered Warnke. He started to calm down. Billy probably hadn't seen the cocaine. He was just a crooked cop out to get his take.

"You *guess* so?" said Billy. "You'd better *know* so. I take care of my people. Like that time I kept the county mountie from searching your car at that speed trap on Route 17. Don't give me any of this 'I guess so' shit, okay?"

"Yeah, right, okay. I appreciate your help, I really do . . . it's just that I've got some cash flow problems right now, and . . ."

"Look, I *know* that you're moving more product than ever, so spare me the poor-mouth routine. Two grand. Now."

"Okay, okay, gimme a minute." Warnke went back to his bedroom. Billy followed him. Warnke knew better than to complain.

"Shit, you really got this place spiffed up," said Billy. "You're not thinking of selling your house and moving away, are you? Fester would sure hate to lose it's only celebrity."

Warnke said nothing. Right now, he just wanted to get Billy Snyder out of his house. He dug through his sock drawer and found his roll of cash. Hunching his shoulders so that Billy couldn't see how much was there, he peeled off two thousand—which didn't really leave a whole hell of a lot.

"There you go," he said, handing the cash over. "If you don't mind, I was just going to get ready for bed."

"Oh, I doubt that very much." Billy took the stack of bills and jammed it into his uniform pants. Then he just stood there in the bedroom, eyeing Warnke.

"Is there anything else?"

"Just one thing," said Billy. He stepped up to Warnke and shoved his face up close, so they were almost nose-to-nose. "Don't screw with the system, Randy. We've got a really good thing going here, and I'd hate to see you fuck it up. I don't like it at all when somebody makes things complicated for me, understand? UNDERSTAND?"

"Y . . . yeah, I get it," stammered Warnke.

"Good. I hope you do. Just keep doing what you're doing, and paying me my cut, and things will continue to run smoothly. Start fucking up by,

say, holding out on me . . . well, things won't be pleasant for you. I fuckin'
guarantee that. You just keep it in mind."

"I . . . I will."

"Good. Now, I've got better things to do that bullshit with a has-been
cartoon clown. Don't bother showing me out—I can find my own way." He
disappeared from the bedroom.

Warnke sank to the bed, perspiring heavily. He absolutely did not need
this crap. Now he'd have to come up with more money to keep Billy off of
his back. Meaning he was in hock to the gangster supplier in Philadelphia
and the local cops. Cash flow problem, indeed. Bad shit.

He briefly considered doing some more blow, but after the scare that Billy
had just laid on him, decided against it. He no longer felt great. Not even
close.

Chapter 4

G oddammit, Hoegenbloeven!" raged Cecilia Schmidt. "That son of a bitch!" She strode rapidly back and forth in her study, carrying a large tumbler of Glenlivet. Her red hair eddied around her head like a firestorm as she paced. "Who the fuck does that asshole Snyder think he is? How dare he tell me how to run my business! Me!"

In the corner of the oak-paneled study sat Ceclia's assistant, Cynthia Hoegenbloeven. She was young, with a dark, smooth complexion that bore no sign of makeup. In contrast to Cecilia's fashionable clothes, Hoegenbloeven was dressed in a shapeless brown shift. Her only nod to fashion was a punky asymmetrical haircut that was much longer on one side than the other. She sat attentively in a straight-backed chair with a pad and pencil in her lap.

"The company is mine, dammit! No one can tell me how to run it. Not the minority stockholders, not my rotten in-laws, and especially not Billy Goddamn Snyder. Who does he think he is?"

Cecilia stopped to refill her drink at the sideboard, then continued her pacing, Ferragamo heels clacking like castanets on the parquet wood floor. She was trailed by a pungent cloud of perfume. Cecilia's sense of smell had been destroyed by cocaine in the 80's, and she practically had to take a bath in Chanel No. 5 to be able to smell it herself.

"I work my ass off for that damn company, and those lousy Schmidts just sit on their fat asses and suck up the profits," she raged. "The fruits of *my* labor! And when I want to make some changes—changes that will make them even *more* money—they have a shit fit! Sure, I had to get rid of some of the dead wood on the board. They were a drag on the company, but the whole family is carrying on like I massacred them!"

In the corner, Hoegenbloeven twitched slightly.

"Jesus H. Tapdancing Christ!" said Cecilia. "Bunch of goddamn ingrates. The company had been losing money for nearly a decade before I took over."

She stopped under a large oil portrait of a blond-haired man in his early thirties. He had a round, boyish face and a broad smile that showed off deep dimples. Cecilia stared up at it and downed the rest of her drink. "My poor Emile," she said. "He was such a sweet man—not at all like the rest of his shitty, stuck-up family." She sighed. "He just couldn't run a business to save his life."

Drained by her outburst, Cecilia flopped down behind the huge mahogany desk. "Shit, Hoegenbloeven, sometimes I wish I'd never heard the name 'Schmidt.' Or 'Fester.' Jesus Christ, why me?" She lifted the glass to her lips, noticed it was empty, let it *thunk* down on the desk. "Oh, fuck it. You can go now, Hoegenbloeven. Send the rest of the staff home, too. I'm going to watch my movie."

Without a word, Hoegenbloeven rose from her perch in the corner and left to walk back to her quarters in the far corner of the estate.

Cecilia slowly rose from the desk, grabbed the Glenlivet bottle from the sideboard and went downstairs. The huge old house seemed empty ever since Emile died. Cecilia had considered moving into a place of her own but decided that would be a sign of weakness. She was now the head of the Schmidt family business, and she was going to live on the family estate, if for no other reason than to spite her in-laws.

The rest of the Schmidts had despised her from the time her engagement to Emile was announced, and absolutely loathed her once the terms of the will became known. Emile had left her absolutely everything, cutting out the rest of the family. There were conditions, though: she owned the huge estate at the top of Morningwood Heights but was not permitted to sell it. The massive stock holdings had all manner of restrictions on how she could dispose of them. Cecilia could try to unload the shares, but the family would tie up the deal in court for years, with no guarantee of her succeeding. Even the underhanded legal ministrations of Nasté, Brutus and Shore would be no match for the long-standing Schmidt family traditions and legal bulwarks.

She went down the front hall to the media room. The rest of the mansion was traditional dark hardwood and polished marble, but the media room was cool, sleek, and modern. It was the only room in the house where Cecilia really felt at home. She flung herself onto the contoured Danish couch and started the tape of *Gone with the Wind,* which was permanently installed in the VCR.

Cecilia had watched the movie hundreds of times. As a girl, growing up in the rough Homewood section of Pittsburgh, she had been entranced by the movie. She had always wanted to be Scarlet O'Hara when she grew up. In effect, she had achieved her dream. Here she was, sitting in her huge house which was easily the equivalent, in size and splendor, of Scarlett's Tara. There was no cotton plantation, but Cecilia was the head of a very successful company—and she had plans to make that even more successful. Not bad for a blue-collar girl from the wrong side of the tracks.

The phone rang. She paused the tape and snatched up the receiver. "What?" she snapped.

There was a mocking chuckle on the line. "Hello, Cici," said an electronically altered voice. It sounded flat and emotionless, like a robot in a cheap sci-fi movie.

Cecilia felt her mouth dry up. "Who the fuck is this? What do you want?" she asked.

"We were just wondering what you're doing this evening. Maybe you're watching a movie, eh?"

Cecilia took a quick look at the windows; the heavy linen curtains were closed. No one could see what she was doing.

"We were just watching a movie, too," the voice continued. "It's very amateur, but not without its entertainment value. It was taken at the 1985 National Plumbers Convention at the Pittsburgh Marriott. Do you remember that? You should, Cici—you're the star of the show."

"You cocksucker!" Cecilia hissed.

"Ha!" the short, barking laugh sounded like bad amplifier feedback. "You should know all about *that*. You do a bit of that yourself, in this movie. You really did show those plumbers a thing or two about how to take care of their pipes. In fact, I believe there's one scene where you take a rather large length of PVC pipe and . . ."

"Yes, all right, all right" Cecilia interrupted. "Just what the fuck do you want?"

"The same thing you've always wanted, Cici. Money. The same motivation you had for gang-banging half a dozen plumbers."

Cecilia ground her teeth. She had done what she'd had to do. It was the quickest way to make the money that she needed to climb out of Homewood. She had tried to be discrete and had mostly succeeded—except for that one three-day binge at the Marriott. By the time the guy with the video camera had shown up, she had been too wasted to care.

"How much?" she asked.

"Oh, a cinematic classic like this does not come cheap. The asking price is one million dollars."

"Jesus Christ! Where am I supposed to get that kind of cash?"

"Sell more pretzels, bitch. Where the money comes from is of no concern to us. We'll give you six weeks to come up with the cash, small bills, used, non-sequential, unmarked. If you don't come up with the cash by the first of June, a copy of this red-hot video will find its way to the home and office of every prominent person in Kerian County."

"You bastard!"

"We will be in touch before the deadline to give you instructions for the drop-off. Of course, you shouldn't even think of going to the police. Six weeks, bitch." There was a click and the drone of an open line.

She sat stunned for a moment, unable to believe what had just happened. She was being blackmailed! Her first thought was that her in-laws were behind it. It was certainly something that they capable of, but the idea didn't hold up. If one of her bastard in-laws had the tape, they'd just release it and not bother with blackmail. Besides, as much as the disclosure would

24

hurt Cecilia, it would also stain the rest of the family. After all, she was a Schmidt—as much as her in-laws hated the fact—and they'd never do anything to sully the precious family name.

Whoever it was, they had her by the short hairs. If that tape got out, she'd be finished. She had to do something. She picked up the remote, turned off the TV and began pacing the room, stopping only to swig from the bottle of Glenlivet.

First, she needed someone who could do a little investigating. She knew that Nasté, Brutus and Shore kept a couple of private investigators on retainer. She snatched up the phone and dialed Pierre Nasté's personal number. No answer. She slammed the phone back down.

If push came to shove, she could pay the blackmailers. It went against every grain of her being, but Cecilia was a firm believer in making sure all her bases were covered. Actually, it would probably be a better idea to just take the money and lie low in South America for a while. If those cocksuckers made good on their threat to release the orgy video, it would cause a hell of a scandal, but it probably wouldn't last long. In Fester, there was always a new outrage just around the corner. Regardless of her course of action, she was going to need some serious cash.

She went upstairs to her study and went directly to the wall safe behind the painting in the corner. The painting was rendered on black velvet and was possibly the worst piece of artwork ever conceived: a picture of a three-piece rock combo, featuring Elvis Presley singing, Jimi Hendrix on guitar, and Jesus playing drums. In gilt script across the bottom it read "Heaven's House Band." It was such a repellant painting that Cecilia figured nobody would ever look for a wall safe behind it.

She rummaged around in the safe and dumped an armload of papers, checkbooks, and cash on the desk. It represented all that she had worked for over the years: all of the money-grubbing, deal-making, back-stabbing, and social-climbing she had done since her early teens was represented in this pile of papers. She began sorting through the pile and jotting down figures on a notepad.

Twenty minutes later, she looked with dismay at the number at the bottom of the pad: her net liquid worth was a little over six hundred thousand dollars. Of course, she was worth a lot more than that on paper, but converting those assets to small, unmarked bills would be nearly impossible.

When she first decided to expand into potato chips, she had begun working on a deal with a local real estate weasel named Lee Plummer. She hadn't gone into detail—she wasn't sure yet that she could trust him—but had intimated that she wanted his help acquiring a large piece of real estate south of Fester. Now it occurred to her that it wouldn't be too much trouble to stretch the deal a little further. With a little creative accounting, she could easily pocket a million in cash and still get her potato chip factory.

Maybe she could move up the next meeting with Plummer, and accelerate the schedule. There was no point in waiting—six weeks sounded like a long time, but it was still going to be difficult to pull together that much cash in such a short amount of time. She checked her watch—it wasn't too late. She got Plummer's home number from her Rolodex and dialed.

The phone rang and rang, but no answer. Cecilia slammed down the phone and cursed. She went back downstairs to refill her drink, shrugged, and grabbed the whole bottle. She slumped down onto the couch and tried to watch her movie, but she couldn't concentrate. Her mind was going in eight directions at once. She just drank and fumed and stared blankly at the screen as Atlanta burned.

Chapter 5

There was no shortage of sleazy bars in Fester, and one of the sleaziest was the Pine Room. It was located in the main lodge building of a defunct children's summer camp on the western edge of town.

Despite its remote location, the Pine Room was immensely popular, and its parking lot was full nearly every night of the week. The real attraction for the Pine Room's clientele—who were almost exclusively male—were the waitresses. They were *very* friendly.

Hospitality was their main service, and even a casual observer would notice that only a small proportion of the "waitresses" delivered food or drinks. The rest were serving up something that wasn't on the menu. Those patrons desiring something beyond a burger or a pitcher of beer could accompany their favored waitress to one of the old camp cabins out back.

Lee Plummer and Mike Berg were installed at Lee's preferred table, watching the girls come and go. Lee looked totally average: he was of average height and average build, with average brown hair. His round, unassuming face framed a pair of restless gray eyes. His conservative business suit was off-the-rack—but off the rack of one of the nicer department stores in Baltimore.

"So how are things down at the ol' pretzel factory, Mikey?" asked Lee.

Mike was a maintenance engineer at the Schmidt Pretzel Bakery, and his primary job was to keep the ovens and conveyor belts in working order. He was a little older than Lee, with an iron-gray beard and a booze-busted nose. He had come directly from the pretzel factory and was still wearing his gray work fatigues.

"Ah, you know," said Mike. "Same shit, different day. As long as the paychecks keep coming, I can't complain." He took a sip of beer, his eyes following a short but well-endowed blond waitress across the room. "Holy shit, can't complain about *her*, neither. Damn, she's so top-heavy it's a wonder she doesn't keel right over!"

Lee regarded her briefly. "Yeah, Darla. She's a real peach, all right. You wanna get some hot wings or something?"

"I wanna get something hot, all right," said Mike. "Damn, did you see that Janet? She's looking better'n ever! You can't hardly tell she just dropped her third frog."

"No, you sure can't," agreed Lee distractedly. "So, you want some wings or what?"

"Huh? Oh yeah, sure."

Lee signaled a passing waitress, an older woman who was actually carrying a serving tray. She diverted from her flight path and stopped at the table. "Howdy, Lee. What can I getcha tonight?"

"Right now, we'd like a large basket of wings, extra hot."

"Coming up. Can I interest you in anything else? We've got a new girl on tonight—have you met her? Her name's Ramona."

"Nope, can't say that I've met her yet," said Lee.

"Well, I'll just send her on over, and have her introduce herself. I really think you'll like her."

"You do that, Lizzy. But for now, why don't you just hustle your buns back to the kitchen and rustle us up those wings?" He took another long sip of his beer as Lizzy made her way to a neighboring table to deliver her tray. "I've been hearing something about a big shake-up down at the pretzel factory. What's the word?"

"Aw, shit, man, I'm just a wrench-turner," said Mike. "They don't tell us diddly-squat. Working at Schmidt's is like being a mushroom, y'know? They feed us shit and keep us in the dark."

"Ah, c'mon Mikey, you know what's going on. You've been working there for nearly twenty years. I know you're connected. Don't yank my chain, okay?"

"Well, everybody pretty much knows that the boss lady went apeshit and canned half the board of directors. Apparently the Schmidts—the *real* Schmidts—are so mad they can't even see straight. Especially since it was all legal, and there's nothing they can do to stop her."

The waitress dropped off the wings, but Lee didn't notice. "So what was behind the shakeup, anyway?" he asked. "What got her to busting balls on the board?"

"The way I heard it, the boss lady's got some big plans. Gonna make some big changes, change the name of the company, maybe some other stuff. I guess she had to get rid of some of those old-school types on the board. Most of 'em don't do anything but collect a paycheck, anyway."

"Hi, Lee," purred a silky voice. "I haven't seen you in a while." An auburn-haired cutie slipped into the booth and snuggled up close to Lee. "Why don't you introduce me to your friend?"

Lee rolled his eyes. He was just on the verge of getting some useful information, and he didn't need this interruption now. He said, "Yeah, sure, introductions. Tammy, Mike. Mike, Tammy. The end. Now if you don't mind, the boys are talking business. Why don't you run along now, okay?"

"There's no need to be so mean, Lee baby." She pouted. "You sure weren't that way last time."

"Yeah, well there's not going to be a *next* time unless you make yourself scarce, Tammy Faye. Scram."

"Don't call me that! You know I hate it when people call me that!" She cast a hurt glance over her shoulder as she sashayed off to another table.

"Jesus Christ, Lee—what the fuck's wrong with you tonight?" asked Mike. "All these honeys in here, and you haven't even *looked* at one of 'em! That's not like you at all. You haven't touched the wings, either."

Lee leaned over the table to try to keep his attention from wandering. "Look, buddy, I'm sorry that I'm on edge here, but I just want to know what the hell's going on at the plant. You know, Carla's parents left her a pretty decent chunk of Schmidt stock. Nothing huge, but if something bad is going down at the bakery, I'd like to be able to unload that stock before it tanks." This wasn't entirely a lie, but the stock that his in-laws had left his wife was only worth about five hundred dollars.

Mike managed to peel his eyes away from Tammy's ass. "Oh, hell, Lee, I'd hang on to that stock if I were you." He leaned in conspiratorially. "The word is that Cecilia Schmidt wants to expand into potato chips. Wants to rename the company, too, which is why the rest of the Schmidts are all worked up. Anyway, the plant is already running at maximum capacity. They'd need to build another facility to handle the potato chip production."

This pretty much confirmed what he had gleaned from his previous meeting with Cecilia. There was just one more vital piece of information that he was after. "So, where do you think they'll be building that new plant? I don't think they've got any more room at the current site."

"Nobody knows for sure. The way I heard it, they're looking at a place over by Weaverville. Some farm that's gone bust. I'd hate to have to commute that far, but I'd be willing to do it if there was a pay raise involved."

Lee sighed and leaned back in his seat. The tract of land that Cecilia Schmidt had approached him about was nowhere near Weaverville, but it was good to know that the rumor mill was way off the mark. He said, "Well, I gotta tell you—that's a big relief. Thanks for putting my mind at ease. I guess I'll hang onto that stock after all."

"Good. Maybe now you can relax and enjoy yourself, get some r'n'r with one of these girlies. I was startin' to worry that you'd gone queer or something."

"Who? Me? You gotta be kidding, Mikey. Fact of the matter is that I've got a hot date with a redhead a little later this week."

Mike socked Lee on the shoulder. "Ah, that's the boy. I swear I don't know how you keep your wife from finding out."

"Hell, Carla's too married to her job to keep track of what I get up to. I just tell her that I'm working late or out playing poker with the guys. She's usually too wiped from her shift at the hospital to pay me any attention."

"Well, I'd be careful all the same if I were you. Word gets around in Fester, and you're getting a reputation . . ."

Lee checked his watch. "Look buddy, I gotta go." He pulled out his billfold and slipped a hundred across the table. "Here, this will cover the tab, and maybe a quick romp with Tammy back there. I appreciate it, Mikey."

"Wow, thanks, pal! You're a good man, Lee Plummer!"

"That's what your wife always says!" replied Lee, and he left the Pine Room with a spring in his step.

Chapter 6

Fester City Hall was a pile of smudged marble and dirty brick that loomed over the intersection of Sixth Street and Washington. The Fester Constabulary Headquarters, which stood right next to it, was even grimmer. It was a hulking, rectangular concrete box that looked like a gigantic cinderblock. Billy Snyder's office was on the southeast corner of the top floor.

It was early in the evening, and Billy was knitting in his office. He had finished up all of his paperwork and was now just waiting for Roscoe Dirkschneider to report in. Although there was technically no assistant chief constable position, Roscoe was the closest thing that Billy had to a second-in-command. Actually, "vice chief constable" would probably be a more appropriate title. Roscoe had a thing for vice.

Billy's office was large, but austere. The small collection of furniture—steel desk, wooden chairs, and a bookshelf crammed with unused law books—was crowded into one corner of the room. The walls were spotless white and unadorned, except for a framed certificate from the Pennsylvania Municipal Police Officers Education and Training Commission behind the desk, and some certificates of appreciation from the Rotary Club, the Jaycees, and the Odd Fellows. The only other objects in the office were a locked metal cabinet on the wall opposite the desk, and a large vertical pipe that stood incongruously near the center of the room.

While Billy's office didn't have much in the way of furnishings, it did boast a fabulous view. However, it rankled Billy that he could only see part of Fester from his corner office. Using contacts from his service in the

Marines, Billy had obtained some surplus military equipment to better keep tabs on his city.

The "pipe" in the center of the room was actually a periscope from a Skipjack-class submarine. It provided a panoramic view of Fester and its surroundings. Billy really couldn't see all that much with it, but it reassured him to be able to keep his eye on all points of the compass. The periscope was well-known in Fester. It comforted the well-off burghers who counted on the constabulary to maintain the status quo, and it made the criminals nervous. Everybody knew about Billy's periscope.

One the other hand, only Billy knew about the contents of the metal cabinet. It was crammed full of surplus military intel electronics, which were tied into the PennBell exchange two blocks away. It allowed Billy to monitor nearly every telephone line in Fester. This gave him considerably more reassurance than the periscope.

There was a pounding at the door, and it swung open to reveal Constable Roscoe Dirkschneider. Roscoe was in his late fifties, with a large, slab-like gut that overhung his belt. His blocky head sported a bristly iron-gray buzzcut and a perpetually pissed-off expression.

Billy put down his knitting and glanced at his watch. "Running late tonight?"

Roscoe clomped across the room and dropped into one of the straight-backed chairs in front of Billy's desk. "Yeah, I stopped by the fag bar to put a little extra squeeze on 'em. Some of the fruitloops got a little mouthy, and I had to teach them some manners."

"Hurt them much?" asked Billy.

"Not too much," replied Roscoe. "There's two of 'em in the holding cells. They'll be awright 'til morning."

"Yeah, so where's the cut?"

Roscoe pulled a wad of cash out of him pocket and began counting it out. "I got an extra hundred from the Embers. This was the Pine Room's week, so they're paid up okay. One or two of the darkie bars in Rivertown came up light, but I told 'em I'd go easy on 'em if they had the money by the end of the week."

"Okay, just be sure they don't skimp," said Billy. "Give those people an inch and they'll take a mile."

Roscoe finished divvying up the cash and handed part of it to Billy. Billy thumbed through it quickly, adding it up. "Seems a little light."

"Yeah, yeah, I told you, some of them Rivertown places were short."

"I know that, but you also said you got an extra hundred from the Embers, right?"

"Oh, yeah," said Roscoe. He handed Billy an additional fifty dollars. Billy shot Roscoe a dark look and tucked the cash away in his desk drawer.

"All right," said Billy. "Anything else I should know about?"

"Nah," said Roscoe. "All quiet on the western front. Only thing new is I'm gonna do some moonlighting. Doc Ziffer is having some sorta wingding at his house this weekend and needs someone to do security. Completely aboveboard, and he pays cash. I don't hafta cut you in, do I?"

"No, that money's all yours," said Billy. "Dr. Ziffer, huh?" He leaned back in his chair, thinking. A week ago, he had listened in on a phone conversation of Ziffer talking with a pharmaceutical company rep. Billy couldn't say for certain, but the two of them seemed to be up to something shady. Billy had overhead enough sneaky conversations over the years for Ziffer's exchange to pique his interest.

It put him in a delicate situation. As the chief constable of Fester, Billy was honor-bound to let Top Hats like Ziffer carry on whatever upper-class, low-brow behavior that they cared to, as long as it wouldn't draw adverse attention to the town. On the other hand, if Ziffer was messing around with drug dealing, then he was horning in on Billy's territory, and was therefore fair game.

Billy's electronic eavesdropping was very useful, but it also had its limitations. He definitely needed to get some human intelligence on what Ziffer was up to. Roscoe had very little intelligence, but if he was going to be up at Ziffer's house during a party, he might be able to come up with some useful information.

"What's up, boss?" asked Roscoe. "You got that funny look in your eye again."

"Probably nothing," said Billy. "But I want you to keep your ear to the ground at that party. I think Ziffer might be moving pills on the side. Let me know if you hear anybody talking about pharmaceuticals. I'll make it worth your while if you bring me back some useful intel."

Roscoe leaned forward eagerly. "You gonna cut me in on some of the drug action, boss? I'm fuckin' sick of just shaking down the bars. The real money's with the drugs, and I want a cut of it."

"Yeah, that's the problem," said Billy. "Whenever you get involved with the drug trade, you end up 'confiscating' too much of the product. Nobody's gonna make money selling drugs if you're taking them all for yourself. And if the dealers don't make money, then neither do I."

"Aw, shit, Billy, you know that ain't true. Sure, I'll take a little sample from time to time, but not much."

"'Not much,' my ass. You and Keith Richards, Roscoe—I don't know how either one of you is still walking around. Besides, you're making good money with the bar racket. That's regular income, and low-risk besides. You should be thankful."

"Shit," said Roscoe. There was a petulance in his voice that Billy hated. He didn't mind the violence, or Roscoe's penchant for demanding freebies from the whores on Adams Street, but the man's appetite drugs was a sore point for Billy. It cut into his take.

"Tell you what," said Billy. "You bring me some information on Ziffer, and it's worth five hundred to me. After that, maybe we can talk about cutting you in on some of the drug action in Rivertown."

"Rivertown?" said Roscoe. "That's all nickel-and-dime shit down there. C'mon, boss."

"Roscoe, don't give me a bunch of lip on this," said Billy sharply. "Just keep your ears open at Ziffer's party. You got that?"

"Yes, Chief," said Roscoe sullenly.

"Also, if you try holding out on me again, even ten bucks, we're going to have trouble. Dismissed."

Roscoe got up and left, slamming the office door behind him. He was like a guard dog that wasn't completely trained. It always paid to keep him on a short leash.

Also, the situation with Warnke was bothering him. Billy needed to keep a closer eye on him. If the clown was getting into the coke, there was no telling what sort of stupid bullshit he might get up to.

Billy checked his watch. It was getting late, but he wasn't quite ready to go home yet. Instead, he raised the periscope and spent the next thirty minutes scanning the town.

Chapter 7

Like most suburban neighborhoods, Krump Acres at night was safe, well-lit, and utterly boring. The teenagers who lived there spent their free time at the Spendmor Mall or on the neon-washed instant-gratification strip along North Jackson Street. Those with fake IDs gravitated towards the campus hangouts around Prosser College, while the truly adventurous would go slumming down in the Rivertown area.

Most of the rest just cruised, around and around the downtown business loop. They drove in their parents' innocuous sedans and minivans, or in their own older cars that were either beat to hell or souped up like crazy.

A tricked-out 1975 Chevy Nova turned off the main drag and slowly wound its way through Krump Acres. It was painted metallic midnight blue, jacked up in the back, with gleaming Centerline mag wheels. The throaty rumbling from its dual glasspack mufflers caused more than one curtain to twitch as it passed through the neighborhood.

It stopped in front of a darkened house on Hicks Lane. The driver, Michael "Bolly" Bollinger, emerged and closed the door carefully behind him. He was a lumpish teenager with a battered motorcycle jacket and greasy black hair that hung nearly to his shoulders. He looked up and down the vacant lawns of Hicks Lane and said, "Okay, Secret Squirrel, the coast is fuckin' clear."

Paul Plummer popped out of the passenger side of the car and ran for the front door of the house, hunched over like an infantryman dodging an artillery barrage. Bolly followed slowly behind, a bemused expression on his face.

37

Paul scuttled up to the door, fumbled with the lock and quickly pushed inside. "Hurry the fuck up!" he hissed. "You're attracting attention!"

"Yeah, Mr. Subtlety, sorry if I'm blowing your low-key routine. We just pulled up in a car that sounds like a B-17. Of course, the nonchalant way you made your exit undoubtedly deflected any suspicion." He went inside and slammed the door behind him.

"Jesus, Bolly, why do you have to be such a sped?" asked Paul when they had gotten to the kitchen.

"Dude, what crawled up your ass and died?" He flopped down in one of the kitchen chairs. "You call me to pick you up at the Grab-n-Gulp, whispering so I can barely hear you, you don't say a damn word on the ride over, and now you're acting like Lancelot Lunk, Secret Chump. What gives?"

"This gives, butthole," said Paul. He pulled the bulging baggie of pot from his jacket and tossed it on the table in what he hoped was a dramatic fashion.

It had the intended effect. Bolly gave a long, low whistle. "Holeee shit, dude! You could stuff a pillow with that much bud! Where the hell did you get the money for that much shit, anyway?"

"I didn't. Get the money, that is. The guy, like, fronted me for most of it." He gave Bolly an abbreviated version of his transaction with Cowboy Bob.

"So, what are you gonna do?" asked Bolly.

"I'm gonna sell it. What did you think I was gonna do?"

"So, what, now you're gonna be a drug dealer? Paul the Pusherman?"

"Hey, don't say that, man!" said Paul. "I'm not a drug dealer! I just, y'know, help my friends hook up."

"Yeah, I guess so," said Bolly. "I think you're gonna need to find some more friends, though."

"Shit, what choice do I have?" asked Paul. "It was easy enough when I was just buying an ounce and getting you and a couple other guys to go in on it. Now I gotta get rid of four times that."

"You coulda just told the guy no," Bolly pointed out.

"Yeah, that's easy enough for you to say—you weren't there," said Paul. "He was acting really fuckin' weird. I didn't want to piss him off."

"Then why didn't you just leave?"

"Because I wanted the goddamn pot, Bolly! So did you! You've been hassling me all week about when I was gonna score, so don't give me this 'Paul the Pusher' bullshit, okay?"

"Okay, okay, slack, slack," said Bolly. He pulled out a grimy nylon wallet. "Might as well go ahead and take some of it off your hands. How much for an eighth?"

"Just an eighth?" asked Paul, "C'mon, how about a quarter, man? I know you got the money—you told me just yesterday that your old man paid you for helpin' him rebuild that truck engine. Besides, this is some good shit. Take a whiff." He opened the Ziploc bag and waved it under Bolly's nose.

"Whew, man!" said Bolly. "That cowboy guy might be batshit crazy, but he sure gets some kind bud. Okay, sped, you're on. I'll take a quarter—but you're packing the first bowl. The second one, too."

"My man!" said Paul with a grin. "Whaddaya say we go on out to the garage and give this shit a test drive?"

"I say fuck yeah!" relied Bolly. "You sure it's cool, though? When are your 'rents getting back?"

"Ah, sure it's cool," said Paul. "My mom's working 'til nine, and my dad won't be home for another couple hours, at least."

Out in the garage, Paul loaded up a ceramic bong that looked like the Grim Reaper. He handed it to Bolly, who torched it up with a Bic. After a few passes, both boys were bent over, wheezing and coughing.

"Oh, holy shit, man," gasped Bolly. "That really is good weed. Hey, you got any tuneage in here?"

"Yeah, my dad's got a radio, but it only gets the shitkicker station."

"What, it can't get the Wop?" asked Bolly. "It should be late enough."

The only radio station that could reliably be picked up in Fester was WKKK, the local country/western station that billed itself as "Kerian's Kickin' Kountry." The area's top rock station, WOPP, was based thirty miles away in Weaverville. It could usually only be picked up in Fester at night, when the ionosphere allowed the signal to blast through the strange interference that screwed up regular reception in the town.

"Nah, the radio's messed up," said Paul. "Only gets the shitkicker station."

"Put in on, anyway," said Bolly. "It's better'n nothing."

"We'll see," said Paul. He snapped on the cracked Motorola on his dad's workbench, and Dave Frizzell began warbling "I'm Gonna Hire a Wino to Decorate Our Home."

"Holy shit," said Paul. "We're gonna need more weed to deal with this."

"Run it, dude."

Paul packed the bong again. As the two passed it back and forth, the wino song gave way to Waylon Jennings.

"Sweet merciful Christ," said Bolly. "I *must* be high—this music's actually beginning to sound good."

"Admit it, man—you're just a shitkicker at heart." This broke the two boys up laughing, and Paul nearly dropped the bong.

They smoked in companionable silence as the country music bleated on. Bolly gazed intently at the track for the garage door. Paul stared into the corner of the garage, regarding his bicycle.

About a year before, he had bent the front wheel. He had gotten his learner's permit a few weeks after that, and since then the bike had sat abandoned in the back corner of the garage. Paul felt a pang of regret, like he had been neglecting a sick friend. His stoned mind began working through all the possible permutations he would need to consider in order to fix the bent bike wheel.

Finally, he said, "Hey, Bolly, would I have to go all the way to Harrisburg for a specialty hammer store?"

"Do what?"

"Well, um, I was thinking about fixing my bike, because the front rim's all, like, potato-chipped, but I don't want to use my dad's regular hammer because it might fuck it up worse, so I guess I need to get a special bike wheel rim hammer, right? I don't think the suck-ass True Value here in town has any bike wheel rim hammers, but there's gotta be a specialty hammer store that sells 'em, right? I just don't wanna have to go, y'know, all the way to Harrisburg to get . . ."

Paul trailed off. Bolly was staring at him with a look of amusement. Why was he having so much trouble explaining himself? It all made perfect sense just a few seconds ago. "So I thought you'd, like, know about a store that sells bike wheel rim hammers," he finished lamely.

Bolly considered this for a moment. "Dude, why don't you just take it to a bike shop?"

"Oh, yeah. I hadn't thought of that."

They drifted off into silence again. After a few minutes, Paul said, "Holy shit, man. I just thought of something!"

"Amazing! Better call *Ripley's Believe It or Not!*"

"No, seriously, man. The Pretzel Fest is in a couple of weeks, right? This weed is going to be awesome for that. We can get totally baked and ride the Viking Ship. And the Whip! And all that other cool shit!"

"Hell, yeah, man," Bolly nodded. "That'll rock."

The boys lapsed back into silence, watching the smoke by the ceiling eddying and swirling, making intricate patterns in space.

Abruptly, Paul said, "I think I'm gonna ask Sara Ziffer to the Spring Dance."

"Dude, I don't get what you see in that chick," said Bolly. "She's not that hot, or anything. I mean she's okay, but definitely not, y'know, a fox."

"Aw, bullshit," said Paul. "Sara's no supermodel or anything, but she's cute and has a hot bod. Kinda."

"Yeah, right," Bolly snorted. "You sure you're not just after the family fortune? Her house up there in Morningwood Heights probably cost a couple million."

"I don't care about that shit," said Paul. "She's just, I dunno, real neat."

"Dude, seriously, she's out of your league."

"What the hell's that supposed to mean?"

"Nothing, man, nothing," said Bolly, holding up his hands. "I just mean that she runs in different circles than you and me."

Paul frowned, and Bolly continued, "Look, right now she's probably at some fancy fuckin' cotillion or something up at the country club, with her cheerleader friends and their Prosser college-boy dates. And here *we* are in a cold garage, smoking dope and listening to lousy country music like a couple of lunkheads."

"So what? That doesn't mean anything. Besides, I've got a couple of classes with her. She's not stuck up."

"You ever talk to her? I mean, have a real conversation?"

Paul frowned but didn't reply.

"That's what I thought. How about last year when you went out for football to get her attention, and she didn't even realize you were on the team?"

Paul's frown deepened into a scowl. "That's not true. I went out for football because it's a good sport and good for the school."

"Yeah, you're Mr. School Spirit, all right." Bolly shook his head. "Dude, you *hated* football practice, remember? You got to play for, what, ten minutes all season? Besides, you *told* me that the only reason you went out for it was to try and impress that Ziffer chick."

"That's bullshit!"

"C'mon, man, I hate to see you getting yourself worked up about her. Sara and the rest of those cheerleaders don't give a rat's ass about sports, anyway. It's all about status and looking good in front of their stuck-up friends. Believe me, you don't want to even bother with someone like Sara Ziffer."

"Goddammit, Bolly!" yelled Paul. "Why are you being such a buzzkill? You don't know shit about Sara. Hell, you don't take any college prep classes anyway, so how the fuck can you . . ."

Suddenly, there was a splash of light on the back wall and a rumble as the garage door began to go up. The door rose to reveal the bright lights and massive grille of Lee Plummer's Cadillac coming up the driveway. The boys froze, the high beams from the Caddy pinning them into place.

Paul and Bolly stepped aside as Lee's car pulled into the garage. A cloud of smoke rolled slowly out of the open door. The garage reeked of pot smoke. Paul and Bolly looked at each other helplessly. They were flat-out busted.

The car engine shut off, and Lee bounded out. "Hiya, guys," he said cheerfully. "Enjoying some music?"

Paul and Bolly said nothing, waiting for the hammer to fall.

"Well, I've had a heck of a day, let me tell you," continued Lee as he walked briskly to the door. "It's been work, work, work, all day."

"That's great, Dad," Paul managed to choke out.

"Y'know, I think I'm going to get myself a drink," said Lee. "I deserve one after the day I've had." He disappeared into the house.

Paul and Bolly looked at each other, wide-eyed. Bolly said, "How could he *not* have noticed that?"

"I don't know," replied Paul. "Let's just get the fuck out of here before he comes back."

They left the garage door up to try and clear out the smell and spent a nervous hour at Perducci's Pizza, shooting pool and guzzling Cokes.

Paul was worried when Bolly dropped him off, but there was no retaliation awaiting him. The garage had pretty much aired out. His mom still hadn't come back from her shift at the hospital. His dad was busy in his study. Paul went straight to bed without saying a word.

Chapter 8

C arla Plummer was suffering from a whopping migraine. She had always been prone to severe headaches, but it was only in the last five years or so had they graduated to full-blown migraines. And this one was a monster.

The migraines always coincided with periods when her husband was busy at work. Lee was away from home a lot, frequently spending late nights slaving away at the office. Lee was so dedicated to his job and to providing for his family that Carla sometimes felt unworthy of his affection.

She had felt this migraine coming on two nights ago, when Lee was pulling a late-nighter preparing for a big proposal. It was clearly a big deal, and Lee had been pretty excited. He said that it would mean big things for the Plummer family—you could see the gleam in his eye.

Carla really didn't care about having a bigger house or a fancier car, she just wanted to keep her family happy and her patients healthy. She certainly didn't care for climbing the social ladder in Fester, but she knew it was important for her husband's business.

She disliked all of the gossipy, backstabbing social one-upmanship that she had to endure. Lee insisted that it was for the good of the business and the family, so she put up with it. Deep down, she hated these small-town gossips and their shallow status symbols.

Carla was in her late thirties, with auburn hair pulled back in a bun and wide-set blue eyes that were just beginning to show evidence of crow's feet. She looked at the watch that was pinned to the front of her white uniform blouse. It was five minutes after nine. Her shift had just ended,

44

and she desperately wanted to go home, but Dr. Michael Ziffer had asked her to stop by his office. You simply didn't ignore a summons from the chief administrator of Kerian Memorial Hospital.

The elevator stopped and opened onto a spacious suite of offices. Most of them were dark, but one at the end of the hallway still had the lights on. An old woman in a blue housekeeping uniform was emptying trash into a pushcart. Carla could see no other people; the offices were usually deserted after six.

She made her way down to the lighted office at the end of the hall. Dr. Ziffer was at his desk, studying a patient folder. He was gray-haired and slightly balding, with a bushy moustache and wire-rimmed glasses. When he saw Carla his face broke into a fatherly smile. "Ah, Nurse Plummer, do come in. It's so nice of you to stop by, especially after a busy shift. Please, sit down."

Carla sat. "It's no problem, Dr. Ziffer," she said. "Although I am a little surprised that you would want to see me. I hope I haven't done anything wrong."

"Oh no, not at all. By all accounts, you are one of the finest, most capable nurses we have on staff." He picked up a folder and waved it in front of him. Carla could see her name written on the tag. "You are not in any trouble at all, Carla. You don't mind if I call you Carla, do you?"

"No, Dr. Ziffer, of course not."

"That's just fine. We don't have to bother with formality here, eh? If I'm not mistaken, your son is in the same class as my girl Sara at Fester High. I'm sure that we've run into each other at school functions. And, please, go ahead and call me Mike."

"Oh, I don't know if I feel comfortable with that. We nurses are under strict orders not to be . . ."

"Oh, yes, that," he said. "So many silly rules we have here. You can call me whatever you're comfortable with." He walked around to the front of the desk and sat down in the chair next to her. "Carla, according to your file you suffer from migraine headaches. I was going to ask you if you were still having problems with this, but it seems obvious that you are dealing with one right now. Judging from the asymmetrical dilation of your pupils, it must be a doozy."

Carla nodded miserably. "It's pretty bad."

"It must be really awful. Frankly, I'm amazed that you are able to work under such conditions. It is a testament to your dedication that you were able to show up at all, much less complete an entire shift."

Carla nodded tentatively, unsure of how to respond.

"Tell me, Carla, what medication are you taking for your migraines?"

"I've got a prescription for Migranal, but I don't like to take it when I'm working because it makes me feel queasy. When I have to work, I usually just take Tylenol."

"Does that really do anything to help?"

"A little, sometimes. It's probably more of a placebo effect."

Dr. Ziffer scowled. "I hate to think what that placebo might be doing to your liver. Look, I won't belabor the point. One of my functions here is to head up our research activities. We are currently pursuing some interesting projects. One of them is a new medication that shows promise for a number of neurological applications, including migraine. Perhaps you would be interested in joining the clinical trial group? I mean the group that is getting the real drug, not the control group."

"Yes. Oh God, yes!" An unexpected wave of hope swept through Carla. She felt like crying. "Anything to relieve this, even a little."

A benevolent smile spread across Dr. Ziffer's face. "Excellent, that's wonderful. You help me get data for my trials, and I help eliminate your discomfort. A win-win situation, eh?"

He went back around his desk and pulled a small bottle from one of the drawers. "I've already prepared a sample for you. It's called Torbuphenol. The instructions are on the bottle. It's preferable that you take it after eating, but not entirely necessary."

He held the pills out to her, but when she reached for them, he pulled them back. "One word of caution, though. There have been reports of some minor side effects: slight distortions in the visual field, minor dizziness, that sort of thing. It's probably best if you wait until you get home before you take the first dose and avoid driving afterwards. Is that acceptable?"

"Yes, yes, certainly. Anything to help with the pain." Carla's hand, still extended, began to shake. She could feel tears welling behind her eyes.

"Okay, very good." Dr. Ziffer gently placed the pill bottle in Carla's outstretched palm. "I won't keep you any longer. I'm sure you want to go home and try the Torbuphenol. I'm confident that it will have a profound effect on your condition."

"Thank you, Dr. Ziffer. Thank you so much!"

"Absolutely, Carla. I'm glad we can help each other out. After all, we're all a big family here at Kerian Memorial, right?"

She held the pill bottle closely to her chest. "Yes, that's right. I can't thank you enough for this."

He flashed the fatherly smile again. "Of course, of course. Now, if you run into any unusual side effects, you should contact me immediately. Otherwise, we'll schedule a follow-up in two weeks to see how you are faring. I am confident that the only effect will be a rather dramatic reduction in your migraine symptoms."

Carla stood to leave. It already felt as if the vise around her skull has loosed a bit. "Thank you again, Dr. Ziffer . . . Mike. I can't tell you how relieved I feel. It sometimes seems like this pain will never let up."

"I'm glad I could be of service," he said. "Now go on home and start feeling better. I have a bit more paperwork to finish and then I will be homeward bound as well." He sat down at the desk and pulled a stack of papers towards him.

Carla turned and left his office. She thought she could hear Dr. Ziffer chuckling to himself as she left. He was such a good man, happy to be able to help out a colleague in need.

Down the hall, the elderly housekeeper was still emptying trash into her cart. "Good night," Carla told her as she passed, but the housekeeper didn't even look up. It didn't matter. Just knowing that she had a shot at relieving herself of her misery made her feel considerably better. She pushed the elevator call button, tapping her foot impatiently as she waited for it to arrive.

Chapter 9

So you blew it with Sara Ziffer, huh?" asked Bolly. He was wheeling his Nova through the streets of Krump Acres, a cigarette hanging casually from his mouth.

"Yeah, sorta," said Paul, who was slumped in the shotgun seat.

"Whaddaya mean, 'sorta'?"

"Well, I was gonna ask her out at the end of Coach Tonka's eighth-period physics class, but I was waiting for the classroom to clear out so wouldn't have, y'know, an audience. Didn't matter anyway, 'cause I kinda got cock-blocked."

"You got cock-blocked? By who?"

"Janie Simmons."

Bolly grunted, took a final drag off his cigarette and flicked the butt out the window.

"Yeah, I know it sounds lame," Paul continued. She and Sara were talking, and Janie kept dragging the conversation out. It was on purpose, I know it. She kept looking back at me and smiling every time she did it. finally, Sara just splits before I could say anything. God, I hate that Janie!"

"What is it with you two?" asked Bolly. "You've hated each other's guts since, like, first grade. What the hell do you guys do to each other?"

Paul shrugged. The animosity between he and Janie was so long-lived that he couldn't even remember what had started it. Something about hair-pulling, he seemed to recall, but he couldn't remember who had pulled whose hair, or why.

"Well, buck up, Romeo," said Bolly. "Sara's bound to be at this party. You can have a beer or two to relax, and then make your move. Smooth, like Billy Dee Williams, y'know?"

"Yeah, I guess so," said Paul doubtfully. "Also, I've gotta unload some of this weed. I'm supposed to pay the dude by today. I brought a bunch of it to sell. I think I can unload a bunch at this party and swing by his house and pay him off later tonight."

"You've got some weed to sell?" said a voice from behind Paul.

Paul jumped, and turned to see an unfamiliar figure sitting in the back seat of the car. "Fuck! Who the hell's that?"

"Oh him? He's new," said Bolly. "He just moved here. I've got a couple of shop classes with him. He's cool. His name's Knob."

Paul twisted around to take a look at the new kid. He had lank brown hair framing a round face, with a thin layer of fuzz above his upper lip.

"Uh, actually my name's Terry," said Knob. "Terry Benson."

"Oh, no," corrected Bolly. "You're name's 'Knob' now."

"Why Knob?" asked Knob.

"Well, at first you were New Kid on the Block," explained Bolly. "Then I tried to shorten it up, but 'N-kob' was too hard to pronounce, so I just rearranged some of the letters, and presto! You're Knob."

"I don't like it," said Knob. "It makes it sound like I'm a dick."

"Tough titty," said Bolly. "In Fester, you're a dick until proven cool."

"Why do I have to have a nickname at all?" asked Knob.

"Because you're new here," said Bolly.

"Well, how long 'til I'm *not* new here?"

"In Fester, pretty much 'til you have grandchildren," said Paul. "Hey man, I need to cop some smokes. Let's stop at a Grab-n-Gulp."

"I dunno," said Bolly. "The constables have been cracking down on selling to minors."

"Yo, I know," said Paul. "Let's go to the one over on Boundary. Maybe Inbred Ted's working tonight."

"That freak?" said Bolly. "He creeps me out, big-time. Besides, Boundary's practically on the other side of town."

"Aw, c'mon, it's not that far," said Paul. "Plus, Inbred Ted's so out of it that we can just cart off a bunch of shit without paying. He'll definitely come across with the smokes."

"Yeah, okay," said Bolly. He yanked on the emergency brake and sent the Nova into a screeching bootlegger's turn that directed the car back in the other direction.

"Holy shit!" exclaimed Knob, as he slid across the back seat and slammed into the door. "Who the hell's this Inbred Ted, anyway?"

"He's a Totenkopf," said Paul, as if that explained the matter definitively.

"What the hell's a Totenkopf?" asked Knob.

"Totenkopfs are a big family of rednecks," explained Bolly. "They live way up in the hills. They're all fucked up. Inbred Ted's probably the only one of 'em that can hold a regular job, and he's still pretty messed in the head."

Paul said, "Yeah, we were in seventh grade with him, but by then he'd been held back so many times that he was, like, eighteen or nineteen years old."

"Come to think of it, it's pretty amazing that he made it all the way to seventh grade," said Bolly. "Probably makes him the genius of the family."

Bolly navigated the car through anonymous, homogenous subdivisions bisected by anonymous, homogenous shopping strips. The sun sank behind the hills as they wound through the faceless sprawl of suburban Fester.

"Well, we're here," announced Bolly. He tromped on the brake and screeched the Nova into a parking slot in front of a brightly lit convenience store. Inside, Inbred Ted Totenkopf was propped up behind the counter. He had a thousand-yard stare in his protuberant eyes and a sheen of drool on his large lower lip. Paul went up to the counter to begin the complicated transaction of purchasing cigarettes, while Bolly went foraging in the back of the store.

"Hey, Teddy, how's it going?" said Paul. "Remember me, man? I need some smokes. Hook me up with a pack of Marlboro Lights."

"Uh," said Inbred Ted. "Huh. Yeah. I remember you from school." A bubble of spit formed on his fishlike lips, swelled, and popped. He laughed and went back to staring out the window.

It took Paul ten minutes to walk Inbred Ted through the complex process of taking the cigarettes down from the rack, ringing them up, accepting his money, and returning the change. Bolly strolled by with a large bag of Schmidt Bavarian Pretzels, a six-pack of Coke, and a fistful of candy bars. He gave Inbred Ted a jaunty wave and continued out the front door without paying. Inbred Ted didn't give him a second look.

Cigarettes in hand, Paul joined Bolly in the parking lot. A beat-up Toyota pulled into the lot, and Janie Simmons got out. Catching sight of Paul and Bolly, she strolled over with a contemptuous grin. She was wearing a low-cut black top underneath an oversized Fester High letter jacket. Her long blond hair was tucked up under a Pirates ball cap.

"Aw, great, just who I wanted to see," Paul groaned.

"Well, if it isn't Beavis and Butt-Head!" Janie exclaimed.

"Yeah, nice to see you too, Miss Simmons," said Bolly with sarcastic gallantry.

"So solly, Bolly," said Janie. "I know *you're* no Beavis, but Plummer is *definitely* in the butthead category."

Paul responded with a classic of his own. "Hey Janie, is that your face or did your neck throw up?"

Janie smiled sweetly and flipped him the bird.

"We're just headin' over to Zack Huff's party," said Bolly. "You going?"

"Nah. We've got a family get-together tonight, some aunts and uncles down from Carlisle. I'm just making a run for chips and sodas. By the way, Butt-Head, way to choke with Sara Ziffer in physics the other day."

This caught Paul flat-footed. "What? I didn't . . . You . . ." he sputtered.

Janie frowned and patted Paul on the shoulder. "Poor Butt-Head. Too stupid to know when he's out of his league."

"Fuck you, Janie!"

She just laughed.

Bolly said, "Well, I'd love to stick around and listen to more of this witty banter, but I've got a party to liven up. See ya, Janie."

"Take it easy, Bolly. Make sure that monkeyboy here doesn't embarrass himself at the party."

Bolly grunted, grabbed Paul by the shoulder and turned him away from

Janie before he could initiate another exchange.

"Goddamn, that bitch drives me fucking nuts," said Paul as Janie disappeared into the store. "Besides, Butt-Head's the smart one."

"You shoulda pointed that out to her," said Bolly. "I'm sure she would have apologized. Y'know, she *is* kinda cute. Nice ass."

"Dude, you're out of your fucking mind."

"Yeah, whatever. C'mon, let's load up and roll."

Bolly backed the car out of the parking lot with a screech and headed towards the party. A few minutes later, he turned to Paul and said, "Shit, dude, if you're so hung up on that Sara Ziffer chick, why dontcha go see a powwower? Get fixed up with a love potion or something."

"That stuff's all bullshit," said Paul. "Besides, there aren't any powwowers around anymore."

"What's a powwower?" asked Knob.

"Powwowers are like, I dunno, these German witchdoctors," explained Bolly. "People useta go to have 'em cure warts, sell 'em potions, say a spell to make the crops grow better. Maybe they'd have 'em throw a hex on their enemies. My old man says they used to be all over the place when he was a kid, but not so much anymore."

"Man, that's crazy," said Knob. "This whole place is crazy. Tribes of rednecks in the hills, German witchdoctors putting hexes on people. What the fuck?"

"Welcome to Fester, dude," said Bolly.

"Besides, there aren't any powwowers anymore," said Paul. "Are there?"

"Yeah, there's probably one or two still around if you know where to look," said Bolly. "Speaking of looking, where the hell do we turn to get out of this subdivision?" Paul was silent as Bolly threaded back through the suburbs. He was thinking about Sara and love potions.

"Hey, Paul," said Knob. "You got any of that weed to sell?"

Paul snapped out of his trance. "Huh? Oh, yeah, man. You're cool, right?"

"Yeah, he's okay," said Bolly. "Knob's a cool cat. That's why I asked him along."

"Okay, sure," said Paul. "Twenty-five bucks for an eighth. Forty a quarter."

"All right, gimme an eighth," said Knob. He pulled out a huge leather Harley-Davidson wallet on a chain and handed over the money. Paul gave him one of the bags of pot from his jacket.

"See, we haven't even gotten to the party, and you've already made a sale," said Bolly. "Good job, Pusherman."

"Don't call me that!" snapped Paul. "I already told you!"

"Looks like I'm not the only one with a new nickname," observed Knob.

"Shit, you fuckers better *not* start calling me that! I'm *not* a pusher!"

"Lighten up, dude, I'm just raggin' ya," said Bolly. "Hey, we're here!"

The Nova slowly cruised past a large brick house with cars filling the driveway and lining either side of the street. A laughing group of teens was strolling up the ivy-lined walk. Bolly went around the next corner and parked away from the other cars on the street. "C'mon, ladies," he said as he shut off the ignition. "Let's bust this party open."

* * *

Forty minutes later, Zack Huff's house party was moving into high gear. His parents owned a cabin up in the Poconos, and often went away for the weekend, leaving Zack in charge. Zack was large and genial, with a booming laugh that sounded like a Grand Canyon echo. He was an outstanding athlete and an honors student but didn't really run with any specific high-school in-crowd; he just sort of fit in with all of them. Consequently, his parties were clique-free events where jocks, nerds, greasers, mathletes, and preps could all congregate without fear of exclusion or intimidation. Any potential conflicts were quickly and decisively settled by Zack himself, who could bench press three hundred pounds.

Paul, Bolly, and Knob stood in the living room, drinking beer out of plastic cups and watching the crowd. Every time the door opened to admit more guests, Paul's head swiveled around to check them out. During the course of his stakeout, he had already consumed four cups of beer, and was starting to get good and relaxed. He felt that a little pot would round off his buzz nicely.

Paul noticed their host walking by and grabbed him by the arm. He said, "Hey, Zack, is there someplace here where we could go to, y'know, toke up? Is that okay?"

Zack regarded him coolly. "What are you saying, Plummer? Are you asking me if you can do illegal drugs in my house? In my *parents'* house?"

"H-hey, look, dude, I didn't mean any disrespect or anything," said Paul. "I mean, if it's not cool, then it's not cool."

"Of course it's cool, fool! Haw haw haw!" Zack gave Paul a meaty whap on the shoulder. "Jesus, Plummer, you're such a sped! Haw haw haw! We'll just go up to my room and have a little session. C'mon, follow me."

"Man, I didn't know you smoked," said Bolly. "I thought you were, like, Mr. Athletics and shit."

"Yeah, well, it helps take the pressure off, sometimes, y'know," said Zack with a shrug. "Just gotta make sure not to get too far into it. You see some of these burnouts walkin' around school, and you know that's all they do. Fuckin' losers."

Paul hunched his shoulders; it felt like Zack was staring at him while delivering this judgment. They went upstairs into Zack's room, and were soon joined by several other stoners who were tipped to the fact that there was a session in the works. Paul managed to quickly unload three more bags of weed.

After the first bowl, Zack, Bolly and Knob went back downstairs. Paul opted to stay upstairs and continue smoking and selling. By the time the bowl had made a few more rounds, he'd almost forgotten that there was a full-fledged party going on downstairs. *Sara!* he suddenly remembered. Surely she'd be here by now.

He stumbled to the stairs and then froze, looking at the scene below. The size of the crowd had tripled since he had gone into Zack's room. The living room was crammed shoulder to shoulder with drinking, dancing, talking, jostling people. The lights seemed too bright; the music too loud. He became acutely aware that he was standing in sight of the whole crowd, like an actor making a big entrance. He fought back an urge to go back to the bedroom and forced himself to continue down the stairs.

Neither Bolly nor Knob were anywhere in sight. Paul shouldered his way through the crowd, feeling intensely self-conscious. Another beer would help take the edge off. Paul lined up by the keg in the kitchen. As soon as he had gotten his beer, he chugged it down and wandered back into the living room. His mouth no longer felt like the Sahara, and he felt like he could successfully brave the crowd again. He spotted Bolly leaning against the wall by the fireplace and worked his way over next to him.

"Hey, check that out," Bolly said, jerking his chin towards a knot of people who were dancing to a Mariah Carey song. Knob was boogeying away with one of the second-tier cheerleaders.

"Lookit the new kid bustin' some moves," said Bolly. "You gonna get out there and strut your stuff, Twinkletoes?"

"I dunno. Maybe when Sara shows up, I'll ask her to dance."

Bolly took a long pull from his beer. "Well, man, she actually just got here. But you're not gonna be too happy about it."

Paul felt a jolt go through him. He scanned the crowd but couldn't see the girl of his dreams. "What? Whaddaya mean? Where?"

"Over there, by the front door."

A group of jocks and their cheerleader dates were standing just inside the entry foyer. The guys were wearing letter jackets. The girls were looking sharp, dressed for a big night, with their warpaint in full effect.

Paul could make out Sara Ziffer in the cluster of new arrivals. The largest of the football players had his arm draped possessively around Sara's shoulders.

Paul sagged. "Jesus. What the fuck's she doing with Garth? That guy's a total dickblister!"

"Yeah, he is," agreed Bolly. "Garth Bowman: wrestler, captain of the football team, and All-American Asshole."

"Jesus fuck! He's the biggest jerk in the whole school! What the hell would Sara see in him?"

"Women," said Bolly philosophically. He shrugged and took another swig.

Garth and his crew pushed into the living room. Paul's gaze fixed on Sara. She was short and slender, with light brown hair and wide blue eyes. She was decked out in heels and a low-cut black T-shirt dress that was cinched around her waist with a belt of golden seashells. Paul thought she had never looked so beautiful.

Bolly said, "Dude, let it go. Sometimes you gotta pick your battles. Maybe we should split—go hang out at Perducci's and play some pinball or something."

"No, man. I'll be okay. I'm gonna go get another beer." He spun away and pushed back into the kitchen.

Paul spent the next hour alternating between drinking beer in the kitchen and staring resentfully at Sara and Garth in the living room. What the hell could she possibly see in that meathead? Garth wasn't even paying attention to her, yet she followed him around like a puppy.

If only she could understand how Paul felt about her, she would ditch that asshole in a heartbeat. He had to let her know, and he had to do it *right now*. No more delays, no more fucking around. It was *go* time; it was now or never.

Bolly sidled up to him and said, "Dude, I can't help the feeling that you're getting ready to do something stupid. C'mon, why don't . . ."

"Fuck off," said Paul without looking at him. "You don't know my feelingsh." He finished his beer, threw the cup decisively to the floor, and wove off through the crowd.

In the corner, Garth and his football buddies were engaged in a push-up contest. Sara stared raptly at this display of machismo. Paul crowded up until he was standing right behind her. Her could smell her hair and perfume, and his head spun. He cleared his throat, but she took no notice. Finally, he tapped her heavily on the shoulder.

She spun around angrily. "Hey, watch it! You made me spill my beer!"

"Sorry, Sara, I jusht . . . I gotta tell you shomething . . .

"What? What are you talking about, Paul? I can't understand a word you're saying."

Paul leaned in close and said, "I love you, Sara!"

She recoiled from him. "Ewww! You're drunk! And stoned! You reek like a frat house!"

Paul's mind reeled, struggling for words that would adequately convey the depth of his feelings for her. Desperately, he blurted, "I wanna have your babies!"

A heavy hand clamped on his shoulder and spun him around. He looked up at the maliciously grinning face of Garth Bowman, who said, "Why are you bothering my woman, you little pussy?"

Paul moved so that he stood toe-to-toe with Garth, who had five inches and at least fifty pounds on him. Paul didn't care. He yelled, "Shcrew you, Bowman! You're a shtupid fuckin' shtupid meathead! You're not . . . not good enough for her! You're jusht a big, bullying douchebag!"

The angry expression on Garth's face was momentarily replaced by a look of comical surprise. Then his mirthless grin returned. "Okay, asshole," he said. "You just signed your own death warrant." He grabbed the front of Paul's shirt, pulling him up so he was standing on his toes. His other hand curled into a fist and began to draw back.

Things seemed to move in slow motion. The crowd had gone silent. The pulsing beat of the music seemed to come from far away. Garth's fist looked as big as a canned ham. Paul winced, waiting for the blow to fall.

Suddenly, Zack Huff thrust between Paul and Garth, shouting "Knock it off, assholes! No fighting! No fighting!" Paul could see Garth's reddened face over Zack's shoulder, shouting. Paul felt hands grab the back of his jacket, yanking him back roughly.

Bolly dragged Paul up the stairs. From behind them, Garth was shouting, "You're dead meat, Plummer! I'm gonna pound you like a piece of cheap veal! *Nobody* calls me a douchebag, you stupid pussy!"

Bolly thrust Paul into Zack's bedroom, slammed the door shut, and leaned on it. The handful of remaining smokers looked at them in red-eyed confusion.

"What's going on?" asked one. "What's with all the yelling?"

"Nothing," said Bolly. "Just a couple of assholes fighting over a piece of tail."

"Hey!" said Paul. "Sara's not a piece . . ."

"Shut up!" commanded Bolly. He snatched the smoldering pipe and thrust it at Paul's face. "Smoke that!"

Paul smoked.

Bolly eyed him critically. "Good goin', Romeo. Now you got the biggest, strongest asshole in school gunning for you."

"I'm sorry, Bolly." Paul could feel the adrenaline starting to sink in. He felt like he was going to throw up and start crying. "I . . . I don't know what I was thinking. Sorry I told you to fuck off."

"Never mind that," said Bolly. "We gotta figure out how to get you outta here without half the football team doing the *lambada* on your skull."

Someone said, "Hey, what happened to the music?" The constant thumping that had been going on all night had stopped.

There was a frantic tapping at the bedroom door. "Cops!" hissed a voice on the other side. "The constables are here! The party's busted!"

A lance of fear stabbed through Paul's guts. He frantically patted his jacket. There were still seven or eight bags of pot in the pockets. If the constables caught him, he'd be up on a felony distribution charge. "Oh fuck!" he cried. "We gotta get outta here! What are we gonna do?"

"The window!" cried Bolly. He jumped to his feet and stuck his head out the window. "We're right above the back porch. We can climb down off the roof."

There was a rush as everyone in the room made a push for the window. They tumbled through the window one by one, slithered to the edge of the porch roof and dropped off the corner.

Outside, there was mayhem in the Huff's back yard. Red and blue lights splashed on the sides of the house next door. Kids were spilling out of the back door and dashing into the darkness. Shouted commands and confused yelling came from inside.

"Jesus, that was close!" said Paul.

"We ain't out of the woods yet," said Bolly. He pointed across the back yard. "That way! Let's book!"

Behind them, a uniformed constable burst onto the back porch, waving a massive flashlight. "Halt! All of you stay where you are!"

"Wait!" panted Paul. "I gotta get rid of this shit!" He scrabbled frantically in his jacket pockets, pulling out handfuls of pot-filled baggies and flinging them away into the darkness.

A voice from the yard cried, "Fuck you, pig!" The constable with the flashlight charged towards the defiant partygoer. Paul and Bolly cut in the other direction and dove through a hedge, emerging in a dark back yard.

A few minutes later, they stumbled out onto a quiet street. The noise and confusion from the busted party could still be heard in the distance.

"Where the hell are we?" asked Bolly.

"We couldn'ta gone too far," said Paul. "Wait, there!" He pointed down the street, where Bolly's Nova sat serenely under a streetlight a block and a half away. They sprinted for it.

Bolly had the ignition turning over before they even had the doors closed. The car started with a deafening roar. As they pulled away from the curb, a dark figure burst from the bushes behind them, running towards the car and shouting.

"Holy shit!" said Paul. "There's another pig! Fuckin' floor it!" Bolly mashed the accelerator to the mat, sending the Nova into a screeching fishtail down the middle of the quiet suburban street. Paul twisted around to watch the figure behind them recede into the distance.

Paul laughed shakily. "Damn, I think we lost him! Now we just gotta get the hell outta this maze."

"Don't worry, man. I'll get us gone." Bolly slowed to a slightly less insane speed and began navigating back towards the center of town. Paul slumped in his seat, feeling sick and scared. The evening that had seemed so promising had turned out to be a total disaster. He had thrown away most of his weed and— even worse—totally blown it with the girl of his dreams.

Behind them, Knob stopped running and watched the Nova's taillights disappear around a corner. He wondered how the hell he was going to get home, and why his parents had ever wanted to move to this insane town in the first place.

Chapter 10

Martin arranged himself in the hard, straight-backed chair in front of Chief Constable Snyder's desk. It was remarkably uncomfortable, and it reminded him of his childhood in the Holy Jesus Christ Almighty Home for Unfortunate Boys. It was as if he had been called into Father McJaggar's office to answer for some infraction. He unconsciously began rubbing the knuckles of his left hand, in anticipation of a smack with a steel yardstick. "What was it you wanted to discuss, sir?"

"I wanted to discuss the Prosser killings. Have you spoken with the parents yet?"

"I've spoken with the Neff family, but I have been unable to speak with the Drehers," Martin said. "Unfortunately, I was unable to learn much of substance from Neffs. No overt signs of problems, drugs, anything like that. I hope to gather some useful information when I talk to the shooter's family."

"Don't worry about it, Prieboy," said Snyder. "I'll handle the case from here. I'll talk to Carl Dreher, and finish tying up the loose ends. I've known Carl for over thirty years. It will be easier coming from me."

"Yes, sir," said Martin. "But why not just come along with me? I'm more than willing to continue the case on my own."

"Prieboy, don't look at this as anything but a bonus. I'll carry the rock the rest of the way. You know as well as I do how often this sort of thing occurs in Fester. The only two people who really know what happened are dead. Let's leave it at that and get this one in the record books."

"Sir, you don't have . . ."

"Don't argue with me, Inspector! Shit, I'm doing you a favor. A little appreciation would be nice."

"Of course. Thank you, sir," said Martin. This was feeling more and more like a dressing down from Father McJaggar. He wanted to finish this conversation quickly. "Is there anything else?"

"Hm, perhaps," said Snyder. "What do you know about Randolph Warnke?"

"He's Fester's resident celebrity," said Martin. "Used to do a kids' TV show in Weaverville. He retired to Fester about four or five years ago. Sometimes he does grocery store openings in his Cowboy Bob persona. Why do you ask, Chief?"

"His name came up. It got me to wondering about him. Just a feeling, nothing more."

"I understand," said Martin. Like any good cop, he understood the power of intuition. It was, of course, no match for diligent investigation and logical analysis, but it had its place. It was like Edison's saying about genius: good police work was one percent inspiration and ninety-nine percent perspiration.

"Well, if you hear anything about Warnke, you let me know. Even if it's big, you come to me first. Okay, Prieboy?"

"Is there something I should know, Chief?"

"Nope," said Snyder. "Nothing to concern yourself with. You're dismissed, Inspector."

***

Martin pulled into his driveway an hour later. He was troubled by the exchange with the chief constable. Of course, he was the Chief; it was his prerogative to delegate assignments and information as he saw fit. Nonetheless, being relieved of the Prosser case and the odd questions about Randolph Warnke bothered him.

Under normal circumstances, Martin would have teased at it, trying to unravel why it bothered him so much. He had cracked more than one case by exploring similar nagging doubts, but this time he would have to leave it well enough alone. He supposed that he just had to trust his chief.

It would help if he could just unwind a little. There *was* one thing he could to do when he was feeling tense and anxious that never failed. He didn't do it often, but it seemed like a good idea right now.

He locked the front door behind him, closed all of the curtains in the living room, and removed a metal lockbox from a cabinet in the corner. He took a deep breath and unlocked the metal box and slowly raised the lid. For several minutes, he just stared at what was inside, then reached in, removed the contents and placed it reverently on the table.

The lurid colors of the comic book jumped out in the light of the halogen spot. The cover was mostly yellow with a broad red swath across the top which backed the title of the publication: *Detective Comics*. Below that was a drawing of a dark costumed figure snatching up a bad guy while two other villains looked on in disbelief. Bold text in the corner announced, "Starting this issue: the amazing and unique adventures of THE BAT-MAN!"

It was issue number twenty-seven, and it had been published in May of 1939. The price on the cover was ten cents, but Martin had paid nearly thirty thousand dollars for it—almost his entire life savings. There were only a few dozen surviving copies in the world.

Just staring at the vivid cover of his prize, Martin felt redeemed. He remembered the day he had found a much-used copy of a Batman comic book while cleaning the lavatory at the orphanage. He knew that he should turn it in to Brother Mordecai, who was in charge of hygiene and discipline. He couldn't specifically remember having been told that comic books were against the rules, but it seemed like a safe bet. Just about everything besides praying and studying was against the rules at the orphanage. Under normal circumstances, Martin would have handed over the contraband immediately. Instead, out of reflexive curiosity, he opened the cover and glanced at the first page.

Thirty minutes later, he had read it cover-to-cover twice, and then hidden it beneath a loose floorboard in a supply closet. Later, Brother Mordecai had thrashed him for the inadequate job he had done cleaning the lavatory. Martin had felt that the beating had been a small price to pay for the amazing relief and escape that the tattered comic book had brought him. For the first time that he could remember, all of the fear, loneliness and uncertainty that made up his life in the orphanage had been swept away. He still felt an echo of that relief and wonder whenever he looked at his prized issue twenty-seven.

When Martin turned eighteen, he had gone straight from his indentured servitude at the orphanage to the Pennsylvania Police Academy. He graduated at the top of his class. Instead of taking a position with the State Police—where he could have had his pick of assignments—he opted instead to take a much less prestigious posting in the Fester Constabulary. This decision was driven by a desire to reconnect with the tenuous roots he had with the town as a young boy, before the car crash that had claimed the lives of his parents.

As a beat constable in Fester, Martin had taken courses in law enforcement at Prosser College, and aced all of them. Seeking more of a challenge, he began taking extension courses in forensics and criminology from the University of Pittsburgh. He had busted the curve on these as well.

Soon, Martin was promoted to chief inspector—the youngest in Fester's history. He excelled at his job, garnering awards and commendations. Martin loved his work and was very good at it. Contemplating his prized comic book always reminded him of this. It helped keep him grounded—especially when things at work became difficult.

For the next thirty minutes, he read through the comic book, carefully turning the pages with tweezers, and brushing away specks of dust with a soft-bristled brush. When he finished, he lovingly returned it to the velvet-lined lockbox. He stared raptly at the comic book for another few minutes before closing the box and returning it to its place in the cabinet. Then, with a broad smile on his face, Martin went upstairs and got ready for bed.

Chapter 11

Lee Plummer gunned his Cadillac down Route 17 towards Weaverville, hoping there were no speed traps. It would not be good to keep Cecilia Schmidt waiting.

When she first approached him about the land deal, Lee was over the moon. The deal itself was a little hinky, though. Schmidt was after a large piece of forested land south of town, known to the old-timers as the Wizard's Woods. It was reputed to be haunted and generally regarded as bad luck. Most of the residents of Fester steered clear of it. Cecilia Schmidt, however, regarded it as the perfect place for her new potato chip factory, and was determined to get her hands on it. Lee had readily agreed to help her get the land.

The land was deeded to Kerian Memorial Hospital, and a mental hospital had stood on the part of the property until it had burned down in the early sixties. The hospital's claim to the land was murky, though, and Lee thought that he could finagle the right to the property away from the hospital.

Of course, he had told Cecilia Schmidt a more confident story, making it sound like he practically had the deal sewn up. Now he was starting to sweat, even though he had made a lot of progress in the last couple of days. A contact in the city clerk's office had just come through with a vital lead, but there was still a lot of work to do. Cecilia Schmidt would undoubtedly be impatient.

Lee arrived at his destination, a notorious dive called the Sharpe Turn, which squatted by the side of Route 17 just outside of the Weaverville city limits. They'd decided their meetings would go unnoticed there. No one would expect Cecilia Schmidt to be in such a place. He paused in front of the entrance, flipped up the collar of his topcoat, and looked around quickly to make sure that there was no one to witness his entry. He pulled open the door and stepped through quickly.

Inside, he was met with a blast of country music and despair. It smelled yeasty and dank, like the carpet in a condemned fraternity house. Most of the space was dark, lit here and there with bare 40-watt bulbs. The only real light came from the garish red and pink neon beer signs behind the bar. A balding man wearing a dirty wife-beater undershirt and an eyepatch made out of duct tape wiped down the warped wooden bar. A handful of despondent-looking regulars slumped at the far end.

Lee moved quickly out of the neon glare of the bar area into the gloom of the seating area in the back. Here, more patrons lounged in high-backed booths and mismatched tables. Lee gave himself a minute to let his eyes adjust to the darkness, and then scanned the room trying to spot Cecilia Schmidt. He couldn't see her, but he could tell that she was there just by the smell of Chanel No.5. He made his way to a booth in the nearly lightless back corner of the bar where Cecilia sat, regarding her surroundings with undisguised contempt.

"It's about damn time you got here," she said, as Lee removed his coat and slid into the stuffing-sprung vinyl seat. He took a quick glance at his watch, revealing that he was in fact five minutes early.

"Sorry, Cecilia," Lee said.

"That's 'Ms. Schmidt' to you, Plummer," said Cecilia. "Don't you forget it. Now let's get down to business so I can get out of this dump. We need to quit fucking around and get the rights to that land. We need to get the assessment and the loan taken care of, and above all we have to keep the whole thing quiet. And we need to do it fast. Like last week."

"Jesus!" said Lee. "Uh, I mean it's not going to be that easy. We can't rush into it without proper preparations . . ."

"'Proper preparations'? Dammit, Plummer! You said you could take care of this without any hassles, and now you're punking out on me?"

"I-I'm sorry, Ms. Schmidt," he said. "Normally, it wouldn't be this much of a problem. This is a special case. I've determined that the hospital doesn't legally own that land, but beyond that it's a little more complicated. I've made a lot of progress in the last few days, but there are still some details that need to be worked out. We need to approach the owners cautiously."

"Cautiously? You pussy! Why do we need to approach them cautiously?"

"Well, according to my source, that land is actually the property of the Totenkopfs."

"The Totenkopfs? Who the hell are they?" Cecilia demanded.

"I keep forgetting that you're not from around here," said Lee. "The Totenkopfs have a reputation, well, for . . . let me put it this way—have you ever seen *Deliverance?*"

"The only deliverance I care about is you delivering on your promise to get the title to that fuckin' land!"

Lee realized he could really go for a drink right now. "Well, it may actually be a little dangerous. The Totenkopf clan is pretty strange. They don't like outsiders and have a history of violence."

A waitress loomed up over the booth. She looked twenty-five going on sixty. Lee ordered a screwdriver. Cecilia just curled her lip in disdain. The waitress shrugged and disappeared. Cecilia removed a large silver flask from her purse and took a long draw.

More people were coming into the Sharpe Turn. A dark figure slipped into the adjacent booth. Someone plugged a quarter into the jukebox, which began wailing "All My Exes Live in Texas."

Cecilia upended the flask. She shuddered and sighed, "Oh, shit, I needed that. Those Scots really know how to take the edge off."

She returned the flask to her purse. She seemed much more relaxed now that she'd had a belt. "Look, Lee," she began, "I know that this must be difficult for you. But certainly, you realize that this will be the best thing for both of us."

"Yes, of course," Lee said. "I'm just not sure that the timing is right . . ."

"Of course, it's right," Cecilia said, with a little more edge in her voice. "We both know that. But there can't be any doubt in either of us. Are you committed to this, or not?"

Lee paused. Even though he still had his doubts about the deal, now was not the time to vacillate. "Yes," he said firmly. "I'm committed . . ."

"You BASTARD!" came a familiar voice from behind Lee's head. He turned around to see a fiery-eyed figure rising up from the booth behind him. It was his wife.

"Carla! What the hell are you doing here?"

"I would ask you the very same question, Lee Austin Plummer! I'd ask, but I already know!" Carla's face was white with fury.

"B-but, dear, you don't understand," Lee stammered. "It's not what you think!"

Carla ignored him. "No wonder you two sneak over here for your little meetings! Hiding away out here won't help! I've heard enough, and I don't care about your excuses!" She drew a ragged breath. "I know what you two are up to! I don't have a problem with letting the whole town know, either. You sneaky jerk!" She swung at Lee, connecting squarely on the side of his face, then abruptly turned and ran out of the bar.

"Don't just sit there, idiot!" Cecilia commanded. "Get after her!"

Lee rose from his seat and began stumbling towards the front door. Jeers and catcalls from the other patrons rose over the blaring jukebox honky-tonk. An anonymous leg slithered out from one of the booths, tripping Lee as he went by. He went sprawling onto the sticky floor. The raucous hooting and laughter intensified as he scrambled to his feet.

As he staggered into the parking lot, he could see his wife's minivan pulling out onto the highway. He stood breathing heavily as the taillights disappeared down Route 17.

"Good going, jackoff," came an icy voice. He turned to see Cecilia staring at him, her arms crossed.

"I, uh, look Ms. Schmidt . . ." he began lamely.

"You heard what she said. Somehow, she knows about our deal. I thought that you would be discrete, but I clearly underestimated what a total shithead you are."

"My wife's been acting a little moody since she got this new prescription," said Lee. "I don't think she knows anything. She just thinks that we . . ."

"Doesn't know anything?" Cecilia shrieked. "Didn't you hear what she just said, Plummer? She's going to screw up the whole deal! She works at the hospital, doesn't she? If the damn Board of Directors gets wind of this, we're fucked!"

"Look, it's just a misunderstanding," said Lee, who was beginning to regain his composure. "She just thinks that we're having an affair."

"Ha!" barked Cecilia. "In your dreams, pal! There's no shortage of idiots in Fester, but there are none so idiotic as to think that I'd be fooling around with the likes of *you!*"

Lee blinked, stung by this assessment. He said, "I'll take care of everything. There's no reason to worry."

"I've got plenty of reason to worry," huffed Cecilia. "But you're right about one thing: you *will* take care of this. If you don't, you will be finished in Fester, in Kerian County, in Pennsylvania. Timbuktu won't be far enough away if you screw this up."

Lee opened his mouth to protest, but Cecilia cut him off. "Not one more word, Plummer, or I'll claw your goddamned eyes out." She wagged a carefully sculpted nail in front of his face. "You are going to get in that pathetic Cadillac, and drive back home, and straighten out your little wifey. Then you're going to call me and let me know that the problem has been taken care of and that the deal is going to go ahead immediately. Now go!"

Lee hung his head and limped back to his car. In the rearview, he saw Cecilia reach into her purse and yank out the flask. Without another look back, he pulled onto the highway in pursuit of his wife.

Chapter 12

Paul cruised slowly down Back Duck Road. It was a desolate rural road that peeled off from Route 23 south of Fester. Ahead on the right was a listing mailbox with the number 13013 in crooked stick-on numbers—his destination. He pulled the minivan past the mailbox and over to the shoulder. Set back from the road was an old-style wooden farmhouse, partially built into the steep hill which rose behind it. There was no driveway, just an overgrown flagstone path that led up to a sagging porch. A hand-painted sign hanging from the porch read "N. Emig, Notery Public."

For the last several days, Paul had been obsessing about Sara Ziffer to the exclusion of nearly everything else. Eventually, Bolly's remark about finding a powwower had taken root in his mind and grown like a weed. He decided to seek one out to provide help with his Sara problem.

The trouble was actually finding one. He had finally gotten a lead from none other than Inbred Ted Totenkopf. "Oh, yuh, I knows a good un," Inbred Ted had said. "You'll want Ol' Lady Emig. She's out on Back Duck Road. She helped fix up m' brain problem." Following Inbred Ted's lead, Paul found a listing in the phone book for an N. Emig at 13013 Back Duck Road.

Now, Paul could feel a clockspring of apprehension unwinding in his stomach. The house was isolated and creepy. The misspelled sign made Paul wonder what sort of bumpkin he was going to be dealing with. He warily climbed the swaybacked steps and halted before the front door.

"Come in, alreddy" said a voice with a strong Pennsylvania Dutch accent.

"Yez lettin' the flies in."

Paul entered the front room of the house. It was incredibly cluttered. Piled on nearly every surface were stacks of newspapers and books. A small green hardbound volume was in its own reading stand on a desk. Paul could see the faded title on the well-worn cloth cover: *The Long-Lost Friend*.

An old woman in a faded pink housedress regarded him with a pair of piercing blue eyes that peered out from an array of wrinkles and crow's feet. "Yez wait here," she said "I'll be right back." She disappeared behind a pile of boxes.

On one wall, there were seven rococo gilt frames. Each one contained a small square of paper covered with careful, ornate handwriting. Paul leaned over and squinted at one of them, trying to make out what was written there: "God is with him who carries this heavenly letter in times of war and peace, and shall be protected from all danger, be it visitation from fire or flood, through the power of our Lord . . ."

"*Himmelsbrief*," said a voice from behind him.

Paul jumped. "Huh?" he asked. "What's that?"

"Them there's *Himmelsbriefs*," said the old woman. "Keep yez safe in all cases and places. My Grampaw Spangler made those. Yez can't have 'em, but I can write yez up one works chust as good."

"Er, no thanks," said Paul. "No, that's, um, not really what I came here to talk to you about."

"Oh?" the old woman said, smiling and raising one fluffy white eyebrow. "And chust what was yez comin' to talk to me about? Yez got a name, boy?"

"Paul Plummer," he said, automatically extending his hand. His father had long ago taught him to do this whenever he met an adult.

The old woman looked even more amused, then stepped forward and gave Paul's hand a hearty pump. "I'm Nettie Emig. Paul Plummer, eh? Yez must be Lee Plummer's boy."

Paul's mouth dropped open. "Uh, yes, that's right. How did you know?"

"Close yez mouth before them flies get in there," cackled Nettie. "There ain't too many Plummers 'round these parts. Yer paw's that real estate seller, got his phiz on billboards all over town. You looks chust like him. Sit down."

She waved vaguely at a couch that was covered with piles of ancient copies of the *Fester Daily Dispatch*. Paul shoved a pile aside and sat down.

"Mind yez, I gots the power," said Nettie. "I got it when I was chust a little girl. I had a vision and saw a huge golden staircase. The voice of Chesus tole me to climb it, and when I reached the top there was this Indian standin' there. He's been my spirit guide ever since. He's called Chief Tonto. He helps me when I'm tryin' for people."

"'Trying for'—what's that?" asked Paul.

Nettie laughed. "When yez try for a person, yez use the power that comes from Chesus to help 'em."

"Oh, yeah. I got you. Can you also use your power to, like, put a hex on people?"

Nettie's face darkened. "Hexes are bad work. Yez need not be messing with the like o' such things, Paul Plummer. The power of Chesus can take a hex off'n someone, but it's the devil's work to put one on."

"I had a hard time finding you," Paul said. "My friend Bolly says that there used to be a lot of powwowers around, but I guess now there's only you and maybe a few others left."

Nettie looked at him sharply. "Yez wrong there, Paul Plummer. There's still plenty of powwowers around. The thing is, anymore there ain't but a few of 'em trying for people. Most of them's chust in it for themselves. Or worse." She stared off past Paul's head. "There's some bad times comin' this way, chust like in my grampaw's day. Folks usin' powers they don't unnerstan to get what they think they need. Dark days, dark days . . ."

She stared off for a few moments more, then snapped back to attention. "But never yez mind that, boy. Chust the ramblin' of an old woman. So providin' yez not here to put a hex on someone, what can I help yez with, Paul Plummer? Yez got warts? St. Anthony's fire? The liver grow'd? I can try fer all o' them, but good."

Paul looked down uncertainly. "Um, no, none of those. Uh, you see, there's this girl and I . . ."

"Ah, I shoulda knowed," said Nettie. "Healthy young man like you. I've got chust the thing." She went to a shelf that was crammed with bottles and jars, and began rummaging around, muttering to herself. "Where the *teufel*? I knowed it was chust here . . . goldangit . . . Ah-ha! Here 'tis!" She pulled out an old peanut butter jar that contained what looked like tiny evergreen branches. She took it over to the desk and sat down, digging in the mound of junk on the desktop until she found a small pad of paper and a pencil stub.

"So, Paul Plummer, I can help yez out. Yez got an eye on a sartain young lady an' yez wants to win her heart. Well, that's easy. I'll need to know the girl's name first." She hovered the pencil expectantly over the pad.

"Her name's Sara—Sara Ziffer," Paul said. "I don't know her middle name."

The pencil remained poised over the pad of paper. Finally, Nettie said, "Sara Ziffer, eh? She'd be one of Doc Ziffer's girls, then?"

"Yeah, her dad's a doctor," said Paul. "He works at the hospital. Do you know him?"

"Oney too well, oney too well," said Nettie. "He's tried to run me out of business a time or two fer 'practicin' medicine without a license.' Don't need no license to do the work of Chesus. No matter, I was able to distract the authorities before it got too bad. Yez needs to keep an eye on them Top Hats—they're always up to sumpin' devious. 'Specially them Ziffers."

She picked up the bottle and stuffed it into a cluttered drawer. "Tell yez what, Paul Plummer. Yez seem like a good lad, too good for the likes o' that simple spell. I'll give yez something special, something that'll help you get yer true love."

"That would be Sara, all right!" said Paul.

"Mmm-hmm." Nettie reached into the pocket of her house dress and pulled out a Crown Royal sack. She pointed to a spot in front of the desk. "Yez stand right there an' don't move."

She stepped up in front of Paul and removed a polished stone from the sack. It was mottled brown, the size of a small egg. She held the stone in both hands for a moment, her mouth moving silently. Then she held it to Paul's forehead and began chanting softly. It was in a strange language, like a mixture of German and Latin. The stone felt warm and smooth on Paul's forehead.

After a few minutes, she moved the stone to the center of his chest and continued the incantation. Paul resisted the urge to fidget and stood as still as he could. It felt like it was getting warm in the room.

Finally, Nettie moved the stone and held it at the front of Paul's jeans, still chanting. Paul suddenly found himself with an enormous erection. He quickly turned his head away, his cheeks burning. Nettie continued muttering for a few more moments before removing the stone.

Paul was embarrassed beyond belief, but he forced himself to turn his head back. Nettie was standing at a window with her back to him, gazing out at a small stand of trees in the yard.

Paul cleared his throat once or twice, but Nettie continued staring out the window. Finally, he said, "Um, is that, uh, it?"

"Yep. Before the full moon, yez'll find yer true love."

"Oh," said Paul. "Um, what do I, uh, owe you?"

"Oh, I don't charge nothin', as my power comes from Chesus," said Nettie. "But if'n yez care to make a freewill offerin', yez can leave it on the Bible there by the door."

Paul was confused. Had the incantation done anything? Paul couldn't tell. He felt a little strange, for sure, but he attributed that to Nettie touching him on the joint and being embarrassed by getting a huge boner.

"Is five bucks okay?" Paul asked.

Nettie shrugged.

Paul took a five-dollar bill from his wallet and left it on the massive Bible by the front door.

As he was about to leave, Nettie turned from the window and said, "Yez take care, Paul Plummer. There's all manner of wickedness afield in Fester these days, so yez be careful. If yez needs help, yez know where to find me."

"Okay, I will," Paul said, still embarrassed. "Thanks, Missus Emig."

Nettie cackled wildly. "'Missus Emig,' that's a good 'un! Yez can call me Nettie—everyone else does. Yez a good lad, Paul Plummer. Now be on your way."

Needing no further encouragement, Paul pushed through the front door. He *did* feel different; lighter somehow, as if some weight had been lifted.

He got into his mom's minivan and started it up. A black sedan was coming down the road. He waited until it had passed, and then pulled a U-turn and headed back towards town.

I will soon have my true love, he thought. It couldn't be too long until the next full moon—he'd have to check the calendar. By then, he and Sara would be together. He wondered how it would happen. Maybe she would come up to him after physics class, and blushingly admit that she had a huge crush on him. They would go to the Spring Dance together, and then get crowned homecoming king and queen in the fall. After that, who knew where it would lead?

Paul was so absorbed with these possibilities that he was scarcely paying attention to the road. He certainly didn't notice that the car which had passed earlier was now trailing him closely. As he approached the stoplight where Back Duck Road intersected Route 23, the driver began flashing the headlights and honking the horn. Paul was rudely snapped out of his wedding plans.

The car pulled into the turning lane to the right of the minivan. Paul looked over and saw the furious face of Randolph Warnke. He was yelling something unintelligible and shaking his fist. Paul's stomach turned inside-out. He had meant to go by Warnke's and pay what he could, but after the debacle at the party he had put it off. Now Warnke had caught up with him and he was *pissed.*

Without thinking, Paul slammed his foot down on the accelerator. The minivan shot into the intersection, narrowly missing a milk truck. He swung the steering wheel wildly, fighting to keep the minivan on the road. The vehicle careened wildly right then left before he managed to regain control.

Paul's heart raced; his system flooded with adrenaline. He looked in the rearview mirror and saw Warnke's car charging through the intersection behind him. Paul knew there was no way he could outrun him. Paul pushed the accelerator down and hoped that he could lose Warnke closer to town.

The black car rapidly filled the rearview. He could see Warnke's face behind the wheel—it was brick red and twisted with rage. Warnke's lips were moving, and Paul could almost hear the profanity spewing from his mouth. Paul's throat closed up and bitter spit flooded his mouth.

The black sedan lurched forward. It struck the rear of the minivan, making it fishtail wildly. Paul grappled with steering wheel, trying to keep it on the road. *Jesus, he's trying to kill me!* he thought. The sedan bumped him again, and Paul was just barely able to keep from running into a ditch on the side of the road.

They were almost to town now, but Warnke showed no sign of letting up. The sedan dropped back a car length or two, probably to make one final charge that would either knock him off the road or into oncoming traffic. At any moment, he expected to feel the impact that would send him tumbling.

He heard the howl of a siren behind him and looked up into the rearview mirror to see a constabulary cruiser behind Warnke's sedan. Paul felt like cheering. The cavalry had come to the rescue!

As he watched, Warnke's car abruptly turned off into a half-built subdivision, but the cruiser didn't follow him. Instead, it rushed up behind the minivan and began flashing its headlights. Paul pulled over.

The constable cited Paul with speeding and gave him a thorough chewing-out. After what seemed like an eternity, the constable finished writing the speeding ticket and let him go.

Paul drove home, his body shaking from the aftermath of fear and adrenaline. He forced himself to go slowly, scanning around him for Warnke's car.

When he finally got back to his house, he staggered from the garage and barely made it to the downstairs toilet before throwing up. All thoughts of powwowers, Sara Ziffer and true love were long gone.

Chapter 13

Roscoe Dirkschneider finished observing the driveway of the Ziffer mansion and turned to go inside. Dr. Ziffer would probably object to the word "mansion," although that was clearly what it was. Roscoe was always irritated by the way the rich seemed ashamed of the wealth that they had spent so much time and effort to acquire.

The mansions up on Morningwood Heights were carefully hidden behind tall fences and dense hedges. Roscoe scratched under the armpit of his rented tuxedo and marveled at the stupidity of it all. If *he* lived in a house like this, there would be a big neon sign out front that said "Roscoe Dirkschneider's Huge Fucking Mansion—LOOK, BUT *KEEP OUT!*"

Inside, the party was in full swing. Roscoe felt distinctly out of place with his ill-fitting tux and his seven-dollar haircut. He never felt comfortable around the Top Hats. The seamy underside of Fester was more to his taste, and he spent most of his work and leisure time there.

Almost all of Fester's Top Hat families were represented at the party. In the corner was Stanley Milkman, whose family owned a regional chain of department stores. He was regaling a group with stories about abusing the wait staff at a spa in Gstaad. Listening and laughing uproariously was Ophelia Schmidt, matriarch of the "real" Schmidts. She was drunk and had been so since Cecilia had sacked her from the board of directors. Of course, Cecilia's name had not been on the evening's guest list.

Roscoe found an alcove by the bar and hung back, watching the crowd and listening in on the conversations. It was all stocks and horses and ski vacations in places with tongue-twister names. Billy must have been crazy to think that he could learn anything by snooping around this party. If Ziffer was up to something shady, he was certainly smart enough not to discuss it at a party in his own home—particularly when he had hired an off-duty constable for security.

Roscoe watched Ken Schinkel, the city attorney, trading shots of single-malt scotch with Dallas Strickler. Strickler was publisher of the *Fester Daily Dispatch*, and also a number of greasy porn mags which sold in less-reputable convenience stores. Strickler lost the drinking contest and handed over a fistful of hundreds to the victorious (and very drunk) Schinkel.

Roscoe wondered what the combined net worth of the people at the party was. Millions. Maybe billions. More money than he could imagine. Not that he had much of an imagination, even when it came to money. A few extra bucks would be nice—he'd be able to afford smoother booze, stronger drugs, and prettier prostitutes. More importantly, he'd be able to get Happy Hal off his ass.

Happy Hal was a bookie in Baltimore, and Roscoe was up to his gonads in debt to him. The whole thing had started out as a lark, but Roscoe had made the mistake of betting heavily on the Pirates and compounded his error by doubling down when they lost. Which they had done a lot in the last year. He cursed the name Barry Bonds—if the guy had shown a little loyalty instead of fucking off to San Francisco, Roscoe would be on easy street. But Bonds had left, the Pirates had sucked, and Roscoe had lost a lot of money.

Now he was deep in debt to Happy Hal. Even working the shakedown of the bars, Roscoe was barely able to keep up with his payments. One of the bookie's associates had paid him a visit last month and had let Roscoe know that Hal was Happiest when he was busting the elbows of some deadbeat who fell behind on his payments.

Roscoe thought about his conversation with Billy Snyder and started to feel angry. Why the hell couldn't Billy cut him in on some of the drug action? That was where the real money was. Sure, Roscoe might have "confiscated" a gram here and an ounce there, but so what? There was still plenty of money to be made, and plenty to skim as well.

Billy hadn't seen it that way and had cut him out of the drug action entirely. The bar protection racket didn't make nearly enough money to fund all of Roscoe's rotten habits, so now he had to do jobs like working security to help cover expenses. He thought that the world was in a sorry state when a crooked cop had to resort to doing straight security work just to make ends meet.

Everything seemed okay inside, so Roscoe went back outside and walked the perimeter of the property. All was quiet. *Fuck it*, Roscoe thought. Ziffer was paying good money, but this gig was boring as hell. He took a quick look around, saw no one, and pulled a plastic flask from his jacket. As he turned it up, a voice from behind him said, "Good evening, Constable."

In one smooth motion, Roscoe pitched the flask under a nearby Jaguar and turned to see Dr. Ziffer standing behind him. *Shit*, he thought. *Totally busted.* Plus, he had just chucked nearly a pint of Evan Williams Green Label. "Uh, hi Doc," he said. "How's it going?"

"Very well, thank you," said Ziffer. "How are things out here? I assume you have the security situation under control?"

"Um, yeah, sure" said Roscoe. "Things are pretty quiet."

"Excellent, Constable, excellent. Perhaps you'd care to take a bit if a break, then. Would you join me in my study?"

Oh shit, here it comes, thought Roscoe. *He's gonna can my ass.* He said, "Sure thing, Doc. You're the boss."

"You are correct. Follow me, please."

Roscoe followed Ziffer back into the house and upstairs into a large study that was nearly as big as Roscoe's entire house. There were towering bookshelves lined with leather-bound books, and fancy-looking paintings on the wall. Ziffer took a seat behind an enormous desk. He said, "Close the door, please. Then have a seat."

When Roscoe was seated in one of the leather-bound chairs across from the desk, Ziffer surprised him by reaching for a decanter on the shelf behind the desk. "Care for a drink, Constable? I'm sure you will find this a bit smoother than whatever you were swilling out there in the driveway."

Roscoe followed his first instinct, which was to deny and play dumb. "Uh,

I beg your pardon, sir," he said. "You must have made a slight mistake. I was just, ah, looking up at the stars out there. I'm an amateur, um, starwatcher."

"Don't treat me like an idiot, Constable," said Ziffer. He slid a heavy tumbler across the desk. "Here, have a drink."

"I really shouldn't," protested Roscoe. "I may not be on duty, but . . ."

"Constable Dirkschneider, you are beginning to try my patience. Drink."

Roscoe drank. The liquor went down smooth. It was definitely better than Evan Williams. He downed it quickly; Ziffer refilled it immediately.

"I don't know, Doc," said Roscoe. "There's still a long time to go before the party's over. I need to stay sharp."

"Don't worry, Constable," said Ziffer. "I have just the thing for that." He opened a desk drawer and removed a small mirror. There was a pile of powder, with a number of fat lines already chopped up. He whipped a hundred dollar bill from his wallet and rolled it up.

Roscoe was astounded. He certainly hadn't been expecting this turn of events. Automatically, he said, "Sir, possession of cocaine, which is a Schedule 2 substance, is illegal under the . . ."

"Will you please shut the hell up, Constable?" said Ziffer with a laugh. "I'm sure I don't have to remind you how things work in Fester. Short of committing murder in front of hostile witnesses, there's very little you can do to someone of my standing. Now, are you going to be a horse's ass, or are you going to accept my hospitality?"

"Well, if you put it that way," said Roscoe. He accepted the bill from Ziffer and did a rail for himself. It went up smooth as a baby's ass. "Holy shit!" he said. "That's some righteous stuff!"

"Pure pharmaceutical grade," said Ziffer. "There are some distinct advantages to being a physician, you know."

"No shit," said Roscoe, helping himself to another line. He could feel the rush hit him, lighting up his nervous system like a pinball machine. He took another belt of the Scotch. It complemented the blow perfectly. He felt good, really good.

He shoved the mirror back across the desk to Ziffer, but Ziffer waved him off. "No thank you, Constable, I'm fine as I am. Go ahead and help yourself, though."

"Thanks, Doc!" said Roscoe. He did a few more lines, chasing them with the whiskey. By the time he finished, he was feeling quite fine.

"Tell me, Constable Dirkschneider," said Ziffer. "What do you think of Chief Constable Snyder?"

"Billy's okay. We came up in the constabulary together, y'know? Started at the same time, practically. Then he married the mayor's sister. Well, he wasn't mayor at the time, but he was still a snooty Top Hat. No offense."

"None taken," said Ziffer. "Tell me, Constable, do you ever feel cheated, having to work as an underling to a man who is—at best—your equal?"

Roscoe looked at Ziffer uncertainly. He and Billy had gone through a lot together. He really didn't feel right badmouthing him in front of Ziffer. Still, the way that Billy had cut him out of the drug action pissed him off, especially with Happy Hal breathing down his neck.

Ziffer regarded him coolly. "Your reticence is understandable, Constable. Not to worry. This is, after all, a party. We should be enjoying ourselves." He removed a silver vial from his desk and tapped out some more cocaine onto the mirror. "Why don't you have another little pick-me-up?"

Roscoe obliged his host, and after three more lines he was practically babbling. "Yeah, so after Billy married Rose he started getting a little big for his britches. His brother-in-law got elected mayor and appointed him chief constable." Roscoe could feel himself getting worked up. The coke that had made him feel good a few moments ago was now making him angry. "Yeah, then he started throwing his weight around. Forgot about his old buddy Roscoe. Sure, he says I'm his right-hand man, but does he cut me in on any of the good rackets? Fuck no! Thinks I ain't good enough. That son of a bitch!" Roscoe was practically yelling now.

"That *is* unfortunate," said Ziffer. "And our chief constable has a long nose. Normally, that would be a good thing for Fester. But Mr. Snyder seems to have forgotten his place and is sticking his long nose into places it shouldn't be."

"Yeah, yeah!" said Roscoe. "I almost forgot about that! He wanted me to snoop around at your party. He thinks you're up to something. Some sort of drug thing."

"I figured as much," Ziffer said, "You know, Constable Dirkschneider, I think you and I can come to an agreement that would solve both of our problems. Are you interested?"

Roscoe was.

"Okay, good. Now shut up and listen closely to what I want you to do."

Roscoe did.

Chapter 14

"Dad, can I go now?" asked Paul.

Lee didn't even look at him. "No. I told you, not until the speech is over. God, you sound like a six-year old."

Paul was supposed to meet Bolly and Knob at the Viking Ship in half an hour. Instead, he was stuck here with his dad on a creaky set of bleachers, waiting to hear a boring speech by the mayor. The speech marked the kickoff of the Pretzel Parade, the beginning of Fester's annual Pretzel Fest.

Beyond the bleachers was the parade staging area. Paul could see various marching bands, beauty queens in convertibles, and pretzel-themed floats as they maneuvered into position and waited for the mayor to blow the silver-plated whistle that signaled the start of the parade.

Beyond the staging area was the Pretzel Fest Carnival, which had opened the night before. The sounds of calliope music and screams from the midway rides drifted over the atonal tootlings of the marching bands. Paul looked at his watch again and said, "Geez, Dad, why do I have to be here at all? This is so boring. I told Bolly . . ."

"I don't care what you told that delinquent," Lee snapped. "It's important that I be seen with my family here—important for the business. Your mother's got another migraine, so it has to be you. Also, could you take off that awful jacket? It really looks lowbrow."

Paul took off his denim jacket and opened his mouth to complain but thought better of it. His big problem now was how to deal with Warnke. Paul sorely regretted throwing away so much weed while scrambling away from Zack's party. He had unloaded the remainder over the last few days (while keeping a bit for himself, of course). Nevertheless, he was still over three hundred dollars short of having the money he needed to pay back the drug-dealing clown. He couldn't ask his parents for the money, and he knew that none of his friends would be able to come up with that kind of cash.

All of the heads in the grandstand swiveled as a small motorcade entered the grounds, and the limousine of Mayor Raymond J. Augenblick rolled to a stop at the base of the grandstand. Actually, "limousine" was an exaggeration. The mayor's official vehicle had begun life as a delivery van for the Schultzie Bread Company and been specially modified for the mayor's use.

Two constables got out of the van and went around to the back. A ramp was put into place, and a few seconds later the constables rolled out the iron lung containing Mayor Augenblick. The mayor's top-hatted head protruded from one end of the tube. At the other a bellows pumped in and out.

Mayor Augenblick had been in an iron lung since being stricken with polio in the middle of his first term. The citizens of Fester were proud of their disabled mayor despite—or perhaps because of—the unusual nature of his malady and the hardware that went with it. His support in town was immense, and he had been re-elected four times. Over the years, accommodations for the mayor's disability had been built into Fester's civic infrastructure. One such accommodation was a steep ramp built into the grandstand. Both constables got behind the iron lung and strained to push it to the top. They muscled it into position and locked the wheels into a frame that was built into the stand. A switch was thrown, and the whine of poorly maintained hydraulics cut through the crowd noise. Slowly, the frame—and the mayor's iron lung—began to tilt upwards. When the mayor was at about a forty-five degree angle, there was a grinding sound, and the frame's hydraulic lift jerked to a stop.

"Goddammit!" said the mayor. "Little help here?"

One of the constables gave the frame a swift kick, and Mayor Augenblick's ascent continued. When he was fully upright, the lift shut off, leaving his face perfectly positioned in front of a microphone. The faint Darth Vader-like hiss of the iron lung's pump was clearly audible through the PA system. In the crowd, several small children began to cry.

Mayor Augenblick began his speech, his comments punctuated by the wheeze of the iron lung's bellows. "My fellow citizens of—*hwaa*—Fester! It is my honor and privilege to—*hwaa*—welcome you to the seventy-seventh annual Fester Pretzel Fest." This elicited whoops and hollers from the groundlings. Although the mayor delivered the same speech every year, the crowd always ate it up.

Mayor Augenblick beamed at the crowd before continuing, "When Karlheinz Schmidt first built his mill on the—*hwaa*—Black River over two hundred years ago, he was laying a foundation not only for his family's prosperity, but for the—*hwaa*—entire community. For from that humble mill grew not only the Schmidt empire, but the—*hwaa*—town that we are all pleased and proud to call Fester, Pennsylvania!"

"Fester sucks!" yelled a scruffy-looking teenager on the edge of the crowd. He was promptly surrounded and beaten by the more civic-minded members of the audience.

The mayor ignored this interruption and continued. "This humble enterprise grew to be the world-famous—*hwaa*—Schmidt Pretzel Bakery, our hometown pride and joy. And we are proud to be known as—*hwaa*—Pretzeltown USA!"

Paul shifted in his seat as the mayor prattled on for another ten minutes. Finally, Mayor Augenblick wrapped up his address. There was a pregnant pause, as if some vital cue had been missed. Finally, the mayor snapped his head to the side and hissed, "Briggs! Goddammit! The whistle!"

The constable standing to his right whipped a silver-plated whistle from his jacket pocket and jammed it into the mayor's mouth. The mayor blew an ear-splitting blast into the microphone. The Fester High School Marching Band struck up "The Thunderer" and began stepping out. Over the PA, the mayor could be heard berating Constable Briggs for missing his cue.

"Can I go now, Dad?" said Paul.

"What?" said Lee distractedly. "Oh, yeah, sure, sure. Do you want to meet up somewhere later?"

"No, thanks. I'll get a ride from Bolly."

Paul slipped beneath the seats and clambered down the splintery wooden supports. As he threaded his way through the parking lot, he swiveled his head back and forth, looking for Warnke. The coast was clear. In fact, there was hardly anyone in the parking lot, so Paul took the opportunity to duck down behind a Chevy and take a couple of quick hits from the pipe in his pocket. Suitably stoned, Paul paid his carnival entrance fee and made his way through the sawdust-covered lanes towards the Viking Ship.

His senses were bombarded by the carnival. Brightly colored booths, garish rides, and flashing neon assaulted his eyeballs. The smells of popcorn, fried dough, and hot sawdust mingled with a subtle olfactory undertone of livestock from the 4-H sheds. A cacophony of clanging bells, blatting buzzers, and shouting sideshow barkers merged into an almighty sonic wave. From the rides came the grinding roar of machinery, low-fidelity rock music, and the screams of thrilled riders.

Paul came to the Viking Ship, which was swinging two dozen screeching passengers in a huge arc to the high-decibel sounds of Def Leppard. Although he was only a few minutes late, there was no sign of Bolly or Knob. He decided to cruise through the rest of the carnival and see if he could spot them.

Paul wandered through the midway, checking the crowd for his friends—and for Warnke. He figured that Warnke wouldn't be anywhere near the carnival, but it couldn't hurt to be careful. As Paul wandered from one end of the midway to the other, he continually looked back over his shoulder, just in case.

Despite his vigilance, he was taken by surprise at the Tilt-A-Whirl. "Hello, pussy," said a voice behind him. A strong hand clamped painfully on his shoulder.

He quickly spun around to confront the malevolently grinning face of Garth Bowman. Behind him, Paul could see Sara Ziffer, and a handful of Garth's football buddies and their girlfriends. "Who's the douchebag now, pussy?" Garth asked.

Before Paul could answer, Garth's fist came crashing down from low

Earth orbit and into Paul's left eye. A nova of bright blue pain exploded across his field of vision. He heard a feminine squeal in the background—he was sure that it came from Sara—followed by loud guffaws from the others.

Before Paul could recover his senses, Garth pistoned his fists into his stomach—*wham-wham!* Paul doubled over, retching, and fell into the dirt.

From miles above him came Garth's voice, "That'll teach ya. You watch your mouth around me from now on, pussy." He kicked a cloud of dust onto Paul's head.

Paul coughed miserably and rolled over. Opening his good eye, he could see Garth's expensive sneakers and the bottom of his pegged jeans. A few steps behind him stood Sara. She paid no attention to Paul, but beaming at Garth, eyes shining with excitement. Paul closed his eye and waited for the next blow. He hoped that it would kill him.

Instead, someone said, "C'mon, Garth, let's get away from this sack of shit and ride the Bobsled again."

"Oh, yes," said Sara. "Let's do that! C'mon, Garth honey!"

"Later, pussy," said Garth indifferently.

Paul moaned and rolled over. He managed to get to all fours, but he couldn't quite get to his feet. His left eye was shooting pains through the back of his skull, and his stomach felt like a clenched fist. Passersby were pointing at him and laughing. Still moaning, Paul crawled around the side of the Tilt-A-Whirl, out of the way of the gawking crowd.

He managed to sit up, his back to the cold metal of the ride's mechanical housing. His breath was shuddering in and out of his chest in noisy spasms that sounded a lot like sobs. His nose was running. When he wiped his hand across his face, it came away with a mixture of snot and blood.

"Jesus, Plummer," said a voice from above him. "You look like shit."

Paul looked up to see Janie Simmons standing above him. *Great,* he thought. He coughed miserably, and finally managed to spit out, "Gonna kick a guy when he's down, huh, Janie? Well, go ahead. I don't fucking care."

"Jeez, you really look like absolute shit," Janie repeated. "Are you okay?"

"Yeah, peachy," said Paul. He dragged the back of his hand across his lower face again. It came away snotty, but there was no more blood.

Janie squatted down in the dust beside him. "Garth Bowman is such an asshole," she said. "That was a cheap shot he gave you."

Paul grunted.

"What did you do to piss him off, anyway?"

"I got into a fight with Garth at the party. Zack broke it up, but I guess Garth's been gunning for me ever since." Paul coughed again and spat into the dust.

"Got into a fight with Garth Bowman, huh?" said Janie. "You sure can pick 'em, Plummer. What was it about, anyway?"

"Sara Ziffer," muttered Paul. "The fight was over Sara Ziffer."

Janie's left eyebrow raised. Paul expected her to begin laughing, but she just shook her head. "So you got into a fight with the biggest jock in school over her, huh?"

"Yeah, so what?"

She shrugged. "I dunno. You and Sara Ziffer. I just can't see it."

"Aw, screw you, Janie. Everybody thinks that I'm not good enough for her. Like I'm some sorta lowlife and she's a princess. Fuck that bullshit!"

"You're such a romantic, Plummer," Janie laughed. "No, don't take me the wrong way. It's just that . . . I mean, what do you see in her?"

"What do I see? What do you mean? She's smart, she's pretty, she's got a lot of . . ." Paul suddenly found himself at a loss for words. "She's great," he finished lamely.

Janie gave him a funny look that was half pity and half something else. She reached into her denim jacket and pulled out a mashed-up pack of Winstons. She fished two out and handed one to Paul. He accepted it with a grateful grunt.

Janie took a drag off of her cigarette and blew a plume of smoke into the thick carnival air. She gazed into the cloud reflectively for a moment, then said "Y'know, Sara Ziffer really isn't all that."

Paul was astounded. "What do you mean? I thought you and her are friends."

"Oh, yeah, we hang around together some, but not much. And you're right—she's definitely smart, and cute, and she comes from a good family and all. But there's something, I dunno, missing. It's like she's hollow inside. Like one of those chocolate Easter bunnies."

"Shit," muttered Paul. He flicked his half-smoked cigarette into the weeds beyond the Tilt-A-Whirl.

"Look, I just wanted you to know that Sara Ziffer is definitely not worth getting your ass kicked for."

"Yeah, well, I'd pretty much worked that one out for myself."

"Really?" Janie crushed out her smoke in the dirt. "So, how are you feeling?"

"Better, I guess. I'll be okay if I can avoid Garth and the Bozo Posse."

"So whatcha gonna do now?"

"I dunno. I was supposed to meet Bolly, but I can't find him. I don't really feel like sticking around right now."

"Well, I got my car here if you want a ride," Janie said. She was looking down and taking a long time dusting off her jeans.

"Yeah, that'd be cool, I guess."

Janie hopped to her feet and held her hand out to Paul. He looked at her suspiciously for a moment, half-expecting her to yank it away at the last second. Then he took it and let her help him to his feet. He winced.

"You gonna be okay to walk?" she asked.

"Yeah, I'll be okay. Let's get the fuck out of here."

Paul and Janie double-timed it back down the midway. Paul didn't care who saw him or who might come after him. He felt used-up, but also strangely buoyant.

They found Janie's beat-up old Corolla in the parking lot and drove back through town to Krump Acres. When they got to the end of Hicks Street, Paul said, "Just let me out here. I don't want my mom seeing me all beat up like this. I'll just sneak in the back door and try and clean myself up before she freaks."

"Okay."

When Paul had gotten out, Janie said, "Hey, Paul?"

"What?"

"Nothing. Forget it." She put the car in gear and drove away.

Paul limped down the street, trying to walk normally. He felt like a shit sandwich without the bread, as Bolly would have said. He was so intent on watching his feet as he walked that he didn't notice the constabulary cruiser in the driveway until he was almost in front of the house.

Paul froze, his mind racing. Why were the cops there? Could it be the dope? He didn't have much more in the house. Maybe they had found the bags he had thrown away as he was fleeing the party and traced them back to him. Could they do that? Maybe they'd traced his fingerprints from the baggies somehow.

Suddenly, he felt incredibly tired, alone and afraid. He didn't care anymore about the pot, about Warnke, and especially about Sara Fucking Ziffer. All he knew was that there was cop car in the driveway, the herald of the latest in a string of disasters. He might as well just get it over with. He trudged up to the front door, ready for the cops to slap the cuffs on him and take him to jail. What the hell.

As he reached for the knob, the door swung open and his father stood there, looking pale and scared. Behind him in the kitchen, Paul could see a uniformed constable kneeling with a camera. Another man in a suit and tie was taking notes. The kitchen was trashed.

"Paul, thank God you're home," said Lee breathlessly. "It's your mother. It . . . something happened while we were away. Carla . . . your mother—she's gone."

Chapter 15

Billy Snyder pushed Mayor Augenblick's iron lung into the drawing room of the Mayor's Mansion. They had just finished up dinner and were retiring to talk business while Gertrude Augenblick and Rose Snyder continued to chat in the dining room. "Now don't you let him have too much to drink!" cautioned Gertrude as Billy pushed the mayor across the foyer and into the drawing room.

Once they were safely in the study, Billy locked the door behind him.

"Jesus Christ, finally," said the mayor. "Help me get out of this damn thing." Billy undid the latches on the iron lung and lifted the cover. The mayor carefully swung his legs out and Billy helped him to his feet.

"Holy shit, I've been looking forward to this all day."

"I don't know why you bother with this fucking contraption," said Billy. "It's got to be a huge pain in the ass."

"Hey, go easy on Ol' Wheezy," said the mayor. "This thing has gotten me reelected four times now. Never underestimate the power of the sympathy vote. Hell, Ol' Wheezy here's been keeping *both* of us in office for years."

"Yes, well, have you ever thought about what would happen if you were found out?" asked Billy

"I'm sure I could bullshit my way out of it somehow. Say it was a miracle of prayer, or some such hogwash. Besides, you and Gertie are the only two people in town who know the truth. She runs her mouth a lot, but she knows that if she spills the beans about the iron lung that she'll be out on her ass in a hurry. As for you, Chief Constable—well, we've both got secrets to keep, eh? Drink?"

"Shit, yes," said Billy. "I've had a hell of a week."

The mayor poured two large glasses of Jack Daniels and handed one to Billy. "Yes, well, I've got my problems, too," he said. "It's budget time, and I need to keep the state auditors out of the books. We don't need them finding out about our little 'emergency fund,' eh?"

"Hell, no."

Billy refilled both of the glasses and they sipped in companionable silence for a while. Finally, the Mayor said, "So, are you on top of this mess with that real estate guy's wife? Whatsername—Plummer?"

"Ah, Jesus, that shit I do not need," replied Billy, and took a long drink from his glass. "Couldn't be worse timing. It's bad enough that we're still dealing with the killings over at Prosser. Now we've got that damned Plummer woman's disappearance to deal with, too. I've had to call in a few favors with the local media jackoffs to keep the coverage toned down."

"So what do you think happened to that woman?"

"I don't know, not yet. I'll put Prieboy on it. He can handle it better than anyone else in the county. Don't worry, Ray. We'll get to the bottom of the Plummer disappearance soon, I'm sure of it."

"You don't think it's Satanists, do you? Maybe they used her for a ritual or something."

"Oh shit, Ray!" exclaimed Billy. "Don't go getting all worked up about Satanists again! Jesus H. Christ!" The mayor had an irrational fear of witches and Satan-worshippers. It had started after he had seen *Rosemary's Baby* at the drive-in.

"I heard that there's been Satanist activity out at the Rosewater Hill Cemetery."

"That was just a bunch of dipshit high school kids. We nabbed them two nights ago. Nothing but a pack of teenage shitheads drinking Iron City beer and knocking over tombstones. There are no goddamned Satanists around here, so quit fretting about it."

Billy checked his watch and drained the rest of his bourbon. "I've got to get going now. I'm meeting with Sherriff Turner for a friendly game of cards."

There was a rapping on the door. "Are you boys done chatting in there?" came Gertrude's voice. "I don't want Ray having too much to drink, now."

"Ah, shit," said the mayor. "No rest for the weary." He polished off his drink and climbed back into the iron lung. "Latch me up, Billy."

Billy sealed the mayor back into the metal tube and turned it on again.

* * *

An hour later, Billy Snyder was sitting in a shack in the woods just outside of the town of Kugels, a run-down logging town in the hills south of Weaverville. The area around the town was crisscrossed with old logging roads and dotted with decrepit hunting shacks. This one was owned by Kerian County Sheriff Robert Q. Turner.

The interior of the shack stood in stark contrast to the dilapidated exterior. The room was furnished with rich oak paneling and thick wall-to-wall carpeting. A modern wood stove at the back of the room radiated a drowsy cherry heat. High-fidelity speakers mounted on the rafters mellowly broadcast Frank Sinatra tunes.

Billy and Turner sat at a large mahogany table in the middle of the room, sipping rye and puffing on cigars. Turner opened a pack of cards and began shuffling. Billy pulled a large roll of bills from his pocket.

"Well let's get down to it," said Turner. "What'll it be then? Five card draw? Ten dollar ante?"

"Aw, what the hell, Bob," said Billy. "Let's make it twenty."

Turner laughed and the cards flew across the table. Billy tossed a twenty into the pot and picked up his cards. Two pair: two jacks and a pair of deuces. He discarded both jacks and one of the deuces. "Gimme three," he told Turner.

"Sure thing," said Turner. "So how's the law enforcement game down in Fester? I'll raise forty."

Billy looked at his hand—the new cards were complete crap. Perfect. "Things are pretty busy right now, but we have it under control," he said, and tossed in more bills. "I'll see you and raise twenty,"

"Very good, very good," said Turner. "You run a tight ship out there, Billy, and I respect that. Why, I can't remember the last time I had to send one of my deputies over to Fester. See you and raise twenty."

"See you and call."

"Ha! Take a look!" Turner turned over his hand, revealing a pair of tens.

"Well, that's got me beat." Billy threw down his cards.

Turner raked the cash to his side of the table. "Got you, Billy. I'm feeling lucky tonight."

The one-sided poker game continued. Billy deliberately threw away good cards, or just folded when he accidentally got a decent hand. Occasionally, he would win one just for appearances, but the bills from Billy's bankroll quickly migrated to Turner's side of the table.

Billy Snyder and Bob Turner had been working law enforcement in Kerian County for a long time. Both were as crooked as worms on a griddle. Early on, they had come to an agreement: Billy would take care of matters in Fester without any interference from the sheriff's department, and Turner would dip his beak elsewhere in the county. This agreement cost Billy a couple of thousand dollars a month.

Turner's backassward sense of morality would not allow for a straight-out bribe. Instead, every few weeks Billy would come out to this cabin and deliberately lose large amounts of money playing poker.

The fire burned down, booze was guzzled, cigars were smoked, and Billy's bankroll diminished. It was starting to get late, so Billy began to wager even more recklessly. Soon he was down to just a few bills.

"Well, that's it, Bob," he said. "You cleaned me out again. Guess I'd better get going. Rose will be wondering where I am."

"So soon, Billy? Sure you can't play another hand? I heard something up at the state police barracks recently that you might be interested in."

Turner had a habit of withholding good information until the end of the evening. Billy always carried a few hundred dollars in reserve, just in case. Billy grunted, and reached for his wallet. "Yeah, I suppose I can play another hand or two," he said with resignation. "What do you have for me? This'd better be good."

"Heh, I thought you might stick around." Turner began dealing out another hand.

"C'mon, Bob, quit yanking' my chain." Billy looked at his cards—a full house, sevens over sixes. He tossed two of the sevens and a six and got three more crap cards.

"Well, I was up at the barracks today, talkin' with ol' Wally Johnson." Johnson had been the commander of the state police barracks at Weaverville pretty much since the Battle of Gettysburg.

"And?"

"Well, he was saying . . ." Turner trailed off and studied his cards with intense interest. "Y'know, I think I'm gonna see you and raise another sixty." He tossed more bills into the pot.

Billy was getting frustrated. "Fuck, yes, here's the damn sixty and I fucking call," he said. "Now what the hell did Wally say?"

"Read 'em and weep, Billy boy. Two pair."

"Goddammit, Bob!"

"Okay, okay. Wally let it slip that he's been having a little problem with his ticker. Gonna retire next month. Doctor's orders."

"What?!" This was big news—very big. Like the Kerian County Sheriff, the state police also had jurisdiction over Fester. While Billy had been readily able to come to a shady agreement with Sheriff Turner that had kept the deputies out of Billy's backyard, Commander Wallace Johnson had been a tougher nut to crack. After a great deal of time and effort, Billy had been able to make a similar agreement with Johnson: the staties kept their noses out of Fester, and the photographs of Wally Johnson entering an Altoona motel with a teenaged prostitute stayed in a safe deposit box in Harrisburg.

"Yep, I thought you'd be interested in that," said Turner.

"Jesus! How long have you known about this?"

"Oh, I guess it was two, three days ago I was up there."

"And you're just getting around to telling me now? Fucking hell!" Billy could feel his pulse racing. He looked at Turner, who was grinning lazily over the tens, twenties and fifties that were stacked by his ashtray. *You fat sack of shit,* Billy thought. He slowly counted to ten. It wouldn't be a good idea to piss off Turner now. With a new commander at the SP barracks, Billy would need all the allies he could muster. He blew out a breath and settled back in his chair, trying to calm down.

"Hey, don't blame the messenger, now, Billy. If it weren't for me, it might've been another week before you'd heard about this."

"Yeah, yeah," Billy muttered. "Just caught me by surprise, is all." He felt the immediate shock of the news beginning to subside. Close on its heels was something even worse—a distant but insistent feeling of panic.

Johnson's replacement would probably be some freshly promoted hotshot from one of the larger cities, a rising star from Pittsburgh or Philadelphia, out to make a mark in Hicksville before moving on to bigger and better things. It could take many months to find and exploit some weakness in the new commander. In Billy's experience, every man had his price. But the interim period would be a major problem, especially if the Pennsylvania State Police decided to take an interest in what was going on in Fester.

Billy pushed back from the table and put his coat on.

"You leaving already?" Turner asked. "We aren't finished playing."

"Yeah, we are," said Billy. He dropped the rest of his money on the middle of the table.

"What's that for?" Turner asked with irritating insincerity.

"It's my contribution to the get-well flower fund for Commander Johnson. I'm not feeling too well, Bob. Must've been something I ate."

"Well, okay," said Turner. "Hope you're feeling better. By the way, you haven't been having any trouble with witchcraft gangs out your way, have you?"

"What?" said Billy. "Witchcraft gangs? Have you been talking to my brother-in-law?"

"No, I just heard that you'd had problems with devil worshippers out in Fester recently."

"That's bullshit," said Billy. "We caught a bunch of heavy metal meatheads fucking around in a graveyard. They knocked over a couple of tombstones, that's all. Simple vandalism."

"Look, Billy, *you* may be appointed by your tin-can brother-in-law, but

I have to get re-elected every four years. If folks in Kerian County think there's a Satanism problem going on, then I have to deal with a Satanism problem, whether it's real or not. Otherwise, I'm out of a job."

"Well, I'd appreciate it if you'd keep your imaginary Satan worshippers the hell away from Fester," said Billy. "I've got enough on my plate as it is."

"I'm just letting you know what I heard," said Turner. "I know you can take care of your own business in Fester. But if you do run into any devil worshippers out there, be sure to let me know."

"Yeah, sure," said Billy as he stalked out the door. "But I know what's going on around my town. I promise you that there are no goddamned Satan worshippers in Fester!"

Chapter 16

As Billy Snyder was leaving Sherriff Turner's cabin, Fester's newest Satanic coven convened their meeting in the basement room of Odd Fellows Hall downtown. During the rest of the week, the same room was used for AA meetings and as a rehearsal space for a group of mimes.

All of the members of the Fell Circle of Mammon, as they called themselves, were new to the devil-worshiping business. They had been recruited over the course of the last two weeks by the group's leader, a woman known only as the Scarlet Mistress. The Scarlet Mistress had approached each recruit individually, promising vast wealth and power if they aided her in serving her dark master, He Who Shall Not Be Named Without Express Written Consent. All of the new initiates had taken on secret names and wore hooded robes so that their real identities were not known to each other. Only the Scarlet Mistress knew who they really were. Her own identity was a mystery to the rest of the group.

As the time for the ritual drew closer, the black-robed figures scurried around the room, preparing it for the ceremony. They were following instructions on a cheat sheet that their leader had provided, and the results were a bit scattershot.

"Hurry, my Dark Siblings," encouraged Brother Diabolical. "The Scarlet Mistress will be here soon!"

"Okay, okay," replied Sister Darkness. "I'm going as fast as I can." She was on her knees chalking a pentagram on the floor. She had a copy of a heavy metal magazine featuring the popular band Quiet Twisted Iron Goat. The magazine had a large picture of the band's stage set, and Sister Darkness referred to it from time to time to fill in the details on the pentagram.

"Do we really need all this incense?" asked Brother Underworld, who was lighting the seventh stick. "This stuff really reeks!"

"Yes, it is as the Scarlet Mistress has commanded," replied Brother Foulness. He balanced precariously on top of an old elementary school desk, draping black cloth over the posters of Marcel Marceau and the Twelve Steps that were tacked to the walls.

"Well, that incense really plays havoc with my asthma," said Sister Inferno. She produced an inhaler from the depths of her robe and took a long hit.

"It is all in service of He Who Shall Not Be Named Without Express Written Consent," said Brother Wicked. "Your sacrifice will be rewarded."

"I sure hope so," replied Brother Brimstone. "I really want to put a down payment on that cabin in the Poconos before the ski season starts."

"Yes, and my little Debbie's going to need braces soon," said Sister Darkness. "Between that and the tuition for her prep school, well, sometimes I just don't know how we'll cope."

"Where are the candles?" demanded Brother Diabolical.

"I've got them right here," said Sister Hellfire. She opened a craft-store shopping bag and produced a handful of bright pink candles.

"Those aren't the right color!" protested Brother Frankenstein, as he fiddled with a boom box in the corner. "It says that the candles need to be black!"

"But these were on sale," protested Sister Hellfire. "Sixty percent off! You don't find many bargains like that. With today's economy, you have to grab a deal when you can."

From down the hall came the sound of high-heeled shoes rapping on the linoleum floor. Brother Diabolical said, "The Scarlet Mistress approaches!" He gave a quick look around the room. The heavy smoke of the incense helped provide a gloomy ambiance. The pentagram chalked on the floor was a little lopsided, but passable. The pink candles seemed out of place, but they were less obvious when the lights were turned down.

The staccato footsteps grew louder. The door slammed open, and in swept the Scarlet Mistress. She stood with her hands on her hips and surveyed the preparations that had been made for the ritual. "Brother Diabolical, have all of the preparations been made to serve He Who Shall Not Be Named Without Express Written Consent?"

"Yes, Scarlet Mistress."

The Scarlet Mistress regarded the lopsided pentagram, the pink candles and an exposed poster of a capering mime. "Yessss, well," she said slowly. "We'll have to work on a few things for next time. Now, everyone take their places around the pentagram. Sister Hellfire light the candles. And someone start the music."

As Sister Hellfire lit the candles, the others took their places around the pentagram and held hands. From the boom box in the corner an ominous organ dirge began to play. The Scarlet Mistress stood at the top point of the star. In a deep, rich voice she evoked the spirit of He Who Shall Not Be Named Without Express Written Consent, asking for his blessings of wealth and material success in exchange for doing his Dark Bidding.

"Now I want you to close your eyes and imagine the thing you want most in life," said the Scarlet Mistress. "A big house in Morningwood Heights, a Rolls Royce, or even a fleet of helicopters. He Who Shall Not Be Named Without Express Written Consent will provide these things if you bow down and serve him." The members of the Fell Circle of Mammon scrunched up their faces, imagining all of the things they thought they needed to give their lives meaning.

"Very good," said the Scarlet Mistress. "Now I want you to repeat after me: 'By all the powers of darkness and acquisition, I offer to He Who Shall Not Be Named Without Express Written Consent my eternal . . .'"

In the corner, the gloomy organ music issuing from the boombox came to a dramatic climax, and was immediately followed by an upbeat, tinkly piano number. A mellow, slightly nasal voice began to trill, "Who can take a sunriiiiiise . . . sprinkle it with dewwwwwww . . ."

"What the fuck?" yelled the Scarlet Mistress. "I thought I told you to make a tape of Satanic music! What is *this* shit?"

"It's Sammy Davis," said Brother Frankenstein. "He *is* Satanic. He hung out with a guy named Lavvy, who was a famous devil-worshiper back in the sixties."

"It's true," said Sister Inferno. "I saw it on a special on cable last week. Him and whats-her-name. Marilyn Monroe."

"It wasn't Marilyn Monroe," said Sister Darkness, who had seen the same program. "It was Jayne Mansfield. She kind of looked like Marilyn Monroe but wasn't as famous. She got her head . . ."

"Will you all shut up?!" shrieked the Scarlet Mistress. "This is the Fell Circle of Mammon, not Hollywood Trivia Night!"

In the corner, the boombox continued its serenade. "The candy man cannnnn . . . the candy man cannnnn . . ."

"And turn that crap off!" commanded the Scarlet Mistress.

Brother Frankenstein went to the corner and shut off the crooning boombox. "I can rewind it to the good part if you like," he said.

"Never mind," said the Scarlet Mistress. "The mood's been spoiled." She drew herself up to what she hoped was a commanding posture. "I know this is our first real ritual, but this is pathetic. If you people don't start acting like real Satanists, you won't get jack shit, you hear me? No big houses, no fancy cars, nothing!" She looked around the lopsided circle, where the rest of the group was staring guiltily at their feet.

"All right," said the Scarlet Mistress. "Let's just get down to business. Our Dark Master has let it be known to me that his will best be served by conjuring the Loud Ones here in Fester, so they might aid in His bidding by sowing discord and chaos. Will you serve Him thus?"

There were mumbles of assent around the circle.

"What was that?" asked the Scarlet Mistress sharply.

"Yes, Scarlet Mistress," said the rest in unison.

"That's better. So we must now bend our wills to making this happen. First things first. Brother Wicked, do you have the contract?"

"Yes, Scarlet Mistress," said Brother Wicked. He picked up a briefcase and handed her a thick sheaf of papers. She looked through the contract, mumbling to herself and occasionally pausing and flipping back to check a previous section.

"This seems to be in order," she said. "I have but one question."

"What is that, Scarlet Mistress?"

"Why do all of the green M&Ms have to be removed?"

"It is as the Loud Ones demand."

The Scarlet Mistress shrugged. "Then let it be so."

Chapter 17

"You've got to be fucking kidding me," said Cecilia to the detective. "This is bullshit."

"Lady, I ain't kidding, and this ain't no bullshit," said the detective, whose name was Vic Electro. He was huge and greasy, and he smelled like an onion's butthole. Cecilia disliked him instantly, but he had come highly recommended from her lawyer, Pierre Nasté. The detective had just finished installing an imposing array of electronic recording and traceback gear on Cecilia's telephone line.

"Don't call me 'lady,' you gelatinous clod. My name is Ms. Schmidt."

"Sorry," said Electro. "I mistook you for a lady." He shifted the soggy unlit cigar stub from one side of his mouth to the other. "I'm just sayin' that we can't trace the number of these blackmailers until they call again."

"Jesus H. Christ! I paid I don't know how much money for you to install all of this crap, and now you're telling me it can't trace the calls?"

"For cryin' out loud, la . . . Ms. Schmidt. It's a tracer, not a frickin' time machine. It can't trace calls that were made in the past."

"Goddammit!" said Cecilia, trying to control her temper. "Okay, okay, but when these bastards call again, you'll definitely be able to trace the number?"

"Look, this is top of the line gear," said Electro. "Made by Ramjack Communications, best in the world. This is the same gear used by the F. B. frickin' I."

"It had better be good," said Cecilia. "It just goddamn better."

Electro plucked the cigar from his mouth, regarded it briefly and reinserted it. "Look, Ms. Schmidt, I know you're nervous, okay? You don't . . ."

"I'm not nervous! I'd better not be nervous, with the money I'm paying for this shit!"

"Right, right, 'course not. These extortion cases are tough on everybody, I know. I've worked dozens of 'em, and we've nailed the blackmailing cocksuckers every frickin' time. Electro Security Services has got a man monitoring this line around the clock. If the call comes from a pay phone, we'll have a car out to it before the bastard can hang up."

"What if the call comes from out of town?"

"Then we call in a favor with the nearest law enforcement agency. We got connections everywhere, la . . . Ms. Schmidt."

"Shit," said Cecilia. "This sounds like bullshit to me. Nasté better be right about you."

"Of course he's right. Me and Pierre go way back. He knows I do good work. Look, Ms. Schmidt, Electro Security Services always gets their man. Or woman, as the case may be," he added with a leer.

"Ugh," said Cecilia. "Enough. You'd better just be able to nail this bastard the next time he calls. Until then, you can get the hell out."

Electro rose from the chair, sweeping his dirty trench coat behind him. "Ha! Y'know, lady, I like you. You've got balls."

"You son of a . . ."

"Don't bother seeing me to the door, I'll find my own way out." Electro waddled to the door of the study, his filthy coat and stink cloud trailing behind him.

Cecilia watched him depart. The detective was a total pig, but he seemed to know what he was talking about.

However, Vic Electro did not exactly fill her with confidence. If the foul detective was her best hope, then it was time to consider the alternative: she might actually have to pay the goddamn blackmailers. Anything to keep that tape from getting out. Regardless of Electro's performance, she was going to need the real estate deal to go through, and soon.

"Hoegenbloeven!" she barked. "Get me Plummer on the phone right away! Call his home number."

Hoegenbloeven got up from her chair in the corner, went to the phone and punched in a number. When the line started ringing, she handed the receiver to Cecilia.

"Plummer residence, Lee Plummer speaking."

"There you are, dammit!" Cecilia snapped. "How close are you to getting the title to that damn tract of land?"

"Ah, Ms. Schmidt," said Lee. "I was wondering when I'd be hearing from you."

"You shouldn't be hearing from me at all, Plummer. *I* should be hearing from *you*. What the hell is going on with our deal? I need results—and fast, dammit!"

"I'm working on it, but as I've explained before it's a complex deal. Besides, I've been having some major issues at home. My wife has, um, disappeared under what might be called mysterious circumstances."

The circumstances didn't seem too mysterious to Cecilia; if she had been Lee Plummer's wife, she would have disappeared ages ago. "Yes, so I've heard," she said. "I'm terribly sorry for you and so forth. I'm sure she'll turn up safe and sound. In the meantime, it's probably best for you to keep your mind occupied with other activities. Might I suggest the deal that you promised you could swing for me?"

"I assure you that it's my top priority," said Lee. "After, of course, finding my wife. The constables have had a lot of questions . . ."

"The constables? You're talking to the constables? What the hell are you doing that for?"

"To find my wife!" spat Lee. "Like I said, she disappeared under suspicious circumstances."

"Jesus, it's not going to help talking to those pigs. They couldn't find their own assholes with both hands and a flashlight!"

"But . . ."

"But nothing. Look, Plummer, I understand your concern, I really do. But believe me when I say that talking to the Fester Constabulary isn't going to help the situation at all. If anything, it will make it worse."

"I don't know, Ms. Schmidt. It would seem pretty suspicious if I stopped cooperating with the constables. Hell, they might even think that *I* had something to do with Carla's going missing."

"Shit, Plummer, don't be an idiot. Of course I'm not telling you *not* to cooperate with the cops. Just don't do anything that's going to draw any attention to yourself, or to this deal. You're going to be a lot better off if you just try to focus on getting this deal to happen as quickly and quietly as possible. Do you get me?"

There was a long pause. Cecilia was beginning to wonder if the call had been cut off when Lee said, "Yes, I think I understand. Of course, Ms. Schmidt, it makes perfect sense, what you're saying. I appreciate your suggestion on how to focus my attention. As I've said, getting this deal done for you is my top priority, and I will redouble my efforts to move it forward as quickly as possible."

"Finally, some fucking sense. It's about goddamn time!"

"Thank you for your confidence," said Lee. "Now, if you'll excuse me, I really should be going. I've got a number of things for your deal that I'd like to get done right away. I'll be in touch soon with an update. Goodbye." Without waiting for a reply, he hung up.

Cecilia stared at the phone, once again speechless. Right now, she just needed a drink. "Hoegenbloeven, get me a drink!" she demanded. "Make it a triple."

Chapter 18

Paul was unenthusiastically spooning up a bowl of Bosco Flakes at the table when his father walked into the kitchen. Lee sat down at the table, looked at his watch, got back up again. "Damn. I don't have time for breakfast. Is there any coffee?"

Paul shrugged. "I dunno. Mom usually makes it."

"Oh, yeah." Lee stood in front of the refrigerator, looking uncertain.

Paul dropped his spoon in the bowl, making a waterlogged *plonk* sound. "Um, have you heard anything from the constables, or anything?" he asked. "Have they asked any more questions?"

"Ah, I talked to that Inspector Prieboy again last night. He said that they were pursuing a number of leads but hadn't learned anything else yet."

"Oh." Paul resumed his desultory breakfast.

Ever since his mom had gone missing, Paul and his father had been prickly with each other. Lee was either sullen or furtive, which was bad enough. Even worse was his salesman mode, when he was full of transparently false optimism and cheer. Paul thought his father was hiding something.

Paul glared at his dad. "Is there something wrong with you?" asked Lee.

"What the hell's wrong with *you?*" shouted Paul. "There you are in your suit and tie, ready for another big day at the office! Am I the only one in this damn family that cares that Mom's gone? 'Cause you sure as hell don't seem to!"

Lee slammed his fist into the refrigerator, sending an array of fruit-shaped magnets cascading to the floor. "Goddammit, Paul Wilson Plummer, you'd just better watch your mouth, or I'll slap it clean off your face! I work hard

106

to support this family, each and every goddamned day. If there's anything I could do to help the constables find your mother, I can and will do it. In the meantime, I've got a damned job to do, and I intend to do it. I provide support for this family, I'm not just moping around here like you always do! What the hell do you think . . ."

"I think you SUCK!" yelled Paul. He jumped up from the table, fists clenched, staring furiously at his father. Lee stared right back, his mouth was working angrily, silently. Both were breathing heavily, waiting for the other to make the next move.

The phone rang.

"I'd better get that," said Lee tightly. He turned away and snatched up the phone. Paul slumped back into his seat.

"Hello? Yes, this is he. What? Where? Was there any . . ."

There was a long pause as Lee listened to the person on the other end of the line. Finally, he hung up. He stared at the phone for a moment, then turned to face Paul. "That was Inspector Prieboy. They've found the minivan. It was empty. There was no sign of . . . foul play."

"Where was it?"

"They found it on a side street by Mill Park. They want me to come down and take a look at it." Lee glanced at his watch again. "I'll call if I learn anything else." He turned and went through the door to the garage, slamming it behind him.

Paul picked up the remainder of his breakfast, tossed it into the sink and went up to his room. He wanted to get high. There was precious little weed left in his stash, but it certainly seemed like a good time to catch a buzz. Maybe not, though. There'd be cops coming by the house later. Reluctantly, he slung his backpack over his shoulder and slouched off to school.

The day went by in a haze. Paul couldn't focus on any of his classes or assignments. Most people seemed to be avoiding him. He sat alone at lunch. There were any number of sympathetic looks from teachers, and behind-the-hand whispers from fellow students. The day was draggy and awful, but he was in no hurry to get home. That would just mean more trouble.

Later, Chief Constable Snyder came by the house to reassure Lee and Paul that no effort was being spared to find Carla. Snyder also took away some articles of his mother's clothing for use with the tracker dogs.

Inspector Prieboy stopped by not long after the chief constable. He spent some time poking around in the kitchen and some time checking out the garage. Afterwards, he and Lee went into his dad's study and had a long talk. Apparently, the recovered minivan was in good condition, but there were no clues as to what had happened to his mom.

Inspector Prieboy also talked to Paul. He asked Paul about what he had been doing on Saturday afternoon. The detective had a way of listening attentively that encouraged Paul to keep talking. Occasionally, he asked a question, but mostly he just let Paul talk. He told Inspector Prieboy about the whole lovesick mess with Sara Ziffer, and the punch-up with Garth Bowman at the carnival.

Paul did not mention anything about Randolph Warnke. There were times he felt like spilling the whole story to the sympathetic constable, but Paul checked himself. Warnke might not actually have had anything to do with his mom's disappearance. It didn't seem like he would go to the bother—or take the risk—of kidnapping someone over couple hundred dollars. Besides, if Warnke *had* kidnapped his mom, why hadn't he left a ransom demand? It didn't make sense, so Paul kept his mouth shut.

The inspector mentioned he wanted to talk to Janie Simmons to see if she might have noticed some details that Paul had missed. That made Paul feel weird, knowing the cops would be calling Janie because of him.

Actually, he felt weird about Janie in general. When he wasn't worried sick about his mother, he had spent an unusual amount of time thinking about Janie. He wasn't sure what to make of it.

He decided he should give her a call, just to let her know that Inspector Prieboy would be getting in touch with her. It seemed like the decent thing to do. He hauled out the phone book and dialed her number.

He was trying to ignore the flutter in his gut when the line picked up and Janie's voice said, "Hello?"

"Um, hi Janie, it's . . ."

"Paul! How are you? I was really sorry to hear what happened with your mom. I sure hope she turns up okay."

"Yeah, thanks. Me too."

"So, were you just calling to talk, or . . ."

"Look, I just wanted to let you know that I talked to this detective. His name is Inspector Prieboy. He wanted to get your address and phone number and stuff, so I figured he was probably going to call you. I just wanted to, y'know, give you a heads-up."

Janie laughed. "You're a little late for that. He just left the house."

"He did? What did he ask you?"

"Well, he was mostly interested in times, you know. What time did we, uh, run into each other at the carnival, what time did we leave, that sort of stuff. Also, he wanted to know if I had seen any weird cars or people or anything when we were driving back."

"Oh."

"That's it, really."

There was an awkward silence. Paul tried to think of something to say but came up empty.

"So, uh," began Janie, and trailed off.

"Yeah," said Paul lamely. "Y'know, I'm really sorry about all this mess, and you having to talk to the cops and all. I bet you're sorry you ran into me at the carnival."

"No, um, actually I'm really glad I did. It was weird, but yeah. I just hope your mom's okay. I hope you and your dad are okay, too."

"Yeah, thanks. We're doing okay. Y'know, you've been pretty cool about this whole thing."

"It's okay. I'm glad I can, y'know, help."

"Yeah . . ." Paul trailed off, again at a loss for something else to say.

"Look, I know things are pretty crazy for you right now and all," said Janie. "But I, uh, just want you to know that if you, um, need someone to talk to, that I'm, y'know, here for you. Sometimes when things are all, y'know, weird and stressed out, it's hard to talk to parents and teachers about it and stuff. If you want, maybe we can hang out or something." This last bit came out very fast.

Just as quickly, Paul replied, "Yeah, that's cool. Uh, maybe we could meet at the bowling alley tomorrow night, or something. Unless, y'know, something happens with my mom."

"What time?"

"I dunno. Seven?"

"Oh, okay, great. That's really great. Look, I really got to get going now. My mom's been riding my ass about getting the dishes done. I'll see you tomorrow night, okay? Bye."

"Uh, bye," said Paul. There was a click and a dial tone. He stood there, looking at the telephone receiver with disbelief. What the hell had just happened? Had he really just made a date with Janie Simmons?

Paul put the phone down. As soon as he did it rang. He jumped, startled. Cautiously, he picked it up. "Hello?"

"Yo, Paul, how's it going?" said Bolly.

"Well, you know, man," said Paul. He was still blown out by his conversation with Janie but didn't really feel like discussing it with Bolly.

"Um, yeah, well I guess that's cool. Hey, have you heard the big news?"

"No, what?"

"What, you haven't heard? Seriously? This is like the biggest thing to hit town in ages!"

"No, sorry, dude, I'm not up on the local scuttlebutt," said Paul. "Guess I've been a little distracted, what with my mom disappearing and all."

"Oof. Hey, sorry, man. I didn't mean any disrespect, but I think this might cheer you up. Dig it: the Goat is coming to Fester *this Friday*."

"Seriously? Quiet Twisted Iron Goat is playing a show in Fester?"

"Yeah, man, believe it. And dig *this*: Lothar the Psycho is opening for 'em!"

"Get the fuck outta here! Bolly, if you're fuckin' with me, that's so totally not cool."

"Hey, check for yourself. The DJs on the Wop have been talking about it between, like, every song. They were supposed to play at Shippensburg University, but the auditorium caught fire and they had to cancel. They rescheduled the show at Wombat Auditorium over at Prosser. Tickets went on sale this morning. I cut class and scored a couple. Got one for you, if you want it."

Suddenly, Paul almost felt like crying. "Yeah, yeah, sure man. Thanks. I mean, thanks a lot, Bolly. Sincerely."

"No prob. I figured it's the least I could do, what with all the bullshit you've had to deal with lately."

"Who else is going?" asked Paul.

"I know Knob's up for it—he's a big-time Goathead," said Bolly. "I haven't seen him much since the carnival, but I got a ticket for him, too."

"Yeah, that reminds me—where the hell were you at the fuckin' carnival? I looked around for you guys for, like, an hour. Then I ran into that asswipe Garth."

"Oh, shit," said Bolly. "What happened?"

"He got me with a cheap shot. And Sara was standing right there, watching."

"Ow! Sorry, man, but we were there. Knob was a little late, but not too late. We looked all over for you, too, swear to God. We must've kept missing each other, or something. Man, I'm genuinely sorry."

"Yeah, it's okay. That's really cool about the show, though. The Goat and Lothar. That's tits!"

"Yeah, I thought you'd be into it."

"Look, I really gotta run," Paul said. "I'll catch you later."

"Rock on, my man," said Bolly, and hung up.

Paul put down the phone and shook his head. What a weird goddamn day it had been. He didn't know if he should even be thinking of having a social life with his mom missing, but he had gone and made a date *and* made plans to go to a rock concert. He felt guilty as hell about it, but also a little excited. He decided to smoke a bowl to celebrate, even though it would stress his diminishing stash. He wasn't sure what he was going to do when it finally ran out.

Chapter 19

Billy sat at his desk, knitting and mulling over how to best deal with the Prosser killings and the Plummer disappearance. The intercom buzzed. "Captain Fahrt on line one, Chief. She says it's urgent."

Beatrice Fahrt was the chief of Prosser College's laughable security force. Billy regarded Prosser Security officers as glorified mall cops—poorly trained and completely undisciplined. The relationship between Prosser Security and the Fester Constabulary was not a good one, and Billy was not especially interested in improving it.

He answered the phone with forced joviality. "Hello, Bea, how are we doing today?"

"Good morning, Chief Constable," Captain Fahrt replied coldly. "I believe we have a few things to discuss."

Billy couldn't imagine that there was anything that he wanted to discuss with Captain Fahrt, but he was willing to humor her. "So, have you cracked the Dreher/Neff case, Bea? It would save me a lot of trouble if you have."

"Please don't patronize me, Chief Constable. You know perfectly well that while we're happy to assist the constabulary's investigation in any way we can, we leave such serious matters in your hands."

"So what can I do for you, then, Bea . . . Captain Fahrt?"

"I just wanted to discuss a cooperative strategy between our two forces to deal with the concert on Friday."

"Concert?"

"Yes, the heavy metal concert that's been booked at Wombat Auditorium for Friday night. Their name is something unusual, let me see . . . 'Quiet Twisted Iron Goat.' Apparently, a pretty big-name act. They're expecting a sold-out show. Surely you're aware of this event."

"What? Yes, of course, of course," said Billy. His mind reeled. Why had he not been informed of this? He struggled to maintain his composure and get Fahrt off the line so he could find out what the hell was going on. "Yes, well, of course. I'd just forgotten about this little show, what with all of the other *real* police business that's been landing on my desk lately. We're, ah, already looking at traffic control strategies."

"Well, that's excellent. Who is your liaison officer for the event?"

Fuck, thought Billy. He didn't have time to deal with this shit right now.

"Constable Briggs will handle this," said Billy. "He knows all about heavy metal. Comes from pushing the mayor's iron lung around."

"I . . . see. Well, I'm glad to hear that you have things under control as usual," Captain Fahrt said. "I look forward to hearing from Constable Briggs soon. I should have my additional manpower request ready by lunchtime."

"Certainly. You can count on us, Bea. Now if you'll excuse me, I have some serious business to attend to. I'll have Briggs give you a call to discuss what you think we need to handle this little Woodstock." Without waiting for a reply, Billy slammed down the phone and roared, "GODDAMMIT!"

He picked the phone back up and called Will Minnick, the city clerk. The phone rang and rang, but Billy stayed on the line. He knew that old Will hardly ever left the office and moved as slowly as a sedated glacier. After fifteen rings, Minnick's querulous voice came on the line. "Fester Clerk's Office."

"Will, this is Billy Snyder."

"Well, Mr. Chief Constable, just how are you doing this fine day?"

"Shitty, Will. Look, I've got no time to chat. What the hell is this about a concert at the college?"

"Oh, yes, that rock-and-roll combo show. Strange thing, that."

"What's strange?"

"This here rock-and-roll heavy metal stuff. The hair and the clothes these kids wear! And the things they sing about! All the sex and the drugs and the perversion, it's enough to gag a maggot!"

"Is that right?" Billy clenched his teeth, waiting for Minnick to get to the point. He knew from long experience that there was no point trying to hurry the old clerk along.

"No, Billy, the reason that it's strange is that the show got approval right away. No review, no permitting fee, nothing. Came straight from the top."

"What do you mean 'straight from the top'?"

"Well, Mayor Augenblick himself gave me a call late yesterday afternoon. Said that a permit application was comin' in and that I was to approve it right away. Said to skip the council review and even waive the fee. Ain't that a helluva thing? Of course, I'm sure you know more about it than I do."

"Yes, well, I'm on top of it. I was just a little surprised that he waived the fee, that's all." Actually, Billy was surprised as hell about the whole thing, but he didn't want Minnick to know that. It wouldn't do to seem uninformed.

"Personally, I'm agin' it," said Minnick. "Such a god-awful racket. And the way they look! The boys look like girls, and the girls look like hoors. Hoors! I tell ya, no good will come of this!"

"I suspect you're right about that," said Billy, and hung up.

Three minutes later, he stormed into the mayor's office. Behind the big mahogany desk, Mayor Augenblick's iron lung was positioned so he could look across the desk through the angled mirror fastened above his head. Constable Briggs sat in the corner, looking bored.

"Briggs, take a break," commanded Billy.

Briggs slunk out of the room. Billy said to the mayor, "What the hell is this about a concert at Prosser this Friday night?"

"Oh, that. Apparently they had to—*hwaa*—cancel a show at Shippensburg and wanted to—*hwaa*—reschedule it here. I said yes."

"And you didn't consult me!" Billy spat. "Do you know how much of a pain in the ass this is going to be? Do you know anything about this damn band?"

"Yes, they're called the—*hwaa*—'Quiet Goats' or something. A folk-rock combo, I—*hwaa*—think."

"It's one of those damned heavy metal bands, not some folk group!" Billy exclaimed. "The crowd is going to be out of control!"

"I figured your—*hwaa*—men could handle it," the mayor said. "It's just a small—*hwaa*—show."

"A 'small show'?" said Billy. "They're expecting several thousand people. A ton of kids, drunk and drugged up, out of control. These bands get them all worked up, especially a heavy metal band. A *Satanic* heavy metal band. Just the other night you were pissing and moaning about Satanists, and the next thing I know you invite some fucking devil-worshipping heavy-metal band into town!"

The mayor looked at Billy coldly. "I didn't have a—*hwaa*—choice, Billy. They *knew*. They threatened to tell—*hwaa*—everyone."

"Knew what? What the hell are you talking about?"

"About *me*, you—*hwaa*—dolt," hissed the mayor. "About the iron lung, and how I don't—*hwaa*—really need it. They said if they didn't—*hwaa*—get the permit, they'd go to the press."

"Jesus Christ! Did they say anything else?"

"No. They didn't—*hwaa*—have to. There are only three people in—*hwaa*—Fester that know I don't really have—*hwaa*—polio. And two of them are in this—*hwaa*—room right now."

"Well, I sure as hell didn't tell anybody!" exclaimed Billy. "Why the fuck would I do that?"

"I don't know. I guess—*hwaa*—not. I suppose my idiot wife has finally let her damn mouth run too—*hwaa*—far. Either way, the decision has been made: the—*hwaa*—show's going to happen, and you're going to—*hwaa*—deal with it."

"So that's the way it's going to be?"

"That's the way it—*hwaa*—is," the mayor replied.

Billy was livid. He turned on his heel and rushed back to his office to begin doing damage control. In the breezeway between City Hall and the Constabulary Headquarters, he was accosted by Martin Prieboy. "Chief, I have something you may be interested in," Prieboy said.

"I'm having a shitty day, Inspector," snapped Billy. "This better be something good."

"Yes, I think so, Chief," said Prieboy. "It involves Carla Plummer's disappearance."

"Okay, well then, what do you have?" asked Billy. He didn't really expect anything that would improve his mood, but with Prieboy you never knew. The kid could come up with amazing stuff from left field.

Martin pulled himself to attention as he prepared to deliver his report. "As you know, sir, Carla Plummer's vehicle was recently recovered near Mill Park. We vacuumed the interior for forensic evidence. Unfortunately, we've discovered nothing of interest yet."

"You stopped me to tell me that?"

"No, sir. During the course of the examination, we noticed that the vehicle had been involved in a collision. The rear bumper had been damaged and there were paint chips embedded in it, indicating that the collision involved another vehicle."

"So what? It was that woman's car, and women can't drive for shit. It's probably got dings and scrapes all over it."

"Yes, sir. However, the damage done to the bumper indicates that this was recent. There was raw metal exposed by the collision, yet there was no weathering or oxidation. I would estimate that the collision occurred less than a week prior to the vehicle's discovery. Neither Mr. Plummer nor his son was aware of any collision that had occurred recently. Mr. Plummer said that his wife had been sick for several days before the disappearance, and that the vehicle was in the garage during that time."

Billy stopped being annoyed and listened with interest. "So you think that this fender-bender had something to do with her disappearance?"

"It's possible, sir. She may have been rammed from behind and forced out of her vehicle once she had pulled over."

"Is that all?"

"No, sir. I've analyzed the paint chips that were embedded in the Plummer vehicle. It's an unusual color—a shade called 'Sable Sunfire.' It was used on a limited number of Chrysler and Plymouth vehicles, and only for the 1978 model year. Not very common."

"Good, Inspector Prieboy. Can you get a list of such vehicles that are registered to local owners?"

"I have already done so, Chief. There are only fourteen, sir," said Prieboy. "One of them belongs to Randolph Warnke. I remember you asking me to let you know if I'd heard his name come up."

Billy thought for a long time before replying. "That's very interesting, Inspector Prieboy. Very fucking interesting indeed. Is there a way you could conclusively prove that the paint chips in Mrs. Plummer's car came from a specific vehicle?"

"With the proper analysis, yes, sir."

"That's good enough for me, Inspector Prieboy. I want you to get a sample from Warnke's car and determine if it's from the same batch of this Black Sun paint."

"Sable Sunfire, sir."

"Right, whatever. Do whatever analysis you need to in order to match it with the paint chips in the Plummer vehicle."

"Wouldn't I need a warrant to obtain such a sample, sir?"

"Don't worry about the warrant. I'll take care of that."

"Yes, sir," said Prieboy doubtfully. "I'm just a little confused about . . ."

"Don't give me a hard time about this, Prieboy!" snapped Billy. "You have your orders, now get going!"

"Yes, sir!" Prieboy executed a perfect about-face and marched off down the hall.

Billy stalked back to his office, his mind whirling. He found it very interesting that Warnke might be connected with the Plummer disappearance. Could Warnke actually have had something to do with it? Stranger things had happened, especially here in Fester. It was also possible that it was only a coincidence. It didn't really matter. What mattered now was there was a connection, however tenuous, between Warnke and Carla Plummer. And that connection could be exploited.

Billy realized there was now a way to wrap all of his problems into one big Cowboy Bob-shaped package and get rid of them all at once. He would start taking care of it immediately. It would require a little trip to the evidence locker first, once the day shift had gone home.

Billy smiled. It was a small, tight smile, full of malice. Things would soon start to turn around, he thought. He picked up his knitting and resumed work on the thumb.

Chapter 20

Paul sat at the bowling alley snack bar and loudly slurped up his Coke—the third of the evening. He looked at his watch. It was ten minutes past seven, and just two minutes since the last time he'd looked at his watch.

He took another long pull on his drink. He could feel the tidal tug in his bladder and pushed the red waxed cup away; he didn't want to spend the entire evening running to the men's room. He'd already done so twice. Each time, he spent several minutes in front of the mirror making sure that he looked presentable before reemerging to continue his vigil.

He checked his watch again: twelve minutes past seven. He was surprised at how nervous he was. He hadn't been out on a date in six months. It felt really funny to be going on a date now—if that's what this actually was. Paul was unclear whether this was a *date* date, or just hanging out.

Another time check: seven-fifteen. Paul took another sip of Coke and surveyed the bowling alley. Dane's Lanes was popular hangout with the high school crowd, and Paul was a little uncertain about meeting Janie there. It's not that he was ashamed to be seen in public with her, exactly. He just didn't relish the idea of being a subject of gossip around the school halls on Wednesday morning because he had been spotted at the bowling alley with Janie on Tuesday night.

Fortunately it was early, and Dane's Lanes was not very busy. There were a couple of middle-aged men with matching work shirts on the lane closest to him. Three geeky-looking guys in West Kerian High jackets were choosing balls from the rack and snickering. A good-looking college girl in a red sweater was examining the bulletin board by the front door. A bunch of hoody-looking dudes in their early twenties were skulking around the pool table, cracking dirty jokes. No Janie.

Paul finished off his Coke with a prolonged gurgle. He checked his watch again and wondered if he was being stood up. Well, maybe that wouldn't be such a bad thing. He felt more than a little guilty about going out on a date right now.

What the hell am I doing here? he thought. Everything in his life was fucked up, falling apart. His mom was missing, and maybe dead. There was a deranged drug-dealing clown that wanted to kill him. And here he was waiting in a goddamn bowling alley for a girl who was probably going to stand him up and then laugh in his face about it later. *Well, fuck that*, he thought. He pushed back his stool and got up to leave.

He looked up and saw that the cute college girl was walking right towards him and smiling. She looked familiar. Paul squinted.

She stopped right in front of him and said, "Hi, Paul."

It was Janie, and she was dressed to kill. This was *definitely* a date.

Paul plopped back down on his stool and goggled. He couldn't really remember ever seeing her wearing anything but jeans and T-shirts. Tonight she was wearing a red sleeveless turtleneck and a short denim skirt. Her blond hair, normally pulled back into a tomboyish ponytail, cascaded down to her shoulders. She was wearing makeup, too—something else that Paul had never seen. The makeup was laid on inexpertly but served to highlight her cheekbones and blue eyes. Paul was astounded. This was most definitely *not* the Janie Simmons that he had come to know and detest over the years.

"Are you going to say hello," she said, "or are you just going to sit there with your mouth hanging open?"

"Ah," said Paul. "Um."

"As articulate as ever, I see," Janie grinned. She seemed pleased with the effect she was having.

"Oh, uh, sorry Janie. It's just that I didn't, er, recognize you."

"I just got my hair done," she said, tossing her head. "Do you like it?"

"Yeah, it's, like, really nice," said Paul. "You look, really, I dunno. Pretty, I guess. I've never seen you like this."

Janie giggled again. "I really don't dress up like this very often. It's kind of a hassle. The makeup is really a pain in the ass."

Automatically, he said, "So you thought you'd dress up and put on makeup so you could hang out at a bowling alley, huh?" The sarcasm slipped out—the force of habit of years of hostility.

Janie's eyes narrowed momentarily but said nothing. Then the look disappeared, and she said, "Well, that's something I wanted to talk about. Are you hungry?"

"Hell, yeah," said Paul. "I was just about to order a cheeseburger. You want something?"

"Well, I was thinking that we could go down to Hutchison's for dinner. This place is a little, I dunno, skeezy."

"Whaddaya mean?" demanded Paul. He was rather fond of the Dane's Lanes cheeseburgers—they had the perfect balance of greasiness and meatiness. Hutchison's, on the other hand, was considered a "nice" restaurant; the sort of place you went on birthdays and special occasions. It was a little too frou-frou for Paul's tastes.

"Well, coming to Dane's seemed like a good idea at the time, but a girl's allowed to change her mind. C'mon, it'll be fun." She grabbed Paul's upper arm and hauled him off of the snack bar stool. As she touched him, he felt an electric jolt travel down his spine and linger a bit in his groin. He felt slightly lightheaded.

"Okay, sure, I guess," he said, a little dazed.

Paul and Janie walked to Hutchinson's, which was only three blocks away. They spent the meal talking about school and friends and laughing at stupid jokes. The only problem was that Paul had to excuse himself to go to the men's room every fifteen minutes or so. All of those Cokes were coming back to haunt him.

In between bathroom breaks, Paul found that he was really enjoying himself. He felt a lot more relaxed than he thought he'd be. He remembered the last time he had been on a date; he had felt tense the whole time, trying to talk and act in a way that would impress his date. With Janie, it didn't really matter; he could relax and just be himself, and she seemed okay with that. Paul glanced at his watch and was surprised to see that nearly two hours had gone by.

"So what do you want to do now?" he asked when the meal was over.

"I dunno. What do you want to do?"

"Well, we could go back up to the Dane's and bowl a few frames or something. Maybe shoot some pool."

"Nah, I'm not really into hanging out at Dane's tonight," she said.

"Okay then, *you* think of something."

"Well, y'know, it's a pretty nice night out," said Janie. She twirled some of her hair around her index finger. "Maybe we could go down and check out the lake."

"Uh, yeah, we could do that. Sure." Paul was surprised by the suggestion. There was only one reason to go down to Redskin Lake on a date: to park on the overlook on the south side of the lake and make out. It was known locally as "Rubber Road."

"Great," Janie said brightly. "The moon's almost full. It'll be pretty on the water. Do you want to drive, or should I?"

"Um, I guess you'll have to drive," said Paul. "I, uh, actually walked here." Even though his mom's minivan was back at the house, the thought of driving it felt really weird.

"Awesome," said Janie. "I'm parked, like, half a block away. Let's go."

They got up, and as they were leaving Hutchinson's, Janie took Paul's hand. Once again, he felt a little shiver run down his spine and circle his hips a few times before fading away. They walked hand in hand to Janie's old Toyota, and soon were heading through town towards the lake.

Chapter 21

Deep in the woods south of Fester, the Fell Circle of Mammon was trying once again to perform an infernal ritual. As usual, they were not having much luck.

"C'mon, c'mon," urged the Scarlet Mistress. "It's getting dark. You cretins need to speed it up."

"I thought you wanted it to be dark," said Brother Underworld.

"Of course I did," snapped the Scarlet Mistress, "but if you don't get that fucking fire going soon, we won't be able to see a damned thing. We've already flubbed one ritual—I don't want a repeat of last time. Hey, where is Brother Blackheart? He's late."

"Oh, I forgot to tell you," said Sister Hellfire. "He can't make it tonight. His wife has aerobics, and he couldn't find a sitter."

"WHAT?" exclaimed the Scarlet Mistress. "This is an important ritual, and he's missing it because of an aerobics class?"

"That's what he said," reported Sister Hellfire smugly.

"Damn him to poverty!" spat the Scarlet Mistress. "This isn't a fucking PTA meeting! Well, he is hereby *cast out!* He Who Shall Not Be Named Without Express Written Consent will *not* treat him kindly. We'll just have to go on without him tonight, and hope for the best. We'll need to start looking for a replacement, too. *Damnation!"*

The Scarlet Mistress stalked around the clearing, watching the rest of the group trying to get the bonfire going. How in the name of Hades had she wound up with such a group of nitwits? Sometimes she wondered if dealing with these idiots was worth the effort.

The visions which had guided her to establish the Fell Circle of Mammon had not made entirely clear the final outcome of her efforts. However, they had been right about the mayor, and how to use his bogus ailment against him to get him to approve the concert permit. The Scarlet Mistress had faith in the visions.

Her faith in the rest of the Fell Circle of Mammon was a little shakier. To bolster their enthusiasm—and to test their resolve—the Scarlet Mistress had decided that a blood sacrifice was needed to make up for the deficiencies of their earlier ritual attempt.

Brother Depraved had been tasked with obtaining a goat to sacrifice. He had perused the classifieds in the *Fester Daily Dispatch* and called a number of farms before finding a farmer named Bair who had a goat to sell.

Farmer Bair had used the opportunity to rid himself of a particularly unruly billy goat named Sir Oliver. The goat was very large and covered with shaggy brown fur, with weird orange-gold eyes that almost seemed to glow. Overall, Sir Oliver was a wicked-looking goat, and a perfect candidate for a Satanic ritual.

Farmer Bair had sedated Sir Oliver in order to facilitate the transportation process. Unfortunately, the sedative began to wear off about halfway back from the farm, and Sir Oliver kicked the hell out of the interior of Brother Depraved's minivan. With a great deal of effort, he and Brother Frankenstein managed to drag the semiconscious goat out of the battered vehicle and tie him to a tree near the ritual circle.

Meanwhile, the Fell Circle of Mammon was still trying to get the ritual pyre ignited.

"You're doing it all wrong," said Sister Darkness. "You'll never get it to start that way."

"I know what I'm doing," replied Brother Foulness, who was bent over the pile of wood. He struck another match. It was blown out immediately.

"Will you people get a move on?" demanded the Scarlet Mistress. "The moon's rising!" She shook her head and walked back to the grove of trees where the cars were parked. The rest of the Fell Circle continued to squabble.

"This is taking forever," said Brother Underworld. "Let me take care of this." He shoved Brother Foulness out of the way and began breaking up small twigs and dried leaves. Three matches later, he finally had a small spark kindled, and began blowing on it. "You see," he said between puffs, "you've got to start small and slowly build it up."

The Scarlet Mistress suddenly reappeared with a large cup in her hand. It was full of gasoline she had taken from a can in the back Brother Frankenstein's pickup. "Get out of the way, you fools!" she commanded. She tossed the contents of the cup onto the tiny spark, and the fire roared to life with a tremendous *whump*. So did the back of Brother Underworld's robe.

"AHHHHHHH!" screamed Brother Underworld. He began running in a tight, panicky circle.

He was immediately bombarded by advice from the rest of the Mammonites:

"Stop, drop and roll!"

"You're just making it worse . . ."

"Throw some dirt on him!"

Brother Underworld's foot caught on a root, and he went sprawling on his face. Unfortunately, the fire was on his back, so he just laid there, combusting.

"We've got to smother the flames!" shouted Sister Darkness. She kicked a few clods of dirt onto Brother Underworld.

"No, that won't work," said Brother Frankenstein. "You've got to beat out the flames." He picked up a log from the woodpile and whomped Brother Underworld squarely between the shoulder blades.

"Oww!" hollered Brother Underworld. "That's not helping, you idiot!"

"I told him he shouldn't have bought that cheap nylon robe," observed Sister Hellfire. "Wool is much better, and less flammable. Sure, it's more expensive, but the extra quality is worth it."

"PUT ME OUT, YOU MORONS!" bellowed Brother Underworld.

"Water! We need water!" cried Sister Burning. "Where can we get some water?!"

"Well, the river is about fifty yards that way," said the Scarlet Mistress. She waved in the direction of the nearby riverbank.

Without another word, Brother Underworld was up off the ground and running towards the river, trailing flame like a comet. The rest of the Fell Circle of Mammon followed closely behind, with the exception of the Scarlet Mistress, who merely stood and observed with disgust.

There was a loud splash. The Scarlet Mistress pulled a flask from her robe and took a quick drink while the others weren't watching. It was going to be a long night.

The rest of the Fell Circle of Mammon trooped back from the river after pulling Brother Underworld from the water. The Scarlet Mistress regarded them with contempt. "What a sorry-looking lot you are. Well, that had better be it for the screw-ups this evening. This is an important, powerful, and rewarding ritual. He Who Shall Not Be Named Without Express Written Consent will not be pleased if you fuck this up. Now, are we all ready?"

"Yes, Scarlet Mistress," they said in unison, like abashed schoolchildren.

"Fine. Then take your places."

The beginning of the ritual actually went pretty well. The sun had set. The bonfire and the surrounding woods made the setting seem appropriately eerie. Plus, the darkness helped conceal the charred and soaked condition of Brother Underworld's robe.

As the Scarlet Mistress continued the invocation, an ambiance of acquisitive malice could be felt. The clearing in the woods fell silent. The only sounds were the gurgling of the nearby Black River and an occasional bleat as Sir Oliver regained full consciousness.

The Scarlet Mistress intoned, "Yea, verily, Dark Father, we have made the proper signs and sigils, and can now feel your presence in this place of darkness. We now offer up to you a living blood sacrifice, so that you may smile upon our endeavors and grant us the wealth that we desire!" She closed the book from which she had been reading and nodded to the Mammonites on either side of her. "Brother Depraved, Brother Frankenstein, bring forth the sacrifice!"

126

The two robed figures scurried off into the darkness towards the tree where they had left the goat. The bleating was now much louder and more insistent, and now there were the sounds of a struggle. Over the crackle of the flames, they could hear Brother Frankenstein yell, "Jesus Christ!"

The Scarlet Mistress winced. Finally, the pair emerged with the goat in tow. The sedative had entirely worn off now, and Sir Oliver was not pleased. He had bitten Brother Frankenstein twice and ripped a large gash in Brother Depraved's robe.

The two Mammonites were having a hard time getting the goat to go where they wanted. Sir Oliver alternately dug in and refused to budge or lowered his head and charged the dark-robed figures who were yanking on the rope.

Once again, the Scarlet Mistress saw that things were edging towards disaster. "Hey, you guys help them! Grab the rope and hold that monster still!"

Brother Wicked and Brother Torment jumped forward to help their struggling comrades with the angry animal. Eventually, they were able to hold the goat in approximately one place, even though he continued to buck and kick wildly.

The Scarlet Mistress watched the furious Sir Oliver with mounting distress. Her mental image of a goat was a small, docile creature about the size of a collie—not this huge, aggressive monster.

The ritual called for slitting the animal's throat with a dagger and catching the blood in a brass bowl. "Fuck that," muttered the Scarlet Mistress. There was no way she was getting her hands near the snapping jaws of the goat. She looked down at the pile of ritual instruments that had been hauled to the clearing. Amongst them was a very large sword. With difficulty, she pulled the huge weapon out of the pile and tested the edge with her thumb. It seemed sharp enough.

"Hold that damned goat still!" she commanded. She dragged the sword over to the goat and intoned, "To He Who Shall Not Be Named Without Express Written Consent, we consecrate this offer of living blood, so that he may smile upon our deeds and reward us with the wealth of Hades!"

She hefted the sword over her head, meaning to take the goat's head off with one swing. At the top of the blade's arc, she wavered. The sword was much heavier than she'd anticipated, and its weight nearly carried her over backwards. "Oh, Dark Father, accept our offering of blood!" she cried.

She swung the sword down.

As the Scarlet Mistress brought the sword down, the goat lunged hard against the rope that was cinched around his neck, pulling all four of the Brothers holding the rope onto their faces. The sword came down, missing Sir Oliver's head but slicing cleanly through the rope.

"Oh shit," said the Scarlet Mistress. She dropped the sword and bolted, with Sir Oliver in hot pursuit. She covered twenty yards in four seconds before Sir Oliver's thick skull connected solidly with her rear end. The Scarlet Mistress sailed majestically through the moonlight, coming to rest in a mud puddle ten feet away.

Sir Oliver trotted to the puddle stood triumphantly over the prone form. He belligerently eyed the rest of the Fell Circle of Mammon, as if to say, *Any of the rest of you want some of this?* Seeing no takers, he turned and loped off into the woods.

Chapter 22

It was a beautiful night at Redskin Lake. In the dirt parking lot off of South Wampler Road, a number of young couples were cuddling, and then some. About a dozen cars were lined up facing the lake overlook. They were evenly split between rusty third-hand beaters in various stages of neglect, and newer minivans and station wagons that had been borrowed from the parents for the evening. From the cars came music, moans, pleas, lies, and promises. This was Rubber Road, Fester's main teen make-out spot.

Inside Janie Simmons's Corolla, things weren't going so hot. Paul and Janie were sitting stiffly, staring out at the twinkling lake vista.

"It sure is pretty tonight," said Janie.

"Yeah, it sure is," agreed Paul.

There was a long pause.

"It's finally beginning to warm up, I think," said Janie.

"Yeah," replied Paul. "About time, too."

"I really don't like it when it's cold out."

"Me neither."

Another pause. From the rusty GTO parked next to them, distorted Metallica throbbed through the rolled-up windows. The GTO bounced on its roached-out shocks, and enthusiastic grunts could be heard intermingled with the heavy metal riffs. The manic bouncing came to a crescendo, then stopped. The Metallica track gave way to one from the new Quiet Twisted Iron Goat album.

"Hey, didja hear about the Goat concert this week?" said Paul, happy to have found a subject for conversation.

"No, what concert?"

"Holy shit, I can't believe you haven't heard about it!" enthused Paul. "Quiet Twisted Iron Goat is gonna play over at Prosser! It's the biggest thing to hit Fester in, like, a zillion years!"

"Really? That's awesome!"

"And even better is Lothar the Psycho is opening up for 'em. They're like the most kick-ass band ever!"

"That's cool!" replied Janie.

"Yeah, do you like 'em?"

"Uh, well, I don't really know that much about them, really."

"Oh, man, they rock! You gotta hear 'em. I'll make you a mix tape or something."

Janie smiled widely. "A mix tape? Really? That would be great! Thanks." She turned towards Paul, and tried to lean into him, but the gear shift poked into her side, thwarting her attempt to move things along.

Paul was oblivious. "You've really never heard Lothar the Psycho, huh? So, like, what do you listen to?"

"Oh, I don't know. Nine and a Half Inch Worms is cool, sorta."

"What? That grunge band? Those guys are a bunch of pussies! All they do is rip off old Sabbath riffs and whine about how much it rains in Seattle!"

"Well, I'm not *that* into them, really," pouted Janie.

They once again lapsed into an uncomfortable silence. There was a roar as the GTO next to them started and backed out. A shiny Chrysler minivan took its place.

Paul sighed and slouched down in his seat. As he sat overlooking the moonlit waters of Redskin Lake, it occurred to him that the constables had dragged the lake just a few days ago, looking for his mother. For his mother's dead body. He felt his throat closing up and knew that tears weren't too far behind. He coughed, trying to choke back a sob.

Janie looked over at him in concern "Paul, what's wrong?"

He turned his head away. "Nothing."

"No, really, you can tell me."

"Look, just . . ." Paul began, thinking he would just tell her to forget about it. Instead, he was amazed to find himself telling Janie everything—the whole sorry story about Warnke, the disastrous party and his mom's disappearance.

Janie sat silently for a minute. Then she said, "Jesus, Paul, that sucks. But you don't *know* that any of that's really happened, though, do you? About Warnke and your mom?"

"Well, no, I guess not."

"You know what you gotta do, don't you?"

"Yeah, I guess so. I'll go talk to Inspector Prieboy first thing in the morning."

"You know it's the right thing to do. Even if Warnke didn't have anything to do with your mom . . . disappearing. There may be other things going on that you don't know about. You could be helping lead the constables right to her!"

Paul wasn't sure if this was true or not. Still, the idea of coming clean with Inspector Prieboy felt right. He didn't know how badly the inspector would rip him for the drug stuff, but at this point it really didn't matter.

"That's so weird, though," mused Janie. "Cowboy Bob turning out to be some freaked-out drug dealer and all. I didn't even know he lived in Fester! Wow!"

"Yeah, maybe the next time I see him I can get his autograph for you or something," said Paul sourly. His nose was still slightly runny and his eyes stung a bit. Now that his emotional storm had passed, he felt embarrassed.

Janie looked over at him. "Geez, sorry," she said. "Maybe we ought to just head back to town."

Paul sighed, "Yeah, that's probably a good idea. I ought to get on home."

"Okay." Janie started up the car and backed onto the road. Her space was immediately filled with a Bondo-spotted Firebird that sported a bumper sticker reading "Jesus Is Coming—Look Busy!"

Janie's car bucketed through the darkness. Highway 23 between Redskin Lake and town was a scenic drive during the day, but featureless at night. On the left, there were the scattered lights of the occasional farm. On the right, there was nothing but the blank darkness of the woods. Janie tuned in a staticky signal from WOPP but turned the volume down. There was no conversation in the car, but it was a companionable quiet rather than an awkward silence. Janie seemed vaguely contented, humming along with the radio and occasionally shooting a glance over at Paul.

Paul was lost in his own thoughts. Oddly, he felt a lot better for having spilled his guts to Janie. He felt cleaned out, as if a storm had roared through his emotional landscape and blown away the bad air that had been lingering there.

"Hey Janie."

"Yeah?"

"Thanks."

"For what?"

"For, y'know, letting me get that off my chest. It's been pretty tough for me the last week. It felt, y'know, pretty weird, um, opening up like that. But good, y'know?"

"No prob, man," said Janie, and gave him a grin.

"Y'know, it's still pretty early, I guess," said Paul. "I'm in no big hurry to go home. Maybe we could go back to the bowling alley and hang out, or something."

"Really? That's cool." Suddenly, Janie slowed down, and seemed to be peering into the woods on the side of the road. "Hey, wait. I have an idea." She slowed the car to a crawl, then pulled off in front of a rusted metal gate that was nearly overgrown with brambles and weeds. Nailed to a nearby tree was an ancient wooden sign that vaguely resembled an arm pointing into the woods. Janie jumped out of the car, fiddled with the rusty lock, and pushed the gate open.

"Where the hell are we going?" asked Paul when Janie had gotten back in. She put the car in gear and began slowly driving down the washed-out gravel road.

"Don't you know what's out here?" she asked.

"Isn't there some old burned-out hospital or something?"

"Okay, so you're not completely ignorant," laughed Janie. "But it's not just

132

an ordinary old burned-out hospital. It's an old burned-out *mental* hospital. Ooooooo!" She leaned over, pulling a spooky face and laughing. The car drifted off the track, nearly sideswiping a tree, but Janie swung the wheel back over just in time.

"Hey, watch it!" said Paul.

"No," said Janie, "you watch . . . this!" The gravel track took a sharp turn around a dense stand of trees. Janie goosed the accelerator, and as the Toyota slewed around the turn, she popped the high beams and stood on the brake.

"Holy shit!" said Paul.

"Pretty freaky, huh?"

The high beams illuminated a crumbling ruin. The charred brick shell poked through the trees to the moonlit sky. Creepers and vines twined through the remains of the Gothic towers and arched windows. The remaining walls and towers cast gray-blue moonshadows across the ruins. It looked like the set of a Hammer horror movie.

"What the hell is this?" asked Paul.

"It's what's left of the Hickory Home Mental Hospital," said Janie. "It burned down in the sixties. C'mon, let's take a look."

The moonlight was bright enough to give them a good view of the burnt-out building, but they left on the headlights. It felt safer; a night light to keep the monsters at bay. The woods around them were hushed. There were bugs humming and the occasional bird call, but the sounds seemed muted and far away.

"Wow, I had no idea this was here," said Paul. "I mean, I guess I kinda knew that there was some old hospital or something out here, but I never knew it was this . . ."

"Big? Imposing? Freaky?"

"All of the above, really. How come you know about this? And about how to get the gate open?"

"My dad brought me out here a couple of times," said Janie. "He's a surveyor. A couple of years ago he was hired to survey the area. Maybe they were thinking of trying to rebuild the place or put up some new buildings or something. I guess not, though, because nothing ever happened."

"Huh, no wonder," said Paul. "This place is really fucking weird."

A branch snapped in the woods nearby. Janie gave a little yelp and jumped towards Paul. He instinctively wrapped his arms around her. It felt good. "Don't worry," he said, trying to sound tough. "It's probably just a squirrel or something." Reluctantly, he let her go.

"Omigod," said Janie with a laugh. "This is a lot creepier than I thought it would be. I've only ever been here in the daytime before."

"Yeah, it feels really weird here," said Paul. "I dunno, old mental asylum, out in the middle of the woods, in the nighttime. I guess it's *supposed* to feel creepy."

"You know what I think the really weird thing is?" said Janie. "That nobody ever pays any attention to this place."

"What do you mean?"

"It's just that . . . well, have you ever noticed that people don't really ever come down here? Not just to the asylum, but to these woods in general?"

"Yeah, so what? It's just a bunch of trees and stuff. There's trees all over the place. Why would anyone want to come here when there's a lake right down the road, and a big state park not much further?"

"Yeah, but this is a lot closer. Think about it—a big patch of woods, next to the river, and right by the lake. You'd figure that people would be coming here all the time."

Paul shrugged. "So what? Like you said, it's pretty creepy."

"Hell, all the more reason for them to come, I'd say. People love haunted houses, but here's an honest-to-God abandoned insane asylum, and hardly anybody ever comes here. You can tell. There's no beer cans or garbage or anything."

"Yeah, okay, so there's no garbage," said Paul. "What's your point?"

"I don't know," replied Janie. "It's like the whole town has a kind of blind spot about these woods. It just seems really weird to me."

"This whole fuckin' town seems weird to me," snorted Paul.

Nearby, an owl hooted. Janie jumped into Paul's arms again, and he pulled her close to him. He thought that he could get used to it.

"Now see, I've gotten myself all worked up," Janie said. She laughed and gave Paul a little squeeze before letting him go. "Hey, there's something back here that's even weirder. C'mon." She grabbed Paul's hand and led him back past the car.

"Where are we going?" he asked, hoping he didn't sound too nervous.

"There's this little building back here, it's super-weird."

They pushed through the brush behind the car. It got darker as the trees grew denser, blocking out the moonlight. The air grew closer and more stifling. It seemed like the woods-noises had stopped entirely.

Janie held Paul's hand even tighter as they pushed further into the bushes. "It's around here somewhere," she said. "Don't want to fall in . . ." They pushed their way carefully through a bramble bush, and Janie came to a sudden halt. "There it is," she said.

They were standing on the edge of a square hole that was about twenty feet wide. "What is it?" asked Paul.

"I'm not sure," said Janie. "I think it's some sort of torture chamber, or something."

"Looks like it's just a big hole in the ground," Paul observed.

"Yeah, well, you can't really see it too well at night," said Janie. "In the daytime you can see down in it. It's got all these little rooms or cells or something, and in the middle is this big, weird metal thing. I think it's where they put the inmates who were bad or dangerous or . . ."

"Hey, waitaminnit," said Paul abruptly. "Did you hear something?"

"What? No. What are you talking about?" said Janie. "Paul, are you just messing with my head? Because that's . . ."

"No. Shhhhh."

They stood quietly in the dark, listening. The woods had gone completely silent. Paul drew Janie closer to him.

"Paul, this isn't cool. You're just . . ."

There was a loud snapping sound nearby. It sounded like a stout branch had been broken—by something big.

"Paul, what is it?"

All of the spit had disappeared from Paul's mouth. He worked his jaw a time or two, unsure if he was going to be able to talk. "Uh, I think," his voice came out in a croak. "I, uh, think it's just another, uh, squirrel. Or something."

There was a snort from the bushes right in front of them. It sounded like it came from a large animal.

"I don't think that was a squ . . ."

There was another snort, followed by a huge crash as something threw its considerable bulk through the brush.

"Fuck!" said Paul. "RUN!"

They turned and took off through the woods. Janie was screaming. So was Paul. Behind them, something big crashed through the bushes in pursuit. Paul held on to Janie's hand as tightly as he could, pulling her along through the grasping bushes and scrub trees.

Janie's feet got tangled in a root, and she went down. Paul turned to help her up. The thing thundered towards them. Janie struggled to get up. Paul hauled on her arm, trying to pull her to her feet. He looked behind him and thought he could see a pair of glowing orange eyes rushing towards them. "Come on!" he yelled. "COME ON!"

Janie got back to her feet and they raced back towards the car. The monster was gaining on them. Paul thought that he could feel the ground shaking as it pounded after them. They broke through the bushes and headed towards the car at a flat-out sprint.

They were about halfway to the car when the monster broke through the bushes behind them. Paul risked a glance over his shoulder. He saw a huge hairy body come crashing out of the brush. The monster was big; its head seemed almost at the same level as Paul's. There were two glowing orange eyes framed by a pair of horns. Horns!

"Jesus Christ!" yelled Paul. He put on an extra burst of speed, dragging the wailing Janie behind him. He slammed painfully into the rear of the Toyota. The monster was just a few yards behind them.

Paul yanked open one of the rear doors, and shoved Janie into the car. The charging black shape bore down on him. As soon as Janie was in, he dove into the back seat behind her and yanked the door shut.

They heard the monster come to a stop right beside the car. It snorted, and then there was a thump as it bashed its head into the door.

"What is it?" Janie shrieked from the floor. "Oh, holy shit, what is it?"

There was another snort and a thump. The car rocked on its tired springs as the monster bashed into it again.

The door lock! thought Paul. He sat up and came face to face with the monster.

Then he laughed.

From the floor, Janie said, "What's going on? Why are you laughing?"

"Take a look yourself," said Paul.

"I don't want to!"

"It's okay," he told her. Then, to the monster, he said, "Shoo! Go on!"

Janie's head popped up. She reluctantly turned to the window and saw the truculent face of Sir Oliver staring in at them.

"It's just a fucking goat!" said Paul.

Janie grabbed her throat and gave a shaky laugh. "Omigod! It scared the shit out of me! Where the hell did it come from?"

"It musta got loose from some farm," said Paul. "Look, you can still see the rope around its neck. Stupid goddamn goat."

Sir Oliver responded to this assessment by lifting his tail and depositing a pile of goat pellets beside the car. He gave its occupants one last contemptuous glare and sauntered off into the trees.

Paul gave a shaky laugh. "Oh, shit."

"Yeah, literally," said Janie, and they both started laughing like loons. The laughter poured out of them in huge gusts as the tension of the evening expended itself. After a few minutes, the convulsive laughter subsided.

Janie looked over at Paul and said, "Omigod. That scared me silly. My heart's going a mile a minute. Feel." She grabbed Paul's hand and pulled it to her left breast.

Unbelieving, Paul gently cupped the round smoothness of her breast. Her pulse was juddering away underneath the warm flesh. He could feel her nipple hardening against his palm.

He looked into her face. A deep flush had risen on her cheekbones, eclipsing the inexpertly applied makeup. Her blue eyes sparkled. It was as if had never seen Janie before in his life; it was like he had known her for a hundred years.

"Oh," said Paul with mild astonishment. "Hey."

And then they were on each other; a tangle of tongues, lips, legs, arms. In an eyeblink, their shirts had disappeared. Paul's hands circled her waist, feeling the smooth, soft skin and the pulsating energy beneath.

He slid his hands up her back, wondering how he was going to get the bra hook undone. Then Janie reached up behind her back, and suddenly the bra wasn't a problem.

Paul exulted in the feel of the smoothness of her body close up against his, her breasts and nipples pressing against his chest. His cock was amazingly, hugely hard. It felt like a crowbar in his pants.

Janie reached down and massaged the bulge in his jeans, pressing and rubbing with the heel of her hand. "Oh, Paul," she breathed. "Oh, wow."

There was a frenzied shuffling of hips and denim, and then they were both naked. Without saying a word, she straddled him. She reached down and encircled his throbbing cock with her hand, stroking it, and it felt so good. Then she lowered herself just a little bit, and he was immersed in the warmth and the wetness of her. It felt wonderful.

Wonderful.

A thought rocketed across his consciousness like a shooting star: "So this is what all the fuss is about . . ." Then conscious thought ceased, and he was lost in the act.

In the Wizard's Woods, the old Toyota rocked and jounced on its squeaky suspension. The remains of Hickory Home had become a one-car lovers' lane. A few yards away in the dark woods, Sir Oliver blandly watched the orgiastically bouncing car, and chewed a mouthful of grass.

Chapter 23

From the *Memoirs of Poppi Totenkopf* (translated from the original German)

E ven though what happened in April of 1763 is over twenty years gone now, I still think of it every day. Wolfgang told us to never, ever talk about what happened, and he would be *sehr* angry if he knew that I was writing this down.

Wolfgang Ziffer is dead now—killed by a pack of rabid shrews—so he will not be able to be angry with me. There are still plenty of those of us who are still alive, however. If they knew what I was doing, they would be just as angry as Wolfgang. So I will not tell them, but I will write it anyway. Those poor Indians deserve to have the truth be known about what happened to them.

We knew there were Indians close to the settlement. Karlheinz Schmidt and I spotted one outside the walls one day when we were plowing. We followed him through the Big Woods to their village on the lake where the *Schwarzfluss* empties out. We knew they were nearby, but we never expected them to come right to our settlement.

When Oswald Milchmensch shouted that there were Indians just outside of the gate, nobody believed him. Since it was nearly noon, Oswald had already been drunk for several hours. He was the settlement's greatest consumer of Uder's turnip schnapps, and it tended to affect his vision as well as his judgment.

At that time, the settlement of Festung Pfalz-Leister consisted of a number of small shacks and the communal building that served as a kitchen, dining hall, and church. The entire compound was surrounded by a tall fence of peeled-bark pine trunks. The fence opened onto the narrow swath of land that stood between the settlement and the river.

There was a narrow plank walkway attached to the inside of the fence seven feet above the ground. Someone was supposed to be on watch at all times. Wolfgang said that we were supposed to be watching out for Indians and wild animals. What we were really looking out for, though, was Herr Grueber's thugs.

On this morning, Oswald was not paying too much attention looking out for bears or thugs. He told me later that he had been standing right by the gate, and the Indians had appeared as if from nowhere. It's more likely that Oswald had dozed off in the springtime sun after imbibing his morning schnapps. When he saw the Indians, he shouted "Ow! Owwwwwwwwww! Savages at the gate! Get Wolfgang!"

I was nearby and clambered up the ladder to the walkway where Oswald was hollering and pointing at the Indians. There were three of them standing there: an old man, a girl, and a large man who looked to be in his mid-twenties. The younger man was standing behind the other two, holding a large bundle wrapped in deer hides.

The girl was gazing up at me curiously, but the two men stared stoically ahead at the closed gate. When the girl saw me gaping at her, she raised her hand in greeting.

Wolfgang Ziffer ran from the *Kommuniteihaus* carrying a musket. He had been the strongman with Herr Grueber's *Zirkus Astoundikus*, and even at the old age of thirty-seven he could whip any man in the settlement. He was huge, with wide shoulders, and very muscular. He shaved his head but kept a big moustache that he groomed meticulously.

Wolfgang shouted up at us, asking how many there were, were they armed and what they wanted. Oswald turned and yelled at the visitors, "What do you want?"

To our surprise, the girl answered in perfect English, saying that they had brought an offering of friendship. Then she said something in a thick, guttural language to the younger man behind her. He stepped forward and laid the bundle in the dust before the gate, unwrapping it to reveal a heap of pottery and trinkets.

Wolfgang had by this time joined us on the walkway above the gate. He leveled the musket at the three redskins and asked them again what they wanted.

"We mean no harm," said the girl. "We have come as friends. Please accept these gifts as a token of our friendship."

Wolfgang observed the party of natives for a few moments and then jumped down from the walkway. Oswald and I climbed down after him. I asked if we should let them in, and Wolfgang told me not to be a *dummkopf,* and that we would go outside the gate to parley with them. As Wolfgang pushed the gate open, the rest of the settlement surged forward, weapons in hand. The redskins watched impassively as the crowd of settlers surged through. Wolfgang Ziffer was at the head of the group, with Oswald and me right behind him.

Wolfgang stood directly across from the old man. They locked eyes for a few moments, and then Wolfgang asked him who he was and what business he had at our settlement.

The girl said his name was Misquashawnak, and that he was the leader of the Sashacannuck people. She said she was Narqualish, his granddaughter, and that the young man in the back was called Chuk.

The old man said something, indicating the skin full of pottery and trinkets with his left hand. Narqualish translated that they had brought us these gifts so that our friendship might grow and prosper, and that we may live as good neighbors.

Wolfgang eyed the contents of the deerskin that sat open at his feet, moving some of the items around with his boot. He said to Misquashawnak that we thanked him for his gift, and hoped too that we may live as friends. As Narqualish translated this, Wolfgang whispered over his shoulder to Horst Schinkel. Horst scuttled out from the crowd, snatched up the skin and disappeared back into the settlement.

Now Misquashawnak began speaking rapidly. Narqualish translated, waiting for the old man to pause before spitting out a quick burst of English.

He said that many, many moons ago, the Sashacannuck people were mighty and covered the land as trees in the forest.

Then the whiteskins came, and with them came the Great Sickness, which took away the young and the old, the weak and the strong. Their villages grew smaller and smaller, like a patch of snow in the springtime sun. Soon there were very few Sashacannuck left.

Then the Peshtank whiteskins came and attacked them. They said that the Sashacannuck had helped the Ottawa massacre whiteskins by the Great Sweetwaters. This was a lie, as the Sashacannuck hated the Ottawa. The Sashacannuck had given their word to the White Father Penn that they would live as friends with the whiteskins and would not harm them. In return, the White Father Penn had promised to protect them, but he did not.

After the Peshtank men had finished their slaughter, the old man led the remaining members of the Sashacannuck towards the setting sun. Their medicine man, Takalpish, had a vision that the Great Spirit would give them a sign when they had reached the place where the Sashacannuck were to settle and make their new home.

After many weeks of traveling, they came to the edge of a lake. Takalpish stopped there to relieve his bladder, but he fell in and drowned. This was the sign that he had promised them, and they began to make their new home there.

Only two moons after they had come to the lake where Takalpish fell in and drowned while pissing, the new settlers came to this spot. Many of the Sashacannuck were wary of making friends with them, as their previous friendship with the whiteskins had ended in betrayal. Misquashawnak said that we will be friends with the whiteskins by our new home, so that we may live in peace and harmony.

The old man finished speaking, crossed his arms, and commenced staring straight ahead. Narqualish looked curiously at the crowd of settlers but said nothing. Then she looked directly at me and smiled. I smiled back and wondered why my knees suddenly felt wobbly.

Wolfgang leaned over and whispered to little Dieter Augenblick, who disappeared back through the gate. After a few moments, Wolfgang said, "I am Wolfgang Ziffer, *fuehrer* of the people of Festung Pfalz-Leister. We welcome you as friends and accept these generous gifts from the great Sashacannuck people."

Narqualish translated this back to Misquashawnak, but she was obviously having trouble with the German names—the name of the settlement came out sounding like "festerer."

Wolfgang continued, and told the Sashacannuck that the *volk* of Festung Pfalz-Leister also came here to seek refuge from those who would harm us. He said that all of us came from very far away, from over the Great Water, many moons ago. We came to this land as performers, working for a man named Herr Grueber. He was a cruel master, who worked us hard and paid us little.

When our circus came to Philadelphia, we ran away. Herr Grueber was angry and hired bad men to track us down and bring us back. We had to keep moving to keep away from Herr Grueber and his men. We kept moving from town to town, but we were never accepted there, and the people made us leave.

I looked over at Wolfgang, wondering if he was going to explain exactly *why* we had been run out of towns like York and Carlisle. Many of our group of refugees from Herr Grueber's *Zirkus Astoundikus* had a fondness for activities that made the citizens of Penn's colony extremely unhappy. Theft, drunkenness, public nudity, profanity, licentiousness, brawling, cruelty to animals, blasphemy, and loitering were all activities that brought out hordes of pitchfork-brandishing citizens to run off our group.

Wolfgang concluded his speech, "So, my new friends, the *volk* of Festung Pfalz-Leister welcome your offer of peace and friendship. Our stories are very similar, and I believe that it is no coincidence that the Great Spirit has led our two peoples to settle in this place. May we both find harmony and prosperity in our new home!"

Little Dieter Augenblick pushed his way through the crowd to Wolfgang's side, and handed him a bundle wrapped in a cloth. With a huge, false smile, Wolfgang turned to Misquashawnak and presented him with the bundle.

The old man unwrapped it to reveal a top hat. He examined it closely for a minute and looked up at Wolfgang.

Wolfgang explained that the hat once belonged to Herr Grueber, our cruel master. We took it from him when we left. It represents the *freiheit* we earned so dearly. It is highly esteemed by the members of our settlement, and that we wished to present it to the Sashacannuck people as a symbol of friendship and goodwill.

Misquashawnak put on the top hat, where it slumped comically to his ears. The old man began speaking again, with his granddaughter translating that the Sashacannuck people thank their new friends and neighbors, the people of Festerer, and that he looked forward to a long and prosperous friendship.

When he had finished, all three of the Sashacannuck turned without another word, and began walking towards the woods to the south. We stood in silence as they disappeared into the trees. At last, little Dieter Augenblick spoke up, asking Wolfgang why he had given those dirty savages the treasured top hat, and said that they would probably just destroy it or throw it away.

Wolfgang replied that no one should worry, because we would get the hat back soon enough.

Chapter 24

The two-way radio on Billy's desk squawked. Roscoe Dirkschneider had just spotted Randolph Warnke leaving his house. Roscoe was to follow the drug-dealing clown and to try to prevent him from coming back for at least half an hour.

Billy pocketed the radio and hurried out to the parking lot. For the last day and a half, he'd had Roscoe staking out Warnke's place in the woods behind his house, waiting for the drug-dealing clown to leave. Billy had stopped by from time to time just to make sure that things were going okay, and to re-supply Roscoe with bourbon and Slim Jims.

Billy knew that it wasn't really a good idea to send Roscoe out on any operation that required patience or finesse, but in this case he had to make an exception. Fortunately, the setup for staking out Warnke's place was textbook perfect. A large tract of vacant woodland backed up to Warnke's property, providing good cover and no witnesses. Even a lummox like Roscoe couldn't screw up this stakeout too badly.

Billy drove at breakneck speed to Warnke's house. A moment's observation indicated that the house was empty. He parked the car around the corner, slung a satchel around his neck and walked around to the back door. A few seconds' work with the lockpick gun and he was inside.

Billy stepped into the kitchen and stopped. Randolph Warnke's kitchen had been tidy the last time Billy had been in here; now it was immaculate. Clearly, Warnke had been using his coke-fueled energy to get caught up on his housekeeping.

He went over to the kitchen drawer where he had seen Warnke stashing his coke. Sure enough, there was a small bag of white powder, along with various pieces of paraphernalia. Billy shook his head. The clown was getting careless.

He dumped about half of the stash down the sink drain and replaced it with a grayish powder from a bag in his satchel. Billy gave the bag a shake. The mixture was not quite as white as the pure coke, but Billy doubted that Warnke would notice.

Billy knew that lacing Warnke's coke stash with PCP from the evidence room was risky, but he didn't care. He needed to get Warnke do something outrageous in order to warrant a messy public arrest. Once that had happened, Billy could justify a search of the premises that would turn up the incriminating evidence that he was about to plant.

He had in his satchel a number of things that would link Warnke to both the Plummer disappearance and the Dreher/Neff killings. Two days ago, he had stopped by the Plummer house, telling Lee Plummer that he needed an article of his wife's clothing for the tracker dogs. He had given Lee a receipt for the coat he had taken, but he had also pocketed a number of smaller items that had not been officially entered as evidence. Items for the Prosser killings were easier to obtain—Billy just let himself into the still-vacant dorm room and helped himself.

Now there was the matter of where to plant the evidence. Billy went to the hallway that connected the bedroom with the living room. Sure enough, there was a trapdoor in the ceiling that led to the attic storage space. Perfect. He pulled down the door and climbed the ladder until he could pop his head through the hatch.

Warnke's cleaning binge had not yet extended to the attic. It was mostly empty, with a few boxes of bric-a-brac jumbled haphazardly in the space. The place was filthy, though. Billy realized he should have brought along some coveralls.

Walking hunched-over in the cramped space, Billy made his way to the very back, where there was a pile of cardboard liquor boxes and a couple of small suitcases. Billy could see that some of the boxes contained Cowboy Bob memorabilia from Warnke's TV days.

He pulled a small suitcase to the side, opened it, and transferred the rest of the contents of the satchel into it, then replaced it with the rest. He walked between the attic door and the suitcase a few times, dragging his feet in order to avoid leaving distinct footprints. Now there was a fairly clear path between the attic door and the place where the evidence was hidden. It wasn't glaringly obvious, but it would be easy enough to spot.

He brushed off his uniform as best he could, hurried down the ladder, and closed the attic door. He checked his watch again: twenty minutes had gone by since Warnke had left.

Making sure he was unobserved, Billy carefully returned to where his car was parked. As he drove away, he considered giving Roscoe a call to see where Warnke was. Billy decided that he wouldn't bother. Warnke would be home soon enough, and then things would get interesting.

Chapter 25

Martin Prieboy was at his desk, reviewing the results of a forensics test that had just come in from the state crime lab in Wrightsville. For Martin, it was the scientific part of his job that he liked the most. This was the *real* Batman stuff. Every superhero got into fights and chases, but only Batman really got down to the scientific nitty-gritty of solving crimes. When Martin got to do that, he felt just like the Caped Crusader.

He finished with the lab report and began to tackle some of the other paperwork that had accumulated. It was difficult for him to focus. He was anxious to report the results of the analysis to Chief Constable Snyder. Unfortunately, his boss was not in the office, and nobody seemed to know where he was. The chief was a busy man, and he tended to come and go at unusual times. It was one of the prerogatives of sitting in the big chair.

Martin's phone rang, and he quickly snatched it up. "Fester Constabulary, Inspector Martin Prieboy speaking. How may I help you?"

There was silence on the line.

"Hello? Is there someone there? Are you in trouble?"

"Uh, no, no trouble," said a shaky adolescent voice. "Um, hello, Inspector Prieboy. This is, um, Paul Plummer."

"Hello, Paul. What's up?"

"Um, you know how we were talking the other day? And you said to call if I, um, remembered anything else? I kinda, um, remembered something that you probably oughtta know about. It's kinda fu . . . uh, I mean, kinda weird."

148

"Well, that's okay. I would welcome anything that you might be able to tell me."

"This is, uh, kinda complicated," Paul said. "I was wondering if we could, you know, maybe talk in person? I was thinking that we could meet up at the Dairy Ferret on Jackson, maybe. Is that cool?"

"That is very much cool." Martin looked at his watch. "Can you be there in one hour?"

"Yeah," said Paul. He sounded reluctant.

"Very good, Paul. I'm looking forward to it."

Paul didn't reply. The line clicked and went to a dial tone.

Martin was very curious about what Paul had to tell him. During the other times they had spoken, Martin could tell that the young man was holding something back. Even a novice investigator could tell when he was being lied to, and Martin was very experienced. Most people weren't very good at telling lies, especially if they were telling them to someone with a badge. Really dumb people told flat-out lies, and these were as easy to spot as a mouse in a punchbowl. The ones who were a little smarter would spin tales that contained a little bit of the truth. The challenge in these cases was to separate the truthful bits of these stories from the outright fabrication.

Most people had "tells" that clued Martin in to whether they were lying. A lot of people would either you look directly in the eye when they were lying to you, or *never* make eye contact when spinning a tale. Martin had once worked with an informant called Scumbag Sammy. The man could not tell a fib without tugging at his left earlobe. Even when Martin pointed it out to him, Scumbag Sammy's hand would always steal up and give his earlobe a yank when he lied, which was often.

At his earlier interviews with Paul Plummer, the boy would blink rapidly at certain parts of his story. Martin was sure that he was concealing something when he did that. He had chosen to let it go. The teenager had clearly been upset and confused. He had a hunch that Paul would shortly get around to telling him the whole story, and the phone call he had just received seemed to bear that out. He would find out soon. However, if he thought that Paul was still being less than truthful, Martin would drag the whole story out of him, one way or another.

He checked his watch. He would have to get going pretty soon. He got up and headed down the hall to the men's room. As he was coming out of the bathroom, the door to the parking lot swung open and Chief Constable Snyder stepped through.

"Hey, Chief," said Martin. "You're just the man I wanted to see."

Snyder looked around at Martin. He seemed surprised to see him. "Oh, it's you," he said. "I didn't think you were on duty today."

"Well, I'm not scheduled, but I thought that I'd drop in and take care of some things. I had some paperwork to catch up on, and so forth."

"Well, that's just fine," said Snyder. "You're a credit to the constabulary, Inspector. And so forth."

The chief constable seemed distracted and out of sorts. His uniform, normally pristine, was rumpled and askew. The necktie was smudged, and there were patches on his knees that looked like some dirt had been ground in. Martin could also see a few odd pink fibers clinging to the cuffs of his pants.

"Are you okay, Chief?" asked Martin.

"Of course I'm okay," Snyder snapped. "As okay as I could be with two major criminal investigations open, the state police breathing down my back and a huge concert to deal with Friday night." He glanced down at his messy uniform and scowled. Looking Martin straight in the eye, he said, "And on top off all that, Rose has me shifting boxes in the basement. Messed up my uniform something awful. Jesus, I need a fucking vacation."

"Well, I'm glad I ran into you. I've had an interesting development in the Plummer case."

"Yeah, great. I could use some good news. Whatcha got?"

"I got the lab results back on those paint chip samples."

"Damn, that was quick."

"Yes, normally, it would have taken three or four weeks. I was able to call in a couple of favors with the lab boys in Wrightsville. You know, if we had our own gas chromatograph, we wouldn't have to wait . . ."

"Fuck that noise, Inspector Prieboy. We are not buying a gas chromatograph. What were the goddamn results?"

"Positive match. Ninety seven point eight percent chance that the paint chips embedded in Carla Plummer's vehicle came from Randolph Warnke's Chrysler."

"No shit? That's good news indeed!"

"Well, the results *are* pretty conclusive. That Hewlett-Packard GC-5890 they've got up in Wrightsville is top of the line. It can . . ."

"Will you please shut up about the damn gas chromatograph?" The chief constable's eyes narrowed, and he tapped his forefinger on his chin. "Okay, here's what we're going to do," he said. "I'm going to bring Warnke in for questioning. I think he might be able to help me with some other, um, concerns not related to the Plummer disappearance."

"Yes, Chief. Actually, I've been meaning to ask you more about your interest in Randolph Warnke, especially since it appears to have a direct bearing on this case."

"That's not important right now, Prieboy. This is a politically delicate matter. I'm going to handle the arrest personally, so keep it to yourself until I've brought him in, understand? Then I'll fill you in on the details—*all* of the details."

"Yes, sir."

"Good. I'm going to take him as soon as I can. Stay near the radio. I'll let you know when I've grabbed him."

"Yes, sir, Chief."

"Good work, Inspector Prieboy. You've been invaluable as always. Now let's keep things cool and handle this properly. I have a feeling that we're going to get a lot of things wrapped up very quickly. Now if you'll excuse me, I have a clown to nab."

"Is there anything I can do to help, Chief?"

"No, I've got it covered. You just sit tight and wait for my call."

Martin watched his boss turn and stride briskly down the dimly-lit corridor towards his office. The chief constable was definitely in a peculiar mood, but Martin didn't want to dwell on it right now. He had an appointment at Dairy Ferret and was running late.

Chapter 26

Every Wednesday night at 7:00 p.m., the Calvary Lutheran Reformed Church called its congregation to worship. Overlooking Juegler Square at Second and Jackson, it was the oldest and largest church in town. Nearly all of the Top Hat families were members.

Wednesday night services had disappeared at many other churches, but Calvary Lutheran clung to tradition with a death-grip. Not only was their Wednesday night service still a going concern, but it was also reasonably well-attended. Not as much as the Sunday services, of course, but you still had to hunt for a seat if you came late on Wednesday.

A big part of the draw was the minister, Reverend Georg Eyler. He was an old-school Teutonic Bible-beater, and his sermons tended to raise a sweat amongst the congregation. Eyler secretly prided himself on giving the most intense fire-and-brimstone sermons this side of Cotton Mather. The energy of his sermons and the fear of approbation if one's absences were noted kept the congregation in the pews all week.

On this particular Wednesday, Eyler was on one of his favorite topics: the abomination of homosexuality in the eyes of the Lord. This sermon topic came up two or three times a year, usually after some news about gay rights had injected itself into Eyler's constricted reality-bubble.

This Wednesday's sermon was particularly inspired. Earlier in the week, while visiting a parishioner who had cable TV—something the good reverend looked upon as worldly and sinful—Reverend Eyler had chanced to see a commercial for a national tour of the musical *La Cage aux Folles*. The experience had unnerved him to such a degree that he had stayed up all night composing his sermon, combining the most vicious passages from Leviticus with articles from his two favorite magazines: *National Review* and *Soldier of Fortune*. With these sources of inspiration, Fester's leading man of God had come up with a homophobic rant that made Anita Bryant seem like an ardent fag hag.

Now Reverend Eyler was winding up his graphic description of the foul and excruciating punishments that the Good Lord had waiting for the "painted, prancing sodomites" once they had arrived in the afterlife. He also none-too-subtly suggested that God would smile upon those who helped hasten the homosexuals' arrival at their final reward.

The effect the sermon was having on the congregation was galvanic. Most of the congregants were following the hellish torments Eyler described avidly. A number of the older men in the congregation were looking around the interior of the church, as if a painted, prancing sodomite might materialize in their midst at any moment. Simultaneously, a number of teenage boys—not yet entirely certain of their sexual identity—were sweating profusely and trying to avoid eye contact with anyone else. A half-dozen women had already fainted after hearing what God had in store for sinful sodomites, but the good reverend was not about to let up.

As Reverend Eyler's hateful rant was building to a fever pitch, a battered Chrysler sedan recklessly wove its way through the center of the city. The car zigzagged across the street and back, hopping curbs and sideswiping storefronts. Fortunately, traffic was sparse downtown after business hours, and the sedan had not encountered any other traffic on this slow Wednesday evening.

The car now moved towards the center of downtown. It bounced off a number of street signs on Fifth Street like a four-wheeled pinball, then turned onto Jackson Street and accelerated. It gained speed as it passed Fourth Street, and by the time it hit Third it was doing well over fifty. As it approached the intersection at Second, the driver locked up the brakes, and sent the car into a screeching turn. It slewed sideways through the intersection, the protesting tires leaving smoking curlicues of rubber on the pavement. The car finally came to a rest by the edge of Juegler Square, with the driver's side tires sitting neatly against the curb.

Behind the wheel of the car was Randolph "Cowboy Bob" Warnke, and he was gooned out of his mind on the PCP that Billy Snyder had mixed in with his coke stash.

It had been a rough week for Cowboy Bob. After nearly getting nabbed by the constables for ramming the goddamn Plummer kid, he had laid low for a while. At first, he amused himself by doing a bunch of blow, but he eventually had to cut back. Things were starting to get out of hand.

He thought that he was starting to hallucinate; he started seeing constables driving by his house, fooling around with his car, and lurking in the woods out back. That scared him badly enough that he laid off the cocaine entirely for several days—an effort that took an enormous amount of willpower and most of the contents of his liquor cabinet.

Eventually, his supply of food and booze and run out and his paranoia had diminished to the point where he could go out. He scuttled out to his car and drove carefully to the Food Ape for groceries and then to the State Store for booze. He kept a sharp eye out for any constables tailing him but didn't see any. He was in the clear.

This made him feel a lot better when he got home. To celebrate, he decided to do few lines. The stuff had seemed funny going up—kind of moldy, somehow. Well, what the fuck—it had been a few days since he had done any blow; his sense of smell had probably improved. He shrugged it off and did up two more fat lines.

The coke—or, rather, the PCP-laced cocaine—hit him hard. He figured that his tolerance had gone down in the days he had been abstaining. His heart kicked like a mule, but in a good way—no painful twinges now. He felt energy pouring through his limbs. He felt great, like the cameras were on and all eyes were on him. It was great, just fucking great. To celebrate, he did another line.

Then things started to get weird.

Instead of just remembering his glory days as Cowboy Bob, he was actually *right there* in the studio. He could feel the heat from the high-intensity spotlights, hear the excited murmur of the studio audience and feel the makeup on his skin. It really was show time back in the studios of WEVL, and he was the star again. It felt amazing, wonderful. He was a celebrity, and he was invincible. Cowboy Bob had never felt so damn good in his entire life.

Then the whole scene faded, and it was like he was being sucked backward through a long, dark tube. The bright lights of the WEVL studio diminished in the distance, became a dot, disappeared. Cowboy Bob struggled to get back to the spotlight, but to no avail.

For a long time, he just sat in the dark tube, feeling cool air blowing on his face. It wasn't unpleasant, but Cowboy Bob desperately wanted—*needed*—to get back to the spotlight. However, he couldn't move, so he just sat in the dark, feeling the wind on his face.

Eventually, he realized he was sitting on his kitchen floor. He slowly got to his feet and with a shaky hand had chopped out more lines. He snorted them up, hoping he would get back to that wonderful place, where he had been the star again for real.

From that point on, things became very hazy and disconnected in Cowboy Bob's corner of the space/time continuum. Sometimes it seemed like he was back in the dark tube. Sometimes it seemed like he was underwater. Sometimes his kitchen would snap into focus and then just as suddenly snap out. At one point, he was talking to Murray Glatfelter, his old producer. Cowboy Bob was explaining to Murray that he needed to get back to the studio, to do his show, to be a star again. Murray started to respond, but then he had turned to dust in midsentence and just blown away. Cowboy Bob didn't care. He just knew that he had to get back to that place where he was the center of attention.

So he got into his car and started driving.

Now he had arrived. Now it was time. Cowboy Bob was ready for his triumphant return to show business.

In Juegler Square, the bells of Calvary Lutheran Reformed Church began ringing. Taking this as his cue, Cowboy Bob stepped from his car, ready to perform for the adulation of his adoring fans.

He was wearing his old cowboy hat and nothing else. He had managed to unearth his old TV show outfit, but he hadn't liked the way the clothes felt on his body. Instead, he had slathered himself head to toe in white greasepaint. A lot of it had rubbed off his back and legs in the car, leaving a Cowboy Bob-shaped imprint on the driver's seat.

Cowboy Bob had a huge erection of which he was entirely unaware. All he knew was that the bells meant that it was time for his glorious comeback performance. He began to do his signature hornpipe dance, his prick bobbing merrily in the early spring breeze.

The members of Calvary Lutheran, still inflamed by the gay-bashing sermon of Reverend Eyler, began to pour out of the front doors of the church. There they were confronted by the sight of an oddly colored naked man with a cowboy hat and a huge hard-on, dancing at the bottom of the church steps. The stunned congregation bunched up at the landing outside the doors, astonished and appalled at the sight.

"Holy shit!" said one of the parishioners. "The Rev was right! It's one a them painted, prancing whatyacallums. Troglodytes."

"That's sodomites, you moron," his wife pointed out.

"It's clearly trying to undermine our American way of life and corrupt the moral fiber of our youth!" said another. "We should do something!"

By this time, Reverend Eyler had pushed his way to the front of the crowd. He briefly surveyed the spectacle of the naked, dancing Cowboy Bob and leveled his pronouncement: "GET IT!"

Brandishing his huge, leather-bound Bible, Eyler led the charge down the steps of the church, with his congregation close behind.

Cowboy Bob was blithely unaware of the danger bearing down on him. In his mind, he was performing at the Academy Awards.

Reverend Eyler was the first to reach the leering, gibbering clown, and bonked him squarely on the head with his tremendous Bible. Cowboy Bob's hat absorbed the first few blows but was quickly knocked away. He was surrounded by the vicious, screaming crowd. Blows rained down on him. He was pummeled by fists, feet, and purses, but continued to dance. The PCP coursing through his system made him impervious to the pain.

In the distance, an approaching siren wailed. The choirmaster, who was secretly as gay as a tree full of monkeys, had called the constables.

Cowboy Bob continued to dance, and the congregation of Calvary Reformed Lutheran continued to pummel him. Finally, Reverend Eyler caught Cowboy Bob in the temple with the brass-reinforced corner of his Bible, and the clown crumpled like a wet dishcloth. Driven to a faith-based frenzy, Reverend Eyler and his brothers and sisters in Christ continued to beat his unconscious body.

The howl of the siren grew louder, and then cut off as Unit Four skidded to a halt in front of the mob. Inside, Roscoe Dirkschneider took one look at the situation, and radioed for backup and several ambulances. He couldn't even see the battered form of Cowboy Bob, but was expecting numerous injuries, most of which he intended to inflict himself.

He popped out of the cruiser. "I order you all to disperse," he said conversationally to the screaming mob, who didn't even notice him.

Seeing that the unruly crowd was taking no heed of his command, he pulled his billy club from its holster. "I'm warning you that you are in violation of the law and must quit this place at once," said Roscoe quietly. He softly tapped his palm with the club. "This is your last warning," he whispered. "Cease and return to your homes."

There was no response.

Roscoe shrugged. He had given them three warnings; now it was time to act. Smiling broadly, he raised his club and waded into the melee.

Chapter 27

Martin Prieboy eased into the Dairy Ferret restaurant on Jackson Street, trying to be as unobtrusive as possible. To this end, he had dressed like a fast food assistant manager: cheap khaki slacks, a staggeringly ugly brown nylon shirt, and a logo-free brown ball cap.

He spotted Paul Plummer in a booth in the corner and slipped into the seat across from him.

Paul started. "Holy sh . . . uh, holy moly. I didn't see you come in."

"Sorry if I startled you," said Martin. "We detectives are trained to be stealthy. We can move like a ghost." *Or a bat,* he mentally added.

"Oh," Paul said. He took a sip from his squashed soda cup.

Martin looked at the young man. He was clearly unhappy. His eyes were glazed, and there were dark circles under them. It looked like he hadn't been sleeping well.

"So, how are you doing, Paul?" Martin asked. "You look a little rough around the edges."

Paul sighed. "My life's been so crazy lately. I mean, it's bad enough, y'know, just in general. And now, my mom . . . I really miss her." He coughed and turned away abruptly.

"I'm sure you miss her," Martin said. "We're doing everything we can to find out what happened to her and get her back."

Paul nodded glumly. "Yeah, I know. It's just that . . . I shoulda . . . I dunno. This is hard . . . I'm scared."

"What are you scared of?" Martin asked gently.

158

"I . . . I'm scared because I did something bad. I'm scared because I'm afraid I might get in trouble. But most of all, I'm scared buh-because my mom is guh-gone, and I think it's muh-muh-my fault!" Paul turned away again, suddenly taking an intense interest in the view out the window.

He couldn't help but empathize with the young man. However, Paul had already withheld information from him, and until Martin was satisfied that he had gotten the entire story out of him, there was no place for sentiment.

Paul turned back from the window, red-eyed. Martin thought he looked stoned—the red eyes and the faded denim heavy-metal jacket spelled *stoner* in Martin's book.

"So, what's that painted on the back of your jacket?"

"Uh, that's an album cover by Lothar the Psycho. They're playing at Prosser this Friday."

"Yes, I understand that is going to be quite an event. Are you planning on going?"

"Hell . . . heck yeah! They're my favorite band. You ever listen to 'em?"

"I can't say I know any of their music. I used to get into Led Zeppelin, though," Martin said.

"Yeah?" said Paul, brightening. "They're cool, too, though. They're like the original metal dudes."

"Heck, yeah. I saw them perform once, down in D.C." Martin was completely improvising now.

"No shit? That's awesome! When did you see 'em?"

Martin pretended to rack his brain. "Huh. Must have been around 1974, I think. Memory's a little hazy, if you know what I mean." He mimed puffing on a joint.

"Yeah, I sure do." Paul gave a little laugh.

"Of course you do," said Martin. He decided it was time to shift into attack mode. "So, Paul, do you have any drugs on you? Are you high right now?"

"What? No, I never . . ." said Paul, blinking rapidly.

"Come on, don't try to BS me. I don't want to bust you. I just want to help find your mom. But I can't do that if you *keep lying to me.*"

Paul slumped and said, "Yeah, okay. That's really what I wanted to tell you, anyway. The whole thing's fuck . . . screwed up. Here's what happened: I got some pot from this guy, but I didn't have enough money. He fronted me the money, but some shit . . . some stuff happened and I didn't pay him back. I think he mighta done something to my mom."

"What was this man's name?"

"Ruh-Randolph Warnke." Paul looked around the restaurant warily, as if Warnke might pop up from behind a booth and attack.

"How do you spell that?" asked Martin coolly. His pulse speeded up, but he maintained his composure. This could be the corroborating evidence that he needed. It would certainly provide a motive for Warnke regarding Carla Plummer's disappearance. Without taking his eyes off the red-eyed teenager, Martin pulled a notebook out of his pocket and scrawled "Warnke" at the top of the page as Paul spelled it out.

"Okay, so, you purchased marijuana from this Randolph Warnke. When did this transaction occur?"

"Um, lessee . . . it was on a Tuesday, like two weeks ago."

"So, on Tuesday the twentieth you purchased marijuana from Randolph Warnke. How much?"

"Uh, four ounces."

"That's a lot of pot for one person. Were you going to sell it?"

"Uh, no, not exactly."

"Horsecrap!" Martin slapped his notebook down, hard. "Are you trying to tell me you were buying that much marijuana just for your personal use?"

"N-no, really I wasn't going to buy that much, but when I got there Cowboy Bob—Warnke—said that he was tired of dealing with small amounts, and that from then on, the minimum was a quarter pound. I didn't have enough for that much, so he fronted me for the difference."

"Paul, I need to know all of the facts. You can tell me everything. I'm not going to bust you for drugs. I just need to know exactly what happened in order to help find your mom. Okay?"

"O-okay."

Martin got the entire story out of him: from buying the weed to the run-in on his way back from Nettie Emig's house.

"So what was the purpose of your visit to this Nettie Emig? This wasn't drug related, was it?"

Paul began to squirm. "It's, uh, well, no. No drugs—really. I, uh, just wanted, um . . ."

"Wanted what, Paul? To sell some of that marijuana?" Martin was getting more interested now. "You're acting very evasive about this. It makes me suspicious and a little bit angry. Now tell me why you went way out to the country to visit this Nettie Emig!"

"It's just that, um, I wanted to buy a, um, love potion."

This was not the answer that Martin had been expecting. "A 'love potion'?" he asked incredulously. "Is that some new sort of drug? Or maybe just a new slang term I haven't heard before? Remember, Paul, you need to level with me. I'm trying to help you here."

Paul's complexion was now the color of a brick. "No, uh, really, I'm not shitting . . . uh, kidding you." He began to speak very rapidly. "Y'see, there's this girl at school, and I think she's really great, but she doesn't even know I exist. So I heard someone say I should go get a love potion from a powwower."

"A powwower?"

"Yeah. They're like a kinda witch-doctor, or medicine man, or, um, woman."

"So I've heard," Martin said. "So did this Nettie Emig actually sell you a potion or any other sort of substance?" He poised the pen over the notebook, ready to take down the details.

"Um, no," Paul admitted. "She just held a rock over . . . me and chanted in some funny language."

"I see," said Martin. "And did she demand payment for this?"

"Um, no not exactly. She said that if I wanted to, I could give a 'free-will offering.'"

"Did you?"

"Yeah, I gave her five bucks."

"I see. Did you at any time feel coerced into paying this money?"

"Um, no, not really. I mean, she said it was, y'know, voluntary. Besides, she was pretty cool and all."

"I see," said Martin. He felt a little bit of empathy for the boy. He had been a lonely, horny teenager himself once—although he had never been so lonely or horny as to consider giving money to a charlatan. "Let's get back to the matter at hand. Where were you when you first noticed that Warnke was following you?"

"Uh, it was right at the intersection of Back Duck Road and Route 23. I pulled up to the stoplight and then I heard him honking his horn."

"So you ran the red light, and he followed you?"

"Yes."

"Then what happened?"

"He, uh, rammed me. He was trying to run me off the road."

"He hit you from behind?"

"Yeah."

Martin felt a funny sensation in the pit of his stomach. This was an important revelation, but it also could mean that his previous theory was now shot to heck. He remained calm and continued, "How many times did he ram the minivan with his car?"

"Two times. He hit me two times."

"You're sure?"

"Yeah, 'cause he dropped back and I thought he was going to hit me hard and knock me off the road on the third one, but then the cop car showed up and scared him off."

"I see. Okay, when you finally got the van back home, did you inspect it for damage?"

"Yeah, I was afraid my dad would notice and that he'd be really pissed. There were a couple of dents in the bumper."

At Martin's insistence, they went out in the parking lot. They squatted down by the rear end of the minivan and took a look at the battered bumper.

"Okay, Paul, can you point out to me the dents that were made the day that Warnke rammed you?" He consulted his notebook. "This was on Saturday, the twenty-fourth, right?"

"Yeah, the Saturday a week before Pretzel Fest." He pointed at two large dents in the rear bumper. "It was these two," he said.

Martin removed his notebook and made another note. Paul had just pointed at the two dents from which he had removed the paint fragments for analysis. "You're sure about that?"

"Yeah, pretty much," said Paul. "Look, the metal underneath is still kinda shiny."

"Good observation," said Martin. "Now, just one more question, Paul. Do you see any dents here that weren't there when you examined the bumper when you got home? Any dents that might have been made *after* you had your encounter with Randolph Warnke?"

Paul scrutinized the bumper and said, "I don't think so. It looks pretty much the same as it did that day Warnke rammed me, I guess."

Martin didn't say anything. What Paul had told him had just thrown a major monkey wrench into his assumptions. If the dents and the paint chips that he had removed from them had come from the incident out on Back Duck Road, then there was no direct evidence linking Warnke to Carla Plummer's disappearance. That meant that the case that he had built up was, in a legal sense, worthless. The unpleasant feeling in his stomach intensified. There was something about the chief constable's interest in Warnke mixed up in here as well.

He remained squatting, staring at the bumper, then straightened up. "Okay, Paul, thanks a lot. I really appreciate your honesty about what went on with Randolph Warnke. It's going to be a real help in my investigation."

"You sure don't look too happy about it," observed Paul.

Martin shook his head. "I've just got to figure out how to fit in a few more pieces into the puzzle, that's all."

"Okay. Can I go now?"

"Absolutely. If you remember anything else, please let me know. I will probably be in touch with some follow-up questions."

"Oh. Okay. Thanks, I guess."

Paul climbed into the minivan and started it up. Martin walked slowly to his car and watched Paul pull out of the parking lot and into the traffic on

Jackson Street. He got into the car but just sat there, thinking. He'd had a lot to process in the last few days, especially concerning Randolph Warnke, and now Paul Plummer had added another twist.

Warnke had had a psychotic break at Calvary Lutheran on Wednesday night, touching off a melee that had left him in a coma at Kerian Memorial. Billy had requested and received a warrant to search Warnke's house, and Martin had led the search team. They had turned up a number of interesting items, including a bag of suspicious white powder in a kitchen drawer, and a pound and a half of high-grade marijuana in the freezer. A search of the attic had led to some boxes that had recently been shifted. Inside those boxes had been a number of textbooks and notebooks with Michael Neff's name in them, as well as a copy of Anton LaVey's *Satanic Bible*. There were also a number of items of women's clothing that Lee Plummer subsequently identified as belonging to his missing wife.

Billy had been pleased, saying that all of this indicated that Warnke was responsible for a host of Fester's ills, including the Dreher/Neff shootings and the disappearance of Carla Plummer. The paint chips proved that Warnke had run the Plummer woman off the road and kidnapped her for some nefarious Satanic ritual. City attorney Ken Schinkel agreed, and announced plans to prosecute Warnke into a deep, dark hole as soon as he came out of the coma.

Martin had been unsure of this. The evidence recovered from Warnke's house seemed too random to make a whole lot of sense. Now, Paul Plummer's story undermined the theory that Warnke had run Carla Plummer off the road. The whole thing seemed fishy.

Martin felt like there was some connection that he wasn't making—something that he had seen recently but failed to understand the significance of. Then it hit him: the pink fiber clinging to the chief constable's pants cuff. It looked to Martin like fiberglass insulation. The chief had said that his wife had him shifting boxes in the basement, but who has fiberglass insulation in their basement? Insulation usually went in the attic. There had been plenty of pink insulation in Randolph Warnke's attic. Had Chief Constable Snyder planted the evidence there?

Impossible. His boss would never do something like that. The idea was ridiculous, and Martin pushed it away.

He started up his car and drove slowly home. He kept turning all of the facts over in his mind, but they still didn't add up. The matter of the pink insulation on the chief constable's pants leg wouldn't go away, but Martin stubbornly ignored it. It had been a long day, but Martin had a hard time getting to sleep that night.

Chapter 28

Lee Plummer was staring down the barrel of a rifle. He had been pretty sure he would encounter a gun or two on this trip up into the hills, but he hadn't expected to see one so soon, or be looking so closely into the business end of it.

The man in camouflage had materialized out of the bushes almost as soon as Lee had gotten out of his Cadillac. One moment the camo man wasn't there; the next he was, holding the muzzle about two inches from Lee's right eye.

It wasn't any sort of hillbilly hunting rifle or shotgun, either. It was a deadly-looking flat black assault rifle with a large scope on top. The camo man didn't look much like a hillbilly, either. He was wearing a faded but clean camouflage uniform, polished combat boots and a green beret with no insignia. He looked like he might have just parachuted in.

"Who the fuck are you and what the fuck do you want?" the camo man demanded.

"I . . . I'm Lee Plummer," Lee said, as if that would explain everything.

The camo man snorted and poked the gun into Lee's eyeball.

"Don't shoot!" Lee cried. "I'm a real estate agent!"

The camo man laughed. "Yeah, right. You look like a fed to me. Maybe a statie. Definitely a cop." He took a step back and lowered his eye to the gun sight.

"Hey . . . hey. Wait a minute. Let's not get carried away here. I really am a real estate agent. I'm not a cop. Would a cop be driving one of these?" He gestured at the Caddy behind him.

The camo man dropped the muzzle of the gun and surveyed the car. Lee could feel his sphincter unclench a little. "Yeah, okay, so maybe you're not a cop. Still, what the fuck is a real estate agent doing up here?"

"Is your name Totenkopf?" asked Lee. Immediately, the gun muzzle was back in his eye.

"That's none of your goddamn business!" the camo man snapped. "You *are* a cop. I shoulda known." He jacked a round into the chamber.

Lee launched into his full salesman routine like his life depended on it. It probably did. He said, "Look, it really doesn't matter what your name is. I just want to let you know that the Totenkopf family has been screwed out of a lot of money over the years by some of the bigwigs in town. I'm here to help the family get back the money they deserve. I was hoping to see a man named Jeffrey Totenkopf. This deal could be worth a lot of money to him and his family."

"That sounds like a lot of bullshit to me," the camo man said.

Lee pressed his case. "It's not bullshit. There's a tract of land south of town, some people call it the Wizard's Woods. I believe that it legally belongs to the Totenkopf family. It's worth a lot of money, but it's going into someone else's pocket."

"How much money?"

"Nearly a million dollars. Maybe more."

The camo man paused and rubbed his chin. "Hmmm. A million, huh? That's a lotta money. And you wanna talk to Uncle Jeff? Awright. I'm gonna frisk you, first. Put your hands up."

"They're already up," Lee pointed out. He'd thrown his hands in the air the moment he had seen the rifle.

"Oh, yeah," said the camo man. Holding the rifle in his right hand, he used his left to pat Lee down. When he finished, he said, "Okay, let's git goin'. And no funny stuff, or I'll blast your ass."

"What about my car?"

"Ain't no one gonna fuck with your car. Ain't no one else around here dumb enough to come up here uninvited."

They marched up the muddy lane, away from the main road. Occasionally,

Lee could hear a car passing on Route 23 beyond. It made him feel lonely and scared. He was only fifteen miles from home, but it felt like he was in another world. He wondered how he had gotten himself into this situation in the first place.

In retrospect, dealing with that damned Schmidt woman had been a huge mistake. His wife was missing, probably kidnapped by one of Cecilia Schmidt's goons. Now, he was being marched into the woods, where he'd probably be given a cornholing and a bullet to the head. And the worst part of the situation, the absolute *worst*, was that he had yet to see one goddamn dime from this deal.

They hiked further into the woods and soon arrived at a small clearing at the end of the road. Standing there was a small, rickety shack. It was tiny—little more than a tool shed, with a few dirty windows and smoke lazily spiraling up from a tin chimney attached to the side.

"All of you live here?" Lee asked in amazement.

"Shit no," said the camo man. "You must be dumber 'n you look. Now git inside."

Lee went through the decrepit door, followed closely by the camo man. The interior of the shack was nearly bare. There were a few ancient-looking pieces of furniture scattered around the floor. The only thing that looked even close to new was a telephone bolted to the wall.

"Siddown there," the camo man commanded, indicated a splintery wooden stool in the corner. Lee sat, and the camo man got on the phone and had a low-pitched, intense conversation. Lee couldn't hear most of it but did pick up a few phrases: "city bozo," "Uncle Jeff," and "fuckload of money."

When the camo man hung up, he motioned Lee to the door with his gun. "Let's go, asshole. It's yer lucky day."

When they were outside, the camo man went to a thick growth of bushes on the opposite side of the clearing, reached in, and gave it a tug. To Lee's amazement, the whole row of bushes swung smoothly outward, revealing another road leading further into the trees. "Get going, Mr. Real Estate Agent."

The concealed road twisted through the trees for another hundred yards or so, then opened up on a large clearing. Lee was amazed; it was like a small village there. There were a number of ramshackle structures around the perimeter of the clearing. Most of them looked like they had been cobbled together from scavenged lumber and sheets of corrugated metal. Near a muddy pond in the corner of the clearing, there were a cluster of grungy mobile homes and corroded RVs. The hulks of rusted-out cars were scattered randomly around the site.

In the center of the clearing was a large farmhouse. It had once been white but had faded to a uniform gray. The front porch was sagging a bit, and one of the downstairs windows had been replaced by cardboard, but otherwise it was in good shape. To Lee's practiced eye, it was a good fixer-upper that could go for a decent price if it were in the right neighborhood.

They crossed the clearing to the farmhouse. The camo man indicated that Lee should climb the steps. When they were on the porch he said, "Yer gonna have to wait here 'til I can find Uncle Jeff." He looked out to where a gaggle of dirty children were playing in a mud puddle. "Harry!" he yelled. "Git yer ass over here!"

A dark-haired boy looked up, shot the camo man the finger, and ran up to the porch. He was filthy, covered in scabs, and was wearing only underpants and an old sweatshirt. He looked to be about nine years old.

To Lee's alarm, the camo man handed the assault rifle to the boy and said, "You keep an eye on this bozo. Don't let him go nowhere."

"Okay, Daddy," Harry said, and giggled. He accepted the rifle, leaning backwards to counteract its weight, and leveled the muzzle at Lee's groin.

The camo man started to open the door, then turned to the boy and said, "And don't shoot him, neither, or I'll snatch ya baldheaded."

"Awww," said Harry. "How 'bout just in the foot?"

"No, not today. Remember, or I'll whup yer ass good!"

The camo man disappeared into the house, and Lee was left standing awkwardly on the porch with the filthy child. He decided to start a conversation and try to distract the boy from blowing his balls off. "So, your name's Harry?" he asked.

"Shut up, bozo," said Harry.

Lee shut up.

After a few minutes, Harry seemed to get bored. The barrel of the rifle sagged to the warped wood of the porch. "You look funny," the boy said.

You're one to talk, you little dirtball, thought Lee. "Yes, I sure do." he said aloud, and gave a nervous chuckle.

"I never shot a bozo before," said Harry. "What kinda bozo are you?"

"What do you mean?" asked Lee, sensing that the wrong answer could be painful.

"It don't matter," said Harry, hefting the gun back into position.

"Remember, you'd better not shoot me, or your dad will be real mad," Lee reminded him.

"Oh, yeah," said Harry with disappointment. He let the gun barrel sag again. After a few more minutes, he dropped the gun to the porch and ran back to the mud puddle. "Don't you run off, bozo," he warned Lee over his shoulder.

Lee looked at the rifle lying on the porch. He looked at the door. He looked at the horrible children frolicking in the filth. Running off didn't seem like a bad idea. He could probably just grab the rifle and take off into the trees before anybody noticed. But, no, he had come too far to back off now. He squared his shoulders and waited patiently in front of the farmhouse door.

Presently, the camo man came back out. He saw Lee standing unattended and the rifle lying a few feet away. "Son of a bitch!" he said. He took a few steps to the edge of the porch and called out to where the children were playing. "Goddammit Harry! I told you to watch this asshole! I'm gonna whup yer sorry ass 'til it bleeds!" Harry looked up from where he was playing, and then ran off into the woods like a rabbit.

The camo man picked up the gun, looked at it, and shrugged. "Well, guess I don't need to hold no gun on ya."

"I'm just here on business," said Lee. "Nothing else."

"Well, awright Mr. Businessman, Uncle Jeff says he'll talk to ya. Yer in luck today—he ain't hardly even drunk yet."

"Wonderful. Let's get down to it."

The camo man followed Lee into the front hallway. On either side of him, Lee could see rooms crowded with an incredible array of junk. Every conceivable space was crammed full of an oddball assortment of items. Chairs and couches jostled with piles of magazines and boxes of newspapers. In the corner was what appeared to be an engine block. Some of the things looked incredibly old. Lee spotted a few pieces of antique furniture, and a milk-cupboard on the wall that had to have been from colonial times. There were also dozens—maybe hundreds—of framed pictures on the walls. Some of them were daguerreotype portraits from the 1800s; some were just pictures cut out of magazines. Before he could take it all in, the camo man hustled him up a narrow, dimly-lit stairway and into another room on the second floor.

It took Lee's eyes a moment to adjust to the low light. Incredibly, this room was even more junk-filled than the ones he had seen downstairs. Lee goggled at the assortment of oddities scattered around the room.

"Awful lot of shit to take in at once, ain't it?" said a voice from the gloom. Lee looked over and saw a man sitting in the corner. It was hard to tell his age—he could have been fifty or ninety. A fringe of frizzy white hair surrounded his wrinkled face. He was wearing a faded and patched pair of jeans and a thermal underwear shirt that had seen better days. Strapped to his waist was a gun belt with an enormous revolver.

"Uh, yes, this is quite a place you got here," said Lee. He stepped forward and extended his hand. "Lee Plummer, Plummer Realty Trust. Pleased to meet you."

The old man just looked at Lee's extended hand blankly, then took a sip from a jelly jar half-filled with dark brown liquid.

Lee stood there for a moment, hand extended awkwardly, then let it drop. "Are you Jeffrey Totenkopf?"

"Might be, might be," the old man said. "Depends on who wants to know. And why. Merle here says you got some sorta business proposition."

"Yes, that's correct," said Lee.

"Well, it's a damn good thing ya caught me in a curious mood," the old man said. "Otherwise we mighta just shot yer city ass and dragged the carcass into the woods for the bears to eat." He and the camo man snorted laughter.

"Awright, Merle, yew git on out of here. Sounds like me 'n this city boy got some business to jaw over." The camo man shouldered his rifle and left.

"Well, now, Mr. Plummer, would you like a drink?" said Totenkopf once Merle had cleared out. The backwoods twang in his voice was markedly diminished.

"Yes, certainly," said Lee. After having a gun held on him for the last half hour, Lee felt he could use several drinks.

Totenkopf rummaged around on a cluttered sideboard. He came up with a relatively clean-looking mason jar and filled it from a jug that was sitting at his feet. He passed it over to Lee, who eyed the dark brown contents suspiciously.

"It's rye whiskey, Mr. Plummer. Give it a try."

Lee shrugged and tossed back a swallow. He braced himself for some foul-tasting popskull, but Totenkopf's liquor went down surprisingly smoothly. He said, "Hey, this stuff's pretty good."

"It ought to be," said Totenkopf. "My family's been making whiskey for over two hundred years. Did you know that that's how the Schmidt family got their start, too? Of course, they couldn't make liquor for squat. After a bunch of people went blind from drinking their shitty whiskey, they decided to switch to pretzels."

"That's amazing," said Lee. "I had no idea."

"Well, it's not something that those stuck-up social climbers would really want to advertise, y'know?" said Totenkopf. "So you got somethin' to tell me about the Wizard's Woods, huh?"

"Yes, that's right, Mr. Totenkopf. I'm working on a deal related to that parcel that might be very profitable for both of us."

"Hmmm. You wanna sell the Wizard's Woods, huh? There's a buncha people down in town that might not be too happy about that, you know."

"What do you mean?" asked Lee.

"The Totenkopfs were among the original settlers in this part of the commonwealth," said Totenkopf. "Back around the time Thomas Jefferson was president, the Totenkopfs were the largest landowners in Kerian County."

"Well, you know that the Totenkopfs used to own those woods, don't you?" asked Lee.

"Of course I know it!" Totenkopf snapped. "Like I said, we used to own damn near half the county! Problem was that we didn't really mix too well with other folks, if you know what I mean. Caused a little problem in the marriage department. We liked to sample our own goods a bit too much, too." He held up his jar of whiskey and downed the rest of it in one go. "Eventually, there came to be a lot of what you might call mental issues with the family."

Lee could well believe it.

"So, yeah, there was a lot of Totenkopfs actin' batshit. Damn sorry thing, too. We went from bein' an important family to bein' outcasts. Around 1930, my granddaddy Horace donated the Wizard's Woods to Kerian Memorial Hospital. It was so's they could build a loony bin there. The deal was that the hospital would provide free headshrinkin' to any Totenkopfs what needed it, in return for the land. Seems like a good deal, too, since ol' Horace ended up bein' one of the first residents." Totenkopf filled up his jelly jar and took a sip.

Lee swirled his jar of whiskey thoughtfully. "Tell me, Mr. Totenkopf, are you aware of any revisionary clause in the deed?"

"Huh? What's that?"

"Well, as I understand it, the document that gave that land to the hospital had a clause that said in the event that the land wasn't used for its intended purpose, it would revert back to the original owners. The Hickory Home asylum burned down in 1960 and was never replaced. If that revisionary clause exists, that means you once again own the Wizard's Woods."

Totenkopf looked surprised. "No shit? Well, how do we find out 'bout this here clause?"

Lee felt the momentum of the conversation swinging his way at last. "That's what I came here for," he said. "The donation deed that's on file at the courthouse conveniently seems to be missing a few pages. I thought maybe your family might have a copy."

Totenkopf narrowed his eyes suspiciously. "Well, look here, if there ain't no record of this clause says we own that land, how'd you come to hear 'bout it?"

"Ah, there are other people in Fester with long memories, too. Someone mentioned it in passing once at the city clerk's office. It kind of stuck with me. Of course, it's just a rumor, but if you could lay hands on a legitimate copy, you would regain ownership of that land. And I could help you sell it pretty quickly once you did."

"Well, that's mighty fuckin' interesting, Mr. Plummer." Totenkopf gestured at the contents of the room, sloshing liquor on his arm in the process. "As you can see, we've got a fair amount of the family history right here. It might take me a day or so to lay hands on this document yer talkin' 'bout, but I reckon I could find it."

"That's good. Very good. That old piece of paper might be pretty valuable for you and your family."

"Yeah, well, we do pretty good with the family business, y'know," Totenkopf said, hoisting his jelly jar of liquor. "Still, there's a lot of mouths to feed up here, an' we could always use some more moolah. Just how much money we talkin' about here, Mr. Plummer?"

"Oh, call me Lee." He smiled a great greasy grin and began to talk business.

An hour later, Lee was on his way back down to town. His sendoff from the Totenkopf homestead was considerably more genial than the welcome he had received. He had concocted a pretty good deal with old Jeffrey Totenkopf, too. The old man had been a wily negotiator, and Lee hadn't been able to screw him over as much as he had hoped. Still, he had managed to get pretty good terms for the sale of the land—terms that the Schmidt bitch didn't need to know about. In fact, it wouldn't be that much of a stretch to cut Cecilia out of the deal entirely. Lee could probably scape up enough money to do the deal with Totenkopf on his own.

However, he wasn't entirely comfortable with the idea. He'd make money in the short term, but in the long run it was never good to get crosswise of any of the Top Hats, even a pariah like Cecilia. And there was still the matter of Carla's whereabouts. Screwing over Cecilia would definitely endanger his wife—she had made that much clear.

Besides, the whole deal hinged on the Totenkopf patriarch being able to find a copy of the original donation deed. While it was far from certain that he would, the condition of the house indicated that pack-ratting ran pretty strong in the Totenkopf clan. If there was a complete copy of the deed anywhere in Kerian County, it was probably in the faded farmhouse that the Totenkopfs called home.

Lee felt confident. For the first time since Carla's disappearance, things were starting to break his way. He'd get a big chunk of money, he'd get his wife back, and he'd be able to get clear of that manipulating bitch Cecilia Schmidt.

As the lights of Fester appeared through the trees along Highway 23, Lee began to whistle.

Chapter 29

Son of a bitch!" shouted Bolly. He had, for the third time in five minutes, dropped a lit joint in his lap while driving.

"Would you just give it up and drive?" said Paul. "We're almost there, anyway. We can finish it when we find a place to park." He reached down and grabbed the smoldering roach from between Bolly's legs.

"Hey, what are you doing?" cried Bolly. "Didja see that, Knob? Plummer just made a grab for my schlong! I always knew he was a homo!"

"Ask your mom if I'm a homo, she'll tell you," retorted Paul.

Bolly snorted, "Plummer, you're such a sped. Whoa, better keep it cool, though. The pigs're getting thick." Bolly slowed the Nova to a crawl.

They were now approaching the entrance to Prosser College, the center of higher education in Fester. Emmanuel Prosser, the school's founder, had once spent three weeks touring the Australian outback, and had come home profoundly affected by his adventures Down Under. As a result, the college had a distinctly Aussie flavor. At the entrance to the campus was a fifteen-foot high bronze statue of a kangaroo, dedicated to the "unique and noble beast" that Prosser had chosen to represent his school.

There were constables on almost every corner of the campus tonight. The traffic was getting heavier, and the sidewalks were thronged with rockers decked out in their finest denim and leather. All were heading towards Wombat Auditorium, where the concert was scheduled to start in less than an hour.

"Holy shit!" yelled Knob, "Didya see the rack on that chick? My God!" He turned and stared out the rear window at a girl wearing a tight tube top

176

and even tighter Spandex pants. "My eyes are buggin' out!"

"Man, where the hell are we gonna park?" asked Paul. "This place is nuts." All around the car, the traffic on the street and the crowd on the sidewalk was getting heavier.

"No sweatsky, bro. Bolly's got it covered." He whipped the car into an alley, narrowly missing a phalanx of punker/metalhead hybrids, who yelled after the car and shot it the finger. He cruised down half a block and pulled in behind the dumpster at the rear of a sandwich shop.

"Hey, won't we get towed here?" asked Knob.

"Nah," said Bolly. "Guy that owns this place is a friend of my old man's. He said we could stash the ride here for the show. Now what the hell happened to that joint?"

Five minutes later, Paul, Bolly, and Knob were on the campus of Prosser College. At the main entrance, someone had placed a ripped Motley Crüe T-shirt on the kangaroo statue. All of the foot traffic had converged on the entrance to the school, and the atmosphere was amped with anticipation.

Dampening the festival atmosphere was the heavy police presence. Constabulary cruisers, their blue lights strobing harshly, were parked at regular intervals along Laurel Avenue along the front of the campus. Knots of constables in riot gear were stationed across the main quad.

"Fuckin' pigs," said Knob. "Why can't they just let everybody have a good time?"

They turned a corner and came face to face with a huge line stretching back from the entrance to Wombat Auditorium.

"What the hell?" said Paul.

"Ah, shit, they must be frisking everybody who comes in," said Bolly. "Jerk-offs."

"So, like, have the cops got any leads on your mom?" Knob asked Paul.

Bolly socked him on the arm. "Don't bring that up, you sped. You're bringing my man down."

"No, it's all right," said Paul. "I'm dealing with it okay."

"Hey, sorry, man," said Knob. "I just wasn't thinking."

"Yeah, yeah, okay—no harm, no foul," said Bolly. "We're here to have a good time, right?" Without waiting for a reply, he pumped his fists in the air and yelled, "Fuck yeah! Rock and roll! ROCK AND ROLL! WOOOO!"

Up and down the line, the other concertgoers took up Bolly's cry, and pretty soon the whole crowd was chanting "ROCK AND ROLL! ROCK AND ROLL!"

The closer they got to the entrance, the more electric the air became. Paul quickly got caught up in the rock show vibe. There was an air of anticipation and excitement, flavored with an undertone of danger that made it all the more appealing.

Pretty soon they had made it to the head of the line and were at the security checkpoint. Nervous-looking campus security officers were taking tickets and patting down everyone who came through the door. When Bolly's turn came he raised both hands and shot a double bird as he was being patted down, to the hoots of approval of the rockers in the line behind him.

Once they were through the door, they shouldered past the concession stands and tables selling grossly overpriced T-shirts, and found their seats in the auditorium. The place was packed. All of the seats were full and the standing room spaces at the back were getting jammed.

The crowd-sound was a constant roar, punctuated by wild shrieks and yells. Occasionally, a chant of "GOAT! GOAT! GOAT! GOAT!" would arise and echo around the auditorium before dying down. There were at least three beach balls being batted around.

Up on the stage, bored-looking roadies ambled around, casually setting up mike stands and fiddling with amplifiers. One of them gave the drum kit a few experimental whacks. The crowd went wild.

The tension continued to mount. Paul thought he was going to go nuts if the music didn't start soon. The crowd had settled into a continuous chant of "We want the Goat! We want the Goat!" A few fistfights broke out as latecomers shoved and jockeyed for better vantage points.

Without warning, the house lights went down. A deafening roar of approval went up from the crowd, followed shortly by a wave of marijuana smoke from those who had managed to smuggle their weed past security.

A skinny, middle-aged man appeared from offstage and strolled up to the main mike in the center. He was sporting a WOPP T-shirt, wire-framed shades, and a bad comb-over.

"Who the hell is that?" hollered Knob.

Paul shrugged.

The man tapped on the mike twice, producing a booming, squealing feedback that rolled through the auditorium. Then, in a rich, deep baritone he said, "Hey, rockers and rollers! I'm Chuck Roxx from WOPP-FM, central Pennsylvania's home of hard rock! Thats-a rock 'n' roll!"

The crowd screamed its approval.

"Are you all ready to have your asses rocked off by Quiet Twisted Iron Goat?"

Louder scream.

"What's that? I can't hear you!"

Crazy loud scream.

"All right! The Goat's coming right up, but first it gives me very great pleasure to introduce . . . Lothar the Psycho!"

The lights went up on the stage behind Chuck, revealing Nappy Batesford and the rest of Lothar the Psycho. Chuck scooted offstage, and Nappy leapt forward, grabbed the mike, and shrieked, "Ya gotta take yer fiiiiiiight to the maaaaaaan!" The rest of the band launched its sonic assault.

Paul went nuts. He was immediately standing up on his seat and stayed there for the entire set. Lothar the Psycho was his favorite band, bar none, and he had wanted to see them in concert for years. In an instant, all of the stress, worries, and strangeness of the last several weeks was swept away by Nappy Batesford's vocals and Dave "Dirtbag" Moosh's wailing guitar. Paul was transported, banging his head like his life depended on it and screaming the lyrics of each song along with Nappy.

Too soon, Lothar the Psycho finished their set and cleared off the stage. They were immediately replaced by the blasé roadies who hustled Lothar's gear off the stage to make room for the headliner.

"Holy shit!" yelled Paul after he had climbed back down off his seat.

"What'd ya think, man?" asked Bolly. "Was it worth the wait?"

"Hell yes! That was fuckin' AWESOME!" He gave Bolly and Knob high-fives, then flopped down into his seat to catch his breath.

The crowd around them was a little bit more relaxed, having blown off some steam with Lothar's opening set. It didn't last long. Pretty soon, they were cranked up to a new level of craziness. It continued to mount as the intermission dragged on. The crowd was again chanting "We want the Goat!" continuously, but unlike before it had an ugly lynch-mob edge to it.

"Jesus, what's takin' 'em so long?" asked Bolly. "I'm starting to lose my buzz."

"Ah, it's all a head game," said Knob. "They've prolly been ready for fifteen minutes, but know that if they draw it out, it'll make it that much cooler when they finally come on."

"Well, I think they're draggin' it out a bit too long," said Bolly. "Things're gonna start getting ugly soon."

Just then, the house lights went down, and the crowd broke into a loud, ragged scream. A deep synth note swelled up from the PA system. Red spotlights came up on the stage to reveal the members of Quiet Twisted Iron Goat in various tough-guy poses. The lead singer, Judas H. Christ, raised his hands in the air and shouted, "Hello Shippensburg! Are you ready to rock?"

The crowd went nuts, not caring that Shippensburg was forty miles away.

"Awright!" shrieked the frontman, "It's time to fuckin' rock! This one's from our latest album—it's called 'Give 'Em the Horn.'" The band launched into the intro and the entire crowd was on their feet, screaming.

Quiet Twisted Iron Goat was only about twenty seconds into their opener when the house lights suddenly came on and the power to the PA was cut. The audience howled in disapproval as the band members looked in confusion at each other.

The howls increased as a pissed-off looking man in a khaki constable's uniform emerged from the wings, strutted to the central microphone, and rudely shoved Judas H. Christ out of the way.

"Holy shit," said Bolly. "It's the main pig, whatsisname, Snyder."

"Yeah, I know," said Paul. "He was at my house last week."

"What the hell is he doing here?" asked Knob.

Snyder gestured to someone offstage and there was a piercing whine of feedback from the mike. "I am Chief Constable William Snyder," he intoned. "This public space is dangerously overcrowded and in violation of Pennsylvania General Statute 40.092. I am shutting this concert down."

A tidal wave of howls and profanity rose from the audience, nearly drowning out a loud, flat bang from the back of the hall. Snyder staggered back two steps with a confused look on his face. He reached down and touched the spreading red stain on the front of his uniform. "Son of a bitch," he said in mild wonder. Then he sat down, hard.

The audience's screams of protest subsided to a confused rumble as they tried to decide if this was real or just part of the act. Another man in a constable's uniform and a man in a suit rushed from the wings to where Snyder was trying to get to his feet. The man in the suit was gesturing wildly offstage. The uniformed constable was barking something into a walkie-talkie.

In the crowd, it began to sink in that they had just seen Fester's chief constable get shot onstage. Screams of fear mingled with shouts of approval for the unseen assailant.

"Holy shit!" said Knob. "Someone just shot that cop!"

"You've got a real good grasp of the obvious," said Bolly. "I think things are about to get ugly, fast. We should book."

The rest of the audience had the same idea. There was a mad rush towards the exits. The side doors to the auditorium burst open and in poured squads of constables in full Darth Vader riot gear. Truncheons drawn, they rushed into the panicked crowd.

Most of the crowd freaked and made a dash for the exits. The more militant members of the audience began fighting with the riot cops. One girl—she was tiny, no more than four-foot-ten—was whapping a cop in the face with a deflated beach ball. The cop tolerated this for two or three whaps, then jammed the end of his billy club into her solar plexus. The girl collapsed to the floor.

Up on stage, a paramedic team worked on the downed chief constable. Sirens and shouts could be heard from outside the building. One of the riot cops popped off a tear gas grenade, blinding concertgoers and constables alike.

In the midst of this chaos, Bolly kept a cool head. As soon as the riot police showed up, he grabbed both Paul and Knob by their necks and hollered "Keep cool, dammit, keep cool! We need to wait for the right opening!"

After two minutes that seemed like an eternity, Bolly pointed towards an exit near the side of the stage. It wasn't the closest, but it was almost entirely free from panicked metalheads, angry riot cops, and tear gas. "There!" Bolly shouted, pointing. "Go! Now, motherfuckers!"

They might have made clean getaway if Bolly hadn't shot his mouth off at the last second. As his hand touched the exit door's crash bar, he turned and hollered, "Adios, you goddamn fucking pigs!"

Immediately, two cops in full riot armor materialized out of a swirling tear gas cloud. One of the cops slammed the butt of his club into Bolly's stomach while the other pounded out a drum solo on his skull. Knob took couple of hits to the face, and one of the baton blows bounced off Bolly's thick head and caught Paul square in the eye. Paul and Knob managed to haul the semi-conscious Bolly through the exit door and into the cool night air. Fortunately, the cops didn't follow.

Outside Wombat Auditorium, cop cars, paddy wagons, and ambulances pulled up to the front of the building, sirens and tires shrieking. A news truck from WEVL-TV bumped up over the curb and tried to bypass the bedlam until one overzealous constable shot out a tire. Cops were dragging handcuffed, hollering, and crying concertgoers out the main entrance and loading them into the backs of the paddy wagons and ambulances. From time to time, an emergency exit would slam open and more people would stagger out coughing and cursing.

Knob and Paul half-dragged Bolly across the campus and loaded him into the back of his Nova. Paul took the keys and drove away from the insanity at Wombat Auditorium as quickly as he dared.

Chapter 30

It was a week after the disastrous concert, and Paul was home alone and feeling like shit. His eye was still swollen halfway shut, and his back was really sore—although he wasn't sure if it was from a blow from a riot club or if he had strained it while dragging Bolly back to the car.

It wouldn't be so bad if he had someone to commiserate with, but Bolly was still laid up from his injuries. His dad, as usual, was absent on some dubious work-related errand. Janie wasn't returning his calls. She'd said something about things being weird. Well, *yeah*.

Paul resigned himself to another dull evening alone at home.

Some weed would have made him feel better, but he was completely dry. In the days following the concert, he had smoked up the rest of his stash. In short order, he had gone through his closet and sock drawer scavenging for shake and stems. Earlier this evening, it occurred to him that maybe he might have dropped some behind his dresser. He kneeled down to check, but there was nothing. He stood up and a bright lance of pain shot through his back. "Jesus!" he exclaimed miserably. What a suck-ass night this was turning out to be. No friends, no family, no weed, and a big pain in the back to boot.

At least he didn't have to worry about Warnke for the moment. Fester had been buzzing with the news that Randolph "Cowboy Bob" Warnke had shown up naked outside Calvary Lutheran, and had been beaten into a coma by the outraged parishioners. So he was out of the picture. Then again, who knew when he might wake up, or be released?

Paul went to the living room, but there was nothing good on TV. Out of sheer boredom, he dialed up into the high numbers and landed on a commercial for a psychic hotline. On the screen was a woman who had been the star of a popular TV series back in the late sixties. She breathlessly explained how the Psychic Chums Worldwide Life-Improvement Network Hotline had saved her life, resurrected her marriage, and helped her lose forty pounds. Paul watched in dumb fascination for a few minutes. The commercial was stupid, it was cheesy, and it was absolute bullshit—but he was still considering giving it a call. What the hell, it was only $2.99 a minute.

He was halfway out of his seat when he realized that he already *had* a psychic chum: Nettie Emig. Paul hadn't thought of her in a while—not surprising, given all of the crazy shit that had started since he had left her house.

He went back into the kitchen and looked up Nettie Emig's number. When he dialed it, however, he got a message saying that the number had been disconnected. Well, he could always go out and pay Nettie a visit tomorrow.

The idea made him feel a lot better. Tomorrow, he would be able to go talk to someone who might be able to help him out. He would be happy to just have someone listen to him and give him a little advice. All he needed now was a good night's rest.

The only trick now was to get some sleep. Ever since the concert, Paul had had a lot of difficulty sleeping. It would be even worse tonight with his back hurting. He suddenly thought about his mom's migraine pills. They might provide relief for his sore back, and they would probably help him sleep, too. They sure had put his mom out like light. Maybe a couple of heavy-duty painkillers would handle the pain in his back and dull the edge of his miserable existence.

There were two rooms in the house that where Paul didn't usually go: his dad's study and his parents' bedroom. Entry to the former was expressly forbidden by his father. As for the latter, Paul had felt uncomfortable there since he was four years old, when he had walked in on his parents rolling around under the covers and making funny noises. Ever since then he had avoided his parents' bedroom if he could.

He tiptoed through the bedroom and into the bathroom. In the medicine cabinet was an unusual white bottle on the top shelf, off to the side by itself. It wasn't the transparent orange plastic typical of prescriptions from the pharmacy, but it did have a printed label. Paul took it down and read:

KERIAN MEMORIAL HOSPITAL LABORATORIES
RX# 06512-1254446X
SUBJECT A309F: PLUMMER, CARLA J.

TORBUPHONAL, 250mg (EXPERIMENTAL)
PFINQ PHARMACEUTICALS

TAKE 2 CAPSULES FOR MIGRAINE
ALLOW MIN. OF 8 HOURS BETWEEN DOSES
PHYSICIAN: ZIFFER, MICHAEL W., MD

He opened the bottle and shook out a couple of the capsules inside. They were a flat, dull gray color, and rather large. They looked like bombs he'd once seen being loaded onto a B-52 in a war movie. They seemed dangerous.

Paul shrugged and took two.

Okay, now what? He thought one of the good things about smoking pot was the instant gratification. With some decent bud, all it took was a couple of tokes and you were good and high. Paul figured that he probably wouldn't even feel anything from the migraine pills for at least a half hour. He went back downstairs and put a videotape of *Boscoville* episodes in the VCR. He had seen all of them at least a dozen times, but it was still better than what was on TV. He cued up his favorite episode, the one where Uncle Bosco convinces Raymond to go hang gliding.

About halfway through the show, Paul realized he was bored. The animation seemed dull and flat, like he was looking at a series of pictures drawn by a marginally talented grade-schooler. He decided he'd had enough *Boscoville.*

He turned off the TV and stood up. His head swam briefly, but then quickly settled. Maybe the pills were kicking in. He couldn't tell for sure. His mouth felt a little dry, so he went into the kitchen and got some water. It felt cold in the kitchen, and he didn't like it. The kitchen felt weird. He wanted to listen to some music. He went upstairs.

Something was *definitely* wrong with the staircase. It seemed to be really narrow, and it towered above him, the perspective diminishing sharply as he climbed stair after stair. After what seemed like a really long time, he reached the top. He looked back down, expecting to see the incredibly long trail of steps that had comprised his epic journey. But no, it was just the stairs, same as always.

He went into his room, flipped on the stereo and flopped onto the bed. There was a Lothar the Psycho tape in the deck—*Bat Patrol*, his favorite. He had been listening to a lot of Lothar since the concert. Tonight, however, the music seemed jangly and discordant, too angry. It made Paul's earlobes hurt.

He got up and took the tape out of the deck, scanning his tape rack for something a little more mellow. He noticed a tape by an obscure seventies' prog-rock group called Blue Nietzsche. It had a weird title: *A Complicated Series of Occult Symbols with No Meaning Whatsoever*. The synth-heavy, jazzy sound had originally not been much to Paul's liking, and he had only listened to it once. *Well, what the hell,* he thought. He was in a weird mood tonight. He put the tape in and flopped back down on the bed.

After a few minutes, Paul realized he was really getting into the music. It wasn't entirely devoid of the heavy guitar licks that he liked, and there a pretty heavy bass line, but it was also pretty laid back at the same time. Paul smiled.

He watched the wall on the other side of the room. It was covered with posters, mostly of heavy metal bands, but there were also a few older ones of baseball players. The posters used to have a lot of meaning for him, but now they seemed like the background scenery in a movie he wasn't really paying attention to.

There were areas on the wall that were bare between the posters. The overhead light made a bright spot on one of the open areas. Paul was entranced by the bright spot. As he watched, it seemed to grow bigger and become tinged with green.

There was now a funny undertone to the music, a sound that swelled and pulsed rhythmically like the buzz of cicadas. It continued to swell and grow louder, until the music of Blue Nietzsche was just background noise. The bright spot on the wall now filled almost all of Paul's vision. The green edges grew more distinct and jagged, moving like plants in a breeze.

Paul couldn't feel his arms or legs or head. He couldn't feel the bed underneath him. There were only the wavering green fronds and the sunny summer hum of cicadas. Through the gently swaying plants, he could see a figure. It was beckoning to him from the sunlit place beyond the wall. Maybe it was his mother. He really missed her a lot. He had to go and see.

With an effortless *whoosh*, Paul went through to the other side.

The sound of the music pulsing from his stereo faded away, replaced by the soothing *chirr* of cicadas. The green haze resolved itself into a dense stand of tall grass, surrounded by majestic trees. The landscape rushed smoothly towards him, filling his vision, surrounding his senses. The rushing feeling reached a pleasant crescendo, and suddenly Paul found himself sitting on a hummock of soft grass, by the edge of a vibrant patch of woods. Off to his left, he could hear the peaceful murmur of a river. The rich, warm smell of the forest was very strong. Paul thought that he had never smelled anything as wonderful in his life.

There was a man standing in front of him.

"Hello, Paul," the man said. "It is good to see you." The man was tall, with skin the color of rich mahogany. He was dressed in tanned animal skins that were decorated here and there with feathers, seashells, and colored beads. The man's dark hair was cropped closely—almost shaved—on one side of his head but hung down nearly to his shoulder on the other side. He smiled and reached down to help Paul up.

Paul grasped his offered hand with no anxiety. The man certainly looked weird, but Paul felt like he was meeting an old friend. "Thanks," he said.

"You are welcome," the man said. "Do you know where you are? Or who

I am?"

"Well, um, not really. I mean, it feels like I've been here before, and that I've known you a long time, but I don't even know your name."

The man said, "There are those who would call me Chief Tonto."

"That sounds sorta, I dunno, hokey. No disrespect. But, um, is that your real name?"

"No. My real name is Pahlasquahaminashinuc."

"Okay, let's just stick with 'Chief Tonto' then."

"Good. Come now, Paul. I have something very important to show you."

Chief Tonto turned abruptly and strode off into the trees. Paul followed. As they got deeper into the forest, the trees got denser, thicker, and much taller. Chief Tonto marched confidently through the trees, turning here and there at landmarks that Paul couldn't discern. He had to hurry to keep up with Chief Tonto's long stride, but the warm breeze at his back seemed to help him along.

Paul knew that they were walking through the Wizard's Woods—at least it was a *version* of the Wizard's Woods. Everything seemed unreal, but at the same time very familiar. He could tell that the river sparkling between the tree trunks was the spirit world's Black River.

The trees and bushes grew denser, but Chief Tonto kept up a steady pace as they proceeded. At times, all Paul could see was the man's broad brown back vanishing into the leaves. He hurried to keep up.

At last, Chief Tonto slowed down. The birdsong had diminished, and the gentle breeze had ceased. Paul sensed that they were almost in the exact center of the woods. Chief Tonto pushed through a thick stand of winterberry bushes and held the branches aside so Paul could come through.

They were in a small clearing in the heart of the woods. The bushes and grasses still came up to Paul's shins, but it was considerably less dense than the surrounding forest. At the center of the clearing was a huge outcropping of rock that looked like a hand with the index finger extended.

"Where are we?" asked Paul.

"You are seeking something, are you not? You have questions," said Chief Tonto. "This is a place where answers lie."

"My mom's missing," said Paul. "Will this help me find her?"

"As I said, there are answers that lie here, but you might not understand them, nor be comfortable with them. Also know that the Other is nearby. A strange one."

"Huh? What are you talking about? What do you mean?"

"Never mind that, Paul," said Chief Tonto. "Watch." He nodded towards the rocky outcropping.

The woods had gone nearly silent. The breeze had stopped blowing, and the birdsong had ceased. The only noise was the buzz of the cicadas, which now seemed ominous rather than soothing. It was darker, too. The tree canopy overhead was so dense that he couldn't see the sky, but Paul knew it had gone dull and gray. It was noticeably colder.

"What . . ." began Paul, but Chief Tonto shook his head and pointed at the hand-shaped rock.

As Paul watched, the rock began to change shape. The moss-covered gray surface began to bleach out and become a washed-out, pale color. The rock's protuberances—fingers—grew more pronounced and skinnier, and bumps and creases began to appear along the joints of the fingers. The rocky outcropping of the index finger was elongating and becoming pointier.

Paul looked over at Chief Tonto, but he had started to fade back into the brush. His legs weren't moving, but Paul could see the tall man moving away from him, sliding backwards. He was growing transparent as well; Paul could see branches and bushes through his body.

"Hey, where are you going?" cried Paul. "What's going on here? Stop!"

Chief Tonto said nothing. As Paul watched, the tall man faded away into the underbrush. Paul was alone now and getting scared.

The woods felt oppressive. Malignant figures seemed to be lurking just out of sight. The cicada-noise took on a harsh, abrasive sound, rising and falling faster and faster.

Paul looked back at the rock. When they had entered the clearing, it had looked like a fat and lumpy glove. It now looked exactly like a skeletal hand thrusting upward from a shallow grave. A wave of fear washed over Paul, loosening his knees and filling his mouth with a taste like bitter aspirin. He wanted to turn and run.

A creaking sound came from the skeletal rock-hand. The index finger was slowly crooking over. Bits of moss and rock flaked off as the finger doubled over. Finally, the finger came to a stop. It was pointing at a spot on the ground a few feet away from where it thrust out of the blood-dark earth. A small hole appeared in the ground where the stony finger pointed. As Paul watched, the hole grew larger, swallowing up the dark dirt and desiccated grasses. It grew wider and wider, yawning open like the mouth of a hungry beast.

Paul tried to move his legs, but they were like lead, rooted to the spot where he stood. The cicada-shriek grew louder and faster. The hole grew wider, swallowing dirt, rocks, leaves. Paul saw a chipmunk dart out from a clump of dead grass, trying to get away. It wasn't fast enough, and it disappeared into the maw of the hole with a tiny yelp.

The edge of the hole was approaching the pointing rock. The bony white hand teetered on the edge for a moment, and then slowly toppled in and disappeared into the darkness.

Paul watched in horror as the edge of the hole grew closer and closer to his immobile feet. He felt the earth beneath his sneakers begin to crumble out from under him, and then he too was toppling over into the lightless, lifeless black hole in the ground.

The last thing he heard before he fell was the maniacal screeching of the cicadas.

Chapter 31

From the *Memoirs of Poppi Totenkopf* (translated from the original German)

E ven though much time has passed since that terrible day in 1763, I still have great sadness when I think about it. I must now tell of what happened, regardless of how it makes me feel—or what I promised afterward. I will never forget it, not as long as I live.

Just before it began, I was with Wolfgang Ziffer. We were crouched down behind a bush at the edge of the clearing in the Big Woods. He was holding a musket. I was right behind him, clutching the shovel that he had given me. He had told me to stay close to him, and to not talk and do everything that he told me to.

From our hiding place behind the bush, we had a clear view of the entire clearing with the strange hand-shaped rock in the center. Wolfgang lifted his weapon and sighted down the barrel towards the rock. He checked that the primer pan was still dry, and chuckled. It sounded like large rocks clunking together.

The rest of the settlers of Festung Pfalz-Leister were milling around in the clearing. All were armed, some with muskets, some with swords. The women carried farming tools, mostly pitchforks and hatchets.

I asked Wolfgang what was going on. He told me to shut my mouth.

I could not just shut my mouth. It was running on its own accord, as it often does when I am nervous or upset. "You told the Indians we were going to have a feast," I said to Wolfgang. "Why are we having a feast here in the woods instead of at the settlement? There is no food! How can we have a feast without any food? Are we going hunting before they come? Is that why you have that musket?"

Wolfgang called me an oaf and told me to be silent.

I was scared of Wolfgang—everyone was. But I couldn't be silent. Something felt wrong about what we were doing. I asked, again, where the food for the feast was.

Wolfgang spat out that there would be no feast, that the Indians were not our friends. He said they were filthy savages, and that we are going to eliminate them for good.

I was stung by Wolfgang's anger. I closed my mouth and sat down next to a tree, feeling confused and scared.

Not long after, Wolfgang turned back to the clearing and called for little Dieter Augenblick. The dwarf appeared noiselessly beside the bush. It was unnerving how quickly and silently he could move.

Back in Germany, Dieter had been a pickpocket and thief before joining Herr Grueber's *Zirkus Astoundikus*. He had spent most of the last month scouting out the trails that ran through the big woods south of the settlement. He had an amazing sense of direction and his tiny size—barely three feet tall—allowed him to go places impossible for a regular-sized man.

Wolfgang asked Dieter which of the paths the savages used when they came up from their village.

Dieter indicated a small footpath on the far side of the clearing.

Wolfgang told Dieter to go down the path a bit, but not too far. When he saw or heard the savages approaching, he was to come back quickly.

Dieter nodded and disappeared from the clearing like a *Geist*.

I have never been a smart man, although maybe I am a bit smarter than most people think. Still, looking back I cannot believe how long it took for me to understand what Wolfgang Ziffer had planned. Perhaps it was because I couldn't believe that even he could be so cruel, or that my fellow settlers would be so mean-hearted as to go along with his plan. Clearly, they had been keeping the truth of it from me. When I realized what was about to happen, I felt sick to my stomach—and angry.

I shouted to Wolfgang that we could not attack the Indians, that they were our friends. I thought of the girl, Narqualish, and how my stomach felt funny when she had smiled at me.

But Wolfgang only declared that he was the leader of Festung Pfalz-Lester and would have no more questioning of his decisions. To drive in his point, he jammed the butt of his musket into my stomach, hard. I fell down, unable to speak, unable to breathe.

He said if I dared question him again, he would turn me out of the settlement. I would be on my own and would never survive.

Wolfgang told the rest of the settlers that the Indians were strange and dangerous. That we could not tolerate their intrusion on this land and the new life that we had struggled to build for ourselves. He asked if anyone objected to his decision and looked directly at me while he was saying this. To my shame, I turned my eyes down and said nothing.

Wolfgang began arranging the rest of the settlers around the clearing. Those with muskets were to hide in the bushes closest to the clearing. Those with knives and clubs were to stay behind them. When the savages had all entered the clearing, he would give the order to fire. While those with muskets are reloading, the rest were to rush in and attack. A few others were to go to the side of the trail and wait until they passed. They were to cut off their escape route when the attack began.

Wolfgang told me to stick close by him. He had a "special job" for me. He pushed back into the bushes and indicated with his musket that I should stand behind him.

Everyone found their places and hunkered down to wait. The clearing became eerily quiet. Occasionally, there would be a scrap of muttered conversation or a cough, but these were quickly shushed by Wolfgang.

Dieter suddenly appeared in the middle of the clearing. He waved his arms wildly, and then scooted off into the bushes. He popped up in front of us whispering, "They're coming. They will be here shortly."

Wolfgang asked how many there were. Dieter said he believed there were about twenty.

Dieter pulled a long knife from his belt. With his small stature, it looked almost as if it were a sword. Its finely-honed edge glittered wickedly in the green-muted sunlight.

Wolfgang gave me a look of warning, then squatted down behind the bush. He sighted down the barrel of the musket and waited.

The woods around us had gone almost totally silent. In the distance, we could hear faint singing and laughter. The Sashacannuck were approaching.

The voices grew louder. At the far end of the clearing, the bushes wavered, and the first of the Sashacannuck appeared. It was the old man, Misquashawnak, followed closely by the girl, Narqualish. She was carrying a plucked goose. More of the Sashacannuck filed into the clearing. Most of them were bearing food for the feast that they were planning on partaking with us, their new neighbors.

Old Misquashawnak must have sensed that something was amiss. Perhaps it was the silence in the clearing. He stopped abruptly and raised his hand, then turned and said something to the rest of his tribe.

Wolfgang took a deep breath and screamed, *"Jetzt!"*

The muskets roared. Most of the musket balls found their targets. There was a chorus of screams as the front ranks of the Sashacannuck went down. The clearing was suddenly filled with acrid gray smoke.

Wolfgang's first shot took old Misquashawnak square in the chest. The old man went down like a rock. Narqualish screamed and dropped to her knees, trying to help her grandfather.

Wolfgang yelled, "Foot soldiers forward!"

The rest of the settlers rushed forward, wielding their swords, pitchforks and hatchets. The surviving Sashacannuck were still in shock from the initial volley of musket fire. They were completely unprepared to defend themselves.

Oswald Milchmensch raised an axe and charged an elderly woman. She held up her hands in a vain warding-off gesture. Oswald brought his axe down, connecting with a meaty *thwack* at the base of her neck. An enormous geyser of blood gushed out, and the old woman went down in a boneless heap.

Amazingly, the Misquashawnak, was still alive. Wolfgang's shot had left a gaping wound in his chest, but he was struggling to sit up. With a shrill cry, Dieter rushed forward and buried his knife in the old man's neck. Misquashawnak fell back again and didn't move.

Seeing her grandfather taken down again, Narqualish screamed and fetched Dieter a roundhouse punch that connected solidly with the bridge of the little man's nose. He tumbled backwards, doing a full somersault that would have been comical in other circumstances. He came to rest at the base of a tree, groaning and barely moving.

All of this was happening right in front of me. Narqualish was wailing over the lifeless body of her grandfather. I watched, frozen with shock, as Wolfgang reloaded his musket and stepped towards Narqualish.

"Why? Why are you doing this?" she cried, tears streaming down her face.

"Shut up, you filthy savage," growled Wolfgang. He grabbed his musket by the barrel and swung it like a club, catching Narqualish full in the mouth. She fell backwards, screaming. Her mouth was a bloody raw mess of torn tissue and broken teeth. She landed on her back, her deerskin dress hiked up to the tops of her thighs.

Wolfgang saw this and stopped. He dropped his musket and stepped towards the helpless girl. I stood up, my horror forgotten as I tried to fathom what Wolfgang was doing. He knelt down and grabbed the hem of her dress. With one brutal motion, he ripped the garment from bottom to top. It fell away in pieces, leaving Narqualish lying naked on the bloody ground.

Unclothed, Narqualish looked even younger and more vulnerable than she had before. Her breasts heaved as her breath whistled in and out of her bloody mouth. Beneath them, her stomach bulged slightly. It was obvious that the girl was with child.

Wolfgang fumbled with the front of his trousers and yanked them down. His *schwanz* was stiff and stood away from his body like a Prussian salute.

Overwhelmed with horror, I cried, "Wolfgang, you cannot do this! This is wrong! *All* of this is wrong!"

"Stay back, Poppi," said Wolfgang distractedly. "I mean to have this savage, and then I will slit her stinking throat." He held down the naked girl with one hand while trying to force her legs open with the other.

I protested, pointing out the girl was with child. Wolfgang told me to shut up.

Narqualish began to scream and struggle even more. Wolfgang grunted and held her down, his hand firmly pressed in the middle of her chest. Breathing heavily, he moved up and prepared to penetrate the terrified girl.

Without thinking, I took my shovel and swung it as hard as I could at Wolfgang's head. At the last moment, he ducked slightly. My blow glanced off the top of his shaven skull, but it was enough. He fell over sideways, dazed.

Like a shot, Narqualish was on her feet, sprinting off into the woods. I saw a flash of skin as she vanished into the brush, and then she was gone.

Wolfgang rolled over and saw me standing over him. I was still holding the shovel held in both hands like a club. I was deciding whether or not I should kill him. For one moment, I was no longer the clown, the last man of the group, the one whom everyone thought a fool. For a brief moment, I had the ultimate power over the strongest man in the settlement.

I hesitated, and the moment was lost.

Wolfgang scrambled to his feet, pulling a knife from his belt. In a flash, he had it pressed against my throat and was threatening to kill me.

For once, I didn't flinch. Staring Wolfgang straight in the eye, I said, "I cannot believe you, Wolfgang. You were going to . . . force yourself on that girl. She was with child, too! What would the others say if they knew?"

Wolfgang said he didn't care what the others thought. Then he stopped. It seemed that he was considering the possibilities. Even if the rest of the settlers did not care if he had raped a pregnant girl, he would still have to explain why he had killed me.

His hand dropped away from my throat, and he put the knife back in its sheath. He took a deep breath and said we had both let ourselves get carried away. It was for the best if we spoke no more of it.

I nodded in reply, my eyes downcast.

Around us, the tumult had died down. Off in the distance, there was a high-pitched shrieking. There was the report of a musket, and the shrieking abruptly stopped. An uncomfortable silence settled on the woods.

The clearing looked like a slaughterhouse. The bodies of the Sashacan-nuck were sprawled around the clearing. One of the younger Indians was lying backwards, draped over the odd, hand-shaped rock. His midsection had been sliced open from stomach to sternum, viscera spilling out of the gaping wound. Blood was everywhere, splattering the green fronds of the bushes, smeared across tree trunks, pooled in puddles that were slowly soaking into the ground.

Most of the Indians had not been able to run from the clearing before being cut down. One old man had managed to dash a dozen yards into the brush before being taken down by a musket shot.

Wolfgang threw his head back and roared out a scream of triumph. The rest of the settlers came back to the clearing. Except for Dieter, whose nose had swollen up from Narqualish's punch, the rest were completely unharmed.

Wolfgang congratulated them saying we had triumphed over the blood-thirsty savages who threatened the peace and prosperity of our new home.

Then he instructed Horst, Rolph, and Friedrich to take muskets and follow Dieter to the savages' encampment and kill any who remained. Then they were to retrieve Herr Grueber's hat and burn the village to the ground.

The rest were to return to the settlement. Except for me. I was to bury the dead savages.

Eager to be away from the site of the slaughter, the others quickly turned and departed from the awful clearing. I watched them leave, overwhelmed by sadness and confusion. When the last of them had disappeared into the trees, I turned and bent to my grim task.

Chapter 32

There was no disguising the contempt in the dispatcher's voice. *"Acting Chief Constable* Dirkschneider wants you in his office right now, Martin," she sneered over the intercom.

Martin thanked her and rose from his desk to attend to the summons. Ever since Billy Snyder had been shot the week before, things at the Fester Constabulary had been chaotic. Even though the chief constable was out of the ICU, it would be weeks before he was able to resume his duties.

After the shooting, Martin had rushed over to investigate the crime scene. The shot had come from a projection booth in the back of Wombat Auditorium. It made a perfect sniper's nest, with an unobstructed view of the stage and almost the entire hall. The room still stank of cordite when Martin entered it. There were no shell casings and no fingerprints. Minute scratches on the lock indicated it had been expertly picked. Unfortunately, Martin had been unable to discover anything else that would help him find the shooter.

The day after the shooting, the investigation had been taken over by the state police. This move had provoked general outrage throughout the constabulary. The constables of Fester all wanted to personally hunt down the asshole who had shot their boss.

They were less unified about the appointment of Roscoe Dirkschneider as acting chief constable. Many constables felt that Dirkschneider was the proper hard-ass for the job. There was also a small but angry minority who regarded Dirkschneider's appointment as a travesty. They regarded him as an idiot, a bully, and an all-around asshole who had no business being the head of law enforcement in Fester.

Martin also felt this way, although he was careful to keep his opinion to himself. Roscoe Dirkschneider had made it plain over the years that he considered Martin to be a candy-ass upstart who was too smart by half. Martin had made it a personal policy to avoid Dirkschneider whenever professionally possible.

Clearly, it wasn't possible to avoid him now. Martin had been summoned to the chief constable's office and he had to obey. Roscoe Dirkschneider was his boss now, and there was no way he could disregard the chain of command, despite his personal feelings.

With a feeling of foreboding, he rapped on the door to the chief constable's office. From within came a muffled, "C'mon in, already!"

Martin entered to see Dirkschneider leaning back in his chair with his feet up on the desk. A man in a shiny suit was sitting stiffly in a chair across from him. He was tall, with a pot belly and receding brown hair going gray at the temples.

"'Bout damn time," Dirkschneider said after Martin closed the door behind him.

"Sorry, um, Chief." said Martin. The word felt rancid in his mouth.

"Never mind. Sit down," said Dirkschneider. "

Martin crossed the room to sit down, tripping over the periscope. There was a wide metal flange where the periscope dove into the floor, and Martin seemed to trip on it nearly every time he was in the room. He caught himself, muttering "goldurnit" under his breath.

"I think you may know Lieutenant Dunbar here," said Roscoe. "He's one of our hotshot colleagues from the state police."

"Only by reputation, I'm afraid," said Martin. "It's a pleasure to meet you, Lieutenant."

Dunbar rose and gave Martin a firm handshake. "Thank you, Inspector Prieboy, the pleasure's all mine. I've heard good things about you." He flicked his eyes towards Dirkschneider and his mouth tightened briefly, as if to say *but not from this bozo.*

"Okay, that's great, you know each other," said Dirkschneider. "Now if the reunion is over, can we get down to business, huh? I was just explaining to Dunbar here why we don't need any state police help here in Fester. We've got things under control, okay? We can catch the cocksucker that shot Billy on our own."

Dunbar nodded at Martin. "I appreciate that it must have been quite difficult to have the investigation of the attempted murder of your own chief taken away from your jurisdiction."

Martin chose his words carefully. "Yes, that decision was not, ah, particularly well-received here. Chief Constable Snyder is an able and popular leader. Many of the constables feel that decision to take over the investigations was a bit, um, premature."

"I can understand that," said Dunbar. "However, the decision was not mine to make. Unfortunately, the commander of the Weaverville SP barracks, Wallace Johnson, suffered a heart attack earlier this week. He's survived, and is expected to recover, but he is not going to return to active duty. I've been put in temporary command of the barracks. It's not easy to step into such shoes at short notice, as I'm sure you know, Acting Chief Constable."

Roscoe muttered something obscene under his breath.

"However, I still have a job to do," continued Dunbar. "There has been a fair amount of concern in Harrisburg about the open cases in Kerian County, and Fester in particular. Especially after this concert debacle, which culminated in the attempted murder of a police officer and a riot, largely provoked by *your* officers, Chief."

Dirkschneider started to turn red. "They'd just seen their own chief shot down on stage!" he snarled. "Whaddaya fuckin' expect?"

"That's no excuse for police brutality," said Dunbar.

"Yes, okay, things did get a little out of hand there," said Dirkschneider. "The responsible constables will be disciplined. But we've got those other cases—the college boys and the nurse—we've got those cases sewn up."

"No, what you've got is a suspect who is unable to be questioned because he is in a coma." Dunbar said. He consulted the file in his lap. "In a coma as a result of another riot situation that *you* were involved in, Constable Dirkschneider."

"That's *Acting Chief Constable* Dirkschneider," he growled. "Besides, I didn't cause that riot. The churchies were already wailing on Warnke's goofy clown ass when I got there. If I hadn't broken it up, they mighta killed him!"

"Be that as it may, without an interview or confession, there doesn't seem to be enough evidence to successfully prosecute this Warnke," said Dunbar. "However, Chief Constable Snyder had already forwarded a memo indicating that a preliminary analysis of the evidence retrieved from Warnke's home may link him to these unsolved cases in Fester. Do you concur with that conclusion, Inspector Prieboy?"

"I must admit," said Martin, "that the evidence did initially seem to provide links between the suspect and these open cases."

"There you go," said Dirkschneider, brightening noticeably. "Ol' Prieboy here's our best investigative man. Hell, best in the state. If he says that Warnke got them kids to kill each other and then kidnapped that nurse, you can bet it happened!"

"Inspector Prieboy," said Dunbar, "how confident are you in this? Is this evidence solid?"

"Lieutenant, I would like to emphasize that those are preliminary findings, based on a very superficial review of the evidence," said Martin.

"Inspector, that doesn't really answer my question. Is there something about this evidence that would contraindicate your initial findings?"

Martin looked over at Dirkschneider. His face was screwed up in a look of puzzlement; he was probably grappling with "contraindicate." Martin said, "Yes, sir. I am actually beginning to have my doubts about how that evidence came to be in Randolph Warnke's possession. The garments that were recovered were never reported as being missing from the Plummer household. It also seems unlikely to me that Warnke would be in possession of some of the evidence that was linked to the Dreher/Neff killings at the college. Most of the items recovered are circumstantial in nature. And none of the evidence had the suspect's fingerprints."

Lieutenant Dunbar pursed his lips and said nothing. A scowl was spreading across Roscoe Dirkschneider's florid face as it began to sink in that Martin was spilling the beans.

Finally, Dunbar said, "So, then are you suggesting that the evidence was planted at Warnke's house?"

"I can't rule it out as a possibility," admitted Martin. He glanced over at Dirkschneider. A deep red flush was rising from the collar of his new khaki uniform, a full three shades darker than his usual beef-and-bourbon complexion.

"So who, in your informed opinion, would have gone to the effort of planting this evidence?" Dunbar asked.

Now Martin began turn to turn red. He remembered seeing the pink fiber stuck to Chief Constable Snyder's pants leg shortly before the search of Warnke's house had turned up the incriminating evidence. Could the chief really have planted it? Martin thought it was possible. As much as he liked and respected Snyder, Martin knew his boss had been under a great deal of pressure to make headway on the Prosser killings and the Plummer disappearance. Deep down, Martin knew that Snyder had planted the evidence.

"I really don't have a good answer to that question," Martin said finally.

"It doesn't matter," said Dirkschneider. "It's just one of Prieboy's crazy theories, anyway."

Dunbar made a brief notation in his folder and snapped it shut. "Well, this has been an interesting discussion," he said. "It appears that I have a few matters to discuss with Harrisburg about the status of these open cases in Fester. I suspect that I will be taking charge of the Dreher/Neff killings and the Plummer disappearance as well as the Snyder shooting. I expect I will be speaking with you again shortly, Dirkschneider." He rose and walked briskly from the office, letting the door close heavily behind him.

A heavy silence followed his departure. It was broken by a gritty rubbing sound, like coarse sandpaper abrading cheap tile. It was Acting Chief Constable Dirkschneider grinding his teeth.

Dirkschneider exploded. "YOU STUPID, GODDAMN, WORTHLESS, DO-GOODING, ASS-KISSING, COCK-SUCKING SONOFABITCH!" He picked up a paperweight from the desk and heaved it at Martin, who easily dodged it. "What the fuck were you thinking, telling that statie asshole all that bullshit! An inside job! Saying that someone planted that evidence! What the fuck is wrong with you, boy? When word of your squealing gets out—and it *will* get out—you'd just better keep the hell away from anyone in a uniform that you see. Mailmen, Boy Scouts, the dog catcher . . ." He sputtered, at a loss for words.

"You need to calm down, Chief," said Martin. "You're going to strain yourself. Your blood pressure . . ."

"Blood pressure? Goddammit! I ought to strain *you*, dickweed! Hell, the only reason that I don't pound you into the pavement right now is that you didn't drop a dime on Billy. At least you've got a little bit of loyalty, you candy-ass!"

"But . . ."

"Shut the fuck up, Prieboy!" Dirkschneider croaked. He was still breathing heavily, but the color in his face had started to recede. "You've really fucked up this time! Jesus! Well, since that SP asswipe is taking over all of those goddamn investigations, I guess we really don't need your sorry ass around here now. As of right now, you are on suspension! Without pay!"

Martin was flabbergasted. "You can't . . ." he began.

"The fuck I can't!" snapped Dirkschneider. "Until Billy comes back, I'm in charge. You are suspended until further notice, Prieboy. Gun and badge. NOW!"

Martin reluctantly removed the items and laid them on the desk.

"Good, that's a start," growled Dirkschneider. "Now get the fuck out of here. Don't stop to clean out your desk. Don't stop to talk to anybody. If you're still in this building in thirty seconds, I will arrest you for trespassing. Now GO!"

Without a word, Martin went.

Chapter 33

Paul woke up with the weirdest hangover of his life. He felt unmoored and disoriented, as if he was observing a movie of his own life. The feeling was simultaneously comforting and a little bit frightening. He had no idea how his mother had managed to cope with these disconcerting after-effects of the migraine medication. She must have built up a tolerance or something.

Paul just barely managed to catch the bus to school, and then spent the day wandering from class to class like a zombie. Surprisingly, his dad was home when he got back. Lee had been spending a lot of time at the office lately, and it was strange that he was home early on a weeknight. There also seemed to be a sense of barely suppressed giddiness about him, as if he was on the verge of closing a big deal.

Whatever he was up to, he wasn't sharing it with his son. Instead, Lee wandered around the house muttering to himself and occasionally chuckling. This was fine with Paul. He didn't feel much like talking to his dad. He had a peanut butter sandwich for dinner and went to bed early.

The following day was Saturday. It was nearly noon before Paul got up, but by then the mental fog from Thursday night's adventure had finally begun to lift. His dad was already gone by the time he tramped downstairs to suck up a bowl of Bosco Flakes. Paul spent the morning loafing on the couch, watching cartoons. When *Soul Train* came on, he went into the garage to try to fix his old bicycle. It was hopeless—the wheel was too badly bent. Paul shoved it back into the corner.

The minivan sat brooding on the far side of the garage. Paul had not been interested in driving it lately—too many bad associations. With his dad's Caddy off-limits and the bike out of action, it was either use the minivan or walk. Lately, Paul had opted to walk.

He remembered about going to visit Nettie Emig. The idea was energizing—surely Nettie could help make some sense of all of the weirdness he had been dealing with. The idea of going to visit Nettie more than overcame the bad feelings Paul had about driving the minivan. He grabbed the spare key off the owl-shaped wooden rack by the door and was soon on his way out of town.

* * *

He pulled off of Back Duck Road in front of Nettie's house. As he stepped from the minivan, a wave of unreality washed over him. The sky had started to cloud up, and the overcast gave a strange, otherworldly tinge to the light. Pewter-colored clouds raced across the sky, casting strange shadows across the sprouting fields and meadows. The wind began to pick up as well, and the misspelled notary sign creaked as Paul mounted the warped wooden steps.

He raised his hand, but before he could knock a voice from within said, "Come in, Paul Plummer, come in."

Paul pulled open the door and went inside. Nettie was just entering the room, carrying a tin tray with a teapot and two mismatched cups. She set it on the corner of the desk and sat in the chair, gesturing for Paul to have a seat on the faded sofa. The old woman was dressed in the same pink housedress she had been wearing the first time Paul had come to visit. "So, young man, yez came back to visit me," Nettie said. "I figgered yez would."

"Well, things have been really crazy with me lately," said Paul. A wave of dizziness came over him. He shook his head. "Yeah, really crazy."

"I knows, don't I chust," said Nettie. "I talked with Chief Tonto last night, an' he tole me that yez'd be comin' out fer a visit."

"He did?"

"Ya, he did. In fact, he tole me that he'd seen yez hisself, just a night or two ago. Said yez'd wandered over to his part of the universe."

Paul was startled. "Yeah, I guess so. I had this, I dunno, a dream, I guess. There was this big Indian guy, I remember, and we were out in the woods, there." Paul gestured out the front window at the thick swatch of forest that rose in the southeast. "Then, something . . . happened. I can't remember exactly what, but it kinda weirded me out. I don't really remember the details, just that it was, y'know, freaky."

Nettie nodded. "That's okay, it'll come back to yez, if need be. How yez feelin' now?"

"Pretty spacey. Detached. It's hard to describe."

"Um hmm. Seems to me like yez still got one foot in the spirit world, Paul Plummer. Not a comf'table place to be in, if yez ain't used to it." She picked up one of the cups and thrust it at Paul. "Here, drink this. It'll make yez feel better."

Paul sipped at the contents of the cup. It was bitter and made his tongue sting. He wrinkled his nose.

"Don't yez be a babbie, now," said Nettie. "Sometimes it's the bestest medicine as tastes the wustest. Now drink."

Paul took another sip, and Nettie nodded in satisfaction. "So, Paul Plummer, have yez found yer one true love?" she asked with a smile.

Paul put down the teacup and shrugged. "Yes. No. I dunno. I've been . . . it's complicated."

"Of coss it is—it always is when it comes to matters of the heart," Nettie said. She laughed and added, "But I reckons yez got what yez was after, ain't I right?"

Paul blushed and said, "Well, yes I guess so. Except it wasn't what I thought. Or who I thought. Instead of Sara Ziffer it was this other girl named Janie Simmons."

"That's chust as well," said Nettie. " You dint want nothin' to do with that Ziffer girl, anyway."

"People keep saying that!" exclaimed Paul. "I'm tired of hearing about how she's too good for me."

"Whoa, hold on there, Paul Plummer, yez got it backwards. Yez the one too good fer that Ziffer girl. All them Ziffers is nothin' but trouble. Like I tole yez, they's been causin' trouble for a wery long time. Nothin' but a buncha bullies."

"Wow," said Paul. "I thought they were, y'know, all respectable and stuff."

"Chust 'cuz people's afraid of 'em don't mean they deserves any respect. But enough of that now, eh? What's really on yer mind, Paul Plummer?"

"I really don't know what I came here for," Paul admitted. "It's just that, I dunno, things have gotten so crazy lately." He began speaking faster, as the pent-up confusion and frustration began pouring out of him.

"My mom's gone missing, and nobody seems to know where. My dad's been acting really strange. He's hardly ever home, and I don't know what he's doing or thinking. And the cops aren't any damn good either, especially since everything went to hell at that concert. I just miss my mom and want her back and sometimes it seems like nobody else even fucking cares!" He realized what he had just said and clamped his hands over his mouth.

Nettie laughed again. "Don't yez worry, Paul Plummer. It ain't nothin' I've never heered before." She took another sip from her teacup and her face took on a serious expression. "I knows yez feelin' confused and angry, boy. Yez caught up in somethin' yez don't unnerstand—somethin' that's eatin' away at the whole town. That much I knows from what Chief Tonto tells me."

"Yeah, but what can I do?" Paul whined. "I'm just a kid!"

"Yeah, yer chust a kid, but mebbe yez gots more in yez than yez knows. Chief Tonto's already tole me that you've taken the first step, even if yez don't unnerstand it."

"But what am I supposed to do? I need some help!"

"Yez already got some help, Paul Plummer. From me. An yez already been a little ways down the path yez need to go down to gets yer ma back. It ain't gonna be an easy one, though, I can tell yez that much."

"But . . ."

"But me no buts, boy. I knows that yez feels alone and afeared, but yez gots to be strong. I knows yez didn't ask to be put in this mess. But because of your pa *and* yer ma, yer in it. Now that you're travelin' in the spirit world, yez got to be cautious. Especially now, since the Other has come around."

"Chief Tonto said something about that. Who—or what—is the Other?"

"A new presence in the spirit world, one that is from Long Ago, like Chief Tonto, but also from the Now. A wery strange and disturbing presence.

"That Dr. Ziffer's got a hand in it, too. He's the one that let the Other out, even though he don't know it. He's messin' with things he don't unnerstand, chust to make a few more dollars that he don't even need."

"Jesus!" exclaimed Paul. "I don't know what's going on here! What the hell am I supposed to do about this Other thing? My God!" Suddenly, he felt scared—really scared. It was bad enough having to deal with his mom's disappearance, but the notion of some sort of evil spirit coming after him was much worse. Paul shook his head. What the fuck had happened to his life? He felt very small and vulnerable.

"Now, don't yez go and get yer shorts all in a bunch," said Nettie. "Yez don't have to worry about the Other. You'll prolly never even run into her. Chust be careful if yez of a mind to pay the spirit world another visit."

"I doubt it," said Paul. "I just want to help get my mom back. What should I do?"

"Yez go out now an' seek yer path," said Nettie. "It's closer than yez thinks."

"But how do I do that? Where is this path?"

"Cheepers, boy, Chief Tonto already took yez right down it. Yez told me yerself that it's right there in the Wizard's Woods."

Paul frowned. "The path is in the woods? Will it lead me to my mom?"

"The path'll lead yez to the truth, an' that's gonna be good enough to help yez find yer ma," said Nettie. "Now finish yez drink, Paul Plummer. Feelin' any better? Things seemin' a little clearer to yez, mebbe?"

Paul finished the dregs in the cup, wincing at the bitter taste. "Yeah, I do feel better. It's like the fog in my head's been blown away. Was that some sort of old powwower recipe or something?"

"Nope, chust tea," said Nettie. "Lipton's."

Chapter 34

The kitchen timer next to the vodka bottle rang harshly, and Martin downed a shot. He made another hash mark on the memo pad by the timer, refilled the shot glass, and reset the kitchen timer.

Martin had decided for the first time in his life to get drunk. And in typical fashion, he was doing it with scientific precision. The kitchen timer rang again. Martin downed the shot, reset the timer, refilled the glass, made another hash mark.

Four shots down now. He covered one eye and looked at the eye chart that he had tacked to the far end of his garage lab. After four ounces of vodka, his eyesight had degraded from 20/20 to 20/40. Martin made a note of this on his pad.

Martin downed three more shots, carefully noting the effects of the vodka on his perception and vision. Then he rose unsteadily and weaved his way into the house. Halfway up the stairs, his stomach began to rebel. He hurried up to the bathroom, just making it to the toilet before the effects of seven ounces of straight vodka reversed his peristaltic process. He thought about making note of this in his experiment journal but decided he would wait until he was capable of bipedal locomotion. In the meantime, it seemed like a good idea to rest on the cool bathroom floor. He closed his eyes, hoping the miserable feeling of dizziness and nausea would soon pass. How did drunkards like Roscoe Dirkschneider handle this night after night?

Martin's lip curled at the thought of Dirkschneider. The man was lazy, mean and stupid. Dirkschneider's decision to suspend him had come as a shock, but there was nothing Martin could do. The man was, after all, the acting chief constable.

Even more troubling than the suspension was the conflict he felt about Chief Constable Snyder. Martin greatly respected the man, and deep down considered him to be a father figure. That made it all the more difficult to believe that he had planted the evidence in Randolph Warnke's house. Still, the more Martin thought about it, the more likely it seemed.

Compounding his sense of confusion and guilt was the fact that he hadn't told Lieutenant Dunbar all that he suspected about Snyder planting the evidence. He had deliberately withheld information from a law enforcement officer. Did it really make him that much different from Roscoe Dirkschneider? It was really just a matter of degree. In time, would Martin also be accepting bribes, beating up suspects and planting evidence?

Right now, Martin needed to focus on what to do with his time now that he had been suspended. He had been a police officer almost from the moment he had been turned loose from the orphanage. He was a full-time detective who lived, breathed, ate, and slept police work. He was darned good at it, too.

Martin didn't really have much of a personal life and didn't really need one. He was doing exactly what he had wanted to do from the moment he had found the Batman comic book hidden in the orphanage bathroom. He had gone on living his dream right up until yesterday, when the acting chief constable had demanded his badge and his sidearm.

After that disaster, Martin had left the constabulary headquarters in a daze. When he got home, he went straight to his touchstone—his precious copy of *Detective Comics #27.* Looking at the garish four-color cover, he knew exactly what he must do.

Martin Prieboy would become a costumed crimefighter.

Now, Martin was methodically plotting his plan to become Fester's first costumed superhero. His immediate goal was to get to the bottom of the Dreher/Neff killings and the disappearance of Carla Plummer. He felt he would thus be able to vindicate himself and get returned to duty.

He realized immediately that no longer being on the force meant he would not be able to use his authority to question people and collect information.

Another more subtle approach was called for.

He considered how Batman might handle this situation. Presumably, he'd never had to deal with a lack of resources, as he was incredibly wealthy. Martin wasn't incredibly wealthy and in fact was going to have some difficulty paying his mortgage now that he'd been suspended.

For inspiration, Martin turned to his extensive library of detective and mystery novels. It contained everything from the Hardy Boys to Hercule Poirot and took up nearly two entire walls in his bedroom. He thumbed through some of the more favored volumes in his collection and recalled that many of the detectives in his favorite books obtained information by hanging around in bars and wringing information from their drunken patrons.

This seemed like a workable solution, but it had a major drawback: Martin couldn't out-drink a Girl Scout. He recalled from an Ian Fleming novel that British spies were trained to hold their alcohol so that they could extract information without compromising themselves. Thus began Martin's program of alcohol tolerance-building.

Having finished this stage of the training, he tried to think of what to do next. Throwing up had made him feel a little bit better, but he was still feeling pretty lousy. Why did people get drunk night after night? It sure didn't seem like much fun to him. Obviously, he wouldn't have to get this hammered to hold up his own in a bar, but he had to be able to hold a few drinks without losing his control. Hence, the crash-course in vodka consumption.

Slowly, Martin pulled himself up from the bathroom floor. He wanted to go to bed, but it was still early. There was a real risk of alcohol poisoning if he continued drinking. He wondered what his blood alcohol content was. There was a Breathalyzer in the trunk of his car. He gave his forehead an exaggerated and painful smack, realizing that he should have been taking blood alcohol measurements all along.

He wobbled down the stairs and out the front door to the car. After five stabs with the key, he managed to get the trunk open. The entire trunk was full of equipment that would be useful for his crimefighting costume. Why hadn't he thought of that before? He reached in to grab a Kevlar vest and realized that the equipment there was technically the property of the City of Fester. It would not be proper for him to appropriate it for his own uses, regardless of how well-intentioned they were.

Frig it, thought Martin. He began pulling gear out of the trunk.

He staggered back into the house and dumped the pile of equipment on a table in the garage. Then he fired up the Breathalyzer and checked his blood alcohol content. The reading was 0.23, meaning that Martin Prieboy was officially schnockered. He made a note of it.

He still had to think of a name for his crimefighting alter-ego. The name had to have something to do with bats. And maybe stealth. Perhaps strength, too.

"Stealth-Bat"? No, it sounded too geeky.

What else was there that would convey the idea of bat-ness? "Flying Mammal Man"? Too long.

"The Echolocation Avenger"? No way—that was even longer. Plus, Martin didn't really have any echolocation capability—at least not yet.

Maybe a specific type of bat. "The Vampire Bat"? No, too much emphasis on the vampire, not enough on the bat.

"The Fruit Bat"? Nope.

"The Madagascan Flying Fox"? Cool, but confusing. He'd have to spend too much time explaining that he was really a bat, not a fox.

Martin was starting to get frustrated. Perhaps something with a bit of German flair, to reflect the Teutonic character of Fester. He remembered listening to an operetta called *Die Fledermaus* in music appreciation class back at the orphanage. He couldn't remember much about it, other than it involved a guy dressed as a bat, which in German was "fledermaus." That name would do just fine.

Martin Prieboy would become the Fledermaus!

With that happy thought, Martin put his head in his arms and eight seconds later was snoring loudly.

Chapter 35

What the hell are you doing here?" asked Dr. Ziffer.

Roscoe Dirkschneider had just stopped by Dr. Ziffer's office to pay a courtesy visit. He had come to Kerian Memorial Hospital to visit Billy Snyder and keep him abreast of the latest events at the constabulary. That visit hadn't gone too well, and it didn't seem like this one was going to go much better.

"I just thought I'd stop by and say hello," said Roscoe peevishly.

"Of course," said Ziffer. "Now close the door and sit down before anyone sees you."

Roscoe reluctantly did as he was instructed.

"I ask again: what the hell are you doing here?"

"I was just paying a visit to Billy Snyder," said Roscoe. "I wanted to let him know how things were going down at headquarters."

"I see," said Ziffer. "And just how was this news received?"

"Uh, not very well," said Roscoe. "He threw a bedpan at me."

"Did he hit you?"

"No."

"More's the pity," said Ziffer. "So, you have come into my hospital and upset my most important patient, and now you've decided to put *me* at risk by showing up in my office. Constable Dirkschneider, I don't want you to come into this hospital again unless you're at death's door. Or beyond."

Roscoe could feel his temper beginning to flare. "Hey, now wait a fuckin' minute," he said. "That's no way to talk to me. I'm the head of law enforcement in this town now. You should treat me with some respect."

"I treat you with the contempt you deserve. You bungled the job."

"Hey, Billy's out of the way now," said Roscoe. "Besides, he's your patient—you can do whatever you want to him, right?"

"I find the suggestion that I may harm one of my patients odious," said Ziffer. "I want no links between me and Snyder's misfortune. I suppose I can work with the situation I have, but you screwed up, Dirkschneider."

"Hey, it was a clean shot. It should have taken him out. That motherfucker is tough as an old boot."

"Yes, indeed. It is unfortunate that he pulled through, but perhaps not too surprising. So, what exactly did you want to discuss with me?"

"Well, about our deal . . ."

"There is no deal!" snapped Ziffer. "The fact that Mr. Snyder is still breathing attests to that. You failed. You should consider what will become of you if he recovers. I understand the state police have taken over the investigation. I would be *very* concerned if I were in your shoes."

"Don't worry about me," said Roscoe. "I can handle myself."

"Then you can handle your official duties and deal with an issue that is of mutual interest to us both: finding Carla Plummer. You need to make this your top priority."

"Why the hell should I?" asked Roscoe. He didn't like Ziffer's attitude, and definitely did not like being told how to do his job.

"Because I told you to!" spat Ziffer. "You forget who holds the leash here—and who wears the collar. I'm a Top Hat, and you're just a guard dog. Now do your damn job."

"All right, all right," said Roscoe. "We'll keep looking. She's probably dead or run off to Reno or something."

"Just find her, you lackey," said Ziffer. "The woman is a very important part of my research, and I need to have her back. If she's in Reno, bring her back. If she's dead, recover the remains."

"Yeah, okay, okay," said Roscoe. "I'll do what I can."

Ziffer sighed. "I guess that's all that can be expected of you, unfortunately. Now if you'll excuse me, I have to go make sure that you have not unduly upset my star patient."

Roscoe stalked out of the hospital in a stuttering rage. It was bad enough having Billy chuck a bedpan at him. Ziffer's snotty attitude was worse. No matter—he would think of some way to get back at Ziffer later. Right now, he had to go make some money. He owed Happy Hal another payment by the end of the week.

* * *

Six stories below them, Billy Snyder stared at the ceiling in Room 323, fuming. His belly was beginning to throb. There was a large tube draining the gut wound, IV tubes in both arms, and a sinister array of electrodes and wires running from his arms, chest and head into the machines and monitors that were stationed around his bed. Billy felt like a marionette.

Roscoe's visit had been the first time Billy had gotten an update of constabulary goings-on since he had been shot. He had not taken the news well. The fact that Roscoe had been appointed acting chief constable was alarming enough. The news the state police had taken over the major criminal investigations was even worse.

The most upsetting bit of Roscoe's update was about Martin Prieboy, and what he had revealed to Lieutenant Dunbar. Billy had never expected his star investigator to stay in the dark forever about the way law enforcement really worked in Fester. Billy had in fact prepared for the eventuality that Prieboy would confront him about the corruption in the Fester Constabulary. Every man had his price, and Billy figured he knew Martin Prieboy's. Billy knew it wouldn't be too difficult to sell him on an end-justifies-the-means philosophy. It had worked on more than one crusading do-gooder.

None of that mattered now. Roscoe had blown the whole goddamn deal by suspending Prieboy. He knew Roscoe didn't like Prieboy, and that he felt intimidated by the younger man's ability and integrity. However, for Roscoe to have cut Prieboy loose like that when he had just revealed his suspicions about the Warnke frame-up was stupidity of the highest order. He should have given him a promotion, not tossed him out on his ass.

Billy knew he had to get the hell out of this hospital, relieve Roscoe of his command and reinstate Martin Prieboy immediately. Then he would have a heart-to-heart with the young detective and convince him to play ball.

Escaping from the hospital would be difficult. The doctors and nurses acted like he was just another patient who had to obey their commands and play by their rules. *Well, fuck that,* Billy thought.

Billy removed the IV tube from his left arm and was beginning to peel the tape from the one in his right when Dr. Michael Ziffer stepped through the door. "Aha!" he said. "Nurse Sprockett said you were causing trouble this evening."

Billy looked up and scowled, "Goddammit, doc, I've got to get the hell out of here. This town's going to hell without me." He continued to yank at the tape on his arm.

Dr. Ziffer stepped smartly to the bedside and smacked Billy's hand away from the remaining IV line. "Nothing doing, Mr. Snyder. I'm glad to see that you have a little more energy, but you're still in bad shape. You need rest, and lots of it."

"Bullshit. I need to get out of this death house and get back to business."

"Mr. Snyder, you are lucky to be alive right now. There is no way that you are getting up and going anywhere for a while. Now, if you can just relax and let us help you, you will be back on your feet and back at your job a lot sooner than if you struggle and make things difficult."

Desperate, Billy tried resorting to reason. "Look, Doc, you've got to help me. Things have gotten out of hand here in town since I've been out of commission. I need to get out of here or Fester is just going to fall apart."

Ziffer chuckled indulgently. "Well, now, I won't argue that you are an important person in this town, but I think you may be exaggerating just a little bit. I don't think Fester is going to 'fall apart' if you're not at your desk."

Billy ground his teeth. How could he get this man to understand? "That lunkhead Dirkschneider has already screwed things up. I need to get back to work before he makes things worse."

Dr. Ziffer's face furrowed momentarily. "Yes, I agree there could have been a better choice for your replacement. The man seems a bit . . . crude.

Still, law enforcement and local politics are not my concern. My concern is making sure you make a full recovery as quickly as possible, and that means you stay put for now."

"Look, can I at least have a phone?"

"We'll see about that tomorrow," said Dr. Ziffer.

"You stupid pill-pusher," Billy snarled. "I'd be better off at home than in this leper colony."

"Oh, come now, Mr. Snyder. You know, for being a small regional hospital, we're really quite advanced. We have cutting-edge technology and we're working on some very sophisticated experimental therapies." He pointed at the drain running from Billy's gut. "We also have one of the finest trauma units this side of Johns Hopkins. You couldn't have picked a better town to take a bullet."

"Oh, that's just fucking great," said Billy. "Yeah, I took a bullet, but I've still got a job to do, goddammit! NOW TAKE THIS CRAP OFF OF ME AND LET ME GET THE HELL BACK TO WORK, YOU CHEAPJACK PILL PUSHER!"

Ziffer shook his head sadly. "No, no, that will never do. You're getting yourself too worked up, Mr. Snyder. That's not going to help anyone, you know." He pulled a syringe out of the pocket of his white coat and uncapped the needle.

Billy eyed it warily. "No way. You're not sticking that damn thing in me!"

"Of course not," said Dr. Ziffer. He stuck the needle into the remaining IV tube and pushed the plunger home.

Almost immediately, Billy could feel his strength draining away. "You bastard," he said weakly. Ziffer ignored him and busied himself reattaching the IV and the electrodes that Billy had pulled off.

Billy knew he should feel very, very angry right now. He had been reduced to the status of a small child sent to bed against his will. In addition to all of the other indignities, now he was doped up like some sort of dirty hippie. He felt like shit.

Dr. Ziffer regarded Billy silently for a moment, then checked his watch. "Well, Mr. Snyder," he said, "this must be a difficult situation for you. Laid up in the hospital, unable to move, completely at the mercy of the staff."

"What the fuck is it to you?" Billy said. It came out in a weak slur.

"You, Chief Constable, are a man who is in charge of the entire law enforcement apparatus, and has a great deal of influence with the mayor. You have your fingers in a great many pies, I think, yes?"

Billy scowled but said nothing. Even scowling was exhausting.

"However, there are a number of, ah, situations here in Fester of which you are not privy to. Situations of some importance to the Top Hat families."

With great effort, Billy said, "Bullshit. You can't tell me anything . . . about this town that I don't already know. I know where all of the . . . bodies are buried."

Ziffer laughed. "Oh, you don't know where *all* of the bodies are buried, I am certain of that. There are secrets buried in Fester that need to stay buried. If they do come to light, they will bring a great deal of unfavorable attention on this town, its history, and to the Top Hats."

"What . . . the fuck . . . you talking about . . ."

"It has come to the attention of the Top Hats that there is an interest in developing the wooded area along the river south of town."

"Yeah . . . so . . . what?"

"We already know it was Cecilia Schmidt who approached a group of property developers about the deal, even though she has no title or rights to the land. We also know she engaged the help of a man named Plummer to help her with this project, and that the man's wife has now disappeared under mysterious circumstances."

This news about Lee Plummer was a surprise to Billy. He tried to work through the implications of this new piece of information. It was difficult with his head fogged in.

"Ah, yes, so you see perhaps there is more to this situation than you understand," said Ziffer. "The Top Hats want to avoid having that parcel of land developed in any way."

"So, what does . . . that have to do . . . with me?"

"Well, let me put it this way. Cecilia Schmidt has a very strong interest in seeing this deal go through. She does not, however, understand the implications of what will happen if it does. She is only concerned with her own power and prestige. I also suspect, Mr. Snyder, that you really do care for this community, and would prefer to avoid any situation that would cast it in a bad light. Unlike Cecilia Schmidt."

"That bitch," muttered Billy. He shook his head. What was happening to him?

"The bottom line is that Cecilia Schmidt has a lot riding on this land deal. Certainly enough that she would go to great lengths to eliminate any obstacles. Obstacles such as yourself."

"Are you suggesting . . . that the Schmidt bitch . . . shot me?"

"She certainly has the motive and the means, I would say. Of course you're the expert on criminality, not I," said Dr. Ziffer.

"That fucking bitch," muttered Billy. "I'll get her . . ."

"Now you're seeing things properly. I knew you could be persuaded with the proper impetus." He patted the syringe in his pocket and disappeared out the door, leaving Billy to sort things out. It was a losing battle, and five minutes later the drugs had done their work and Billy was unconscious.

Chapter 36

The Rivertown section of Fester, in the southeast corner of downtown, was the oldest part of the city. It was an ugly pastiche of run-down houses, neglected stores, and vacant lots. The only businesses in Rivertown that didn't seem to be tottering on the edge of insolvency were bars and pawn shops.

Many shady figures slunk through the muggy May night in Rivertown, engaged in nefarious errands and dirty deeds. Yet there was one figure moving through the darkened desolation with more stealth and cunning than all the rest.

It moved like an oiled shadow from crumbling alley to darkened doorway to swaybacked fence. Occasionally the figure paused, as if it were gauging the extent of all that went on in this dilapidated corner of Fester. Having silently observed and evaluated, the darkened figure moved on.

The Fledermaus was on the prowl.

Martin Prieboy had spent most of the previous two days assembling his all-black crimefighter's costume. Most of the stuff he had on hand: a spare Kevlar vest, black leather boots and gloves, a black balaclava. All of this was topped with an extra-large ninja outfit he had purchased at a martial-arts supply store in Weaverville. He had tried making a cape out of a black leather duster he had picked up in a secondhand store, but it had only gotten in the way, and Martin had ditched it.

Unfortunately, without the cape, the concept of "bat" was entirely absent from the ensemble. To counter this, Martin had hot-glued some pointy ear-like protrusions on the top of the balaclava. He detested having to resort to such superficial decoration, but he thought he might eventually be able to mount a flashlight or microphone in them. That would require some more work in his garage lab—which was now officially known as the "Fledermaus Cavern."

While the overall outfit may have been lacking, Martin was pleased with the Fledermaus Utility Belt he had assembled. It had started out as a regulation duty belt, but he had modified it a great deal. It still held some of the standard equipment: handcuffs, flashlight, first-aid kit, a survival knife, a portable police scanner, and a can of CS tear gas. There was a small forensics kit for on-the-spot crime scene analysis. Martin had added a collapsible saw, a set of lock picking tools, a tiny acetylene torch, and a box of wooden kitchen matches.

There was no pistol—the Fledermaus had no need for such a clumsy weapon. Instead, he had included some special devices of his own design. The best was a small electronic device he called the Shrieker. It was about the size of a billiard ball. When activated, it emitted a blindingly bright light as well as an extremely loud screech. Martin's initial test of the device in the Fledermaus Cavern had sent the neighborhood dogs into a frenzy of howling.

Thus had Martin Prieboy equipped himself to fight evildoers as the Fledermaus. This evening, he was making his inaugural run at costumed crimefighting. He hoped to be able to bag a major perpetrator, arrest him, and hand him over to the constables. He had chosen the Rivertown area as being the most likely part of Fester to find lawbreakers blatantly operating in the open.

So far, the Fledermaus had not had much success. He had already skulked around the neighborhood for almost an hour but had not witnessed any criminal behavior. He wondered if the troublemakers of Rivertown took Tuesdays off. It didn't seem likely, and there still seemed to be a fair number of people out on the streets, but they always seemed to be at least a block away from wherever he was lurking.

The Fledermaus crouched behind a pile of old tires on the edge of a vacant lot. Earlier, there had been a number of young hoodlums in the lot, but they were gone now. He looked down Second Street. There was a boisterous group gathered in front of a place called Dutch's Tavern. Dutch's was a notorious dive; a haven for gambling, prostitution, and drug dealing. It seemed like a likely spot to collar a lawbreaker.

The Fledermaus bent over and darted away from the tire pile and began making his way down the street towards Dutch's. He moved carefully, picking spots that were dark and offered concealment.

By the time he got within a half block of Dutch's Tavern, he realized the rowdy, laughing crowd that had been there a mere five minutes before had evaporated. The sidewalk in front of the dingy watering hole was deserted. Gaudy beer-light neon splashed on the cracked and vacant sidewalk. An errant breeze blew a drift of yellowed newspaper across the barren street. Several blocks away, a dog barked.

The Fledermaus scratched his forehead. The balaclava itched. He wondered where the patrons of Dutch's had gone. He looked back up Second Street and could see a small clot of young men fooling around in the vacant lot where he had just been. He turned and sneaked back, but by the time he got there they were gone.

"Darn and heck!" hissed the Fledermaus. He was frustrated by his inability to even spot an evildoer, much less bring one to justice. He looked up at the decaying row houses that lined the street and wondered if he would be better off flitting from rooftop to rooftop. Unfortunately, that was easier said than done. For the moment, the Fledermaus was going to have to rely on foot travel and sheer cunning.

He carefully began working his way north. He went up to Fifth Street, which was sort of a no-man's land that marked the border between Rivertown and the rest of downtown. He then headed west for a few blocks and began carefully making his way down Jefferson Street back towards the heart of Rivertown.

He tried to be exceptionally stealthy, so that his reentry to Rivertown would be completely unnoticed. Carefully, he moved from shadow to shadow, checking to make sure he was not being observed.

From down the block, a pair of headlights appeared. The Fledermaus shrank back into the doorway of a boarded-up grocery store. The car gained speed as it approached. As it passed the doorway where the Fledermaus was concealed, a whiskey bottle sailed out of the car's window and shattered on the sidewalk just a few feet from his hiding place. Over the receding engine roar, he could hear a voice calling, "Get outta Rivertown, you pointy-ear ninja muthafuckah!" There was a swirling hoot of laughter as the car drove off.

"Dang it!" said the Fledermaus. How could they have seen him? He slipped out of the doorway and made his way back down the street. He cut down an alley that paralleled Second Street, and then carefully climbed over a fence into another vacant lot. It was deserted and had a good view of the entire block. The Fledermaus crouched down into the back corner of the fence, where the shadows were deepest. He waited.

After forty-five minutes, the Fledermaus was ready to give up for the evening. Just then, a figure staggered into view. He was hunched over and weaving perilously with the gait of a veteran wino. The Fledermaus watched him with a laser-like focus. The wino only had to make one false move, and the Fledermaus would swoop down and bring him to justice.

The wino stopped in the middle of the block and began having an argument with someone who was not there. It occurred to the Fledermaus that he could arrest the man for public intoxication, but he decided to just wait and watch.

The wino concluded his one-sided discussion and began staggering back the way he came. Then he swung around in another ragged about-face and took a few faltering steps in the original direction. Abruptly, he careened to the right, out into the street.

The Fledermaus tensed. This was the moment for which he had been waiting. He carefully tracked the wino's slow and unsteady progress across the empty street. As soon as the wino stepped across the centerline of Second Street, the Fledermaus had him. It was time to swoop in and serve justice! He rose from his hiding place and shouted, "Halt, in the name of the law!"

The wino stumbled in a circle, trying to determine the source of the voice.

FESTER

The Fledermaus rushed forward to apprehend the miscreant.

The wino saw him and backed away, yelling, "Stay away, you sumbitch! I ain't got no money! Leave me alone!"

The Fledermaus reached around and pulled the handcuffs from his utility belt. Gently but firmly, he cuffed the wino's hands behind his back, and then began tying up his legs with a length of the nylon line.

The wino was gibbering in fear. "Please doan hurt me! Watchoo want? I ain't done nothin'."

"I am making a citizen's arrest," replied the Fledermaus. "You were apprehended in the act of jaywalking!"

"Jaywalking?" replied the wino. "You stupid sumbitch! You arrestin' me for *jaywalking*? What the fuck wrong with you?"

"You are in violation of Pennsylvania General Statute 31.002. You were creating a hazard to yourself and other citizens in the vicinity."

"Cit'zens in the vicin'ty?" cried the wino in disbelief. "You see any muhfuhn cit'zens in the vicin'ty?" The wino twisted his head around to get a good view of his captor. "Holy shit! What the fuck you doin' runnin' aroun' dressed like dat? You must be crazy, boy! Who the fuck are you?"

The Fledermaus drew himself up to full height before replying, "I am . . . the Fledermaus!"

Instead of the awe and respect that he had hoped this introduction would produce, the wino began laughing. "Hee hee hee! You mus' be the weirdo folks is talkin' 'bout. Ever'body in Rivertown know you prowlin' 'round, fool. They avoidin' you like the plague."

"Nonsense," said the Fledermaus. "I am the very paragon of stealth! I am the Fledermaus!"

"You sho' got the *brains* of a mouse, runnin' aroun' dressed up like that! Hee hee hee!"

Nonplussed by this reaction, the Fledermaus lowered the guffawing wino to the sidewalk and finished tying him up with the nylon line. He wrote out a short note and stuck it to the wino's chest. He turned and began to retreat to the shadows.

"Where the fuck you goin'?" screeched the wino. "Doan leave me here all

224

tied up! These damn kids aroun' here'll eat me alive!"

"Don't worry," said the Fledermaus. "The constables will be here shortly to collect you."

"The Johnnies! They'se even worse than them damn kids! Shit, man, this crazy. Just untie me. I promise never to do, um, whatever it was you caught me doin', ever again!"

The Fledermaus retreated back to his vantage point, and spent some time watching the wino struggle against the rope and the cuffs. After a few minutes, he seemed to go to sleep.

The Fledermaus realized he would have to call this in. It took nearly twenty minutes to find a working pay phone. He picked up the receiver and realized he didn't have any change. Another problem: he would have to add some cash to the utility belt. Fortunately, 9-1-1 calls were free. He punched in the digits.

"Nine-one-one," said a bored operator. "What is the nature of your emergency?"

The Fledermaus paused, trying to think of how to phrase things. He couldn't just tell the operator that he had apprehended a wino for jaywalking; she would think it was a crank call. He tried to think of what would bring the constables to the scene quickly. "There's a bunch prostitutes fighting on the corner of Second and Washington," he said, "They have knives!" The Fledermaus had heard that some of the constables patrolling Rivertown would respond quickly to any call involving prostitutes. The streetwalkers usually came across with fringe benefits in exchange for not being booked.

He hung up quickly and hurried back to where the perpetrator was detained. When he got there, the wino was gone. "Goldurnit!" he hissed.

A quick search of the area revealed that he had managed to scooch his way into a nearby alley. The Fledermaus dragged the protesting wino back to the side of the street.

"You sumbitch!" yelled the wino. "Jus' let me alone, dammit! I ain't done nothing!"

"You broke the law," said the Fledermaus. "The constables are on their way."

"Shit, the damn Johnnies goan throw yo' crazy ass in the joint, not mine. They take one look at you an' know you need locked up."

"They will never see me, for I will fade into the shadows. But I will be watching, oh yes." The Fledermaus was too busy dramatically fading into the shadows to see the wino rolling his eyes.

About three minutes later, a patrol car came screeching to a stop on the corner. Two constables jumped out and began scanning the area for signs of the promised cat-fight. They seemed disappointed to find only a tied-up wino with a note pinned to his shirt. The wino tried to explain what happened, but the constables didn't believe him.

"What, you muhfuhs think I tied myself up an' then called you Johnnies to come git me?" shouted the wino. "Read the note, sumbitch. Think I wrote dat?"

One of the constables snatched up the note and ponderously read aloud, "'I have captured this evildoer in the act of jaywalking and am arresting him to help rid this fair city of the blight of crime.' Signed 'FM.' Well, I guess you didn't write this note, Willie, since you can't read or write."

"Who the hell is FM?" asked the other constable.

"I dunno. Freddie Mercury? Hey Willie, was Freddie Mercury up here singing you a song?" the first constable guffawed.

"No, no, it was probably Ferdinand Marcos," laughed the other constable.

The Fledermaus carefully slipped over the fence and stole down the alley, the laughter of the constables still ringing in the street behind him. Clearly, he should have been more specific with the signature.

Overall, his debut as the Fledermaus was not the rousing success he had hoped. Still, he had managed to apprehend a lawbreaker, and turn him over to the constables. The wheels were in motion, and it was only a matter of time before the name of the Fledermaus was respected far and wide.

Chapter 37

Well, what is it? Do you have the number or not?" demanded Cecilia Schmidt. She was staring at Vic Electro's broad, dirty back as he bent over the telephone traceback equipment. She had just received another blackmail call, upping the price of the videotape to $1.5 million. Electro, to his credit, had shown up at her house almost as soon as the blackmailing bastard had hung up.

Electro pulled the soggy cigar stub from his mouth and studied it carefully. "Well, we got a number," he said finally. "It came from this area code, but I'm pretty sure it's a frickin' fake."

"A fake?" asked Cecilia. "How can that be? What is it? What's the number?"

"867-5309."

"Yeah, and how do you know it's a fake number?"

"Well, two reasons," said Electro. "First, there ain't no 867 exchange in this area code. Second, it's the chorus from a pop song that was real big about ten years ago. Aintcha never heard it? It's pretty catchy." Electro began to warble, "Jenny, Jenny, who can I turn tooooo? Eight six seven fiiive, three oh niii-yeee-iiiine . . . eight six seven . . ."

"Shut up! For God's sake, shut up!" shouted Cecilia. "I thought you said that this was the best tracing equipment out there! Why can't you get the real number the call came from?"

"Yeah, that," said Electro, studying his cigar stub again. "Like I said, we're using a Ramjack rig here. There's no frickin' doubt that this is top-of-the-line equipment. The trouble is that the scumbag that's been callin' you must be using Ramjack gear, too. They got a voice scrambler, right? They gotta be using a setup that can spoof the number as well as alter the voice."

"Yeah, well, that's just fucking wonderful," said Cecilia. "Are you going to be able to trace the call or what, you greasy tub of guts?"

"Whoa, whoa . . . no need to get personal here, lady . . . uh, Ms. Schmidt," said Electro. "I gotta make a few calls, might have to call in a few favors with my contacts at Ramjack. Don't worry, Ms. Schmidt, we'll get the bastard."

Cecilia stared at the malodorous detective in disgust. "The only thing I'm worried about is getting you the hell out of my house—NOW!"

"Okay, I can see you're upset," said Electro as he waddled quickly to the door. "I'm gonna make good on this, you'll see. I'll check with Ramjack and make the necessary adjustments to the system. We'll get this scuzzball, don't you frickin' worry about that. Electro always gets his man!" This last promise came as the detective heaved himself through the doorway.

Cecilia stood at her desk, panting in anger. She should have known that nasty sack of crap wouldn't come through. It looked like she was going to have to go with Plan B after all. She slumped into her chair and barked, "Hoegenbloeven, go find Lee Plummer and bring him up here NOW!"

* * *

Ninety minutes later, Lee was in Cecilia's study. He was not in a good mood. He resented being dragged out of the Pine Room, especially when he had been in the process of chatting up the new waitress, Ramona. He had left the Pine Room very reluctantly.

Cecilia and Lee glared at each other in the study across the expansive mahogany surface of Cecilia's desk, taking loud, passive-aggressive sips from their tumblers of Glenlivet. Finally, Cecilia drained her glass, slammed it to the table, and said, "Well, enough of the social niceties, Plummer. We need to get some shit straightened out right fucking now."

Lee eyed her with distaste. Entering into a business relationship with Cecilia Schmidt had been a colossal mistake. For the first time, however, he felt that he was in a position of control. He had to make sure that the

Schmidt bitch was aware of it, too. It was time to apply some leverage.

He opened his mouth to snarl something nasty at her, and then abruptly closed it again. Perhaps it would be better to take a more subtle approach. "Certainly, Ms. Schmidt," he said obsequiously. "It must really be important for you to summon me out here."

"Hell yes, it's important. I'm just glad that Hoegenbloeven here was able to find you so quickly. Jesus, Plummer, you really need to get one of those pagers or something. I can't be sending people all over the county to track you down every time I need to speak to you."

"Golly, I certainly am sorry about that, Ms. Schmidt. You know, I've looked in to getting one of those pagers, but the reception out here is just atrocious. Nevertheless, I will endeavor to be more available to you until we are able to settle this deal. Perhaps I should leave a message with you whenever I am going to be away from my home or office."

The sarcasm sailed over Cecilia's head without ruffling a hair. "Yes, that would be fine. You have Hoegenbloeven's number; call her and let her know what you're up to."

"Sure thing, Ms. Schmidt," said Lee, suppressing the urge to grind his teeth. "Now, what is it that you wished to discuss with me?"

"What the fuck do you think?" Cecilia said. She shoved her empty glass across the desk in the general direction of Hoegenbloeven, who went to the sideboard and refilled it.

"I assume that you would like an update regarding the status of the parcel of land," said Lee.

"Very good, Einstein," said Cecilia. She tossed back half of her new drink in one swallow. "I'm sick and tired of dicking around on this. So, we get title to the land, and then we get it appraised. By you."

"That's right," said Lee. "I've already set up a dummy corporation, just to make sure the trail's not obvious. Next, the dummy corporation hires me to perform the appraisal. We should do a little site work first. Nothing major—clear a few trees, do a little grading, maybe lay a few pipes just for the look of it. Then I can appraise the property for at least twice its current market value. Then, based on that appraisal, we can get a loan against the property that will more than cover what we paid for it."

"Yeah, great," said Cecilia. She leaned forward. "Now, how quickly can we get the loan against the inflated appraisal?"

"Oh, it will take a few days to get all of the paperwork taken care of, once the title's in the clear. We have to make sure that all of the T's are crossed and the I's dotted."

Cecilia sat up and had another belt of scotch. "Yeah, that's good, whatever. Now, how much can we get the loan for?"

Lee reached into his jacket pocket and whipped out a calculator; he never went anywhere without it. He began punching on the keys and muttering to himself. "Escrow fees, yeah, maybe a couple of points there. Closing costs. Standard grease to move things along at the bank. Throw in a couple of thou for some superficial site work, yeah . . ." He began punching the buttons more rapidly, and then finished with a flourish.

"Well," said Cecilia impatiently, "what is it?"

"Of course, it all depends on how much money we have to put up in the first place," Lee said. He saw Cecilia fidgeting, and decided to let her hang for a little bit. It served the bitch right. "You know, that's going to affect a number of factors that might have a significant impact on the overall . . ."

"Goddammit, Plummer, what's the fucking number? How much money?"

"Somewhere between seven and eight million dollars."

Cecilia slumped back in her chair and sighed. "Thank Christ. At least seven million, huh?"

Lee nodded. "Of course, the loan's going to have the be paid back, eventually . . ."

"Shit, don't sweat the petty stuff, Plummer. Not that it's any concern of yours." She took another belt of Scotch. "If you must know, I'm going to have the pretzel company buy a chunk of it for the new plant. I'm sure they'll be able to pay a fair market value, especially since I cleared all of the dead weight off the board." She chuckled. "As for the rest, I've got a developer from New Mexico who's very interested in building a retirement resort. They think they're sharp, but I'm sharper."

Lee used his best ass-kissing tone of voice. "Sounds like you've got it all worked out, Ms. Schmidt."

"Fuckin'-A right. This calls for a celebration." Cecilia hoisted her glass. "Hoegenbloeven, get us some drinks." Hoegenbloeven rose quickly and stepped across the room to fill the glasses. Cecilia received her drink and took an uncharacteristically small sip. "So, at the end of it all I end up with a couple of million in the bank *and* the damned property. Then I've got the land for my new potato chip factory, and I can sell off the remainder to the hippy-dippy developers from the Land of Enchantment. By the time all is said and done, I'll be up like ten million or so!"

Lee took a knock from his glass. He watched Cecilia for a moment before saying, "I object to your choice of personal pronouns."

"Huh?" said Cecilia. "What the hell are you talking about?"

Lee drained his drink and snarled, "I, I, I—that's all you think of! I'm the one doing all the damn work here. You've barely lifted a fucking finger!"

Cecilia glared at him. "You'll get your cut, little man. Five percent, just like we agreed."

"Yeah, well, the situation has changed a bit since we arrived at that figure. I've had to put up with a lot of shit, especially from you. That cut's going to be more like fifty percent. And, of course, we haven't even discussed the *real* incentive."

Cecilia was outraged. "What? Have you lost your damn mind? Fifty percent? That's insane! I'm running this show, you pissant little shack seller. This isn't some split-level deal for a measly couple of grand, this is the big league!"

Lee felt a small tremor of intimidation, but bit back on it. The whiskey helped. "Before you go off on another lady-of-the-manor tirade, let me remind you there's one crucial piece of this puzzle that you haven't considered. Without the rights to that land, *everybody's* cut is exactly zero."

"So what's your point? You said that you could get the rights, said that the Totenkopfs had some sort of deed . . ."

"That's right. And I'm the only one who can get it."

"Bullshit, Plummer. You're hardly the only . . ."

"Real estate guy in town who can obtain that contract? Think again.

There's no one else with the smarts or the balls to get that deed. Shit, I almost had my head blown off going up there to talk to those lunatics."

"So what are you saying?"

"I'm saying that I'm no longer your lackey. From here on in, we're equal partners, or the whole deal's off."

"You bastard!" Cecilia shouted. "You gutless little sack of shit! Why, I'll just go up there myself and get the fucking deed from those hillbillies myself."

"Too late," said Lee. He pulled out a folded piece of paper from his jacket and waved it in front of his face. "I've already gotten it."

"Let me see that!"

"Hell no," retorted Lee, and stuffed the paper back into his pocket. "It's just a copy, anyway. I wouldn't be walking around with the original, now would I? And technically it's not a deed, anyway. It's the original contract for the donation that the Totenkopf family made to the hospital. It contains the revisionary clause stating that if the land ceases to be used for the intended purpose, then the land reverts back to the Totenkopfs. The hospital seems to have conveniently forgotten about that particular clause."

"So what good is it then?"

"It means that the Totenkopfs legally own that tract of land, and we can contract with them to gain the rights to the property. Or buy it outright."

"So what's to stop me from just going up there and making that deal with those rednecks myself?"

"Two things, really. First, they'd probably just shoot you the moment you showed up. And second, I'm the only one who has the original donation document with the revisionary clause." Lee patted his jacket pocket with a smug smile. "Oh, the hospital probably has a copy somewhere, but I don't think that they're in any hurry to find it. No, I'll have my fifty-percent cut, as well as the other incentive."

"You keep saying that. What are you talking about, you crummy little cocksucker? You're not getting half of the cut, and as far as any other compensation goes, you can just . . ."

Lee lowered his voice to a hoarse whisper. "No. First things first. I want my wife back."

Cecilia's jaw dropped open. "Wh-what? I don't . . . You've lost your goddamn . . ."

"Don't try to act surprised," said Lee. "I should have figured that you were behind it from the moment Carla disappeared. You were after her ever since she turned up at that scuzzy bar in Weaverville. So before anything else happens—and before you see a damned dollar—I WANT MY WIFE BACK!" Lee rose from his chair in a dramatic show of spousal loyalty that was markedly absent an hour earlier, when he was putting the make on the newest prostitute at the Pine Room.

Cecilia had recovered her composure enough to chuck her mostly-empty glass at Lee's head, but it missed by nearly a foot. "You filthy little shit! How dare you accuse me of such a thing? Get the fuck out of my house! GET OUT!"

Hoegenbloeven leapt from her small, straight-backed chair and took Lee firmly by the arm. She began pulling him towards the door as Cecilia continued to scream profanities and threats.

Just before he was hustled out the study door, Lee turned and said, "Your show of indignance is almost believable, you blackmailing bitch. Remember, if Carla isn't home by tomorrow morning, the whole deal's off. I might even go to the cops!"

Lee's knees were shaking a little as he walked to his car. He felt a little scared, but mostly elated. He had stood up to the Dragon Lady of Fester and lived to tell the tale.

To hell with Cecilia Schmidt, Lee thought. He was pretty sure he could swing the deal with Totenkopf on his own now. He didn't need her, so why bother with her abuse? He'd get the rights to the Wizard's Woods himself, and sell to the highest bidder. And if that turned out to be someone other than Cecilia Schmidt, well wouldn't that just be a damned shame?

He paused by the car to catch his breath. Then he pulled the Chinese take-out menu from his jacket pocket, crumpled it up and threw it on the granite-block driveway before climbing in and driving back to his office.

Chapter 38

Martin Prieboy was at the Pine Room, pretending to drink a neat bourbon. His alcohol tolerance training had not really been working out well. He couldn't stand the taste, and even one or two drinks got him dangerously intoxicated. Instead, he had mastered the technique of taking a large sip and surreptitiously letting it slide back into the glass.

He was also having to do some fine tuning in his role as a costumed crimefighter. His second mission had not been much better than the first. It had been carried out in the scrubby East Fester area, where the Fledermaus had surprised a gang of Latino teenagers spray painting the side of a warehouse. Most of them had gotten away, but the Fledermaus apprehended a fat one who couldn't run very fast. When the constabulary patrol car had finally arrived, the miscreant was duly carted away. Martin scanned the newspaper for the next several days but had seen no mention of a mysterious costumed crimefighter, or even of the arrest of the vandal.

He decided to try another strategy—disguised undercover work. He had gone down to a thrift store and assembled a convincing blue-collar costume: a pair of battered Red Wing work boots, faded Carhart twill trousers and a worn blue chambray work shirt. Martin's literal-mindedness refused to entertain anything else—when he went blue collar, the collar had to be blue.

With his new disguise in place, Martin installed himself at the Pine Room and carefully nursed a glass of Jack Daniels. The other paying customers of the Pine Room seemed surly and angry. Most had rebuffed Martin's attempts to strike up a conversation with a rude "mind yer own fuckin' business." Those who did want to talk poured out lengthy litanies of how miserable their jobs and marriages were, and how it was entirely the fault of the darkies, the PRs, the gays, the Republicans, the Democrats, or just "them."

One of the waitresses stopped by and made an extraordinary suggestion. Martin didn't know how to respond. What she suggested was certainly immoral, probably illegal, but had a furtive appeal that Martin found disturbing. He politely declined, but came away from the encounter feeling, well, strange. His head felt a little bit dizzy, and he accidentally took a real sip of his drink. The coughing fit this brought on helped bring him back to reality. The temperature in the bar seemed to return to normal, and his pants didn't seem so tight in the area south of the waistband.

Having been brought up in an all-male orphanage run by monks, Martin didn't know how to interact with women. Relationships had been infrequent and rarely involved physical intimacy. His dedication to his job had gotten in the way of his love life, but he never really regretted it. It occurred to him that this might be an impediment to some types of undercover work. Most of Martin's contact with women had been on a strictly professional basis.

The word resonated with him for some reason—"professional." Suddenly, Martin realized he had just been propositioned! He was so stunned that he almost took another sip of his drink. No wonder so few of the "waitresses" were carrying drinks or food! His mind reeled. The girl had seemed so intelligent and nice—but she was a prostitute! And how was this sort of activity allowed to go on right out in the open?

Another man sat down next to him and Martin pushed aside his concerns about vice at the Pine Room to resume his role as a working stiff having a drink.

The man introduced himself as Frank and began cataloguing all of the things that were wrong with his life, Fester, the United States of America, and existence in general. Then, Frank added that "me and some other folks know what to do about this bullshit, and we're gonna, too."

"What do you mean?" asked Martin.

"Look, it's all a matter of who you know," said Frank. "And who you're willing to a few favors for, if you know what I mean."

"Uh, no, not really," admitted Martin.

"Well, it's really just a matter of . . . look, you're not some sort of narc, are you?"

"Not me," said Martin. "Heck no. Just a regular guy looking to get ahead. Just like you." Frank sounded like he might spill the beans on something important. Martin offered to buy him a drink.

"You bet, fella," said Frank. "I knew you were an all-right guy,"

The drink came and Frank downed it quickly. Martin got him another and let him drink most of it before prodding him for more information. "So, you and some folks have got something going on, huh? What's that all about?"

"Yeah, well . . . look, are you a religious fella? Go to church every Sunday, stuff like that?"

"Ah, no. That's really not my thing, you know." Which was true. His upbringing in the Holy Jesus Christ Almighty Home for Unfortunate Boys had seen to that.

"Yeah, I didn't think so. You look too smart for that."

"I'd like to think so."

Frank was starting to slur his words. "Well, me and some folksh got this thing going on that'sh really gonna help us out. Get us the good things in life, y'know. We just gotta do a few favorsh for the big man."

"The big man? Who's that?"

Frank looked slyly up and down the bar before continuing. "You know, the guy who can get thingsh done. The big man . . . downstairs." He mimed devil horns by the side of his head with his index fingers and made grunting sounds. "Y'know who I mean?"

Martin did. Back at the orphanage, Father McJaggar had done a similar imitation of the Devil during his Sunday homilies, especially when lecturing his wards about the dangers of smoking and playing cards. "Yes," said Martin, "I'm with you."

"You are? That'sh great!" slurred Frank, "You seem like a good guy, but not *too* good, y'know what I mean?" He mimed the devil horns with his fingers and grunted again.

"I'm a man who knows what he wants," said Martin. "And I'm not afraid to go out and get it." He punctuated this braggadocio by taking a big sip of his drink, which he let slip right back into the glass.

"Yesh, I thought sho," said Frank. "You and me shee things the same way. What'd you shay your name was, fella?"

"Wayne," said Martin. "Wayne Bruce."

"Well, Wayne, my little circle of friendsh happen to be in need of someone to help serve ol' you-know-who." Finger-horns and grunting. "It'd definitely be worth your while. Whaddaya shay?"

"I'm up for it," said Martin. "I don't mind getting my hands dirty, if the payoff's big enough." He took another faux sip of his drink.

"Good man," said Frank. He gave Martin a hardy whack on the back, which caused him to accidentally swallow most of the bourbon in his mouth. He began sputtering and coughing.

"You okay there, Wayne?"

"Yeah, yeah, sure. It's this cheap booze. I'm after the finer things in life, you know?"

"Absholutely," said Frank. "I think you'd be a great addition to the group."

"Well, you can count me in, pal," said Martin. He had to fight to keep the excitement out of his voice. He thought that he could really be on to something here—if he could crack a ring of devil-worshippers, he'd be sure to be reinstated to the constabulary.

"Well, if it was up to me, you'd be in like Flynn," said Frank. "But it'sh not. You gotta be cleared by the bossh lady first. She's the one with the direct connection to you-know who." He scrawled a phone number on a bar-napkin and gave it to Martin. "Here—call thish number and talk to Shcarlett. She's the head honcho."

"'Shcarlett'?"

"Yeah, Shcarlett. Like Shcarlett O'Hara from that movie, y'know, *Blowing in the Wind*."

"Right, got it."

"That'sh great! She'll be glad to hear from a sharp guy like you." Frank pushed his stool back and got unsteadily to his feet. "Look, I gotta get goin'. Give Shcarlett a call, you won't regret it."

"I'll do it tonight. Hope to be seeing you soon, Frank."

"I'm sure I will . . . brother. You take 'er easy now, Wayne." He weaved off towards the entrance.

Martin waited a few minutes, then decided to call it a night. He had already succeeded beyond his wildest expectations, and there was no point in hanging around any longer. He debated driving home, but since he had accidentally swallowed some alcohol, he had the bartender call him a cab instead. He wanted to get home and make a phone call.

* * *

Bolstered by his success at the Pine Room, Martin decided to branch out and try a different disguise and a different bar the very next night. His choice was a bar called the Embers. It was just as notorious in Fester as the Pine Room, although for very different reasons. The Embers was Fester's sole gay bar, and the constables busted the place on a regular basis. Martin knew gay bars were allegedly the scenes of wild, lewd parties and flagrant drug abuse. He thought it would be worth investigating. Besides, he remembered how Father McJaggar had fulminated against homosexuals back at the orphanage, so he figured they must be up to *something.*

The disguise Martin had chosen for the Embers was more complicated than his working-man outfit. He sat in his car, putting on his makeup. He had never actually been in a gay bar, but he had seen footage of a gay pride parade in San Francisco and figured that was a good enough basis for his outfit.

After putting the finishing touches on the makeup, Martin got out of the car and made his way towards the entrance to the Embers. He was having trouble walking; the six-inch heels on his go-go boots were severely interfering with his balance. Also, it had been raining heavily all day, and the slick pavement made walking even trickier.

The Embers was discreet. A small, unlighted sign bolted to the window-less cinderblock wall announced the name of the bar. The parking lot was fenced in, and the main entrance was tucked away in the back corner. Martin figured he should make a grand entrance. He paused to take a breath and get in character, then pushed open the door to the bar and tottered inside.

Martin's appearance had a galvanizing effect on the patrons of the Embers. It was not, however, the one that he had been hoping for. The men who were arrayed around the bar and on the dance floor stopped and stared in slack-jawed amazement at the apparition who had just entered.

In addition to the high-heeled boots, Martin was dressed in a pair of very tight electric-blue short-shorts that had been pulled on over a pair of inexpertly-shaved legs. The shorts were held up with a pair of rainbow suspenders that bore a button reading "I ♥ Dorothy!" Underneath the suspenders was a maroon leopard-print tube top. Additionally, Martin had donned a long, blond wig in a style that had been fashionable when Farrah Fawcett was still selling posters. His lips were slashed with a deep vermillion lipstick, and inch-long false eyelashes were adhered to his heavily shadowed lids. Martin Prieboy looked like the Drag Queen from Hell.

All conversation in the bar stopped. The patrons stared, aghast. They were all very neatly dressed, mostly in slacks and button-down dress shirts. A few of the men on the dance floor were wearing tank tops and cutoff jeans, but that was as flamboyant as it got. Suddenly, Martin was glad that he had left the feather boa in the car.

He batted his eyelashes and wobbled over to the bar, trying to mince while retaining his balance. It wasn't easy. All of the eyes in the Embers followed his progress, and then turned away once he had seated himself.

The bartender was a slight man in his mid-thirties. He was wearing wire-rimmed glasses and a spiffy tweed vest, and had a small, neat moustache that curled up slightly at the ends. He looked Martin up and down and said, "Buddy, you have got to be kidding me."

"I don't kid, thweetie," lisped Martin, gamely trying to maintain his act. "I'm therious ath a heart attack."

"Oh, please, no," said the bartender. "Seriously, cut it out. It's embarrassing."

"Oh," said Martin.

The bartender looked at him blankly. "I might have thought you were a cop," he said, "but no cop would be so stupid as to come in here dressed like that. Not even in Fester."

"I'm no cop," said Martin. He slumped in his stool. "Gosh, I don't really know what I am anymore. I just thought . . . well, I don't know what I was thinking."

The bartender eyed him critically for a moment and seemed to come to a decision. "Well, okay, I guess you're not a cop. There's something off about you, though."

Martin sighed. There was something about this place that made him feel anxious. "I've been dealing with a lot of . . . changes in my life lately."

"I think we can all relate to that," said the bartender. "Nothing wrong with a little experimentation, you know? But, Jesus Christ, you've got to be a little more careful about your, um, sense of style. That sort of thing might be okay for some of the clubs in Philadelphia or New York, but this is fer-Chrissakes Fester here. You could get the shit beat out of you for walking around dressed like that."

"I'm sorry," said Martin. "I just didn't know."

"S'all right," said the bartender with a shrug. "What can I get for you?"

"Um, vodka martini," said Martin, picking a drink name at random. He pulled off the wig and plucked off the false eyelashes. They stung a little coming off.

The bartender returned with the martini and handed a fresh towel to Martin. "For the gunk on your face," he said. Martin swabbed off most of the makeup. The towel came away caked in multicolored goo.

When he finished, the bartender hunkered down and squinted at the results. "There, that's a lot better. You're a handsome man. You don't need all that makeup." He stood up and extended his hand. "My name's Sam."

Martin took the proffered hand with a slight bit of reluctance and said, "Hi, uh, Sam. My name's, um, Alfred Butler. You can call me Al."

"Okay," said Sam. "So, um, Al, what's your story? You new in town, or did you just decide to finally come out?"

"Both, I guess." He took a bogus slurp from his vodka martini and looked around the interior of the bar. All of the other patrons had gone back to their business and were paying him no attention. This had been a stupid idea, strutting into a gay bar dressed like an extra from a roller-disco movie. He sighed.

"What's the matter, Al?" Sam asked.

"Ah, I don't know. I'm just feeling a little . . . confused." This was the truth. Martin was put off by the difference between what he had expected from the Embers and how it actually was.

"Well, look, there's no rush, man," said Sam. "This place is low-key. Just take it easy until you start to feel more relaxed. Most of the guys here are good dudes. There's a few assholes you have to look out for, but that's pretty much the case anywhere."

"That's good to know," said Martin. "I feel pretty foolish right now."

"Well, you look pretty foolish, to be honest," said Sam. "But don't worry about it. What happens in here doesn't go beyond the front door. For good or ill."

"What do you mean?" asked Martin.

Now it was Sam's turn to sigh. "It's not easy running a place like this in a town like Fester," he said. "You've probably noticed that this town is hardly a Mecca of enlightened thought."

"Yes, I've noticed."

"In fact, you've probably moved to the most backward, narrow-minded little shithole of a town in the entire northeast."

"Aw, it can't be as bad as that."

"It's bad enough to be a gay man in a place like this," Sam retorted. "You'll find that out fast enough if you go parading around town dressed in something like this." He picked up the wig and gave it a shake.

"Gosh, no," said Martin. "I've learned my lesson."

"That's good," said Sam. "It's tough here. And running the town's only gay bar is no picnic, let me tell you. There's a real bastard of a constable, named Dirkschneider. He's the fucking chief constable now. He used to come in here all the time."

"What?" said Martin, amazed.

"Oh, he wasn't here to socialize," said Sam bitterly. "He was here for a payoff. I'd give the bastard a couple hundred, and half the time he'd still haul in some of the boys or bust the place up."

"This guy sounds like a real jerk," said Martin.

"That's the understatement of the year," said Sam. "That guy's a dyed-in-the-wool asshole. All of the constables are, if you ask me."

"That seems unfair," said Martin. "Surely not all of them are assholes."

"They might as well be. I pay those khaki-shirted bastards nearly a thousand a month, but when we need some help, do we get it? Shit." Sam spat on the bar and wiped at it angrily with the bar rag. "Whenever some group of yahoo rednecks decides to lay in wait outside and beat up on my patrons, do those pigs want to know about it? Hell no!"

"Golly," said Martin. "It sounds pretty tough."

"Sometimes I think they want to get rid of us entirely. Run us off, or even kill us off. They sure don't mind when someone gets beat up—or even killed. Like poor Mikey Neff. That kid that got shot at Prosser last month?"

"Yes, I've heard about that." Martin leaned into Sam, focusing in on him intently. "What's that have to do with what you've been saying?"

Sam shrugged. "Mikey was a good kid, came in here from time to time, but not too often. He had a boyfriend in Harrisburg, so he didn't step out here in Fester. Liked to keep a low profile, not that it did him any good."

Martin's voice was low and intense. "Are you suggesting that Mike Neff was killed because he was gay?"

Sam fluttered his bar rag. "I don't know, I don't know," he said. "All I know is that he was a gay man, and the scumbag that killed him is the son of one of the biggest queer-bashers in town. Did the constables want to know anything about that? Fuck no!"

Martin patted at his chest, instinctively feeling for a notebook that wasn't there. "So, you're say that Tom Dreher's father, Carl, is homophobic?"

"Oh Lord, yes," said Sam. "He's been out in front of the bar with a protest sign half a dozen times. And the apple doesn't fall far from the tree, you know."

"That's just circumstantial evidence," Martin pointed out.

Sam gave Martin a long look. "Whatever, Kojak. All I'm saying is that it never came up, not in the paper, not by the constables, nothing."

"Maybe the constables didn't know," said Martin. How had *he* not known? It bothered him that he was just now learning about this aspect of the case.

"Say, what's up with you?" asked Sam. "First you go all Dick Tracy on me with your 'circumstantial evidence,' and now you look all spaced out."

"Sorry," said Martin, "it's been a long week." He reached down into the leotard top and pulled out a wad of dollar bills. "I think I'd better get going." He dropped the cash on the bar and got up to leave.

"Well, be careful, Al," said Sam. "And feel free to come back any time. Just dress a little more, uh, casual, okay?"

"Yes, thanks, Sam," said Martin. "It's been an enlightening evening."

"Hey, you're forgetting this," said Sam, waving the Farrah wig.

"Keep it," said Martin. "I don't think I'm going to need it anymore."

Outside of the Embers, Martin sat in his car, trying to scrub off the rest of the makeup. It has been an interesting couple of nights for him. First, there were the prostitutes in the Pine Room, what Frank had told him about the Satanic ring in Fester, and the call he had made later. Now, there were the patrons of the Embers, who didn't seem at all wicked like he had been taught to believe. Finally, there was the issue of Mike Neff, who may have been killed because of his sexual orientation.

Martin had a lot of thinking to do, and a lot more work to do as well. That could wait, though. All he really wanted to do now was go home and change his clothes.

Chapter 39

The Scarlet Mistress pulled her car off of Highway 17 and into the weed-choked parking lot of the abandoned factory. It was a low corrugated shed that squatted at the back corner of the lot, as if it were trying to hide. A rusted, bullet-pocked sign that read "P-Rite Corp." hung askew over the front doors.

The Scarlet Mistress guided her car to an overgrown corner of the parking lot and into a slot formed by the encroaching bushes. She was being extraordinarily cautious. After the disasters of the last several meetings of the Fell Circle of Mammon, she knew she had to tread more carefully.

The previous meeting had started off well enough, but someone had accidentally kicked a ritual candle into the corner of the room, where it had ignited a number of AA flyers and a poster of Marcel Marceau. The Mammonites had not been able to extinguish the fire before fleeing, although the Fester Fire Department had managed to keep it from spreading to the rest of the historic building.

It had been the latest disaster in a string of many. However, the Mammonites' mishap at Odd Fellows Hall had inspired a new plan. Another vision showed her a way to rectify all of the groups previous shortcomings—a Final Offering to He Who Shall Not Be Named Without Express Written Consent. Of course, it was really *She* Who Shall Not Be Named Without Express Written Consent, but the Scarlet Mistress didn't think the rest of the group needed to know that.

The Scarlet Mistress really couldn't remember a time before She came into her life. Everything before that was just a thick fog. Her long-term

244

memory didn't really extend back more than a month or so, if she tried to remember. Her life before then—well, it really didn't matter anymore. *She* was who the Scarlet Mistress lived for; *She* was the one she served. Whatever She wanted, the Scarlet Mistress moved to obey.

Not all of Her instructions made sense. The effort to bring the Loud Ones to Fester had been especially opaque. Regardless, the effort had borne fruit, and caused much confusion and consternation in Fester. It had also nearly killed the Main Cop, which really would have been a coup. The fact that it hadn't rankled the Scarlet Mistress. Worse than that, it had displeased Her.

But now She had an even better plan.

As a result of the Odd Fellows mishap, the Scarlet Mistress had decided to hold the meetings outside of Fester. It was especially important now, as the plans for the Final Offering were coming together. There could be no risk of discovery, so she had chosen the new site carefully. The P-Rite Corporation building was located just outside of Mellonville, about fifteen miles north of Fester. It had gone belly-up fifteen years earlier, undercut by cheap imports from Japan and Taiwan.

The Scarlet Mistress opened the trunk of her car and removed a flashlight and a huge pair of bolt-cutters. She glanced up at the sky. Even though it was still early in the evening, the low layer of clouds blotted out most of the light. Everything was washed with tones of gray and dark blue. It had been raining very hard for the last several days. Downtown Fester had received over four inches in less than forty-eight hours. The Scarlet Mistress could see the swollen Black River on the other side of the two-lane highway. The river looked dark and dangerous.

Satisfied that the evening was dark enough to provide cover, she went to the side of the building. There was a dented steel door set into the corrugated metal siding. She gave the door a quick check with the flashlight, and quickly cut off the padlock. The door swung outward with a creak.

The Scarlet Mistress gave the interior of the factory building the once-over. There was little worry of anyone seeing the light; the building was mostly windowless. Most of the factory was just open space. Here and there, rusted bolts stuck up from the cracked concrete floor, indicating where the production machines had once stood. In a corner was a pile of rusting metal junk. Scattered around the floor were shards of porcelain and evidence of teenage partying: busted-up beer bottles, squashed cigarette butts, used condoms, and discarded underwear. In one corner, someone had spray-painted "Qweit Twisted Iron Goat RULEZ!!!"

The Scarlet Mistress snorted when she saw this. She was still angry that the concert scheme had not come off exactly as desired. Perhaps it was just as well, though. The new plan was even better, and she would let the others in on it tonight.

Also, there was the matter of the initiation of the newest member of the Fell Circle of Mammon. The Scarlet Mistress was still a little uneasy with the idea of bringing in a new member, especially now. However, she knew the circle had to number thirteen; that was the rule. Every two-bit headbanger and wanna-be Wiccan knew a coven had to number thirteen members. The Scarlet Mistress, worried about the lack of results and nagged by the feeling that she was running out of time, had decided to take on the new man, even though she had not been able to give him a thorough vetting.

It troubled her that the new man had been recruited by Brother Frankenstein. He claimed he could vouch for the new guy, that he had known him for ages. He was probably just some schmoe he had met in a bar, knowing Brother Frankenstein. That guy was an idiot. Then again, everyone in the group were pretty much idiots. Just as long as they were greedy enough to be obedient, that was all the Scarlet Mistress really cared about.

She checked her watch—it was almost time to start. She went back outside and concealed herself in the bushes behind the parking lot. Soon, cars began pulling into the lot. The Scarlet Mistress watched the rest of the Fell Circle of Mammon fumble their way into the P-Rite factory. The last car to pull into the lot was driven by Brother Diabolical. He got out and led a blindfolded figure into the factory.

The candidate was named Wayne, and he was new to Fester. The Scarlet Mistress had given him a telephone screening. He seemed pretty straight—an accountant who had recently relocated from Hershey. No arrest record, no major money problems. More importantly, he had come across as being acquisitive, and smart enough to hold down a job, but not smart enough to question the obvious inconsistencies of a group of upper-middle-class devil-worshippers. In short, he was a perfect candidate for the Fell Circle of Mammon.

The Scarlet Mistress gave the group enough time to follow the instructions she had given them for setting up the meeting. She then went to the door at the side of the factory and paused to listen. The Fell Circle was nattering away.

"What is this place? It smells funny."

"It's a factory that closed down a while ago. They made porcelain plumbing fixtures—mostly urinals."

"Ewwww. A urinal factory? No wonder it smells funny."

"They just made 'em here, they didn't *use* 'em, nimrod."

"Why'd we have to come all the way out here, anyhow?"

"Because you almost set the last place on fire, dimwit."

"I didn't almost set the place on fire, *she* did."

"Shhh. Don't say stuff like that. She'll be here any time now."

The Scarlet Mistress slammed the door open and strode imperiously into the factory. The rest of the Fell Circle of Mammon stood solemnly around the candle-lit pentagram that had been chalked on the floor. She stood with her hands on her hips surveying the ritual space. The only thing that detracted from the somber atmosphere was the smiling cartoon urinal with safety goggles that had been painted on the back wall. The slogan "Squirty sez 'Be Safe!'" was stenciled under the picture.

The Scarlet Mistress turned away from Squirty the Urinal and addressed the Fell Circle of Mammon. "Brothers and sisters, take heed," she intoned. "We have come through difficult times and trials in the service of He Who Shall Not Be Named Without Express Written Consent. But know that our struggles have not been in vain. I have foreseen that we are on the cusp of success. Soon we will successfully serve our Dark Lord and he will reward us greatly. Bring forth the candidate for admission into the Fell Circle of Mammon!"

Brother Diabolical went to a supply closet in the corner and returned with the newcomer. He was wearing a black robe similar to the others' and was still blindfolded.

"You have chosen to join in our cause, to serve He Who Shall Not Be Named Without Express Written Consent," said the Scarlet Mistress. "Do you swear, upon your life and the threat of eternal torment and perpetual bankruptcy to uphold the ideals of our Dark Master, to commit deeds of great foulness in His Ebon Name and to unquestioningly obey His chosen avatar, I, the Scarlet Mistress?"

"I do," said the new man.

"Very well. You now must be sworn to secrecy. For if you reveal the means and methods of the Fell Circle of Mammon, your body will be ripped asunder by demons of the abyss, your soul consigned to the darkest regions of Hell, and your bank accounts emptied and given to the poor! Do you swear to keep secret the nature and doings of the Fell Circle of Mammon?"

"I do."

"You have given your oath," said the Scarlet Mistress. "You may remove your blindfold."

He did as instructed.

"In order to maintain this secrecy, you will be known by a name of your own choosing to your brothers and sisters in the circle. Only I, the Scarlet Mistress, will know the identity by which you are known in the Realm of the Weak. Within the Fell Circle of Mammon, you shall be known by your new name and by that name only. Candidate, introduce yourself to your brothers and sisters."

The new man paused and looked at the rest of the Fell Circle of Mammon. In a deep, dramatic voice, he said, "I am . . . Brother Bat."

"Very well, Brother Bat," said the Scarlet Mistress, "prepare to be initiated into the Fell Circle of Mammon."

The Scarlet Mistress reached into her cloak and produced a large and impressive-looking document covered with fancy-looking calligraphy. "I have here the contract by which your soul will be bound to He Who Shall Not Be Named Without Express Written Consent for all eternity. It is legally binding in all fifty states, as well as Guam and Puerto Rico. Extend your left hand that you may consecrate this contract with your blood."

Brother Bat held out his left hand, and the Scarlet Mistress produced a small, sharp dagger that glittered wickedly in the flickering candlelight. The rest of the Fell Circle of Mammon shifted uneasily, and there were a few gasps. Their own initiations had not involved any daggers or blood; theirs had been more like a real estate closing.

The Scarlet Mistress stepped forward quickly and slashed a cut in Brother Bat's outstretched hand. Brother Bat did not flinch or quiver. A line of blood welled up in the shallow cup of his palm. The Scarlet Mistress held out the fancy contract, and Brother Bat pressed his hand to the bottom of the document, leaving a smeared bloody handprint.

The Scarlet Mistress held up the blood-smeared document and said, "It is done! Our number is again thirteen and we shall now go forth and do the bidding of He Who Shall Not Be Named Without Express Written Consent.

"Now listen up, because our Dark Master has vouchsafed me a new plan that will please Him and cause him to reward us greatly. Now listen closely, for we must put this plan into practice very soon."

"When?" asked Brother Underworld.

"Friday night at midnight."

"Where?" asked Sister Hellfire.

"The Old Mill," said the Scarlet Mistress. "Now quit interrupting me with one-word questions and let me explain."

Chapter 40

G ee, you sure know how to show a girl a good time," said Janie.
"I'm so glad you talked me into cutting school for *this*."

Paul and Janie were slunching through the thick muck in the
woods near the shell of the Hickory Home mental hospital. The heavy rains
of the past few days had turned almost every lawn, field, and patch of woods
in western Kerian County into a swamp. The sky was growing cloudier,
threatening rain again, as the beginning of the annual Wight Winds pushed
the last bit of the storm front through the area.

"No, seriously," Janie persisted. "What are we doing out here?"

"It's about my mom," said Paul. "I think she may be hiding or camping out
here or something." He was trying to push his way through a dense stand
of bushes, and his feet kept slipping in the mud.

"Well, I hope she brought some scuba equipment," said Janie. "When you
suggested coming out here again, I thought you wanted to make out or
something, not stage a manhunt. What made you think that your mom's
out here, anyway?"

Paul pushed his way through the bushes and held a branch aside so Janie
could get through. "Well, this may sound kinda weird," he said, "but I went
to see a powwower. She told me that my mom was out here in the woods."

"A powwower?" said Janie. "That's amazing. I didn't even know there
were any of them around anymore. I can remember my grandmother
talking about going to powwowers to get love potions and junk. Isn't that
crazy?"

"Yeah," Paul snorted. "Totally nuts."

"So what happened, did this powwower tell you to look in the woods, or what?"

Paul hesitated before telling her more. Would she understand? The Old Janie sure wouldn't, but Paul was trying hard to forget the Old Janie. He took a breath and plunged on. "Well, kinda. She did this, uh, ritual, I guess. Afterward, I kinda, uh, had, like a vision or something. Or a dream. There was this big Indian dude, and he led me into the woods—these woods—and showed me a rock that looked like a hand." Paul shivered, remembering how the rock had turned into a skeleton hand.

"Hm," said Janie. Paul expected a smartass rejoinder, but none came.

They shoved their way through a dense patch of briars and came to a clearing. Paul took a step out into it and was immediately soaked to his ankles. "Shit!" he sputtered.

"Where the hell are we going, anyway?" Janie asked.

"Um, I dunno," admitted Paul. "I was hoping you could help."

"Me help? How could I help?" asked Janie. "It was your . . . vision, or whatever."

"You're about the only person I know who's ever been out here. All I remember was that it felt like it was this patch of woods, y'know, near the burned-down loony bin."

"You *felt* like it was? Too bad the loony bin burned down, man. You could probably stand a visit there, talking like that."

"Well, shit, thanks a lot," snapped Paul. "The whole thing is weird enough as it is. I thought you'd be cool about this."

Janie put her hand on Paul's arm. "I'm sorry. But you've got to admit that the whole thing sounds pretty, I dunno, funky. Powwowers and rituals and visions of other worlds."

Paul paused before continuing. "Well, also, I just wanted to, y'know, just hang out."

"Really? That's sweet," said Janie. "I know I've been kinda hard to reach lately. To be honest, I got a little freaked out after we came out here and, y'know."

"Yeah, I know," smirked Paul. "Wait, what do you mean, 'freaked out'?"

"I dunno," said Janie hesitantly. "I mean, we didn't use protection. I was scared as hell that I might, y'know, be pregnant."

"Oh shit," said Paul. His stomach lurched. The thought hadn't even occurred to him. "You're not, are you?"

"No," said Janie. "I got my period a couple of days ago. So that's why I've been acting kinda weird. Also, I just didn't want you to think I was, y'know, a slut or something."

"I didn't think that," said Paul immediately. It seemed to him this remark required some sort of follow-up qualification, but he couldn't think of anything else to say.

"Well . . . that's good," said Janie. "To make it worse, my folks have been fighting again. It's the Wight Winds."

"Man, I hate those," said Paul. "Everybody acts so weird when they get going. It truly blows. Look, maybe we should just split. I can come back by myself later."

"No, no, that's okay. I want to help you. Really."

They looked at each other for a long moment. Janie opened her mouth as if to say something else, and then quickly snapped it shut.

Paul cut his eyes away from hers. "Well, I guess we'd better get going."

"Yep, guess so."

Paul turned and continued slogging his way through the clearing. It was even wetter and boggier in the middle. Janie said, "Jesus, Plummer, you can really pick 'em, though."

Paul turned to say something sarcastic in response, but his feet got tangled up in a submerged root. He went down, falling full on his face, raising a wave of muddy water as he hit. He rolled over, sputtering and spitting out brown water. He tried to stand up, but his feet slid out from under him and he fell back on his ass.

Janie doubled over with laughter. She tried to say something, but then got a look at the expression on Paul's face and broke up again. Finally, she got herself under control. "I take back what I said earlier," she wheezed. "You *do* know how to show a girl a good time. That was the funniest thing I've seen in, like, forever!"

"That wasn't funny!"

"Oh, but you should see yourself! It's hilarious!"

Paul sat in the muck and glowered.

"Oh, c'mon, Drippy, don't pout," Janie said. "I'll give you a hand."

Janie reached out to give Paul a hand up. Paul grasped her wrist and gave her a hearty yank, pulling her down into the mud with him.

"You bastard!" she squealed.

"Okay, *now* it's funny," said Paul. "Wanna mud-wrestle?"

"Wanna kick in the nuts?"

"Okay, then," Paul said, "Let's keep going. It looks like it might start raining again."

"Yeah, it would sure suck if we, y'know, got wet or something," said Janie with a grin.

They slogged their way across the rest of the bog and were soon back in the woods where the ground was slightly drier.

"Which way should we go now?" asked Janie.

"In my, um, dream, I think that the rock was sorta that way." He pointed in the general direction of south.

"So what's up with this rock that you're talking about? What's supposed to be there? Your mom?"

"I don't know, exactly. I just know that whatever's there will help me find her."

"How do you know that this rock's even real?" asked Janie. "Maybe it's something that your mind made up in the 'dream.'"

"I don't think so. I can't explain it, but it just seemed *real*. It's got to be out here somewhere." Paul tried to think how he could make Janie understand that what he experienced was no dream or hallucination; it had *been real*.

They continued to push south through the woods. Paul started feeling as if he'd been here before. He couldn't say how, specifically. There were no trees or landmarks, but once again, it just seemed familiar. "I think we're getting close," he said.

"I hope to hell you're right," she replied. "It's kinda hard to tell with all these trees, but I think it's really starting to cloud up. Let's make tracks."

The farther they went, the more certain Paul was they were getting near to the rock. There was another titanic crash of thunder, and the pattering sound in the treetops got louder. Rain began to pelt them. The ground grew soggier, and little gullies and streamlets flowed with rainwater.

"Hey, Paul, I really think we ought to head back to the car now."

"No, no, this'll pass pretty soon, I think."

As if to give lie to that prediction, there was another even louder clap of thunder. It was now raining heavily at the forest floor, which meant it was coming down in buckets above it.

Janie started to say something else, but Paul plunged into a stand of juniper bushes, leaving her no choice but to follow.

He could almost feel the pull of the rock—it was ahead and off to the left Paul turned that way and began to hurry, hopping over the little streamlets swollen with rain.

The thunder was coming at regular intervals now. The rain was now pouring down from the boughs of the trees like a shower. Both Janie and Paul had been sluiced clean of the mud from their tumble in the bog.

Paul came to a stop, looking around wildly. They were so near—he could feel it.

"Paul, let's go," said Janie. A whiny note had crept into her voice. "This really sucks, and I'm starting to get scared."

"No, we can't go now," Paul insisted. "We're almost there." He looked around wildly, trying to figure which way to go next.

"No, we're *not* almost there, we're almost lost. And almost drowned!"

"Janie, we're really close. It's right around here somewhere, I've got a feeling."

"And I've got the car keys, and I'm going to use them." She turned to go.

About thirty feet away was another big stand of winterberry bushes, their waxy leaves fluttering madly in the rising wind. Suddenly, Paul knew that the hand-shaped rock was just beyond it. "C'mon!" he yelled. He grabbed Janie's hand and began pulling her along towards the winterberry stand. Janie shrieked, but offered no resistance.

Paul charged headlong into the winterberry, legs pistoning madly as he tried to keep his footing in the slippery muck. Janie was slipping and sliding, too, but managed to keep up. The rattling of the raindrops on the leaves sounded like a drum roll.

With one hand firmly grasping Janie's, Paul bulled his way farther into the winterberry bushes. The going was slow. It felt as if hands were reaching out to hold him back. Paul used his free hand to claw his way through the dense branches and pulled the protesting Janie along behind him. At last, they staggered out of the bushes and into a small clearing, breathing heavily.

It looked different from the clearing he had seen in his vision; it was smaller and more densely covered with bushes and plants, but it was definitely the same place. In the middle of the clearing was the rock, just as he had seen it. It looked like a lumpy glove, with the forefinger extended to the sky that was now dumping water on them. A small rivulet of water ran through the middle of the clearing, and it seemed to be getting bigger with each passing moment.

"Holy shit," said Janie, "you weren't kidding. It looks just like you said. Are you're sure that you've never been here before?"

"Only in the, y'know, vision, dream . . . whatever. But it looks exactly like it did when I saw it in the dream. Exactly."

"Fuckin' freaky."

There was another rumble of thunder from directly overhead, and the rain poured down even harder. It was like standing in a shower.

"Okay, great," said Janie, "we found your rock. Now can we get the hell out of here before we drown?"

Paul shook his head. "We can't have come this far for nothing. I thought we were going to find my mom here, or something. Or at least a clue. Shit, I dunno."

"Well, in your vision or whatever, what happened?"

"The rock kinda turned into a skeleton hand and pointed at the ground. After that, I don't really remember anything."

"Where on the ground was it pointing?"

"Oh, I dunno, I guess right about there," said Paul, indicating a spot on the bank of the storm-swollen streamlet.

As they watched, a surge of water coursed down the little stream as the rain grew even heavier. Part of the bank of the stream crumbled as it was undercut and was carried away in the swirling current. There was a yellowish glint in the dirt. As Paul and Janie watched, more and more dirt washed away, revealing a large, round stone that was a dirty shade of yellow, like old ivory.

"That's a weird-looking rock," observed Janie.

Paul continued to stare at the object as more and more of the dirt around it was carried away by the rain-swollen stream. "That's not a rock," said Paul slowly. "That's a skull. I think it's human."

Another freshet of water cleared dirt away, revealing an eye socket and part of another. Paul and Janie carefully picked their way over towards it, wanting to get close enough to see it, but not too close.

"That can't be your mom," Janie pointed out. "It looks like it's been buried for ages. It's gotta be really old."

Paul just continued to stare at the skull. It was now almost entirely exposed. The blank eye sockets seemed to stare at him like an accusation.

There was a titanic crash of thunder, and Paul snapped. Without another word, he turned and ran, with Janie close behind.

Chapter 41

From the *Memoirs of Poppi Totenkopf* (translated from the original German)

The sun had almost set when I came back to the walls of Festung Pfalz-Leister, with my gruesome task completed. The dwindling light filtered through the clouds, giving the landscape a grim, purplish hue. My slumped shadow was nearly lost in the surrounding gloom.

I had spent the entire afternoon in the woods, burying the bodies of the Sashacannuck killed in the massacre. As near as I could tell, it was all of them. Dieter had reported that there were only twenty-two of them living in the village by the lake. I had buried twenty-one. Only the girl had escaped alive, so we must have killed all the rest.

The gate to the settlement was closed and barred when I finally arrived. Despite my exhaustion, I raised my shovel and slammed the butt of the handle repeatedly on the gate. Uder Goetz was on watch duty, and he sounded more drunk than usual. When I told him it was Poppi and to open up, he said, "Poppi? I know of no Poppi!" Then he laughed.

I had a flash of fear. What if Wolfgang had already banished me from the settlement for hitting him with the shovel? If I were exiled, I would have no friends, no one to count on or to help me out. What would happen to me? What would I do? I was deeply frightened. It didn't occur to me until much later that the girl, Narqualish, was probably asking herself the exact same questions just then.

There was a thud and a creak as Uder unbolted the gate and swung it open. Sure enough, he was drunk, almost unable to stand up on his own. He was hanging from the gate, riding on it like a child. He greeted me, then turned his head and threw up.

What a homecoming, I thought. As I dragged myself through the gate, I could see that the entire settlement was only slightly less drunk than Uder. They must have started celebrating their great victory as soon as they had returned.

Most of the group welcomed me home with a great drunken roar. Karlheinz Schmidt staggered up to me with a bottle of schnapps and shoved it into my hands. I turned the bottle up and drank deeply. This was the good stuff, not the normal homebrewed muck that we made from whatever vegetables were in surplus. The schnapps hit my belly like fire, the warmth of the liquor radiating out from the core of my body. I took another drink. Karlheinz said I deserved it, and that Wolfgang told everybody about what I did.

This stopped me cold. I lowered the bottle. But Karlheinz went on to say that Wolfgang was hailing me as a hero. He'd told the settlement how the savage girl ambushed him and nearly castrated him, but Poppi hit her with the shovel and saved him. And then, after all that, he volunteered to stay behind on the burial detail.

"You are a hero, Poppi!" said Karlheinz. "Drink up!"

I started to say something, but instead turned up the bottle again. I was trying to make sense of what Karlheinz had just told me. Wolfgang Ziffer had already spun a false tale about the encounter with the girl. What other lies had he told? I wanted to shout out that the whole thing was wrong, wrong, *wrong,* and that we had all been willing participants in a cruel and pointless slaughter.

Instead, I drank.

I was hurting inside about what we had done that day—hurting worse than I ever had, before or since. However, after hearing Karlheinz's—and thus Wolfgang's—official version of the day's events, I decided that the smart thing to do would be to keep my mouth shut. Despite the treachery and horror I had participated in, what motivated me the most was the desire to belong. I recalled how I felt when I had gotten to the gate and Uder challenged me: that moment of fear that I might not be let back in. I did not want to be an outcast, to have no home or community. The thought was horrible.

Across the compound, I could see Wolfgang leaning up against the wall of the meetinghouse, drinking from a large leather tankard. Our eyes locked, and for a brief moment, I felt a flash of anger. This had all been Wolfgang's idea: the false feast invitation, the ambush, and the attempted rape of the pregnant girl. He was a bad man. My eyes held Wolfgang's, but Wolfgang did not look away. Eventually, I did.

Wolfgang pushed himself off the wall and began walking towards the central square. "Poppi is back!" he bellowed. "The hero of the day has returned! Now we can truly celebrate! My friends, gather around!"

The rest of the settlers, who were all in various stages of inebriation, formed a loose circle around Wolfgang Ziffer. Dieter ran up with a small wooden box for Wolfgang to stand on. He didn't really need it. He was the strongman and was a good three inches taller than anyone else in the settlement, but he mounted it anyway. He now stood head and shoulders above the rest of us and spoke to the rest of the settlement.

He said that today, we had succeeded in a difficult task. It was not a pleasant duty, but it was a vital one, and everyone here should be proud of what was accomplished. He said that the final obstacle to our settlement's growth and prosperity had been removed. The savages who would have hampered us, taken our land, and attacked our settlement had been eliminated.

Then he told us that despite the valiant actions we had undertaken to secure prosperity for our children and grandchildren, there would be those who would not understand why we had to do what we did today. Wolfgang stared directly at me as he said this.

He said that there may be those who would tell false stories about what happened today in the woods, and that we cannot allow this to happen. Then he dramatically pulled out a wicked-looking hunting knife and a large sheet of paper, which was something of a rarity in those times. Written across the top was, "An Oath to keep Secret the Justified Elimination of the Savages that threatened Festung Pfalz-Leister." (I still have this document, too. I took it from Wolfgang's hut when the shrews got him.)

Wolfgang said that to put the whole business behind us and to ensure that there will be no false tales of what went on this day that we would now take an oath—a blood oath—to never speak of what occurred today in the woods. We would keep this in the community, never to be told, on pain of death.

Wolfgang went first, sliding the glittering blade of the knife across his open palm and raising a thin line of blood. He dipped his finger in the blood and wrote out his name on the paper. He turned and passed the knife to Horst Schinkel, who added his own bloody name.

I suddenly felt faint. The day's events had mentally and physically exhausted me, and the last thing I wanted to see was more blood—especially my own.

The knife made its way around the circle of settlers. Each sliced a cut in their palm and signed in blood, although many could not write and merely made an X. Line after line of bloody signatures began to fill up the blank spaces on the sheet.

I was the last one in the circle. Uder Goetz handed me the knife, its edge now streaked with blood from all of the others.

"Now, with Poppi, we will complete the circle," said Wolfgang. "This secret will stay buried." He was staring at me intensely, as if daring me to object.

I shook my head, denying Wolfgang's unspoken accusation. I reversed the knife in my hand and swiftly drew the tip of the blade across my palm, cutting deep. Blood welled up from the gash in my palm. I looked from the fresh line of my own blood to the gory names on the parchment in front of me. The smears and squiggles of blood looked like the sprawled bodies of the slaughtered Sashacannuck. My head swam, and for a moment my knees felt weak.

I looked up at Wolfgang, then around the circle. The rest of the settlers were watching me intently. Once again, my eyes locked with Wolfgang's. It occurred to me that if there was a time to denounce Wolfgang and what he had done, it was now.

A feeling of immense sadness and exhaustion swept through me. Wolfgang was right. It was time to put this awful day behind me. All I wanted to do was sleep for many hours.

I turned my hand over and slammed it down onto a blank spot on the paper, as hard as I could. The blood that had pooled in my hand splattered widely; everyone nearby got splashed with the spray of red droplets.

I looked around again, daring someone to say something. Then I looked at my hand, which was bright red and coated to the wrist. I opened my mouth to say something—I do not know what—and then I fainted dead away.

Chapter 42

Fester City Attorney Ken Schinkel was lounging at his desk in City Hall. He had his feet up as he idly sifted through the paperwork that had accumulated in his inbox. Most of it went into a pile he would hand off to one of his assistants. A few would receive his personal attention, provided he could fit them in before his five o'clock racquetball appointment. The rest went in the trash.

The intercom buzzed. "The mayor on line one," said Schinkel's new secretary. She was a bleached blonde whose name he couldn't quite remember. That wouldn't stop him from trying to screw her—maybe even this afternoon. If she didn't put out, or caused a fuss afterward, she could easily be replaced.

"Okay, babe," he said. "And keep your schedule clear for later this afternoon. I've got an important case I'm gonna need your help on."

Anticipating an enjoyable romp, Schinkel picked up the phone. The lecherous grin quickly faded from his face as Mayor Augenblick spoke.

"Ken, we got a big—*hwaa*—problem. Top Hat stuff."

"Oh, what, did Myra Milkman's gardener mess up her rosebushes again?" snorted Schinkel.

"No, this is dead—*hwaa*—serious," said the mayor. He lowered his voice to a whisper. "Red Hand serious."

"Jesus Christ! What the hell happened?"

"Some kids say they found bones by the Red Hand. A—*hwaa*—skull."

"Oh, holy fucking shit! Give me the details."

The mayor filled him in. By the time Schinkel hung up, all pleasurable thoughts of racquetball and sexual predation were gone.

He stared blankly at the Currier and Ives print on the opposite wall. This situation could be bad. Really bad. "Shit!" he said out loud. "Why me?" His feet hit the thick carpet of his office and he bolted out the door.

Two minutes later he shoved his way into the chief constable's office, where Roscoe Dirkschneider was in the process of dialing the phone. Roscoe had a smug look on his face that made Schinkel want to belt him. Schinkel quickly stepped to the desk and cut off the call.

"Hey!" said Roscoe.

"Who have you told about this mess in the Wizard's Woods?" demanded Schinkel.

"Oh, just the mayor so far," said Roscoe. "I was just going to call the newspaper . . ."

"Jesus Christ, no!" shouted Schinkel. "Didn't the mayor tell you to keep this quiet?"

"Yes, but . . ."

"No buts, you lunkhead. You have no idea what's going on here, do you?"

The arrogant smirk was fading from Roscoe's face. "Dammit, Ken, why are you bustin' my balls?"

"Yes, it's nice to see you doing some actual police work," said Schinkel. "But we'll wait until the mayor gets here before discussing it further."

Schinkel lowered himself into one of the uncomfortable wooden chairs with which Billy Snyder had furnished the office. Presently, Constable Briggs wheeled the mayor's iron lung into the office and retreated into the waiting room.

"Okay," said the mayor, "what the—*hwaa*—fuck is going on here?"

"The Plummer kid and his girlfriend showed up just after noon," said Roscoe. "They say they found a skull in the woods south of town. I dunno, maybe they were high or something. You know these kids today just . . ."

"Shut up, Dirkschneider! Where were they when they—*hwaa*—found this skull?"

"In the woods outside of town, a little bit south of the old loony bin. I was going to call the newspaper, but I thought I'd let you know first."

"Jesus—*hwaa*—Christ! Look, Dirkschneider, you are to tell nobody about this! Absolutely—*hwaa*—nobody, do you understand me?"

Roscoe looked genuinely puzzled. "But Mr. Mayor, I don't get it," he said. "I think . . ."

"Shut the fuck up!" shouted the mayor. "You're not getting—*hwaa*—paid to think, you're getting paid to—*hwaa*-take orders! So listen up good, because if—*hwaa*—you fuck this up, it's your—*hwaa*—ass."

"Yes sir, Mr. Mayor," said Roscoe sullenly.

"Okay, right. Now where are these kids, Dirkschneider?" asked Schinkel.

"I put them in a holding cell."

Schinkel was appalled. "What?! Have you lost your mind?"

"You said to keep them secure," protested Roscoe.

"Not by—*hwaa*—locking them up, you cretin!" hissed the mayor. "If I could use my hands, I'd—*hwaa*—slap my forehead." He turned his head to the attorney. "Ken, slap my forehead." Schinkel gave the mayor a slight smack above the eyebrows. "Okay, now go get those kids out of the cell."

Roscoe began to rise from his seat, but Mayor Augenblick cut him off. "Not you, meathead. You've—*hwaa*—messed things up enough already. Schinkel, go—*hwaa*—get someone to unlock the kids, and bring—*hwaa*—them in here. Try to smooth things over. Better—*hwaa*—yet, get them out of here entirely. Take them to one of the nicer—*hwaa*—rooms over at City Hall."

"What about me, Mr. Mayor?" Roscoe asked sullenly.

"Roscoe, you are a monumental—*hwaa*—shithead. I should fire you on the spot. I'm not going to, though, because—*hwaa*—I need you to perform some police—*hwaa*—duties for a change. Take your—*hwaa*—goons and go down to the woods. Find this skull, and any other remains, and—*hwaa*—bring them back here."

"That might be difficult. That's a big patch of woods. Shouldn't we call the sheriff's office and get some tracker dogs?"

There was a long silence. Finally, Mayor Augenblick said, "Ken, go on and get—*hwaa*—those kids. I want to have a chat with our acting chief—*hwaa*—constable here."

Schinkel nodded and left. As much as he would have liked to hear Dirkschneider getting his ass chewed off, he knew that right now damage control was much more important.

He hurried into the holding cell area. The two teens were sitting forlornly in the one closest to the door.

Now was the time to really pour on the charm. Smiling his biggest, jury-winning smile, Schinkel said "Hey kids, how are you doing? My name's Ken, and I'm the City Attorney. I sure hope you're enjoying this exclusive tour of Fester's municipal facilities. I guess you've probably seen enough of Constabulary Headquarters by now. What do you say we get a snack and go back to City Hall for a little chat?"

Soon, Paul and Janie were sitting in a well-appointed conference room in the mayor's office. Ken Schinkel was sitting at the head of the table, smiling personably. He was good at that.

"So, kids, the chief constable tells me that you found something in the woods. Something that might look like bones?"

"They *were* bones," insisted Janie. "Or at least a skull."

"Well, we're sure going to check on that," said Schinkel. "That's obviously very important to us, as is the case of Paul's mother's disappearance. Of course, it's a very sensitive matter. We want to make absolutely sure of what you kids think you saw before making a big deal about this. We wouldn't want to compromise our efforts to find Paul's mom, right?"

Paul and Janie nodded uncertainly.

"Good. Now, who have you told about these things that you thought were bones?" Schinkel asked.

Paul and Janie looked at each other and shrugged. "Nobody," said Paul. "We came right here."

"That's good," said Schinkel. "That's very good. You kids did the right thing."

"Then why did they put us in that cell?" demanded Janie. "We didn't do anything wrong! Jesus!"

"Young lady, I will thank you not to take the Lord's name in vain in this office," Schinkel said. Then he put on his best winning grin and said, "I told the chief constable to make sure that you were safe. I am afraid that he was perhaps a little . . . overzealous. Acting Chief Constable Dirkschneider has had a lot to contend with since the unfortunate incident at that concert."

"My dad says he's a real bonehead," said Janie.

"Your father must be a very perceptive man," replied Schinkel, tapping the side of his nose. "Now, how are you kids doing? Comfortable? Would you like some more pretzels?"

"No, I'd like to know what happened to my mom!" Paul blurted out.

"Yeah," added Janie. "And what's the story with that skull we found?"

"Of course," Schinkel said soothingly. "Paul, I want you to know that finding your mother and returning her safely is our number one priority right now. I also don't want you to get too worked up about this 'skull'"—he made air quotes with his fingers—"that you think you saw in the woods. So what we're going to do now is drive down to the woods where you kids think you saw this skull-shaped object." Schinkel chuckled indulgently. "Then we'll find out for sure about these alleged bones, okay? I'm just waiting on a call to let me know when a car is ready. We've got a number of vehicles in the shop today for maintenance."

"We could take my car," suggested Janie.

"Oh, no, no," said Schinkel, waving his hands as if to ward off such a ludicrous idea. "We wouldn't want to put you out. Besides, there are issues of liability and so forth. We'll just wait for a patrol vehicle to become available."

An hour passed. Schinkel made increasingly strained small talk as the minutes crept by. Finally, the phone at the end of the conference room table rang. Schinkel snatched it up, listened briefly, and said, "Yes, good, good. Well, it's about time. Yes, we'll be right down."

He led Paul and Janie down to the parking lot behind City Hall, where a patrol car was waiting with a grumpy-looking constable behind the wheel.

"Seems like there's lots of cars available today," observed Paul, looking around the lot.

Schinkel waved his hand dismissively. "Yes," he said, "and this one's ours. Shall we go?"

They drove out of town and pulled into the track that led to the shell of the mental hospital. The disused road had a churned-up look about it, as if there had been a number of vehicles that had recently passed. They parked by the old hospital and trekked their way through the undergrowth, with Paul and Janie leading the way. After a few false starts, the teenagers were able to find their way back to the clearing with the hand-shaped rock.

"Well I'll be," said Schinkel. "It really does look like a hand. Now, where did you see this skull-shaped rock?"

"It wasn't a rock, it was a skull," said Paul, "and it was right there." He pointed at the place where the running water had exposed the skull. With the rain stopped, the rivulet had dried into a shallow run of mud.

"Well. I sure don't see any skulls," said Schinkel. "Do you, Constable Gross?" The constable shook his head.

"It was right here!" Paul insisted. "Maybe the water washed it farther away. It was raining pretty hard."

Janie looked around at the clearing skeptically. "Y'know, it looks like someone else has been out here recently," she said. "The ground looks all churned up and stuff. Like right where we saw that skull, it looks like it's been, y'know, dug up and filled in."

"Of course it's churned up," said Schinkel. "Your little boyfriend here was just saying how hard it was raining."

"What sort of rain makes a footprint like this?" Janie was pointing at an impression in the soft earth that was clearly from a man's shoe.

Schinkel looked annoyed. "That print's probably just from me or Constable Gross here."

"How can it be?" said Paul. "We just got here and neither of you have been on that side of the clearing."

"I don't know," snapped Schinkel, "Maybe it's from a hiker. Look, we're wasting time here. I've got better things to do besides tramping around in the woods chasing after imaginary bones."

"Imaginary?" said Paul. "What do you mean? We both saw that skull. It was right here! It might have something to do with my mom, and you're just blowing it off! You bastards!"

"Now you just calm down, young man, and watch your damn language," said Schinkel. "I know you think you saw a skull, but let's take a step back and consider things. It was raining. You were lost in the woods. You were probably a little scared, too, right? Your mind can play tricks on you under such circumstances. You probably just saw an old piece of wood or an oddly-shaped stone and thought it was skull."

Janie snorted and said something under her breath that sounded like *bullshit*.

"What was that, young lady?" asked Schinkel sharply.

"Nothing."

"We ought to at least look around a little bit," said Paul. "Maybe the rain washed it away or an animal took it somewhere."

"Oh, okay," said Schinkel with exasperation. "If it'll make you kids feel better."

Paul and Janie scoured the area around the clearing. Schinkel and Constable Gross leaned up against the hand-shaped rock, smoking cigarettes. After ten minutes, Schinkel announced, "Well, I think that's enough, okay? Let's get going."

"But we haven't . . ." Paul began.

"I said that's enough," said Schinkel. "I'm wasting the city's valuable time here. I have important work that I should be doing, not chasing some ridiculous story about skulls in the woods."

"Y'know, this whole thing smells fishy to me," said Paul.

"I don't care how it smells to you, young man. We've looked around and seen no skulls, bones, or buried pirate treasure, for that matter."

"That's okay," said Janie. "We can come back later and look for ourselves."

"I don't think so," said Schinkel. "You shouldn't have been out here in the first place. This is private property, owned by the hospital. If I hear of you messing around out here again, I will charge you both with trespassing. Constable Gross is going to stay by the entrance to make sure no one else comes sniffing around. Furthermore, if I learn of any more unsubstantiated talk about 'skulls in the woods,' I will have to consider charges of obstructing a police investigation. Now let's go."

Chapter 43

Hey, Chief," said Martin Prieboy. He stood at the door to Billy Snyder's hospital room, rapping tentatively on the partially opened door. "Are you decent? It's me, Inspector Prieboy."

"What?" came the gruff reply. "Prieboy? Is that idiot Dirkschneider with you?"

"No, Chief, I'm alone."

"Okay, then, c'mon in."

Martin was always a little hesitant whenever he was in the hospital. The institutional feel reminded him too much of the orphanage in Hershey. The doctors were like Father McJaggar, and the nurses like the brothers who had overseen his austere upbringing. Martin always kept his voice down in the hospital for fear of getting his knuckles smacked.

Martin hesitantly entered the room. It was clean and sterile-looking, and entirely devoid of decoration. Snyder was lying in bed, staring truculently at the ceiling.

"For Christ's sake, Prieboy, quit dawdling and get in here."

Martin came in and lowered himself into a chair. "Um, so how are you doing, Chief?"

"How the fuck do you think I'm doing? I'm stuck in this goddamn white-washed prison, flat on my back with a bunch of tubes and wires running out of me like I'm some sort of damn washing machine. That goddamn Dr. Ziffer is like a warden. He won't let me have a phone. Hell, I had to argue for two days just to get a fuckin' clock in here. Between Ziffer and that goddamn Nurse Sprockett, I can't even pee without getting a form signed

269

in triplicate. Jesus Christ, what a mess!" Snyder sank back into his pillow, exhausted by his outburst. "Huh. Okay, enough of my bellyaching, though. I want news of the real world. How are things down at Headquarters?"

Martin shifted uncomfortably in his chair. "Uh, I wouldn't really know, Chief. Roscoe . . . uh, the acting chief constable suspended me. Didn't anyone tell you?"

"Yeah, that's right. Roscoe the Shithead told me himself. I threw a bedpan at him. Too bad it was empty. So I guess this isn't an official visit, is it?"

"Well, no, not really," said Martin. "I really just wanted to see how you were doing." He paused. "I do have something to ask, though."

Now Martin started to feel really uncomfortable. He was certain Chief Constable Snyder was not going to like his question. He looked around to make sure there wasn't another bedpan within reach of the bed.

"Um, well Chief, I think that the acting chief constable was, uh, a little bit upset by the state police . . ."

Snyder sat bolt upright. "The motherfuckin' staties! Jesus Christ! They have no business sniffing around in Fester! We've always been able to take care of our own business here! I know that things have been pretty fucked up lately, what with the mess at Prosser College and that Plummer woman disappearing. But that's all taken care of. Hell, the perp is lying not fifty feet down the hall from right here. Damn shame he's still in a coma. We can still pin the Prosser shootings on him as well as the Plummer disappearance. We've got him cold. Solid evidence—you saw it yourself."

Martin began rubbing the knuckles of his right hand with his left, another old habit from the orphanage. He did it whenever he thought he was about to get into trouble. "Well, uh, Chief, I don't know how to say this, exactly. At this point, I'm not sure that Warnke had anything to do with the Prosser shootings at all."

"What? What the fuck are you talking about? Goddammit, Prieboy, what sort of trouble are you stirring up?"

"Well, I've been doing a little checking around. I found out that Michael Neff was a homosexual. We know that the night before the shootings, Thomas Dreher had visited Neff in his dorm room."

"Yeah, so what?"

"Well, after I learned that, I went and talked to some of Dreher's friends. They weren't very forthcoming at first, but I kept at it."

Snyder was now watching Martin very closely. "Yes, and what did you learn?"

"One of them, a bartender named Romeo Hoffman, admitted that Thomas Dreher had come into his bar the evening before the shooting, and he was very agitated. He drank heavily. When Hoffman asked Dreher what was wrong, he wouldn't go into detail. All he would say was that he had some business to take care of. When pressed, Dreher said that he was 'going to take care of some faggot.'"

Billy continued to regard Martin silently. Martin rubbed his knuckles and continued. "I surmise that when Thomas Dreher went to visit Michael Neff the night before the shootings, something happened between them. Perhaps Neff made a pass at Dreher, maybe he only revealed his sexuality. Whatever happened that evening, it upset Dreher a great deal. It seems pretty likely to me that Dreher killed Neff because he was gay."

"Ridiculous!" spat Snyder. "That's all conjecture! I know what's going on here. Warnke is the mastermind—he's running a Satanic coven. The Prosser killings and the Plummer disappearance are part of it!"

Martin began rubbing his knuckles even harder. "Actually, Chief, I've, uh, infiltrated the Satanic coven here in Fester, but I'm pretty sure that they had nothing to do with either of those crimes. They all seem pretty . . . inept. I'm still trying to find out what they're up to, but it's certainly not murder and kidnapping. They're pretty much just a bunch of money-hungry dingbats."

Snyder's mouth worked as he struggled to absorb this new bit of information. "Prieboy, what the hell are you saying? You're not even on duty! What the hell are you doing infiltrating a Satanic coven? You've got no business doing that!"

"Gee, I don't see why not, Chief. With all due respect, what I do off duty is my own business, provided that it falls within the confines of the law. There would be no problem if I joined the Elks or the Rotary Club. Why not a Satanic coven?"

271

"Never mind that, Prieboy! You have no idea what you're getting yourself into . . . what you're getting *us* into. Back the fuck off!"

Martin was rubbing his knuckles furiously now. He said, "I have to ask . . . I, uh, think . . . look, did you, um, plant that evidence in Randolph Warnke's house?"

The room was silent except for Snyder's heavy breathing. "Get out now," he said tersely. "You . . . you've fucked up big time, Prieboy. I thought you were a team player, thought you were smart enough to know shit from Shinola. I was wrong. Maybe the worst mistake of my life."

Martin swallowed hard. His knuckles were raw from rubbing, and his stomach was in knots. Unbelievably, he could feel tears welling up. "Look, Chief . . ."

"Don't call me that!" roared Snyder. "You're suspended! I can see now that Dirkschneider made the right decision. As soon as I get out of here, I'm going to make sure that you're off the constabulary for good!"

"But . . ."

"No buts! No talk! I treated you like my own son and you've gone behind my back! Get out of here NOW!" Snyder slumped back into his bed, breathing hard. His face was milk-pale except for two hectic red spots high on his cheeks.

Martin hesitated for a moment, still frantically rubbing his knuckles. He had never felt this bad in his life, not even when Brother Mordecai had caught him ogling the ladies' underwear section of the J.C. Penney catalog. Without another word, he marched uncertainly from the room.

* * *

Later that evening, Billy stared at the ceiling, his mind going a mile a minute. The visit from Martin Prieboy had disturbed him immensely. His golden boy investigator was poised to upset the entire constabulary apple-cart. Well, he figured he might still be able to talk some sense into the kid, if he could keep his temper in check.

Then there was the matter of who had shot him. Billy had spent a great deal of time pondering who had was responsible for the shooting. Cecilia Schmidt seemed a likely suspect, at least according to what Dr. Ziffer had told him. However, Ziffer might have his own reasons for pinning it on that damned Schmidt woman. The whole thing didn't sit well with Billy.

One thing was certain: he was not going to be able to make progress on any of these problems lying in this fucking hospital bed. Things were spinning out of control, and for the first time in a long time Billy began to worry about being implicated in something he couldn't wriggle away from. That was simply unacceptable. He had to get out of the hospital tonight.

One of the nurses popped her head in the door to check on him. He didn't turn his head or acknowledge her and continued to stare blankly at the ceiling. After a moment, she withdrew. Billy looked at the clock on the bedside table. It read 10:34. Good—she was right on time.

Billy could hear the footsteps recede down the hallway and stop. The nurse—her name was Freitag—was checking on the other patients on the floor. When she was done, she would go on a fifteen-minute break. Billy continued to listen until the nurse had finished checking the other three patients between Billy's room and the elevators. At last, he heard the elevator bell ring and the doors slide open as the nurse went down to the basement cafeteria for her break. He sat up and swung his feet to the floor.

Billy checked the clock again—10:39. He knew that he had about eight minutes before another nurse came down the hall. Three East was not a very lively place even during the day, and it was even less so at night. Billy had already memorized the patterns of the ward. This was partially out of boredom, partially out of old police habit, but mostly because he knew that he would have to break out from the hospital. Now the time had come.

He sat up in his bed. His gut still hurt like hell, but it had definitely improved over the last week. Most of the IV tubes and all of the electrodes had been removed. The nurses occasionally allowed him to walk to the bathroom in the corner of the room to use the toilet. Billy had deliberately exaggerated his difficulty in getting around, just to keep their guard down.

His head swam a little as he sat up, but it settled quickly. He swiftly began removing the IV tubes that were still connected to him. Once disconnected, he removed the half-empty IV bag from the pole and yanked the pole from its socket at the base of the bed to use as a makeshift cane. He tied a pillowcase around the end of the pole to provide traction and muffle the sound.

He used his improvised cane to push himself up to a standing position and took a few tentative steps. It wasn't easy. The IV pole was too short, and he was practically doubled over to lean on it.

Billy looked back over at the clock—it was 10:41. He had to get going. He clumped to the door and stuck his head out in the hallway. It was empty. During this small window of opportunity, the only member of the nursing staff on duty was the unit clerk. As long as Billy stayed away from the nurses' station, he should be safe.

He shuffled out into the hall. The bastards had taken his watch and wallet, so he had no way of telling the time once he was out of the room. He began counting off the seconds to himself. At this point, he reckoned he had until a count of four hundred to be off of Three East and on his way to freedom.

. . . sixteen, seventeen, eighteen . . .

Billy thumped grimly down the corridor. His goal was the stairwell door at the end of the hall. Hardly anyone used the stairs. Once he got past that door and into the stairwell, he was practically home free.

. . . ninety-two, ninety-three, ninety-four . . .

Billy continued down the hallway, occasionally casting an angry look back over his shoulder. He was really starting to ache now, even though he had only walked forty feet. He found himself slowing down and forced himself to move faster. His belly was on fire, but he gritted his teeth and kept going.

. . . two hundred nine, two hundred ten, two hundred eleven . . .

Behind him, the elevator bell *bong*ed.

Shit! thought Billy. He was busted! Well, fuck it—they'd have to run him down. He kept moving forward, expecting at any second to hear a nurse start hollering at him.

Nothing happened.

Billy looked back over his shoulder. Down at the elevator, a huge Black man in a housekeeping uniform emerged, pulling a trash cart. The

274

housekeeper gave him a cursory glance, then turned and pulled the cart down towards the utility room at the other end of the hall.

. . . three hundred seventy-five, three hundred seventy-six, three hundred seventy-seven . . .

The door to the stairwell didn't seem much closer. He was bent over almost double now, the pain in his gut battling it out with the ache in his back. His breath came in harsh, gasping whistles. He could feel his heart thudding in his chest.

. . . four hundred ten, four hundred eleven, four hundred twelve . . .

Billy was now past his time limit. Nurse Freitag would be back from her break very soon. Billy's head bumped into something. He looked up. He had reached the door to the stairwell. He put his free hand on the push bar and once again looked over his shoulder. The hallway was clear—he had made it!

With a sigh of relief, Billy pushed open the door and stepped into the stairwell.

Nurse Sprockett was standing right there on the landing.

"Mr. Snyder!" she said with mock surprise. "What are you doing here? I just came back to pick up some papers, and I find you here in the stairs? You should know better than that! We need to get you back in bed at once!"

Billy glared at her. *Pick up some papers, my ass*, he thought. She had known what he was up to the whole time. She had probably stood here watching through the wire-reinforced window as he had made his agonizing way down the hall. He said, "That's *Chief Constable* Snyder, you c . . ." and then he collapsed.

Nurse Sprockett looked at Billy impassively, and bent over his motionless form, saying, "Tch, tch, tch, Mr. Snyder, you really need to know who's in charge around . . ."

Billy rolled over quickly, swinging the IV poll as hard as he could. He caught Sprockett on the side of the head. She went down limply. Billy checked to make sure she still alive. She seemed to be okay, steady pulse, regular breathing. She'd just have a hell of a lump on her head when she came to. Served her right for being such a bitch.

Billy rested for a moment, then got to his feet. A swarm of black dots exploded in front of his eyes. He took a couple of deep breaths and cleared his head. He had to get moving and clean up this mess. Take care of his business, his town.

He made it to the bottom of the stairwell, moving as quickly as he could. There was a notice that the exit door was alarmed, but he could see that the cable to the alarm box had been pulled, probably by some orderly who used the door to cop a quick smoke break. Or maybe sneak out pharmaceuticals. Billy made a mental note to look into it later—there might be a buck to made there.

He pushed the door open a crack and took a quick look—nothing. The door opened on a concrete pad that supported large pieces of air-conditioning equipment. He slipped out, and eased the door closed behind him. A blast of wind hit him, cutting through his thin hospital johnny. It suddenly occurred to him that he was completely unequipped—no uniform, no ID, no sidearm, nothing.

Over the howl of the wind he could hear a siren. It grew louder, then abruptly cut off—another ambulance pulling into the emergency room entrance. The Wight Winds were staring to kick up. Billy knew that Fester's emergency services were going to be busy tonight. *That's it!* he thought. There was bound to be a constabulary presence at the hospital tonight.

"It's an ill wind that blows no good," he muttered to himself. It had been one of his father's favorite sayings. Billy had never really appreciated it until now.

Keeping low, and using the IV pole for support, he circled the building, trying to stay behind whatever concealment was available. He was very tired, but he had to keep moving. He got to the edge of the building and looked around the corner to the emergency room entrance. An ambulance was in the process of unloading. Across from the entrance was a constabulary cruiser, a constable leaning up against the driver's side door smoking a cigarette. Perfect.

He waited until the EMTs had wheeled their patient into the emergency room, then made his move. He took a deep breath, then strode towards the cruiser with as much authority as he could muster while wearing a flimsy gown that opened at the butt.

He was about ten yards away before the constable spotted him. "Hey, old timer," he said. "You shouldn't be out here. We better get your cracked old ass back inside before . . ."

"Constable, ten-HUT!" Billy barked. "Just what the holy *fuck* are you doing smoking on duty?!" The kid's jaw dropped open. Billy was gratified to see a storm of conflicting emotions cross the young constable's face as he snapped to attention. At least the kid recognized him. Now he just had to keep him off-balance.

"What? I . . . I . . . Chief? What are you . . . shouldn't you be . . ."

"Goddammit, constable, I don't have time for any bullshit! This is an emergency! I need the keys to your cruiser and your sidearm."

"But . . . but . . . Acting Chief Constable Dirkschneider . . ."

"Is relieved as of this moment. Are you questioning the orders of your commanding officer, you miserable little fuck?"

"No . . . no sir."

"Good. Keys and sidearm—NOW!"

"Yessir!" The kid fumbled the keys and pistol out of his belt and handed them over.

"Good. There's a woman unconscious on the third floor landing in the east stairwell. She is to be charged with assaulting a police officer. Have her examined, then take her down to headquarters. Get going, Constable—MOVE IT!" He smacked him on the ass with the IV pole. The kid took off running.

Billy slid into the driver's seat of the cruiser and keyed the ignition. First, he'd go by his house and put on a spare uniform. Then he'd drive up to Cecilia Schmidt's mansion for a little chat about his assassination attempt.

As he was approaching the parking lot exit, he was astounded to see the Schmidt bitch's fancy Mercedes go shooting past the hospital entrance, headed south. Uniform or not, he couldn't let this opportunity pass. Billy gave himself a very slow three count, then pulled out into the street and began to follow her.

Chapter 44

W hat's wrong?" asked Janie.

"I dunno," Paul replied, staring at the bedroom ceiling. He felt shitty and didn't want to look her in the eye.

"It's not anything I did, is it? I mean, I hope that I'm not . . ."

"No, no, it's not you," Paul cut her off. "It's me." The whole thing sounded like a bad movie.

"It's just that, y'know, things were getting really hot. What happened?"

"I dunno." Paul sighed again and rolled over.

"Maybe it was the whiskey."

"Yeah, maybe."

The evening had started out promisingly. Janie had come over after dinner, with a bottle of Jack Daniels she had swiped from her parents' liquor cabinet. They were planning on going to a house party down by the school. Instead, they had ended up drinking most of the booze and fooling around on the couch.

Since Paul's dad was again out for the evening, things got hot and heavy in a hurry. Just to be on the safe side, they relocated to Paul's bedroom. Soon, the bed was a tangle of twisted bed sheets, hastily discarded clothes, and sweaty limbs.

Then something happened. Paul looked over at the alarm clock. It was 10:43. His erection, which just moments before seemed as if it were hard enough to cut glass, rapidly subsided. It disappeared with such sudden speed that Paul could almost hear it go, like a rapidly receding train whistle. *WHOOT-HOOooot*. Goodbye, hard-on.

This was immediately followed by a burst of guilt and shame. Jesus, here he was in bed with a hot girl, and he couldn't even maintain a stiffy. Seventeen years old and impotent. God, what if he never got an erection again? Even worse, what if this got out around school? He'd forever be known as Limp-Dick Plummer. He'd never live it down.

Maybe he was a homo. He didn't feel like a homo, had never been attracted to other guys or anything like that, but maybe this was how it started. Holy shit, he'd have to leave town just to keep from getting the shit beat out of him.

Janie sighed. "Ah hell, it's no wonder you're, um, distracted and all. I can't blame you for, y'know." She waved vaguely at the bed. "After that shit with the cops in the woods and all."

"Those fuckin' bastards!" exclaimed Paul. "What the hell are they trying to hide? You were right—there was no way that could have been my mom. I mean, that skull looked like it was a zillion years old. Why'd they bother covering it up?"

"Hell, who knows?" asked Janie. "My dad says that everybody in the city government is crooked as a dog's hind leg."

Paul glared at the Quiet Twisted Iron Goat poster on the wall, contemplating the overall rottenness of adults everywhere. "Cocksuckers," he muttered.

Janie ran a hand up his thigh. "Do you want me to try using my mouth?" she asked.

"Huh?" Paul snapped back to the here and now.

"I can try, y'know, sucking it, if you want," she said, gently squeezing his cock. "Jenny Conrad was talking about it in the locker room the other day. She said the secret is to never use your teeth. Or maybe it was to always use your teeth. I forget."

"Uh, okay! Let's try it with the 'never' way first."

Janie gave him a crooked grin. "That's the spirit!"

She slipped down between his legs, and Paul could feel himself getting hard even before she slid his cock into her mouth. A wave of relief washed over him as Janie began pumping away, clumsily but enthusiastically.

Just as things were really getting going, Paul once again glanced at the alarm clock. As he watched, it flipped from 10:58 to 10:59. Just like before, he could feel the desire draining out of him with astonishing speed.

To her credit, Janie kept at it, but it was no use. Her face appeared, flushed and flustered, rising from the floppy pile of male hydraulics that had been working at full efficiency just moments earlier.

"What happened?" she asked. "Everything was going good."

"Shit, I don't know," said Paul. "Something feels wrong."

"What, was it the teeth?"

"No, not that," Paul shook his head. "I dunno. All this weird shit . . ."

"Yeah, sure, I know," said Janie with resignation. She began picking through the pile of clothes at the foot of the bed.

"Look, I'm really sorry. I feel like shit, really. It's fucked up. It sure isn't you, though. Don't worry about that." He reached out to stroke her breast, but she turned away and put on her bra. "Shit," he muttered. He bent over and retrieved his underwear from the pile on the floor.

Janie continued getting dressed. "Oh well," she said. "Shit happens, I guess."

"Something really feels out of whack tonight," said Paul. "I don't know what it is, but every time I look at the clock, it just feels weird. Like time is running out."

"What do you mean?"

"I dunno. Just that all of the stuff that's been going on—it seems like it's all kinda coming together, like right now. I dunno, it's all just fucked . . ."

Janie finished pulling on her shorts and slid over to where Paul was sitting. She stroked him lightly on the back of the head. Paul jumped, then began to relax.

"Janie, I'm really . . ." he began.

"Shh—no," she replied, putting her finger to his lips.

Paul turned and looked at her for a long moment. Their eyes locked, and Paul felt something twitch in his solar plexus. It was like the night they had ended up in the back seat of Janie's car out in the woods. But it was also different from that, too. It felt more . . . important, somehow, and yet less immediate than the churning vortex of lust he had felt that night. "Sometimes, Janie, I don't know what to make of you."

Janie smiled, but said nothing.

"I mean, all those times in school when we were kids," he said. "All the shitty stuff we did to each other, and now we're, y'know, here. You know, I don't even remember what started all of it."

"You don't?" asked Janie.

"No."

"I do."

"Really? What was it?"

"It was back in kindergarten," Janie said with a distant look in her eyes. "One day at recess—I remember it was in the fall, because the trees were just starting to turn. I don't know what possessed me. I saw you standing there by the swing set, and so I just ran up to you and . . ."

"What? Punched me? Kicked dirt on me?"

"I kissed you, you fuckin' idiot." She turned away. "That's all I really wanted to do all along," she said in a small voice.

"Oh." Without thinking, Paul leaned over and gave her a sweet, simple kiss on the lips—a kindergartener's kiss. He leaned back and smiled. "Like that?"

"Yes, exactly like that."

Paul felt a stirring in his shorts. He thought that he could probably go ahead and make good on his earlier deficiencies, but somehow it didn't seem right, now. Janie's reminiscence and the long-lost purity of the kiss made sex seem just a little bit wrong now. Inappropriate. "So, what do we do now?" he asked.

"We go and find your mom," said Janie. "The cops sure as hell aren't gonna."

"Yeah, and neither is my dad," said Paul. "But I don't know what to do. Nettie said that the answers were in the woods, but there was only a skull—and that disappeared. So now what do we do?"

"We start at the beginning," said Janie. "Where did it all start?"

"Downstairs in the kitchen, I guess. It was all trashed the day mom disappeared."

"Hell, we've already been there," said Janie. "That's no good. What next? Where did you say they found your mom's car?"

"Mill Park, down by the creek."

"Then that's where we'll go."

"What, you mean now?" asked Paul.

"Hell yeah, let's go," replied Janie. "We need to get this whole thing straightened out, fast. Maybe then we can get laid."

Chapter 45

The wind blew steadily across Fester, as it had for several days, chasing away the remnants of the storm system that had drenched the area. The Wight Winds whipped up from the southwest, funneled through the ridges and valleys of the Allegheny foothills, and roared nonstop through Kerian County and Fester.

By Friday night, the winds had thoroughly dried the soaked city. They had also begun to work on the nerves of the residents. The Wight Winds blew hot, and when they did tempers got hot, too. The constabulary had put on extra patrols for tonight and the rest of the weekend, knowing that there would be an increase of drinking, fighting, stealing, spousal abuse, and other rotten behavior.

In Mill Park, a cruiser occasionally glided by, looking for suspicious activity. While safe enough during the day, most people avoided Mill Park at night. It was located very close to the Rivertown district and was the site of after-hours drug dealing and gang activity.

The centerpiece of the park was the Old Mill, a re-creation of the grist mill erected by Karlheinz Schmidt in 1764. The Schmidt family had donated the land for the park and the reconstruction of the mill in the early fifties, when the main pretzel bakery was relocated to the east side of the Black River.

As midnight approached, a dozen dark-clad figures furtively made their way through the park towards the Old Mill building. If a cruising constable had caught sight of them, the result would have been immediate. Twelve black-robed figures lurking in Mill Park near midnight could not mean anything good, especially when the Wight Winds were blowing. Fortunately for the Fell Circle of Mammon, their approach to the Old Mill went largely unnoticed.

"Come on, come on," urged the Scarlet Mistress. She looked nervously over her shoulder as the rest of the Fell Circle struggled with their burdens. They crept through the trees, hunched low as they crossed the baseball diamonds and playground, and finally came to the entrance to the Old Mill.

"Where the hell is that new bastard, that Brother Bat?" snarled the Scarlet Mistress as she looked at her watch. She turned on Brother Frankenstein. "You vouched for him, and now he's letting us down. If he doesn't turn up, I'll have your ass."

"I don't know what's wrong," whined Brother Frankenstein, dropping the gas can he had been carrying. "He said he was going to be here."

"Well, he's not," said the Scarlet Mistress. "We'll just have to make do without him. After we're done tonight, it won't make any difference, anyway."

"I thought that we needed to have thirteen people to do anything," pointed out Sister Inferno.

"Shut up," retorted the Scarlet Mistress. "I'm sick of trying to get you boneheads to do anything right. He Who Shall Not Be Named Without Express Written Consent is interested in results, and tonight, for once, we're going to provide them."

"What are we doing, anyway?" asked Brother Underworld.

"Well, we're standing in front of a wooden building, and have fifteen gallons of gasoline," said the Scarlet Mistress. "I'll let you work out the details by yourself, Einstein."

"You mean we're going to burn down the Old Mill?" asked Sister Inferno.

"You catch on quick," said the Scarlet Mistress acidly.

"Not only that, but the way the wind is blowing, we're might just catch half of downtown on fire," added Brother Diabolical.

"Damn straight," said the Scarlet Mistress. "Starting with the hospital." Kerian Memorial Hospital was directly downwind of the Old Mill.

"We're going to burn down the hospital?" asked Brother Torment, aghast.

"Ideally, yes," said the Scarlet Mistress. "You can't make an omelet without breaking a few eggs."

"I don't know about burning down a hospital," said Sister Hellfire. "Someone might get hurt."

"Yeah, and where will they go to get better?" added Brother Torment. "There won't be a hospital if we burn it down."

"Look, do you jerks want unimaginable wealth or not?" asked the Scarlet Mistress. "If I had known that you were going to be such a bunch of pussies, I'd have just done this myself."

There were mutters of reluctant assent from the rest of the Fell Circle of Mammon. Sure, burning down a historical site, a hospital, and large chunk of downtown may have its drawbacks, but unimaginable wealth made it worth the risk.

"Right," said the Scarlet Mistress, seeing that the rest of the group was still behind her. "Let's bust this place open."

Brother Diabolical stepped forward with a large crowbar and was applying it to the doorjamb when the door swung open. "Hey, the door is unlocked!" he exclaimed.

"Beautiful," said the Scarlet Mistress. "He Who Shall Not Be Named Without Express Written Consent is with us tonight. Now, who's got the flashlights? Wait until we're inside before you turn them on."

The Fell Circle of Mammon filed into the Old Mill, lugging gasoline, flashlights, and ceremonial paraphernalia. The flashlights winked on as they entered the darkened space, revealing the wooden interior of the mill. It had been reconstructed as exactly as possible from historical documents.

"All right, let's get this show on the road," said the Scarlet Mistress. "It's time for this town to suffer so that we may gain!" She gave her best diabolical laugh and said, "It's time for Fester to burn!"

"Not if I have anything to say about it!" came a voice from the rafters.

The flashlight beams converged on the voice, revealing a dark-clad figure wearing a hood and a belt from which hung a variety of mysterious implements. He was standing on one of the rafters and holding on to a length of black rope that had been fastened to the ridge beam.

"Who the fuck are you?" demanded the Scarlet Mistress.

"I am . . . the Fledermaus!" said the dark figure. "And I am going to put a stop to your evil scheme!" He leapt up from the rafter on which he had been standing and swooped down towards the cluster of surprised Mammonites. He would have landed right in the middle of them, but his dramatic arc was interrupted when his head connected solidly with another rafter. There was a loud *thunk*, and the Fledermaus dropped to the floor like a sack of flour.

"What the hell just happened?" asked Brother Diabolical.

"A spy!" hissed the Scarlet Mistress. "I should have known. But now he's no longer a threat. Truly, He Who Shall Not Be Named Without Express Written Consent is looking out for us. Let's see who this really is." She reached down and pulled up the mask.

"Holy shit, it's Brother Bat!" exclaimed the Scarlet Mistress. She turned on Brother Frankenstein. "Yes, the man *you* recruited. I should have known better than to trust your judgment, you moron."

Brother Frankenstein began waffling, but the Scarlet Mistress cut him off. "Never mind, it might be just as well. Tie him up and leave him in the corner. When the ashes cool down, maybe they'll blame him for the fire."

"What, we're going to leave him here?" asked Sister Inferno.

"Hell yes," snapped the Scarlet Mistress. "Now get that damned pentagram drawn and let's set Fester ablaze!"

It was five minutes to midnight.

Chapter 46

On the other side of Mill Park, Lee Plummer crouched in a clump of bushes, cursing under his breath. A constabulary cruiser had just driven down Adams Street, a spotlight beam sweeping the playground on the west side of the park. He waited until the cruiser was out of view and emerged from the bushes. He had a death grip on a battered briefcase. It had once belonged to his father, and currently contained $100,000 in fifties and hundreds—the down payment for the title to the Wizard's Woods. Lee's old man would have had an embolism if he knew his old briefcase would ever contain that much cash. The man just couldn't hang on to money to save his life.

Hanging on to money was Lee's priority right now. Once he'd decided to cut Cecilia Schmidt out of the deal, he'd had to raise ten percent of the sale price on his own. Pulling together $100,000 in cash on short notice had not been an easy feat, but he had managed to pull it off.

He had been so intent on setting the deal up that he really hadn't been thinking too clearly about certain aspects. Certainly, the plan to meet crazy old Jeffrey Totenkopf at midnight in Mill Park wasn't the best of ideas. Yet here he was, lurking around in one of the most dangerous spots in Fester with a satchel full of cash.

Lee had spotted some sort of gang a few minutes before the cruiser had come by. About a dozen black-clad people had come skulking through the playground on the far side of the park. They seemed to be carrying bulky objects, and were clearly up to no good. Fortunately, they had been a good hundred yards away and had passed out of sight without paying any attention to him.

Lee carefully made his way to the fountain in front of the Old Mill, running bent over from tree to bush to bench. Finally, he was within sight of the rendezvous point. He crouched down and waited.

At midnight on the dot, a lone figure strolled through the park towards the fountain. He was wearing grease-spotted work pants and an old hunting jacket. It was Totenkopf. He was alone and empty-handed. He stopped at the fountain and looked around.

Lee tried a whip-poor-will call.

"Shit, Plummer, is that you?" Totenkopf said loudly. "That's gotta be the worst bird call I ever heard. You dumb-ass city boy!"

Lee emerged from behind the bench. "Hey, keep it down, will you?" he said. "Do you want the whole town to know what we're up to?"

"Shit, ain't no one gonna see us. And even if they do, we're covered. You got the money?"

"Right here," said Lee, hefting the briefcase. "I want to see the property deed."

"Yeah, and I wanna see the cash."

Lee held up the briefcase and quickly opened it, allowing Totenkopf a quick glimpse of the bundles of cash inside. "Woo-wee, that's a lot of foldin' green," Totenkopf said.

"Yeah, it's all there. And more to come," said Lee. "Now let me see the deed. If it doesn't have that revisionary clause, then there's no deal."

"Yeah, yeah, okay," said Totenkopf. He reached into his greasy jacket and pulled out an envelope that had once held a Publishers Clearing House Sweepstakes entry form.

Lee opened it and took out the papers folded up inside. They were stiff and brittle with age. Lee squinted but couldn't really make out the writing in the dim light from the streetlights on the edge of the park.

"What's a matter, city boy—cain't read it?"

"Um, no. It's a little dark."

"Shee-it, dincha bring a flashlight? You'd make a suck-ass secret agent, you know that, Plummer?"

"Hey, meeting here was your idea. I don't see why we couldn't have met at a restaurant or a truck stop."

"Fewer witnesses here. Don't get your shorts in a bunch—I gots a lighter." Totenkopf pulled a battered Zippo from his jacket pocket. Lee had to hunch over to shield the dim flame from the gusting winds, but finally he was able to read the crabbed legalese on the parchment. He skimmed through the entire document, muttering to himself. By the time he was done, the lighter was hot in his hand. "Yes, this seems to be in order. Mr. Totenkopf, we have ourselves a deal."

There was a loud click from a tree close to the fountain. "I'll take that deed," came a voice from the darkness.

Lee and Totenkopf looked over in surprise. Standing a few yards away was Cecilia Schmidt, with Cynthia Hoegenbloeven standing close behind her. Cecilia was holding a large revolver and pointing it in their direction. "Don't either of you move. I'm a very good marksman, and I can take your head off with this thing, no problem."

"I dunno who you are, lady, but you're makin' a big fuckin' mistake," said Totenkopf.

"Ha! My only mistake was trusting this lousy little turd. Plummer, put down that briefcase and step back."

Lee dropped the briefcase. "You rotten bitch. I just want to get my wife back. What have you done with her?"

"What the fuck are you talking about, you moron?" Cecilia sounded genuinely mystified and seriously pissed. "I have no idea where your damn wife is. Now step away from the briefcase. And lay that deed on top."

"Fuck you, lady," said Totenkopf. "I don't know how you found out about this, but you're crazy if you think I'd come out here alone." Totenkopf turned his head to one side. "Show 'er, Merle," he called out.

Immediately, a small red dot appeared on the side of Cecilia's head. A dark figure rose from a clump of bushes thirty feet away. "Put the gun down, lady!" called Merle Totenkopf. "I got you bracketed! I'll take you apart piece by piece!"

Cecilia didn't flinch. "This is a .44 Magnum revolver," she said loudly.

"The trigger takes about five pounds of pull, and I'm probably putting four and a half on it right now. If I so much as twitch, this old hillbilly's brains will be splattered all over the park!"

Jeffrey Totenkopf looked over at Merle and then back at Cecilia. "We-ell, looks like we got us a right Mexican standoff here, don't it?" He turned and looked at Lee, who was sidling towards the briefcase and the deed. "Shoulda figgered you'd screw this up, Plummer."

"It wasn't me," Lee protested. "I don't know how she found out about this. The conniving bitch probably tapped my phone."

"Of course I had your phone tapped, you dumb shit," said Cecilia. "Right after your little outburst at my house the other night. That pig Electro wasn't good for much else, but he tapped your line no problem. Hoegenbloeven, go fetch the deed. Plummer, you just step back."

"Or what?" sneered Lee. "You'll shoot me? You move that revolver off Totenkopf there and ol' Merle will ventilate your thick skull."

They all stood there, frozen.

Suddenly, from twenty yards away, the Old Mill exploded in a maelstrom of noise and light.

Chapter 47

Roscoe Dirkschneider was working late. This usually meant shaking down a few bars, putting the squeeze on a couple of hookers in Rivertown, then holing up at the Iron Door bar until he passed out.

Tonight, though, he was at the office, and not in a good mood. He was late with a payment to Happy Hal, and he was worried about the bookie's vengeful and violent temperament. Troublesome though that was, Roscoe had more immediate concerns.

Things had been busy at the constabulary for the last several days, and it looked like tonight was going to be a real bastard. There had already been reports of three assaults, an armed robbery, an attempted rape, and a flasher in the Krump Acres area. The Wight Winds were working their dark magic on the town.

Roscoe would normally have left this dirty work to his underlings, but as acting chief constable he felt he ought to at least put on a show of being on top of things. Also, that weaselly Lieutenant Dunbar from the state police had been sniffing around again, and Roscoe didn't want Dunbar thinking he wasn't on the job.

Dunbar made him very nervous. The statie wasn't just working on the unsolved cases, he was also asking a lot of questions about other things. Roscoe had already had two interviews with Dunbar, and they hadn't gone well. Dunbar had asked a number of pointed questions about Roscoe's income and had also made an observation about the surprisingly high number of suspects who had "fallen down" and hurt themselves while in

Roscoe's custody. These things had made him very nervous indeed.

Dunbar was also asking questions about Roscoe's activities on the night that Billy had been shot. Looking back, he realized he had told the state police investigator a number of things that were verifiably false. Dunbar was likely to discover Roscoe's lies. If that happened, Roscoe would definitely have more to worry about than working late on a Friday night.

He hated being under so much scrutiny, but there was nothing he could do about it right now. If things got a little hot, he could just lay low and get back to business later. It was a strategy that had worked for him for his entire career.

First, he had to make sure things didn't get out of hand around town. It was always a pain in the ass when the Wight Winds blew, and the residents of Fester acted even crazier than usual. He stalked out of his office and into the bullpen, which was practically deserted. Even though extra shifts had been brought on, most of the constables were out on calls. It was a busy Friday night.

As Roscoe poured himself another cup of coffee, he could hear another call coming in on the 9-1-1 line. He strolled over to the dispatchers' cubicle. Marie Strausbaugh was on night dispatch duty, as she had been since shortly after Marconi had invented the radio.

"What's doing, Marie?" he asked.

"Well, just had a fight at the bowling alley, and another report of a flasher, this time in the parking lot of the Jackson Street Food Ape," said Marie. She had a voice like a gravel crusher. She took a drag off her unfiltered Camel. "Also, we just had another call about some kids messing around in Mill Park. Third call tonight 'bout that."

"Yeah, who's on it?"

"No one, yet. Nearest car's Unit 3. That new kid, whatsis name, Gross. He cleared at the emergency room at Kerian Memorial about fifteen minutes ago. Probably sucking down some coffee in the cafeteria. I was gonna send him after he checked in."

"Never mind," said Roscoe. "I'll take care of this myself."

"You sure?"

"Oh yeah, I'm sure," replied Roscoe. He needed to get the hell out of the office. He thought busting a few teenaged skulls down at the park would help take the edge off. He went back to the office and selected his largest billy club, then headed down to the parking lot with an anticipatory grin on his face.

He'd almost made it to his car when he heard the click of a gun behind him. "Hands in the air!" said a hoarse voice. "Make one move, Dirkschneider, and you're a dead man!"

Chapter 48

Paul and Janie were almost out the front door when the phone rang. Paul could see the clock in the living room—it was quarter to twelve. He almost kept going, but at the last second he picked up the phone.

"What's up Paularino?" Bolly asked.

"Not much," said Paul. "What the hell you calling so late for? It's almost midnight."

"Yeah, yeah, I know. I dunno, I'm feeling kinda weird. Restless, y'know? I figured you'd be up."

"So, uh, what's up? I was kinda getting ready to . . ."

"Well, it's kinda strange," said Bolly. "I was hangin' out with Knob at the bowling alley, right? We were just playin' some pinball and shit, and a bunch of these math club dweebs come in, being all loud and dorky. And the next thing I knew, Knob and one of these dweebs are goin' at it like a coupla gladiators."

"Yeah, so?"

"Well, so Knob and the geek are goin' at it," said Bolly. "I'm tryin' to pull 'em apart, but the rest of the dorks are just egging on their butt-buddy. Next thing I know, this constable busts in, takes one look at Knob and the dweeb, and starts bouncin' his billy club off their heads. He didn't say a word, just started wailin' on 'em. An ambulance hauled 'em both off to the hospital."

"Oh, shit," said Paul, wincing. "Sounds like the damn concert all over again. Knob must have bruises on his bruises."

"So, yeah, it's been a weird night," said Bolly. "Anyway, I just got home after that mess at the bowling alley, but I'm not tired or anything. Wanna hang out?"

"Yeah, well, I was just hangin' out with Janie . . ." Paul began.

"Janie? Janie Simmons?" Bolly said with a laugh. "What the fuck?"

"Well, y'know, we've been hangin' out a lot lately and stuff," said Paul cutting his eyes to where Janie was standing. She was watching him with intense interest.

Paul steeled himself for a barrage of crap, but all Bolly said was, "Well, ain't that some wild shit? So I guess you guys are kinda, um, busy, huh?"

"Actually, we were just gonna go down to Mill Park."

"Say what? Whatcha wanna go down there for on a Friday night? Y'know, if you're lookin' for a make-out spot, I can suggest a bunch of better places than that."

"Uh, it's kinda weird, but we're gonna go take a look at where they found my mom's car," Paul said. "I mean, if these fuckin' constables aren't gonna find her, then maybe we can."

"I can dig it," said Bolly. "So you and Daphne are gonna pile into the Mystery Machine and do some sleuthing, huh? Well, if you need some help, I can be Shaggy."

"Yeah, that's cool. You wanna meet us down there?"

"Sure thing, man. Where at?"

"Well, they found mom's car on Washington Street, close to the Old Mill. So right there, I guess."

"Fuckin'-A," said Bolly. "See you soon."

"What was that all about?" asked Janie when Paul hung up the phone.

"Uh, that was Bolly. He says he's gonna meet us down at the park, y'know, help us check it out." He shrugged on his Lothar the Psycho jacket.

"Okay," said Janie. "I can drive, if you want."

"Yeah, that's cool." Paul said. "Let's go."

Fifteen minutes later, Janie's old Toyota pulled up to the curb on Washington Street on the north side of Mill Park. A pair of headlights was coming the other way. Abruptly they swerved across the road and came to a screeching stop right in front of Janie's car. Bolly stepped out from his jacked-up Nova.

"Hello, young lovers," he said in a cheesy game-show-host voice, as Paul and Janie climbed out.

"Cram a sock in it, Bolly," said Paul. "Let's just look around and see if we can find anything."

"Um, I don't mean to sound negative or anything," said Bolly, "but what sort of clues, exactly, were you hoping to find out here in the middle of the night?"

"I dunno," admitted Paul. "I think I was just trying to get some, y'know, inspiration to help find—"

"Hey, look at that!" said Janie. She was pointing across the street into the park. The bulk of the Old Mill loomed up to their left, backlit by the parking lot lights at Kerian Memorial. There was a clear view of the open space and the fountain in front of the Old Mill. There were three people clearly silhouetted next to the fountain. They were engaged in an intense discussion. As they watched, one of the figures raised its arm and the other two shrank back.

"Holy shit!" said Bolly. "That chick has a gun! It's huge! Like Dirty Fuckin' Harry!"

Janie grabbed Paul's arm. "Let's get out of here! This is seriously fucked up!"

Suddenly, the night was torn by an incredible pulsing screech. It sounded like a bad bearing that had been amplified to Motörhead-concert decibel levels. An intense white light burst from within the Old Mill, spilling from every crack, gap, and nail-hole.

The light clearly illuminated the three figures by the fountain. One of them was indeed holding a gun. The second one looked like a farmer or something. The third was very familiar. "Holy shit, it's my dad!" Paul shouted, his words nearly drowned out by the deafening noise coming from the Old Mill. He began running towards the fountain.

"Paul, no! It's too dangerous!" said Janie. She took off after Paul.

"You guys are total assholes," remarked Bolly to no one in particular. He shrugged and began running after his friends.

Chapter 49

Over the course of his career, Dr. Michael Ziffer had spent a lot of time burning the midnight oil. Med school had been tough, and his residency even tougher. He remembered regularly pulling thirty- and forty-hour shifts in those days, and he did not miss them at all.

Tonight, he was at the office late, and was not happy about it. It had been a busy day. One of his patients, Randolph Warnke, had unexpectedly come out of a coma that morning. There had been a rush by the local constables and the state police to get in and question him. This had devolved into a fight over jurisdiction in the hallway of Three East that Ziffer had ultimately had to referee. He had allowed the state police investigator, a man named Dunbar, five minutes to talk with Warnke, and that was it.

That wasn't what was bothering him tonight, however. He sat at his desk, toying with a bottle of Torbuphenol, and considered his predicament.

The trial of the drug had not gone smoothly. Pfinq Pharmaceuticals was paying Kerian Memorial a large amount of money to perform trial tests of the new drug. Pfinq was also paying Ziffer a substantial sum under the table to administer the program. As far as the rest of the board of directors knew, Torbuphenol was an experimental non-opioid migraine remedy. Ziffer knew that the drug was nothing of the sort. According to his contact at Pfinq, Torbuphenol was being developed with funding from a secret national security slush-fund. It was intended to be used as a population docility drug, something to be dumped in the water supply or sprayed over an agitated population in times of unrest.

The problem was that the drug didn't work as expected. His star test case, Carla Plummer, had apparently had some sort of psychotic break and disappeared. A few of the other test subjects had had minor adverse reactions, but many had shown no response whatsoever. The only one who had exhibited close to the results they had hoped for had been a woman named Hoegenbloeven, but even she stopped showing any results after the first week.

Pfinq had not been happy with the preliminary test results. They would have been even less thrilled had Ziffer not omitted the disastrous situation with the Plummer woman. If the press got hold of this information, it would be a public relations nightmare for Pfinq, Kerian Memorial, and especially for Dr. Michael Ziffer.

Compounding the problem of the Torbuphenol trials was the ill-advised deal he had made with Roscoe Dirkschneider to get rid of Billy Snyder. Instead of a nice, easily dismissed accident, Dirkschneider had orchestrated a public assassination attempt in front of several thousand people at a rock concert. Even worse, he had failed to eliminate his target.

Ziffer was considering how he might extricate himself from this mess when there came a meek tap at the door. "Housekeeping," came a muffled voice from the corridor.

"Shit," said Ziffer distractedly. "Come in."

The door opened, and a small, lumpish woman dressed in a blue rayon housekeeping uniform leaned in. "Just needta empty the trash," she mumbled.

"Yes, yes," said Ziffer. He turned his enormous leather chair to face the window as the housekeeping peon scuttled into the office and began emptying the trash into a plastic sack.

Ziffer's office window overlooked the Old Mill and the rest of Mill Park beyond. Past that, one could see the Wizard's Woods south of town and, on a clear day, sparkling glints from Redskin Lake.

He was startled by a bright light that burst through the trees on the near end of the park. He leaned forward in his chair, peering through the window. The light was incredibly bright. It seemed to be coming from inside the Old Mill. It pulsed and flashed, casting weird shadows over the edge of the park.

"What the hell is that?" Ziffer exclaimed.

"That's yez own doin'," came a voice from behind him. "Yez and yez kin."

Ziffer swiveled angrily back. The housekeeping peon was standing in front of his desk. She had her hands thrust deeply into the pockets of her housekeeper's tunic. And she was glaring at him. "What the hell are you still doing in here?" he demanded. "You can't talk to me like that! Don't you know who I am?"

"Oney too well," said the woman. "Yez Ziffers been causin' trouble 'round Fester since yez got here. 'Bout time someone put a stop to it."

Ziffer was outraged. "Who the hell do you think you are, to talk to me like that?"

The housekeeper snorted. "Surprised yez don't reckernize me, given yez sicced the law on me more'n oncet."

Ziffer squinted. "Oh, shit. You're that crazy hoodoo woman from Back Duck Road. Emig. I don't know how you managed to weasel out of prosecution those times I reported you. This time you're trespassing, and I'm calling security."

"Not with the phone line cut," said Nettie. She nodded towards the side of the desk, where the cord from the phone had been neatly severed. It dangled impotently by the side of the trash can.

"No matter," said Ziffer. "I don't have anything to worry about from you, you old bag." He rose menacingly from his chair.

Nettie looked disgusted. "Yez chust don't gets it, do ya? None o' yez Ziffers ever did. Yez all the time thinkin' yez superior chust 'cuz yez gots big muscles or a lotta money. Well, yez don't knows nothin' about the spirit world."

"The spirit world?" scoffed Ziffer. "Don't waste my time with that nonsense."

"Then yez is a bigger idiot than I thought. The spirits knows things, Michael Ziffer, and they tells me. Like them woods yez likes to stare at from yez fancy office here. They told me that long ago, yez kin Wolfgang Ziffer had a whole mess o' people killt fer that land. I knows it, and yez knows it, too."

"That's ancient history, you old hag," sneered Ziffer.

"Yeah, there's powerful spirits as still remembers it like yestiddy," said Nettie. "An' they tells me yez still up to evil. Poisonin' people for material gain. Arrangin' for peoples t' be killt. Yez Ziffers is all alike. Well, I aims to put a stop to it, finally. The spirits are with me."

"Spirits? I've had enough of this nonsense." Ziffer drew himself up to his full height, and made to move around the desk, intending to throw this troublesome witchdoctor out of his office, and maybe kick her down the stairwell before fetching security.

"Siddown," said Nettie. Her hand rustled in her pocket.

Ziffer's legs suddenly felt like they had come unhinged. He fell back into his padded office chair with a loud *fwup*. All of the strength had disappeared from his legs.

Nettie cackled. "Hee hee hee. Not such a big man are yez now, Ziffer? Yez should have never messed with what yez don't know. The spirits is wery angry, and they lends their power to me."

"That's nonsense," said Ziffer. "I just . . . felt like sitting down. I don't have to sully my hands dealing with the likes of you." He couldn't hide the rising panic in his voice. His legs felt like two tree stumps. What the hell had the old witch done to him?

"Hee hee hee. Yez chust felt like sitting down, huh?" Nettie pulled her hand from her housekeeper's tunic. In it was a small doll dressed in a white smock. There was a small tuft of human hair on the head, and another one underneath the tiny wire frame glasses on the face. The doll was an eerie replica of Ziffer, right down to the red shirt beneath the white coat and the gray slacks on the legs. The legs were bound with a small piece of rough twine.

"What . . . what the devil is that?" demanded Ziffer.

"Don't yez knows? It's Dr. Michael Ziffer!" said Nettie. "It's called a *Doppelpuppe*. My grampaw taught me how to make 'em."

"A voodoo doll!" hissed Ziffer.

"Yep, pretty much," agreed Nettie. "But yez don't have to worry none, since it's all superstitious nonsense, right?" She shoved her thumb underneath the doll's right arm and lifted it up. Behind his desk, Ziffer's right arm did the same. There was no conscious thought; his arm just shot up of its own accord.

"I did that on purpose!" he said lamely. His eyes were wide with fear. They settled on a letter opener, a souvenir from a long-ago family skiing trip to Switzerland. His left hand began creeping across the desk towards the dagger-like opener.

"Ah, ah, ah—none o' that, now," admonished Nettie. "It's time yez stood still." She pulled another small length of twine from her pocket and quickly tied it around the arms of the *Doppelpuppe*.

Ziffer's right arm *thump*ed to the desk and laid there alongside the left. There was no feeling in either one of them. The letter opener and the dead phone sat just beyond his motionless fingertips. "Hysterical paralysis," he insisted. "It's just stress. All this work . . ."

"Yeah, whatever," said Nettie. "All the dark work yez been doin' has taken the spunk outta yez, all right. But that's gonna change."

"You stupid witch! This is nothing, do you hear me? Nothing! I'm a respected man of medicine and the leader of this community! You have nothing on me! I will destroy you and burn your house to the ground! You don't stand a chance, you ignorant old crone! I'll show you . . ."

"Time to shuts yez mouth, Michael . . ." Another piece of twine was rapidly wrapped around the doll's head.

Ziffer stopped talking in mid-sentence, his mouth hanging open. The only motion from his body was from his eyes, which flicked back and forth from Nettie to the closed office door.

Nettie stood over him and shook her head. "It's a shame," she said sadly. "Yez Ziffers been a stain on this community since yez come here. It's time fer yez to take yez own medicine."

Nettie leaned forward and snatched the bottle of Torbuphenol from Ziffer's desk. She struggled with the cap, but finally got it off and looked in. "'Cept it ain't really *yez* medicine. This muck is based on a plant called dragonslip. It oney grows here in central Pennsylvania. Us powwowers

301

use it to calm folks down, ease the childbirth. Yez and yez drug company buddies done turned it from something good inta something to hurt folks. To control 'em. Well, it's time to see about controllin' *yez*, Dr. Ziffer."

Ziffer's eyes were locked on the bottle; the look of outrage was replaced with one of fear. The bottle was practically full—nearly thirty doses. It was enough to put a herd of horses into a coma.

"Time fer yez to take yez own medicine," Nettie repeated. She stepped behind Ziffer, tilted his head back, and dumped the contents of the bottle down his throat. She gently closed his mouth, and held her hand over it, gently stroking his throat with the other. Ziffer tried to fight it, but there it was no use. He reflexively swallowed, feeling the huge gelatinous lump of pills slide down his gullet.

Nettie walked out in front of the desk and took a rag from her pocket. She wiped off the pill bottle, and anything else she might have touched. By the time she had finished, Ziffer's eyes had begun to glaze over.

"I gots to get goin', Doc. Busy night . . . and the Other is nearby, I can feel it. I'll have to say goodbye now." Nettie walked slowly to the door. She turned and looked at Ziffer's motionless body behind his desk. "Oh and say 'hello' to Chief Tonto for me," she said quietly. "Yez bastard."

Chapter 50

The Fledermaus slowly clawed his way back to consciousness. His head was a throbbing blot of pain. He could hear chanting sounds, but they were eclipsed by the rushing sound of blood in his ears. He closed his eyes and took three deep, even breaths. The pain subsided, and he opened his eyes. He tried to move, but his arms and legs were bound. He rolled over. His hands were tightly tied behind his back. It probably wouldn't be too hard to get loose, but he wasn't sure that there was time. The Fledermaus could now clearly see the Fell Circle of Mammon; it looked like they were finishing up their ritual.

". . . and look upon our fiery offering with favor and grant us the rewards that are our due, we ask in your unholy name," said the Scarlet Mistress. She clapped the big black book in her hand closed with a loud snap. "Okay, you dingbats, let's torch this goddamn dump. You two, Brother Frankenstein and Sister Burning, start sloshing around the gas. Brother Diabolical, where the hell is that detonation timer?"

The Fledermaus watched as the Mammonites prepared to torch the Old Mill, and clearly they intended for him to burn with it. The Scarlet Mistress was a great deal more ruthless than he had given her credit for. The Fledermaus still hadn't quite figured out her real identity. The others' had been easy to discover.

There was no time for speculation now—he had to escape before the building went up in flames. He tried working his wrists against each other to loosen the knot, but to no avail. If only he could reach the knife in his utility belt, he could cut through in no time. That was no good—most of the tools were on the front of the belt.

Time was running out. The two Mammonites had slung gas all over the interior of the Old Mill, and the air was heavy with a sweet petroleum reek.

In desperation, the Fledermaus felt along the back of the utility belt. There had to be something there that he could use. By twisting his upper body, he could just reach a pouch underneath his left kidney. There was a lumpy roundish shape in there—a new Super Shrieker. It was untested but should be even louder and brighter than his original design.

On the other side of the room, the Scarlet Mistress had finished her preparations. She was holding a small plastic box with a button and a digital timer. Two wires led from the box into a can of gasoline. "Okay, when I say go, make a run for it," she said. "The timer will delay for two minutes, and we need to be out of the park when it goes off."

Brother Diabolical happened to notice the Fledermaus reaching for the Super Shrieker. "Hey, it's Brother Bat!" he said. "He's awake."

The Fledermaus knew it was now or never. He rolled onto his stomach while simultaneously thumbing the switch on the Super Shrieker. He released the device perfectly, and it arced away from his body, landing squarely in the middle of the astonished Mammonites.

Nothing happened. It was a dud.

"What the hell is that?" asked Brother Frankenstein. He leaned over to take a closer look.

"Don't touch it, you idiot!" yelled the Scarlet Mistress. She slapped her hand on the timer, and there was a small beep.

"Oh, it's okay," said Brother Frankenstein. "It's not . . ."

Suddenly, the Super Shrieker burst into life, filling the building with a blinding white light and a skull-cracking screech.

The Fledermaus curled up in a ball and rolled away from the source of the din. He buried his face in his armpit, trying to block out the brutal assault of light and sound. He could feel *thuds* on the walls as the Fell Circle of Mammon bounced around the interior of the Old Mill like pinballs, trying to find the door.

The light and noise went on and on, filling his head to the breaking point.

The Fledermaus was in the middle of a cocoon of overwhelming brightness and sound, and there was nothing else in the world besides it, forever and ever.

Then it stopped.

For a few moments, the Fledermaus wasn't sure what had happened. He rolled over and opened his eyes. His ears were ringing, but he could see fairly well.

He looked around. The Old Mill was empty. The Fell Circle of Mammon had managed to find their way out the front door.

He rolled over and got to his feet. The reek of gasoline still filled the air, and he knew he had very little time to escape before the timer ignited the building. He began hopping towards the door.

He had no idea how much time had passed but figured that it was only about thirty seconds from when the Super Shrieker had gone off. He hopped quickly towards the door, each bound taking him closer to safety. The door loomed closer and closer; he was going to make it.

From behind him came a muted *thump*, and then the world around him erupted into an inferno.

Chapter 51

The standoff by the fountain was temporarily upset by the deployment of the Fledermaus's Super Shrieker. Merle Totenkopf seemingly had the upper hand in the situation. The eruption of noise and light caused him to briefly shift his attention away from the city slickers he was covering with his assault rifle.

Cecilia Schmidt was much more focused and wasn't distracted by the commotion from the Old Mill. She didn't flinch, but immediately spun on her heel and loosed a shot from her .44. In the bushes, Merle Totenkopf dropped his rifle and disappeared from view with a startled squawk.

"All right, you fuckers, I'm calling the shots now!" she said. "Give me the deed, if you please."

No one was paying any attention. Lee Plummer and Jeffrey Totenkopf gaped at the Old Mill as the pulses of light and high-pitched screeching continued.

"Hey! HEY!" shouted Cecilia. "Hello? Lady with a gun here! I've got you covered and all that!"

Jeffrey Totenkopf gave her a brief glance, and said, "Hey, where's Merle?"

"I shot him," Cecilia informed him.

Lee Plummer ignored the entire exchange. "Holy shit, who is that?" he exclaimed.

The front door of the Old Mill flew open, and a number of dark-robed figures staggered out, holding their hands over their ears. They bumbled comically about the lawn. Behind them, the Old Mill continued to throb with light and noise.

Even Cecilia was momentarily distracted. "What the fuck?" she asked, as two of the dark figures ran headlong into each other and tumbled over backwards.

"Put the gun down, Cici," came an authoritative voice from behind them.

Cecilia turned and found herself staring down the barrel of a service revolver held by Billy Snyder. "Goddammit, Snyder!" she cried in exasperation. "You always manage to screw things up! Shit!" She dropped the .44 with a loud clatter.

"Is that why you tried to have me killed, you conniving bitch?" Billy's tough talk was at distinct odds with his appearance. He was still dressed in a hospital johnny and was propping himself up with the IV pole cane. However, his hand was holding the pistol steadily at Cecilia's head.

"You asshole," Cecilia sneered. "I didn't have anything to do with that! Why would I want to kill you?"

"Because I knew about your shady land deal, of course," said Billy. "You thought I'd put a stop to it."

"Shit, no," said Cecilia. "Why would it matter to you? I'd just pay you a bribe, you crooked son of a bitch. I'd already factored that into the project budget."

Billy seemed a little unsure, but he kept the pistol on Cecilia anyway. "I don't know about that . . ." he began.

"None of you know!" cried Cynthia Hoegenbloeven. "This is all wrong! It always has been! And now it's going to end where it began!" The rest stared at her, open-mouthed. None of them, even Cecilia, could remember her ever uttering a word.

"What the fuck are you talking about, Hoegenbloeven?" demanded Cecilia. "Have you been into the cooking sherry?"

"Okay, none of you move!" another voice boomed out of the darkness. "This is the state police, and we have you surrounded!" A man in a raincoat loomed out of the gloom with a drawn pistol. Behind him were three uniformed state troopers, who also had their guns drawn.

"Jesus Christ," said Lee. "Is there anybody in this park who isn't shoving a gun into someone else's face?"

Billy dropped his gun on the grass. "Okay," he said. "I guess at this point I'm supposed to say 'who the hell are you?'"

The man in the raincoat said, "I'm Lieutenant Dwayne Dunbar, Pennsylvania State Police. Are you William J. Snyder?"

"No, I'm Bozo the fuckin' clown," said Billy. "Can't you see my clown costume?" He flapped the hem of his hospital robe.

"Cute," said Dunbar. "You are under arrest for a long, long list of charges, including corruption, malfeasance, aiding and abetting a criminal syndicate, drug trafficking, promotion of prostitution, bribery, tax evasion, mail fraud, wire fraud, contributing to the delinquency of a public school system, extortion, assault, robbery, grand theft auto, grand theft sailboat, grand theft bicycle . . ."

"Okay, okay," said Billy. "I get the picture."

"It might interest you to know that we have Roscoe Dirkschneider in custody as well."

"Well, good for you, Dunbar," said Billy. "You'll get a gold star from the teacher for sure. I'll bet his list of charges is even longer than mine."

"Actually, it is," said Dunbar. "One of them is attempted murder. Of you."

"What?" said Billy. "Roscoe? That asshole!"

"See, I told you it wasn't me," said Cecilia.

"You shut up," said Dunbar. "*You're* under arrest for assault with a deadly weapon." He produced a pair of handcuffs and cuffed Billy to Cecilia, then turned to one of his men. "Go check on the guy in the bushes, make sure he's okay."

Billy was fuming. "Roscoe! I've treated that meathead like a brother. Well, a step-brother, anyway. I can't believe he'd try to kill me."

"Believe it," said Dunbar. "He's up to his eyeballs in hock to a bookie in Baltimore. Guess he wanted to cut you out of the action."

"What action?" demanded Billy. "Is that all the evidence you have against me? The word of a crooked bastard like Dirkschneider?"

"Nope," said Dunbar. "One of your fellow patients regained consciousness this morning, as well. Randolph Warnke had some interesting things to tell us about your involvement in his drug distribution ring."

"What an amazing police officer you are," said Billy. "You've got the testimony of a corrupt half-wit and a drug-dealing clown. No prosecutor is going to touch a case like that."

"We'll see."

A voice came from another figure that had drifted in from the edge of the park. "Dad? What's going on? Are you okay?"

"Paul? What the hell are you doing here?" asked Lee.

"At least he ain't sticking a gun in anyone's mug," remarked Jeffrey Totenkopf, who had been watching the proceedings with amusement.

"Say, aren't you worried about your nephew over there?" Lee asked him.

"Naw," replied Totenkopf, "he's tough. Been shot lotsa times. I shot him myself last fall."

The trooper that Dunbar had sent to rescue Merle came back empty-handed. "There's no one there, Lieutenant. The branches are crushed, and there's some blood, but not a lot."

"Jesus," said Dunbar. "Call it in. Tell 'em to send an ambulance out here, just in case."

"That's my Merle. He's a tough'un," said Totenkopf. "Hey, what about them goobers over there?"

Totenkopf pointed to the front of the Old Mill, where the members Fell Circle of Mammon continued to stagger out of the screeching building like clowns emerging from a circus car.

"Okay, you boys better round them up, too," said Dunbar to his men. "Let's figure out what the hell is going on around here."

As the troopers moved out to round up the disoriented Mammonites, the noise and light flooding out of the Old Mill abruptly stopped. The howling of the Wight Wind now seemed gentle and soothing in the sudden silence.

The troopers gathered up the robed figures that had emerged from the mill. As they prodded the Mammonites back towards where the rest of the group was standing, one broke away from the pack and tried to make a run for it.

"Stop that one!" ordered Dunbar. "Judging from the costume, that's probably the ringleader."

One of the troopers brought down the escapee with a flying tackle. He hauled the Scarlet Mistress to her feet and began to drag the struggling figure to Lieutenant Dunbar.

Most of the other Mammonites had their hoods flipped back in the confusion following their hasty departure from the Old Mill. The others could recognize some of the faces. Paul was surprised to see Coach Tonka. There was also Pastor Eyler, who was desperately looking around as if some divine chariot might swoop down and whisk him away from this mortification. All of the others looked familiar, too—people from the upper-middle-class circle of Fester whom they saw on a regular basis. The only one whose identity remained concealed was the leader, who's deep, fur-fringed hood kept her face in darkness.

"Just who the hell are you people and what are you doing here?" asked Dunbar.

"We are the Fell Circle of Mammon," the Scarlet Mistress replied haughtily. "If you know what's good for you, you will not interfere in our workings!"

Dunbar regarded her skeptically. "Yeah, I'll keep that in mind. And just who the hell are you?"

"I am the Scarlet Mistress! You have crossed me at great peril to…"

"Shut up," suggested Dunbar. "Let's see who you really are, Mistress." He reached out and yanked back the deep hood.

There was a gasp from the crowd.

"Mom!" said Paul.

"Carla!" said Lee. "What in the world?"

The rest of the Fell Circle of Mammon gaped. They had never seen—or even suspected—the true identity of their leader.

The Scarlet Mistress looked around, dazed. "Fuck, I was so close! And I would've gotten away with it if it weren't for you meddling ki . . ." Her eyes rolled up in her head, and she collapsed.

"Jesus!" said Dunbar. He turned to one of the troopers. "Check on the status of that ambulance, pronto!"

A small figure in a blue uniform pushed her way into the crowd standing around the downed Scarlet Mistress. "Make way, yez, make way," she said.

310

"I'm from the hospital." She knelt down by the collapsed woman and checked her over. Then she reached into her pocket and pulled out what looked like a polished stone egg.

"Nettie? What are you doing here?" exclaimed Paul, who recognized the charm.

"Hush up, Paul Plummer," she said. "I'm tryin' to help yer ma." She held the egg to the unconscious woman's forehead and began chanting in a low voice.

"Who the hell is this and what the hell is she doing?" asked Dunbar. "You don't look like a doctor to me."

"Never said I was a doctor," said Nettie. "Said I was from the hospital." She tapped the name plate on her uniform that said "Netitia Emig, Housekeeping."

"Aw, cripes!" exclaimed Dunbar. "This night just keeps getting weirder. Just get away from that suspect right now, before I charge you with practicing medicine without a license."

"Good luck with that," said Nettie. "'Sides, I'm done with her anyway." Nettie stood up and returned the stone to her pocket.

Carla Plummer's eyes fluttered, then opened. "Lee? Paul?" she said uncertainly. "Where are we? What . . . what's been going on?"

Behind them, there was a barely-audible *fwump* and an orange glow shone through the cracks in the boards of the Old Mill. Fanned by the rushing Wight Wind, the flames were soon licking out of the shuttered windows.

Lieutenant Dunbar stared at the growing conflagration in distress. "Now what? Trooper Jessup, call some fire trucks out here! Quickly! That thing is going to go up like a pile of old papers. And call up to Weaverville and get the arson unit out here, too." He turned to the gathered Fell Circle of Mammon. "And you jokers are all under arrest for arson. Holy Christ, could this night possibly get worse?"

"There's someone inside there!" yelled Brother Frankenstein, who was actually Coach Tonka from the high school.

"What?" exclaimed Dunbar. "Are you sure?" He motioned two of the troopers to go check it out.

"She's right," said Brother Torment, who was Lee's old poker buddy Mike Berg. "He was going to turn us in, but he knocked himself out. She tied him up and left him in the corner."

"Terrific, now it's a murder investigation as well," said Dunbar. "All right, everyone here who doesn't have a state police badge is under suspicion of *something*. If anyone moves, I'm going to shoot them. Jessup, give me that radio." He grabbed the radio microphone from the trooper who had been calling in the requests and spoke directly with the watch commander at the Weaverville SP barracks. He requested further state police backup, fire trucks from surrounding communities, more ambulances, two mobile crime scene units, air support—almost everything short of the National Guard.

The crowd surrounding Dunbar gaped silently as the Old Mill burned like a torch, fanned by the relentless Wight Winds. One of the troopers who had rushed over to try to save the person trapped inside, ran back to report to Dunbar. "There's no way anyone in there could escape," he reported. "The fire just spread too fast. You can tell there's accelerant, too. The place reeks of gasoline."

"The rest of you black-robed clowns, get down on the ground and put your hands behind your heads," said Dunbar. In the distance, the howls of sirens on the trucks from Firehouse #1 competed with the wail of the Kerian Memorial ambulances, which had just made the turn onto Adams Street. Their strobing red lights could be seen splashing the fronts of the houses across the street from the park.

"Look!" cried Janie. "There's someone moving in there!"

They turned and stared at the inferno that was the Old Mill. Silhouetted in the doorway was a dark figure that was moving in strange fits and jerks.

"Christ on a crutch!" exclaimed Dunbar. "Trooper Smith, get a fire extinguisher, right away. Jessup, pull one of the cars up right here, and hit the lights. Christ what a mess!" He was beginning to wish that he had never heard of Fester. The state police had always tacitly avoided the place, and now Dunbar understood why. The town was a madhouse.

The troopers ran to their tasks. In Jessup's car, the unhappy face of Roscoe

Dirkschneider could be seen peering out from the rear window.

The dark figure in the burning building continued to hop towards the door. He had just hopped out the door as the rear wall of the building collapsed, sending up a column of flame and a wave of heat. He managed three more hops past the threshold before toppling forward onto his face. "Ouch, my freaking nose!" he cried.

Ignoring Lieutenant Dunbar's commands to freeze, the crowd rushed forward to aid the dark figure who had miraculously escaped the blazing building. He rolled over on his back and observed the crowd that had gathered around him.

"Hey, Chief," he said when he spotted Billy. "You look funny in that gown."

"Holy shit, Prieboy, is that you?"

"Yes, sir. I told you that I'd infiltrated the Satanists!"

"Inspector Prieboy?" said Dunbar. "How on earth did you survive that fire?"

"Oh, it's my special suit. I made it myself in my lab at home. Good thing I treated it with an industrial-strength fire retardant. I just forgot to put any around the mouth. Burned my lips pretty good."

"You're lucky you didn't burn your ass off, boy," said Totenkopf, shaking his head. "You city people are crazy. I can't wait to get back out to the woods. The deal's off, Plummer. I'm takin' my deed and gettin' the hell away from here."

"Oh shit, I forgot about that," said Lee, looking back towards the fountain. "And the money. Where is it?"

"Well, you put it down right there, just before half the town showed up wavin' guns," said Totenkopf. He pointed back towards the fountain, but the space where the briefcase had been was empty.

"Shit, it's gone!" said Lee.

Dunbar took a quick headcount. "Someone's missing. Who is it?"

"Ha!" said Totenkopf. "Someone musta slipped off when the Human Torch here was making his grand entrance."

Everyone looked at each other in confusion. Finally, it hit Cecilia. "Hoegenbloeven!" she cried.

"Gesundheit," said Dunbar.

"No! It's my assistant, Hoegenbloeven! She's taken the money and run!"

Chapter 52

Is your mom going to be okay?" asked Bolly.

"I hope so," said Paul. "She's awake and stuff, but she's still pretty out of it."

The ambulance carrying his mother had just departed from Mill Park to make the short trip to Kerian Memorial. Lee Plummer had accompanied his wife, instructing Paul to go home immediately.

"Of course she'll be okay," said Janie, giving Paul a squeeze.

"Awww, don't you two make a cute couple?" said Bolly.

"Fuck you, Bolly," they replied in unison.

Things in the park had settled down. The Fester Fire Department was hosing down the smoldering remains of the Old Mill. It was a total loss. By the time the first fire trucks had arrived, the wind-driven flames had totally consumed the structure. Fortunately, the wind had died down, and they had been able to contain the blaze before it had spread to the hospital and beyond.

Billy, Cecilia, and Roscoe were bundled off for questioning at the state police barracks in Weaverville. A paddy wagon containing the rest of the Fell Circle of Mammon was following close behind.

Standing away from the police, Paul, Bolly, and Janie conferred with Nettie. "Just what the hell happened?" asked Bolly. "None of this makes any sense."

"Fester ain't much of a sensible place," Nettie replied. "But what went on here makes sense enough, I reckon. If'n yez knows a few things about this town's history."

"Well, what then?" asked Paul. "What happened to my mom? And how much did you know before?"

"I'll be honest with yez, Paul Plummer. I had my suspicions all along, but it weren't 'til last night that Chief Tonto let me in on all of it."

"Chief Tonto?" said Janie. "Who's that?"

"My spirit guide."

Janie opened her mouth to reply, but Paul touched her on the arm and she shut her mouth with a snap.

"All this goes back more'n two hunnert years," said Nettie. "Back then, the original settlers o' Fester come acrost some Indians livin' nearby. They was egged on by Wolfie Ziffer to kill the lot of 'em. There was oney one of 'em who didn't want to go along."

"Yep," said Jeffrey Totenkopf, who had sidled up to the group. "That was my ol' great-great-great-great granddaddy, Poppi. The Totenkopfs pretty much been suckin' hind tit ever since."

"Anyways," said Nettie, "Ziffer an' the rest of 'em lured the Indians out into the woods and ambushed 'em by that rock what looks like a hand. Murdered all of 'em but one. Top Hats have been coverin' it up ever since."

"This still doesn't explain any of what happened tonight," Paul pointed out.

"I'm getting' to that," said Nettie. "All this mess started when Doc Ziffer went in with the guv'mint and a big drug company to test out a new drug they'd whipped up. S'posed to keep folks from getting' riled up, but it din't work out that way. Yez see, that drug was made from a plant called dragonslip. Powwowers have knowed about it for ages. The Sashacannuck knowed about it, too. In small doses, it would help ease pain and calm yez down. However, if you et a large enough amount, it would . . . sorta open yez up."

"Open you up?" asked Janie. "How?"

"It opened yez up to the spirit world, young missy. Could be wery dangerous if yez wasn't prepared. Paul can tell yez 'bout that, I reckon."

Paul nodded vigorously.

"Paul's ma was one o' the ones who got the drug from Ziffer. It opened her up, but someone was able to take control of her. Got her to forget her normal life and start gatherin' up a buncha boneheads to stir up trouble here in Fester."

"Who?" asked Paul. "Who did this? Was it that 'Other' you told me about?"

"I always knowed yez was smart, boy," said Nettie. "Right on the first try."

"But who is this Other?" asked Bolly. "Where's he come from?"

"That I din't know 'til tonight," said Nettie. "And it ain't a 'he,' it's a 'she,' and she's been here all along, in a way. See, when the original Top Hats murdered all them Indians, ol' Poppi Totenkopf helped one of 'em get away. So the Sashacannuck line continued, and there been descendants of 'em livin' here all along. One of 'em got holt of Doc Ziffer's new drug, and it did somethin' different to her. Musta been her Indian heritage or whatnot, but she became what I guess yez'd call possessed."

"By who?" asked Janie. "Or what?"

"I don't know fer sure," said Nettie. "Maybe she don't know, neither. If I hadda guess, I'd say it was a spirit of them murdered Indians, lookin' for revenge. Anyway, she set out to stir up what trouble she could for Fester. She was able to get aholt of Paul's ma real good, on account of the effects of Ziffer's drug—it gave 'em a connection. The Other jest walked Mizzus Plummer around like a puppet, getting' her to do all the dirty work while she lay back in the bushes."

"Lady, you gotta be kidding!" said Bolly. "All that's crazier than a shithouse rat!"

"Yeah, yez gots a better explanation, boy? This is Fester. The whole town's purty damn crazy."

"Never mind that," said Paul. "What about the Other? Who is she?"

"Ah, I knows who it is," said Nettie. "She was chust here, too. But now she's gone. She can sense me, and keeps her distance. She knows my power."

"Yeah, but who is she?" repeated Paul.

"She's that damn Schmidt woman's assistant," said Nettie. "The one who took the deed and the money and lit off."

"Where'd she take off to?" said Bolly.

"I bet Paul can answer that," said Nettie. "Yez was chust there with young missy."

"The hand-shaped rock!" said Paul. "We'd better tell the cops."

"Sure, why not?" said Nettie. "Ain't gonna do no one no good, no how."

"Well, I'm done talkin' with cops," said Jeffrey Totenkopf. "Besides, since we're all about rightin' long-time wrongs, I might as well go have a chat with the rest of the Top Hats. I gots a swar-ray to attend up to the country club. See ya."

Lieutenant Dunbar had set up his command post in the middle of the park. He was assisted by Martin Prieboy, who had been treated for minor burns to his face. The EMTs had suggested he go to the hospital for further examination, but he had refused.

The state police had managed to locate Merle Totenkopf. Despite taking a .44 slug to the shoulder, he had covered nearly two miles through dense brush before being spotted and picked up.

The whereabouts of Cynthia Hoegenbloeven were still a mystery. The high winds had prevented the state police choppers from taking off from their pad in Weaverville. Dunbar was frantically directing the ground search from the command post by the fountain. He wasn't too pleased when Paul, Janie and Bolly approached him.

"What do you kids want?" asked Dunbar impatiently. "Why don't you go home? You're getting in the way."

"I think I know where that woman with the money went," Paul said. He gave Lieutenant Dunbar an edited version of the events that had led them to the finger rock in the woods, carefully avoiding the mention of experimental drugs and Indian spirits.

"For crying out loud!" said Dunbar, when Paul and Janie had finished. "Just when I thought this night couldn't get any stranger. Okay, let's check it out. Inspector Prieboy, do you know where this abandoned mental hospital is?"

"Not exactly," admitted Martin. "I've never been there, myself."

Dunbar had taken out a survey map of the county and spread it on the hood of the cruiser. "It's not on the map. That's about par for the course."

"I can show you how to get there," offered Janie. "My dad did some survey work out there. He took me a couple of times."

"Okay, you can ride with us," said Dunbar. "Prieboy, you follow us."

"Hey, what about us?" asked Paul. "I know where it is, too."

"Oh, for Christ's sake, I'm not taking half the high school with us," replied Dunbar. "Can't you kids keep out of my hair? Just go home. Please!"

There was a burst of chatter from the radio in one of the police cruisers. "HQ says the wind's died down," reported one of the troopers. "The choppers can fly now."

"Excellent," said Dunbar. "Get one in the air right now. Keep them apprised of our 10-20. Now let's go!"

Dunbar, Janie, and two of the troopers piled into the State Police cruisers while Martin sprinted off to his car. Paul and Bolly were left to watch the fire department crew begin rolling up their hoses.

"This blows," said Bolly. "All this excitement, and we're left here with our thumbs up our asses."

"This whole thing still feels pretty creepy," said Paul. "Maybe I should just go home."

"Y'know, that cop never said we *couldn't* go to the woods," Bolly said. "I bet we could still catch up with 'em."

"Okay, yeah," said Paul. "Fuck it—let's go!"

They sprinted back to the Nova. Bolly jumped across the hood, Dukes of Hazzard-style, but misjudged the distance and went flying into a bush.

"Will you quit fucking around?" yelled Paul as he yanked open the passenger door.

"I meant to do that," said Bolly as he climbed in.

Nettie Emig materialized out of the dark and tapped on the driver's side window. "Hey, if yez kids is headin' out to the Wizard's Woods, I sure would 'preciate a ride," she said.

"Yeah, sure, climb in," said Bolly. He let Nettie in, keyed the ignition and pulled out with a screech.

The Nova roared into the night, following the police cars and a state police helicopter that swooped eerily above the woods. Bolly kept the accelerator to the mat, and they soon arrived at the ruins of the Hickory Home mental institution.

The scene was weirdly lit by the spotlight from the hovering helicopter and the headlights from the police cars. In the center of the clearing was a Chrysler New Yorker, its engine still running and driver's door standing open. Some of the state troopers were searching around the car while others probed around the perimeter of the clearing.

Lieutenant Dunbar stood outside his cruiser yelling into a radio microphone over the noise of the helicopter. "Dogs! We need tracker dogs right away!"

"We don't need any tracker dogs," said Janie. "I'm sure she went that way. To the clearing where we found the skull." She waved wildly to the south.

"Yeah, she's got to be there," agreed Paul.

"What the hell are you kids doing here?" demanded Dunbar.

"You didn't say we couldn't," responded Bolly. "It's still a free country, man."

Dunbar shook his head and hollered something into the radio. The helicopter turned and began to move away to the south. The search team, with Paul and his friends in tow, headed into the brush.

A few minutes later, one of the state cops fielded a call on his walkie-talkie. "It's the chopper," he reported. "They've spotted something in the woods, about a hundred yards due south." Up ahead, the helicopter was seen hovering over the woods, the searchlight flicking back and forth through the trees like a restive spirit.

A few minutes later, the search party broke through into the clearing where the hand-shaped rock stood in the center like a heathen idol.

"What is this?" asked Dunbar. He swept his flashlight across the clearing.

At the base of the rock was a pile of crumpled clothing. The briefcase that Lee had been carrying earlier was beside it. There was no sign of the money that had been in it. There was a hat sitting on top of the rock—a silk top hat, battered and ancient. It was sitting top-down just underneath the finger portion of the rock, looking as if it were waiting for the world's oldest magician to come along and pull out an antiquated rabbit.

One of the troopers examined the hat. "Hey, there's something in here," he said. Five flashlight beams converged on the hat, revealing a handful of ashes. "Wait a minute, there's something here that isn't quite burned."

Everyone leaned in to look at the singed scrap of paper that the trooper was holding. "Looks like a legal document," said Lieutenant Dunbar. "It's very old, though."

"It's probably got something to do with the deal my dad was working on," said Paul. Dunbar made a note in his notebook.

Bolly reached out to touch the ancient top hat, but Lieutenant Dunbar smacked his hand away. "Don't touch it—it's evidence. We'll need it when we bring the case against this Hoegenbloeven woman."

"Shee-it," said Nettie. "Yez ain't never gonna catch her. She's gone."

Dunbar flashed his light on the pile of clothes at his feet. "This woman is on the run in the woods of the middle of the night, apparently stark naked, and carrying an armload of money. We'll catch her." He barked an order into his radio and the helicopter began to move away.

Nettie watched the police chopper recede, shaking her head. "Nope, never see her again," she said to herself.

Lieutenant Dunbar gave her a sour look. "Don't you have someplace else to be, old-timer?"

"Well, all this excitement's done wore me out," Nettie admitted. "I'm gonna walk home."

Dunbar watched her go, then said, "Okay, boys, go back to the cars and get the evidence kits. Let's secure the scene. Inspector Prieboy, I'd be deeply grateful if you get these damn kids out of here and back to their homes where they belong."

"Certainly," said Martin. "Let's go. You've been a great help, but I think the Lieutenant's right. Let's head back to town."

"Just a sec," said Bolly. "There's something funny about that rock."

"What do you mean?" asked Paul and Martin together.

"Well, you've always said that this funky rock looked like it was holding up its index finger, right?"

"Yeah?" said Paul.

"Well, maybe it's, like, the light from the flashlights or something, but I

321

think you got the finger wrong."

"What do you mean?"

"It's not holding up the index finger—it's holding up the middle one," Bolly said, nodding towards the rock. "It's flipping Fester the bird."

Chapter 53

The Top Hats had convened an emergency damage control session in the Founders Club House, a part of the Highland Country Club that was so exclusive that most members didn't even realize it existed. It was small building, located in a far corner of the club grounds near a number of similar outbuildings. From the outside, it looked like a large storage shed, but the interior was all carefully polished wood and oiled leather. The main salon was lined with portraits of Top Hat family members from ages past.

Representatives of nearly all of Fester's Top Hat families had convened there, with the exception of Michael Ziffer. The Founders Club phone lines, which were normally used for quick calls to stockbrokers were now being employed in an effort to reach him.

"I've tried his office five times," reported Stanley Milkman. He ran a hand through his thinning ginger-colored hair. "I tried calling his wife, but she just says that he's at the hospital."

"Ah, to hell with—*hwaa*—him," rasped Mayor Augenblick. "We can't just wait around for him to finish up with whatever—*hwaa*—candy striper he's teaching how to take his blood pressure. Just get—*hwaa*—Wally up here, pronto." Wallace Ziffer, Michael's younger brother, was regarded as a wastrel. He ran a string of used car dealerships located, at the family's insistence, outside of Kerian County.

"Yes, it figures you'd say such a thing," said Dallas Strickler, publisher of the *Fester Daily Dispatch*. "You Augenblicks have been after the Ziffers' position in this community for ages. I would not put it past you to make a power grab now, when the chips were down."

"Now, now, this is no time for acrimony," said Ken Schinkel diplomatically. "We clearly have a crisis on our hands, and we need to make sure all of our founding families are represented."

"Shee-it!" came a voice from the corner. "That hasn't happened in over a hunnert an' fifty years!" The assembled Fester aristocracy was astonished to see Jeffrey Totenkopf step out from behind a long damask drape in the corner. He looked slowly around the room, then pulled a can of Skoal from his jacket pocket and shoved a huge wad of it behind his lip.

There was a muffled gasp of horror. Most of the assembled Top Hats thought a homeless person had infiltrated their sanctorum. However, Ray Augenblick knew who Totenkopf was. They had cut a deal or two together during Augenblick's early campaigns. "Jeffrey—*hwaa*—Totenkopf," he wheezed. "To what do we owe the dubious—*hwaa*—pleasure of your company?"

"Aw, I'm here for pretty much the same reasons as you all," said Totenkopf. "I just come up from town. It's been a pretty busy night out by the Red Hand, too."

This elicited another gasp. Even though all of the Top Hats knew about the massacre at the Red Hand, discussing it in anything louder than a hushed whisper was taboo. To have this rustic bumpkin show up at the Founders Club and start hollering about the Red Hand nearly defied belief.

"Mister . . . Totenkopf, is it?" began Schinkel. "I am sure that . . ."

"None o' your bullshit, Schinkel," said Totenkopf. "You know damn well who I am. I've paid you off a time or two, that's for damn certain. The rest of you stuck-up bastards, too. Things is about to change here in Fester. I know you all don't much like the idea, but that's the way it goes."

"Oh, this is ridiculous," said Milkman. "I'm going to call security." He reached for the telephone receiver, but Schinkel grabbed his hand.

"Not so fast, Stan," he said. "Let's hear the man out."

"Thank you, Kenny," said Totenkopf. "I reckon I don't have to go into too much detail here, other than to say that some kids found bones from them Injuns that our families killed off way back when."

"I have no idea what you are talking about," huffed Strickler. "Go ahead, Stanley. Let's have this vermin removed."

"Okay, I guess I gotta spell it out for ya," said Totenkopf. "The secret that all of the Top Hats been hiding for the last two hunnert some odd years is about to get out. Gonna make Fester look bad. It's jest a matter of *how* bad."

"Ahhh—*hwaa*—shit," muttered Mayor Augenblick.

"Jest so," said Totenkopf. "Our ancestors tricked and murdered them Injuns to get this land. Slaughtered 'em like hogs out there in the Wizard's Woods. Everybody did a first class job of coverin' it up. But sure enough, somebody turned up them bones in the woods, and now it's just a matter of time before it all comes out."

"I wouldn't be too sure of that," said Strickler. "I'll be able to keep a pretty tight lid on how this gets reported. I've got a lot of friends in the media, you know. They'll keep it quiet if I tell them to."

"That's as may be," allowed Totenkopf. "I'm sure if it was jest a couple of bones in the woods, you could keep it hushed up real easy. But things is more complicated than that. What complicates it most is this." He reached into his jacket and pulled out a thick sheaf of pages. "This here's a copy of my great-great-great-great grandpappy Poppi Totenkopf's memories. I found it when I was huntin' down that deed. I guess Poppi Totenkopf was the only one who didn't like the idea of killin' them Injuns. Didn't stop it from happenin', unfortunately. You hoity-toity folks been treatin' us Totenkopfs like trash practically ever since."

"So—*hwaa*—what?" said Mayor Augenblick. "You Totenkopfs have been acting like—*hwaa*—trash practically ever since ever since. Running around in the hills like a pack of goats, having—*hwaa*—sex with anything that moves, including your own . . ."

"Whoa, whoa, whoa there!" said Totenkopf. "Let's not go pointin' fingers about incest, 'specially in *this* company. We all know it's a mighty small gene pool in the Top Hat families.

"Besides, my great-great-great-great grandpappy's story, well, it *moved* me. I could really feel for the plight o' them Injuns. Our ancestors done 'em dead wrong, and I think we need to set that to rights. Now, I don't wanna stir the pot here—ain't hardly nobody needs to know about it but us in this room."

"Your 'story' means nothing," said Stickler. "Anyone could have written that."

"Perhaps," said Totenkopf. "Still, I gots some brainy types over at the University of Pittsburgh lined up to analyze it, for verification and whatnot. Say, you don't have a spittoon in here, do ya?"

"Of course not," sniffed Ophelia Schmidt.

"Too bad," said Totenkopf. He hoicked a wad of tobacco juice at a nearby potted palm and wiped his chin with the back of his hand.

"Why should we care about your 'experts'?" said Strickler. "They can verify when it was written and maybe even who wrote it, but that's all. It does not mean that it's true."

"Perhaps not," said Totenkopf. "Don't really matter anyway. 'Cause I also found *this*." He pulled another sheet from his jacket, this one larger and covered with loose-handed calligraphy and large rust-brown splotches. "This here's the pact that ol' Wolfgang Ziffer got everyone to sign after the massacre, coverin' it all up. Haw, here's the funny part: he got them all to sign it in blood. Now, I gots some other brainy types down at Johns Hopkins that say they can do DNA tests and match them up to the different families."

"For a hillbilly, you sure seem to have a lot of connections at big-time universities," observed Strickler.

"That's because we sell them college eggheads big-time quantities of weed," said Totenkopf. "We got lots of friends on campus."

He made a show of looking around the room. "Say, where's Doc Ziffer? Seems like he should be around to hear all this, 'specially as it was his kin that started all this mess."

"Never mind about Michael. Just tell us what you—*hwaa*—want, Totenkopf." said Augenblick.

"I'm getting to that. I jest wanted all of you to appreciate the humor of the whole situation, first. Ol' Wolfgang Ziffer was the leader of the pack out here back in the day, an' he wanted to get rid o' them Sashacannuck

Injuns somethin' fierce. He almost did it, too. 'Cept one of 'em got away.

"Anyway, after the massacre things went on pretty much as before. Wolfgang and the rest of the original settlers built this town and their fortunes without havin' to share it with no pesky Injuns. However, there was still one or two of them Sashacannuck lurkin' around and harborin' a grudge, you know.

"Mighta stayed that way too, if Mike Ziffer hadn't decided to go messin' about with his mind-control drugs. Granted, this bit's hearsay, but I got it from a reputable source out on Back Duck Road. Anyway, Ziffer done stirred the pot with his secret drug testin'. Seems he riled up the spirits, I guess you could say. Guess they were keen to get some overdue payback. Looks like they will, too, now that the story's sure to get out."

"You miserable old bastard!" exclaimed Milkman. "You would love to see us all ruined. Made to look like greedy, bloodthirsty fools! You'd happily tear this town apart, wouldn't you?"

"Now, that's not very charitable of you, *Milchmensch*," said Totenkopf. "Besides, you got me all wrong. I love this place just as much as you all do, and I have no interest in upsetting any apple carts. I jest wanna have some things set to rights, the way they shoulda been."

"Okay, now we finally—*hwaa*—come to it," said Augenblick. "What do you want, you miserable buzzard?"

"Forget the buzzards, let's talk turkey," said Totenkopf. "First off, you bigwigs on the hospital board need to rebuild that mental hospital out in the Wizard's Woods. Christ knows we could use one 'round these parts. I've got a copy of the original deed that says that land belongs to the Totenkopfs unless there's a functional loony bin on the property. You all build that hospital and everything's jake. You don't, and I'll sell the land to Cecilia Schmidt."

"Jesus!" said Ophelia. "You wouldn't dare! Besides, do you know how much a new psych facility will cost?"

"Nope, and I don't care. You can have a fuckin' bake sale if you want. I figger most of you sittin' 'round this room could pay for the whole thing and not even break a sweat."

"Okay," said Mayor Augenblick. "I think we can—*hwaa*—manage that. What else?"

"Next thing," said Totenkopf. "I want those poor Injuns out by the Red Hand dug up and given a proper burial. Find a nice plot of land down by the lake and give them a decent burial and a memorial. Ol' Stricky here can prolly keep the publicity down."

"You're damn right I will," said Stickler. "If we do these things and you hand over the manuscript and the pact? So what? You'd still have the copies."

"They's only copies," said Totenkopf. "You can't DNA test a photocopy."

"Okay, so you'd hand over the original documents if we rebuild the mental hospital and rebury the, um, remains," said Schinkel. "Is there anything else?"

"Oh, jest one other small thing," said Totenkopf. He took a deep breath and looked around the lush interior of the Founders Club. "I'm tired of you all treating the Totenkopfs like pond scum. We deserve to take our proper place among the Top Hats. So, I want a lifetime membership to this here snotlocker country club for me and my immediate kin."

They had no choice but to accede, but for the Top Hats it was the unkindest cut of all.

Chapter 54

C hief Constable Martin Prieboy was sitting at his desk, slowly and exactingly typing a report. He had moved into Billy's old office and had kept it as spare and clean as had his predecessor. Even though he'd been chief constable for over a year, he hadn't gotten around to replacing Billy's framed certificates on the wall. However, he had gotten rid of the cabinets full of illegal electronics. He'd have to do something about the periscope as well. It was a nuisance.

Following Roscoe and Billy's arrests, Martin had been appointed chief constable. Martin had a shrewd idea that Lieutenant Dunbar had had something to do with that. Martin immediately had his hands full with the aftermath of the strange goings-on at the Old Mill and the woods. To further complicate matters, Jeffrey Totenkopf had been killed in a suspicious house fire two nights after the events at the Old Mill. The old man had a habit of smoking in bed, so the coroner had ruled it an accident. The rest of the family had escaped the blaze, but they were not in the least convinced that old Jeffrey's mishap had been accidental.

The crime scene out in the clearing with the strange hand-shaped rock had been thoroughly documented and then turned over to a group of forensic archaeologists from the University of Pennsylvania. They disinterred the remains, carefully documented them, and then reburied them all in a private ceremony on the shore of Redskin Lake.

The secrecy associated with this activity had the perverse effect of attracting a great deal of attention in Fester. Wild stories flew through the town about a UFO crashing in the Wizard's Woods. The fabulous debut of Martin's improved Super Shrieker, and the police helicopters seen in the area that night added grist to the rumor mill. The polite archaeology professors and students were said to actually be mega-ultra-secret government scientists studying alien bodies and crashed saucer technology.

This fuss continued for a few months, and then was overshadowed by a string of Bigfoot sightings in the hills west of town. By the time that construction started on the new Michael Ziffer Mental Hospital, the tale of the crashed UFO had been woven into the rich tapestry of Fester's famous bullshit stories.

While Martin was dealing with the fallout of those crazy days, he had also set about cleaning up the Fester Constabulary. He had gotten rid of the worst of the rotten apples. Several others whose skill and experience had outweighed their crookedness had been kept on with a probationary status. Martin had managed to wrangle a pay increase for the constables, while making it very clear that he would not tolerate those who supplemented their income with extralegal means.

This had not been a uniformly popular decision. A lot of the constables who had been relieved of duty had left muttering under their breath about what they would do to the new chief constable if they ever got a chance.

Martin also made clear to the business owners in Fester that the constabulary extortion racket was over. He instituted a corruption hotline for local businesses to make official complaints if any law enforcement personnel ever hit them up for protection money. Martin even made a special trip to the Embers to let Sam the bartender know that violence against Fester's gay community would no longer be tolerated, and any complaints would be investigated thoroughly.

Martin's old nemesis, Roscoe Dirkschneider, was cooling his heels at the state penitentiary in Camp Hill, where he was serving twenty years for his amazing variety of crimes. He was stuck in solitary confinement for his own protection, as many of the inmates at Camp Hill had begun sharpening toothbrushes and bedsprings the moment they heard that Roscoe would be joining their population.

Billy Snyder had left the constabulary in disgrace but managed to avoid Roscoe's fate. It was thought that Billy had avoided prosecution through blackmail. He was generally regarded to be Kerian County's version of J. Edgar Hoover, and over the course of his long career he had managed to gather dirt on just about every person of importance. It was whispered that Billy had brought to bear his extensive "black bag" files of a large number of county officials and potential witnesses and had thus avoided prosecution. Regardless, he had been relieved of his office immediately after his arrest and was now living in a small house up in the hills near Kugels.

Randolph Warnke had mostly dodged his drug distribution charges, after his defense lawyers had shown that a person or persons unknown had caused him to involuntarily ingest a highly dangerous dose of PCP. Warnke received a suspended sentence and a stretch of mandatory rehab in a clinic in Weaverville. He was just glad to be out of Fester.

Cecilia Schmidt and Lee Plummer had been indicted for attempted fraud, but with the aid of the law firm of Nasté, Brutus and Shore they had escaped serious repercussions. The inability of the prosecution to obtain any testimony from Jeffrey Totenkopf had greatly aided their case.

There was no sign of Cynthia Hoegenbloeven. She had simply disappeared into the woods, butt-naked, with $100,000 in cash. A search of her quarters had turned up sophisticated telephone equipment that could be used to electronically alter the user's voice and prevent traceback. Based on Cecilia Schmidt's testimony, it was surmised that Hoegenbloeven had been blackmailing her employer. Her connection to the ancient top hat that she left by the rock, and why she had chosen to make her escape in the nude was a mystery to all but the Top Hats, and they were keeping silent on the subject.

Martin pulled the page from the typewriter and inserted a fresh sheet. He was on the fifth page of a deposition regarding Carla Plummer. Despite the fact that she had tried to kill him, Martin was of the opinion that she should not be charged with attempted murder or arson. In the days after the fire at the Old Mill, it became clear that Carla Plummer had not been in her right mind for some time. She was still under observation in the Psychiatric

Ward of Kerian Memorial Hospital. Her improvement had been slow but steady, and she was expected to eventually make a complete recovery.

The same could not be said of Dr. Michael Ziffer, who had been found catatonic in his office the morning after the Old Mill fire. He had ingested a huge amount of an experimental drug that he had been testing. It appeared that the dose had been self-administered—an unsuccessful suicide attempt.

On top of this incredible caseload, Martin also kept in contact with Paul Plummer. He made a deal with Paul that he wouldn't be cited for his drug possession as long as he quit smoking entirely and applied himself to his schoolwork. Martin met with him several times during the school year to check up on him. Paul had maintained a decent GPA and would be a senior in the fall. Martin encouraged him to apply to several colleges other than Prosser; it would do Paul good to get away from Fester—at least for a little while.

Martin finished typing the last page of the report, then carefully proofread the entire document. Satisfied it was concise, accurate, and free of spelling errors, he set it aside. He had put in a long day, and it was almost time to go home.

Martin looked around his office. Making sure he was not being observed, he opened his desk drawer and removed a small, glossy poster. He read the poster for probably the twentieth time, feeling a surge of satisfaction.

It was an advertisement for ComiCon '94, a huge comic book convention that was going to be taking place in Pittsburgh in a few weeks. "MEET THE REAL-LIFE BATMAN!" proclaimed the poster's copy. "Live and In Person! Chief Constable Martin Prieboy and His Amazing Crime Fighting Suit! Hear His Amazing Story of His Battles with the Forces of Evil! See the Suit That Allowed Him to Escape Certain Death in a Fiery Inferno!" Beneath this was a large and lurid four-color illustration of the Fledermaus escaping from the burning mill. There had been a few liberties taken with the illustration: Martin's chest wasn't nearly as large or well-defined as that of character in the poster. Also, he was striding purposefully through the door of the burning mill, rather than hopping. Despite these inaccuracies, Martin was pretty pleased.

He grinned and put it back into his desk drawer, then got up and walked over to the window. On his way past, he gave a swat to the periscope in the middle of the room. It was ridiculous, and certainly had no place in his office. Martin thought he would donate it to a children's museum.

The view out of the office window was just fine on its own. Martin scanned the vista as the afternoon shadows lengthened in Fester. On the office building across the way, two workmen in coveralls were tinkering with some air conditioning equipment. The traffic on the street below was starting to get heavier, stacking up at the stoplight on the corner. On the other side of the river, the smoke rising from the Schmidt Bakery smokestacks tapered off as the shift change approached.

Martin gazed serenely across the city, thinking of the things he had ought to do before his trip to Pittsburgh. He turned from the window to get ready to go home.

As he was walking back to his desk, Martin tripped over the periscope flange for the umpteenth time. As he stumbled, he heard a flat report and a crash as a high-caliber slug shattered the window and buried itself in the opposite wall.

It also nearly buried itself in Martin's cranium. The bullet passed through the space his head had occupied only a fraction of a second before, grazing him and taking off a small strip of scalp. A garish splash of blood and hair splattered the white wall and Billy's framed certificates behind the desk.

Martin bounced back up, pistol in hand, ready to return fire. The blood from the head wound ran into his eyes, preventing him from taking a shot. By the time he had cleared his vision, the shooter had gotten away clean.

"Gosh double-darn it!" exclaimed Martin. He knew that he would have to cancel his trip to Pittsburgh now. He had work to do—and so did the Fledermaus.

About the Author

Crawford was born and raised in York, Pennsylvania. He has received degrees in engineering and architecture, which of course led to an interest in writing novels. His first novel, *Jackrabbit* (2019), was a retelling of the career of Depression gangster John Dillinger. His writing frequently concerns crime and history, with dark humor used to highlight the foibles of human nature. He currently lives and works in Portland, Oregon.

You can connect with me on:

- http://sweetweaselwords.com
- https://twitter.com/SweetWeaselWrds
- https://www.facebook.com/SweetWeaselWrds

Subscribe to my newsletter:

- http://sweetweaselwords.com/contact

Also by Crawford Smith

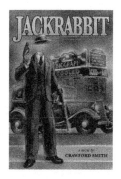

Jackrabbit

What really happened to John Dillinger? It's 1934, and America is in the middle of a crime wave. John Dillinger, a.k.a. the Jackrabbit, has become America's first celebrity criminal. Now desperate to escape the perilous life that he's created, the Jackrabbit concocts a daring plan to disappear. As the FBI draws the noose tighter, the Jackrabbit knows that time is running out. Will his audacious scheme work, or will he go down in a thunderstorm of lead?

Powwows

Deep in the woods lives a wizard called the Professor. In the depths of the Depression, the residents of Fester, Pennsylvania call on "powwowers" such as the Professor to heal ailments, tell fortunes . . . and exact revenge. When an upstart powwower threatens to horn in on the Professor's business, he starts making plans for his own revenge. The sinister forces he sets in motion spiral out of control, and soon threaten to consume the leading citizens of the town.

Made in the USA
Monee, IL
01 December 2022

19282895R00193